THE SORCERESS

Books by Nathaniel Norsen Weinreb

THE BABYLONIANS

THE SORCERESS

THE SORCERESS

NATHANIEL NORSEN WEINREB

DOUBLEDAY & COMPANY, INC. GARDEN CITY, N.Y.
1954

LIBRARY OF CONGRESS CATALOG CARD NUMBER 54-9836

PRINTED IN THE UNITED STATES
AT THE COUNTRY LIFE PRESS,
FIRST EDITION

MTS.
archemish
THE GREAT SEA
ASHER
NAPHTALI
Kedesh
Hazor
Nahatol
Kitron
Harosheth
ZEBULON
Golan
MT. TABOR
ISSACHAR
PLAIN OF ESDRAELON
Taanach
EASTERN MANASSEH
WESTERN MANASSEH
Jordan River
Shiloh
EPHRAIM
GAD
Ramah
DAN
BENJAMIN
JUDAH
REUBEN
Gaza
SALT SEA
River Arnon
SIMEON
MOAB
PALESTINE
Scale of Miles
0 5 10 15 20 25 30

SALEM COLLEGE
LIBRARY

For G. and S. MURCHISON

NOTE

Deborah, Barak, Jabin, and his general, Sisera, actually existed, as witnessed by their stories in the fourth, fifth, and sixth chapters of the Book of Judges. The great chariot battle between the mighty forces of Canaan and the undermanned but courageous tribes of a partially united Israel on the Plain of Esdraelon actually took place. The eloquent poem—the Song of Deborah—describes this battle in the Book of Judges as well.

For the love poem on the swallow, the dream interpretation, and Deborah's verdict as a judge I am greatly indebted to "Ancient Near Eastern Texts Relating to the Old Testament," edited by James B. Pritchard, Princeton University Press, 1950. I am also grateful for the research material found in the excellently documented bulletins of the American Schools of Oriental Research at Yale University. For the biblical text and commentaries I have used the beautiful translations of the Soncino Books of the Bible, published in London.

And last—but far from least—this book could never have been written without the constant and devoted help, patience and understanding of my editor at Doubleday and Company—Mr. Lee Barker.

N. N. W.

PART ONE

THE STONE FROM HEAVEN

1

AT FIRST Dael was only slightly aware of the kiss of cold metal piercing through the film of perspiration on his back. With his eyes intent and concentrated on the fire of the forge before him, his hands busily pumping the leather bellows, he thought that a mere, if welcome, west breeze was giving its chilly caress to his skin. But as the pressure increased, as little fingers of pain slapped insolently at him, Dael turned his head, startled as his throat was nicked by the naked sword blade thrust out at him.

The young man's eyes, already narrowed and reddened by smoke, traveled painfully from the broad blade to the arm, hairy and powerful and girded by black horse-leather cuffs heavily studded with brass, that held the weapon. As his vision focused sharply again, Dael's gaze swept higher, to the expanse of shoulder protected by links of mail, finally to the bearded and weather-beaten face whose grim features were shadowed by the laminated leather helmet worn by the soldiers of King Jabin of Canaan.

"Up, and away from the fire," the soldier's guttural voice was commanding, his free left hand gesturing swiftly. The weapon pressed harder as Dael arose from his knees. "Move wrongly but once," the mercenary's tone warned harshly, "and your blood quenches the fire."

Lithely and easily but carefully, Dael stood up, stopping only as the sword leveled at his breast. "Stand you there," the soldier ordered, pointing to a corner of the smithy where two others in the service of King Jabin had already forced a tall, lanky man with a sparse red beard and a black patch over the left eye.

As Dael joined his father, the smithy began to fill with other fighting men, all with drawn swords, who rushed through the opened doorway and began smashing everything within their sight. Before Dael and Abinoam could draw two full breaths, the room began to be filled with shouts and curses, commands and the crashing of lamps, the metallic clangor of iron hitting the stone floors, and the ripping, tearing sound of wood.

One soldier kicked carelessly at the fire, scattering sparks and ashes to the ground. Others began sweeping heavy hands over the remaining shelves where lay the finely wrought handles of iron, lampstands, chisels, hammerheads and saws, intricately shaped cups and jars, chains of iron, plowshares and bridle bits. These were indifferently knocked down, to be stuffed into large goatskin bags that still other soldiers were bringing into the forge chamber. In another corner a wizened, misshapen scribe was already furiously marking down the number of rough ingots of crude iron that lay piled against a wall, while another sweating mercenary began to lift the metal bars and hand them to his companions on the outside. The noise increased—the sputtering and dying indignation of the fire, the ringing protests of iron against stone, the dull booming of deadly battle-axes that smashed the forge and sent newer sparks streaming from their edges. Sound mixed with sound, intermingling, confusing, all weaving together in a blanket of noise that dropped heavily now over the thoroughly amazed and angered craftsmen.

Abinoam was the first to cry out. His face working so that the meager, three-pronged beard moved up and down fiercely, the single eye narrowed, he lunged forward, only to be stopped by the press of sword against his heart. The huge hardened fists clenched and the knuckles flowered into white, frustrated knobs of bone.

"What means this abomination, this outrage?" Abinoam's tremendous voice roared. He choked with quick rage. "By whose authority enter you here to destroy?" The single clay-colored eye glared from one soldier to the other, seeking an answer, finally resting hotly upon the scribe, with his bent shoulders and concentrated face, the lips puckered over his task.

"You there—scribe!" the trumpet-like voice blasted over the now-wrecked smithy. Abinoam's lips parted in a snarl, the teeth gleaming a pale yellow against his wet lips. "Stand before us and reveal unto us whence comes the authority for this!"

Without looking up from his reed pen, which was leaving its crimson little tracks over the parchment, the scribe made answer. "By the authority of him who rules this land, by Jabin, King of all Canaan," the reply came, carelessly, almost casually. "For thus has he ordered. From this day on, no smith of the people of Israel, who dwell within Canaan, can practice his craft in the land. For thus has Jabin ordered, and his words are law, and not to hear them is the death. And death it will be for all those who work with iron or who hoard the metal illegally. . . ."

"Words, mere words," Abinoam rasped. "Show me the decree from the king. Let us behold the new law ourselves."

For a moment the scribe's faded blue eyes looked at Abinoam. Then the little man shrugged, placing down the parchment and tugging at his belt with his freed hand. Almost disdainfully he pulled out the tightly wound scroll, flipped it open. "So be it," he sighed. "I will read it for you. I——"

"My son knows the mysteries of the written word," Abinoam snapped. "Let his eyes behold the new law and his tongue mouth it for me."

The scribe's eyes showed sudden surprise for a moment. Then he shrugged again and threw the scroll over to Dael, who began to read, his voice even and deep as he uttered the words to his father:

" 'To all the smiths and toolmakers and jewelers and workers in metal of Isreal.

" 'Let this be known to you, by the might and power of Jabin, King of all Canaan.

" 'From this day hence, none of the children of Israel may work in any form of metal. Especially is the forging of iron forbidden, and if any smith or craftsman is so found doing, he will die by the king's hand. And if any craftsman possess the iron metal, he does so illegally and will be slain for the posession of it.

" 'From this day forward, iron becomes the monopoly of Canaan. If the children of Israel need to have their plowshares sharpened, they will do so at the forges of the king and nowhere else in the land. And to disobey means to be slain. No forge fires shall burn in the homes of any smith or craftsman of Israel.

" 'So it is ordered, by Jabin and by Baal, who witnesses all and whose wrath will fall upon those who disobey. . . .' "

Dael tossed the scroll back to the scribe. "And it bears the king's seal and signature," he added tonelessly.

The glare faded out of Abinoam's eye. Weakly he sagged against the wall. "But why so, why so?" he demanded, his eye taking in the complete destruction now around him in the smithy, the bags bulging with iron ingots and articles, even the shavings confiscated. He stared dully as the soldiers found a chest of cedarwood, pried it open, and began to extract from it a treasure of metal artifacts, gleaming chains of silver, polished mirrors of brass with strangely fashioned handles of gold, silver cups of graceful design, golden rings entwined and coiled like serpents, tiny statuettes of goddesses whose naked limbs shone in silver, gilded earrings that blinked as they swung from hand to hand.

"Those too?" Abinoam asked dully. "Can you not spare them? They are of my son's making. They represent all the wealth he possesses, all he has earned, all he wants to——"

"Of metal be they," the scribe's piping voice reached them, "and thus can no longer belong to you." His hand caressed a miniature lamp of gold before it disappeared into the hairy throat of the goatskin bag. "Wonderful workmanship," he murmured.

"But why so?" Abinoam repeated again, anger once more heating the gleam in his eye. "We make nothing here to harm the king. We fashion no evil. We are men of art and creation. We make the tools and jewels which are for peaceful purposes."

"You make also weapons," the scribe said accusingly, "weapons which you and your people plan to use against Canaan. Think you we knew not this—that at your forges were sharpened spear points and arrowheads, that in your fires were dipped the sword blades to drink our blood? Oh, far and piercing is the eye of Jabin, and his ears extend all over the land to know who plots against him." The scribe lowered his severe gaze on the racing pen as it skirted over the smooth surface of the sheepskin parchment. "We knew this, and the king acted wisely and swiftly," the little official went on blandly. "Also known to the king are the names of those who would plot against him and destroy the gods of Baal."

Father and son looked at each other. Abinoam could not be sure, but he thought he detected a flickering gleam of chagrin and reproval in the darker eyes of his son.

"Then the king's judgment is fruited with lies and slanders," Abinoam said thickly, the cords in his scrawny neck quivering again. "For neither smiths nor fashioners of weapons are we here. We are toolmakers and creators of jewels to bring pleasures, not bloodshed. See for yourselves that only useful implements and tools and innocent baubles were found here, harmless vessels that could never——" In his eager enthusiasm the father had stepped closer to the scribe.

Abinoam stopped, grimacing suddenly, as the point of the sword in the hands of his guard nudged his naked chest. With a grin the Canaanite soldier pressed the weapon a little harder, in a circular, grinding motion. The pressure-whitened flesh suddenly crimsoned. A drop of blood appeared, joined by others until a red stream ribboned over Abinoam's gaunt ribs.

"Your tongue is too nimble, old one"—the soldier smiled cruelly—"but I can make it lighter yet with one cut of my blade. Cease your woman's chatter before I sever the sound from you for all time."

Dael, who had been motionless all this time, moved now, ignoring the sudden stiffening of the sword that was being held against him. "Why not speak to *me* thus, swine-worshiper"—the voice came quietly—"instead of to an old and helpless man?"

"Ho!" Abinoam's guard exclaimed in pleasure, regarding him with grim humor. "What have we here? A fighting cock among the nomads of Israel?" He turned to one of his colleagues. "Watch the old one," he said with relish, "while I oblige this one." Arrogantly and deliberately he swaggered toward Dael, looking him over carefully, one hand on a hip, the other still holding the sword.

"You are well built," the soldier said, his tone still level, almost friendly, "and might give a good account of yourself. Now. Repeat again what my ears have heard."

Dael's eyes held those of the mercenary, then dropped to the sword in the Canaanite's grasp. "Weakly indeed must the manhood run in you," the toolmaker answered quietly, "if it must be held up by steel. . . ."

In the suddenly silenced room the clang of sword dropping to the stone floor rang loudly.

"We are even now," the soldier said, his eyes already alert. "Let us see if your strength brays as falsely as your tongue." And with that, the Canaanite's hand coiled back, the cruel brass studs glistening on forearm before they swept forward with smashing force to lacerate Dael's face.

But the soldier's hand struck only at the air. He lurched forward, propelled by his own momentum, and hurled into the wall. While he turned around to look for Dael, his head snapped back twice, quickly, as the craftman's fist pounded into the bearded jaw. Reeling and staggering, the Canaanite put up both hands to protect his face, grunting suddenly and then screaming with pain as Dael sank both fists into the pit of the stomach. Before the mercenary could double up in sharp agony, Dael's bunched knuckles hammered again at mouth and jaw. Moaning softly, the soldier sank to his knees, dropping full length on the stone floor, his head rolling in the blood that streamed from lip and nostril now. He quivered once, raised a leg. Then he lay still.

Instantly three other soldiers were rushing at Dael, their blades raised high. His back flattened against the wall, Dael heard the shrill voice of the scribe: "Stay your blades, soldiers! Hold! Remember the order of the king. No blood is to be shed! Hold your metal!"

As the little official rushed into the group, they backed away from him, scowling but making no further advance. Scolding, the scribe ushered them out of the smithy, telling them to wait outside. One of the soldiers lingered, waiting for the fallen Canaanite to rise groggily and to help him walk through the doorway.

Silently Dael watched them depart, then turned to the scribe. "I thank you for my life," he said simply. "Had it not been for your words, I would——"

"Not my words," the scribe answered, "but those of Jabin. He commanded that no blood be spilled this day. Nevertheless"—and the little one's eyes looked at Dael carefully and calculatingly—"you were both foolish and daring. You have made an enemy of this Dargan. He often prided himself upon his fighting abilities and longs to enter one of Jabin's gladiator schools. Now, with what you have done to him——" The scribe grinned suddenly. "You were like the lightning itself!" he said. "Have you ever——"

He stopped as Dael turned from him and went over to Abinoam, putting a hand over the older man's shoulder. "If you have done with us now," Dael said, "leave us to what we have left. Go now, for you have finished your work and finished it all too well. . . ."

The scribe closed his mouth tightly, cast another look at the havoc of the room, and then, without speaking, took narrow little steps to the doorway and disappeared. Dael and Abinoam could hear him utter some commands, heard the deeper voices of the leaders of ten who ordered their men to march away.

Then there was only silence.

Without speaking, the two men allowed their eyes to pass over the disordered, smashed ruin of what had been their workshop. The floor was littered with dust from the soldiers' sandals, with tufts of hair from the bags. Jagged and split planks of wood, their raw wounds still gaping from the peg holes, lay scattered around in mute testimony of destruction. Even the adobe walls bore deep scratches and niches, running in zigzag fashion, where the mercenaries' hands had snatched at the shelves. Near the wall a drying smear of blood showed where Dargan had fallen. Thin slivers of iron, which had been chipped off the large forge, pointed slim and accusing fingers in all four directions, while a tiny hand bellows lay like some mutilated animal, its leather belly ripped open, gaping against the fragments of door sockets and fleshhooks.

Dael silently strode over to the far corner of the smithy and looked down at what remained of his favorite bellows, a double bellows constructed of inflated skins, now limp and flaccid in injury. Gently he stooped down and picked up the wreckage of the strings attached to foot pumps, which had kept the air pouring into the fire from the clay-nozzled reed pipes. His wide, strong craftman's hand stroked the cracked surface of the clay lovingly.

"Broken . . ." he muttered absently. "As broken as our lives and livelihood and future now." His fingers dropped the remains of the bellows. Without realizing it, he was rubbing his palms against the dirtied leather apron that shielded the gray, short skirt in which he was donned.

"What do we now, Father?" he asked without looking at Abinoam, knowing that the answer which might come was as empty and futile as the question.

Abinoam adjusted the leather strap over the eye patch so that it snuggled closer against his skin. His one good eye met that of his son, but there was no hope, no gleam of suggestion within it. The tight, severe mouth drooped, the red beard sagged. Looking at him, Dael was suddenly aware of how tired and how old his father appeared now.

"If only they had spared us the golden and silver articles," Abinoam said. "Then, at least, there would have been enough for you, my son, to continue your work and study in Egypt. Now——"

"There will be no dream of Egypt and its smithies and craft of jewelry making for me," Dael heard himself answering, unable to stop the thick regret and anger that clotted his throat. "We have to think of merely living now, where to get bread and cheese and keep a shelter over our head. . . ."

Abinoam looked away from the reflected agony in his son's soot-colored eyes, agony that seeped out all over the young man's features, cementing the corners of his lips with hard lines. For Dael's words were sharply edged with truth. Toolmakers and craftsmen had they been for all their lives, Abinoam for six decades, Dael for two, ever since the time when, at the age of five years, he had been instructed by his father at the forges. For twenty years Dael had learned the skill and craft, learned it well, working with a technique of his own, embroidered with an imagination and daring that had sent soaring his dreams of furthering his talents at the fabulous forges of Egypt, where the master craftsmen labored to produce the world's finest metal artwork, the rings, amulets, bracelets, and jewelry that brought fantastic prices. With this goal in mind, Dael had slowly, and with sweat, accumulated the silver and gold artifacts of his creation, saving them as security for the time when he would be able to go to Egypt and study. This dream had sustained him, had been full of rich promise. With the cups and rings and bracelets that Dael had fashioned, he would be able not only to pay his passage to the Nile but to offer his savings for continued study and the ordinary expenses of living in Memphis.

But now the dream, like the forge, was shattered, broken, smashed beyond repair or hope.

Abinoam continued to look at the littered floor, afraid, ashamed to raise his gaze lest his son read the depths of despair there. For Abinoam knew full well that their futures were ruined, that poverty and ruin stared with a hideous grin at the bleakness of the life that was left to them. They owned no land, these two; not in their possession were any fields weighted with the heavy fruits of the olive and its precious oil. To them were assigned no flocks of sheep, goats, or cattle. What they owned had lain in their minds, in their gifted hands and the bars of metal which had gone to forge their sole treasures. Now all this was gone, confiscated by the whim of a king.

Nor was there anyone to whom they could turn for help or appeal. Within all of Israel there was not one who might lay the tender hand of aid upon their bowed shoulders. For, although the tribes of Israel had already dwelled in Canaan for one hundred and fifty years, since the great general Joshua had carved out his initial victories against the Canaanites, the fact remained that the latter still held the edge of power in the land by virtue of their armed might and ruled with the heavy weight of the two-bladed sword. All laws and regulations stemmed from King Jabin's throne room, and those who refused to obey met slavery or death, or worse.

Like a choking web, strangling freedom and economic liberties, was the confederacy of the kings of Canaan, of which Jabin was the head. No Israelite could escape the tolls and taxes imposed upon him by the Canaanite ruler. No man of Israel could travel in safety over the highways unless he had paid for the privilege. One tenth of everything was Jabin's ironclad law, and he enforced it with flame and blood.

And what did the tribes do about it? Abinoam's beard quivered in indignation and his lips stretched in a sour smile.

Nothing.

For even the children of Israel were divided among themselves, having no geographical or political unity at all. Jealous over their allotted territory, of matters of ritual and procedure, they looked with wary and suspicious eyes upon each other. The rich priests and their lowly servants, the Levites, owning no property at all, concerned themselves mainly with religious matters and shrugged away the political and economic problems that faced the bulk of the complaining masses. Other tribes—like rich and haughty Judah, had disassociated themselves completely from their former fellow nomads, had intermarried with Canaanite women, and refused—completely and finally—to be involved in the skein of troubles that Jabin cast over the chosen peoples. Others, like doughty little Dan, had also forgotten their common desert origins and busied themselves, with their Canaanite partners, in affairs of ships, sailing, and the seas.

Of all the twelve tribes, only five still plotted and dreamed and hoped for freedom from the yoke of Canaan. Benjamin, in its tight little mountain districts to the south, had ever been a thorn in the sides of the fat Jabin. Foremost were they in fomenting revolt and guerrilla warfare against the overlords of Baal, the Canaanite deity. Ephraim, Naphtali, Zebulon, and Issachar, knowing they faced certain ruin unless their taxes were lightened and the tolls on the roads lifted, had shown a fierce eagerness to unite with Benjamin and, once and for all, destroy the enemy in their midst. Even one of the tribes that stemmed from the proud seed of Joseph—Western Manasseh—had expressed approval of revolt against Jabin. The sleek, sophisticated merchants of Western Manasseh were finding Jabin's demands too great.

But the other tribes, Reuben, Simeon, Judah, Gad, Asher, Eastern Manasseh, and of course the priestly Levites, were either too aloof, indifferent, or assimilated to join the others in an attempt to rid themselves of Canaan.

Still, Abinoam mused, there was one factor that still held Israel in a loose grip—the worship of the one god, he who was known fearfully as Yahweh and more popularly as Jehovah. At least in this—with the exception of those in Judah who embraced the strange gods and goddesses—there was unity. Not one of the tribes had as yet forsworn completely Jehovah for other divinities. And with this knowledge Abinoam took a deep breath and thought: Other men like myself still can retain a kernel of hope, can still sow that seed on even a partially plowed field and see the fruits of freedom blossom.

He glanced up quickly at his son, saw that Dael, too, was lost in thought, then looked away once more. Perhaps it was still not too late. True, he, Abinoam, was old and it mattered not what the arms of fate held for him. But the son should still have his chance of making the long trip to Egypt and learning there to perfect his artisanship and return as master toolmaker or jeweler to the land of his birth.

Abinoam sighed heavily. Very well, he would take his life in hand and appear before Jabin himself and plead with the monarch for leniency. Not for himself. For Dael. Perhaps Jabin would so be disposed to give Dael special privileges of continuing his work until enough could be accumulated for the journey to the Nile.

Tightening his leather eye band again, Abinoam knew he would have to speak to Achan and have that single authority of Israel in the village appear before Jabin with him.

For Achan was the judge of Kedesh, that little settlement that nestled in north central Canaan, no more than an hour's walk from mighty Hazor itself, the great capital city of Canaan, where dwelt Jabin. Like all the other settlements of Israel, Kedesh's domestic and religious affairs were presided over by a judge, or *shophet,* a man chosen for his wisdom and learning who dispensed justice and mercy within the ranks of the children of Israel. A former Levite, able to read and write, familiar with the religious laws as well as the political and economic statutes of Canaan, Achan's task was to keep law and order among his flock. Like the other judges, he handed out his opinions, interpretations, and solutions of family or domestic problems or those of religion to all who appeared before him.

Beyond that his authority was limited. At best, all the shophet could do was merely to suggest and hope that his rulings would be obeyed, not so much by any force but by the inner consciousness of the supplicant. As a symbol of authority, Achan carried with him the oxgoad, a sort of scepter. A grim smile trembled and was hidden on the older craftsman's bearded lips. Now, with the monopoly on iron declared, poor Achan would not even have a metal-tipped oxgoad to bear proudly.

Still, according to procedure, Achan would have to appear with him before Jabin. Abinoam sighed again. There was little love lost between the shophet and himself. Far too often had Achan voiced his displeasure at Abinoam's tirades against the aloof ones of Israel, the stormy mouthings against the worship of Baal, the Canaanite god of fields and fertility, who was making inroads against the one and only Jehovah among Israelites. Many times had Achan severely and hotly condemned Abinoam for the destruction of the Baal altars which had been erected on the high places. "How can there be peace and unity in the land," Achan had accused Abinoam, "if you persist in heating the anger of the Canaanites and their poud priests by resisting their religion?"

It was no secret in Kedesh that Achan, perhaps like Jabin himself, considered Abinoam a dangerous radical, a revolutionary, a frothy-mouthed and misty-eyed fanatic who, with his followers of the Jehovah worship, were intent upon the complete destruction of Israel, so that its people would be drowned in their own blood and their bodies roasted in the fires set by Jabin and his mighty men of valor.

Abinoam looked up again, his single eye finding Dael, who was still moodily staring out of the smashed doorway.

"My son . . ." The old man's voice was gentle. "Grieve not. For on the morrow I take the shophet with me and approach Jabin in his throne room to ask for leniency, for time for you to accumulate enough wealth to journey to Egypt."

Dael turned around slowly, his eyes wide with utter disbelief. He took a step forward, his hand outstretched in mute protest. Watching him, Abinoam marveled how such a son could have sprung from his loins and from the womb of the tiny, dark-haired Joanna, now long since returned to the earth. In height and breadth and in muscular power Dael seemed like one of the fabled giants of old. How had my seed been able to blossom into such manhood? Abinoam wondered again, pride suddenly swelling within him until it forced a smile to leap into life on his gaunt face.

"I so do," Abinoam asserted. "Fear not. Jabin seeks no additional bloodshed. He will not harm me. Your ears have heard the words of the scribe who was here."

"Then, if you so believe, the years have indeed soured your

reasoning," Dael said shortly and bitterly. "Or perhaps what has this day occurred here has maddened you completely." He darted a scornful glance around the room. "You go and plead with the very man who ordered this destruction?"

"For thy sake, my son," Abinoam said softly, using the familiar, personal phrase. Hearing it, Dael took a deep breath, his hands suddenly hanging limp at his sides.

"My father," he said, trying to control himself, knowing the love Abinoam bore him and yet feeling resentment, "seek not Jabin. Nor go there with Achan, whose hatred against you all know. For what is Achan but the puppet of Jabin, whose will he exercises at every given opportunity? Appear before the king—and"— Dael swallowed heavily with sudden fear—"and he might enslave you before his throne. It is folly for you to do this, my father, Let us wait. Perhaps——"

"I fear not Jabin nor what he might intend," Abinoam said, his voice stronger and confident now. The head drew back, higher, the three-pointed beard jutting. The single eye closed. "I fear not, because Jehovah is with me in all I do, follows me into the light and into the shadows. For Jehovah is my shield and my sword, and His countenance, blessed be it before all men, will light my way and guide me to safety."

Incredulously Dael stared at his father. Then the dams of rage and frustration broke in a torrent of words that rushed from his tongue and pounded against the ears of the older man.

"You are maddened!" Dael cried out. "This Jehovah of yours has set fire to your mind. Jehovah—a cruel, sly, and selfish god of war!" He felt the spittle in his mouth and he spat on the floor. "There is *my* sacrifice to this Jehovah of yours!"

"Dael!"

Abinoam's face was stern and unrelenting, and the eye flashed with shocked anger. "You are wrong. You trod in the pathways of evil to so think. Jehovah is the All, the good——"

"Jehovah is cruel and smeared with the blood of all his victims,"

Dael answered, his voice iced and cold, his words mouthed with deliberate insult. "*You* and your followers call him a high god of peace. I name him one of carnage and hate and bloodshed, who enforces his cruel will upon all who will not follow him. And *I* be one of those. . . ."

"My son, my son . . ." Abinoam's voice had risen to a whining moan of despair. But Dael could not be stopped now. All the pent-up bitterness and frustration, the blasting of his dreams exploded within him.

He waved a wild and trembling hand around the room. "Think you that Jabin ordered this destruction merely because of iron and craftwork?" he demanded. The huge fists bunched and remained clenched. "You know the true cause of what happened today. Not because of iron did Jabin do this but because he considers *you* a danger, a fanatic, a destroyer of Canaanite altars, a boil on the peace of the land. It is a warning, my father, and one that must be understood to be obeyed."

"Evil twists your tongue, son!"

"Not evil but wisdom," Dael raged, slamming one fist against the wall helplessly. He was breathing hard, his breast undulating like the leather skin of one of his bellows. His eyes hardened with the anger that seethed within him.

"By fighting the Baal worship, by incurring the wrath of the haughty and jealous priests, you, and those who follow you, are considered by Jabin as a geat danger to all of Canaan. Can you not understand that? What happened this day is a warning for you to desist—yet you would so foolishly appear before Jabin to beg! Oh, you will beg——beg for your life. . . ."

"I will beg for you, my son."

"Not for me." Dael laughed harshly. "For I care not for this monster of Jehovah who feeds on blood while he murmurs peace. Oh no, my father, plead not for your son but for yourself, for it is your life which Jabin holds in his palm. How long, think you, will the king tolerate your abuse of the gods of Canaan, your slurs and mouthings and preachings, your destruction of altars? Indeed, I believe that were it not for your fanaticism this raid upon our forges would never have occurred. Thus is always the way of Jehovah—a way of terror and death and destruction. . . . It is not the iron that bothers Jabin, it is *you,* whom he considers a troublemaker and a revolutionary who plots against the state——"

He stopped, staring at his father, waiting for an answer. When none came, he continued, his voice softer now.

"Can you not see, my father? Were you less bitter and uncompromising in your attack against Baal, this new ruling might never have left the lips of Jabin. It is his warning to you that next time he will kill you. While there is yet time, forget this Jehovah. We can move elsewhere. We are craftsmen, and it may be given us to find work elsewhere. But continue not this crazed fight against the priests of Canaan. For surely they will destroy you as you follow the word of this Jehovah of yours."

"Jehovah is All," Abinoam repeated again. "And He will bring the peace to the land. What blinds *your* eyes, my son, is the fact that Israel needs a war god now to lead him against his enemies. But when the foes are conquered, and when our burdens are lightened, when true freedom is forged in the fires of warfare, Jehovah will then become a wise and kindly god of peace who will reign over his people."

"And when will that be, my father? When our bodies feed the vultures?" The thin film of sarcasm broke in Dael's words.

"Perhaps." Abinoam's eye was closed again. "But the battle must go on. There is only one god, and his name is Jehovah, and I will fight for that. . . ."

Dael stared, his face relentless. He stepped closer to the older man, thrusting out his hands at Abinoam. "Behold these!" he cried out. "In them, in their strength and cunning lies the only true godliness. That believe I—not in any deity. For my hands fashion with love many articles of beauty. Love and beauty through work. There is *my* god, and one of peace as well!"

For the first time a faint smile whipped over Abinoam's features. "And who gave you those hands but Jehovah?" he asked softly.

Dael's deep breath labored in his throat. Once more he sagged; again his arms hung limp. Once his mouth opened as if to say something, then the lips closed tightly. With a stiff back he turned and began walking to the door.

"You will come with me on the morrow when I see Jabin?" Abinoam called out.

Dael wheeled and faced his father again.

"I will not be there," he answered curtly. "I beg of no man for something in which I bear no belief." And with that the tall, powerful figure, silhouetting the lighted doorway for a moment, disappeared into the outside sunlight.

Abinoam, left along, kicked aimlessly at some broken splinters of wood. The movement made a soft, sighing sound, similar to that which was coming from his own lips now. . . .

2

IN THE SMALL ivory-tiled anteroom reserved for all those who would have audience with the King of Canaan, Abinoam and Achan, the judge of Kedesh, waited impatiently and not without a certain amount of anxiety. For they knew not what the temperament of the ruler might be, whether he would grant them the privilege of casting his royal glance upon them and opening his divine ears to their plea, or whether rage and anger would stir him until they boiled over them.

Curiously, Abinoam, not without a hidden smile, glanced at his companion, Achan, who had reluctantly and with grumbling decided to be at the toolmaker's side when he approached Jabin. For this formal court occasion Achan had donned the full garb of his office. Clutched tightly in his hairy hands was the ever-present oxgoad, nearly four cubits, or the height of a tall man, in length. Abinoam had breathed with relief when he saw the tip of the goad had been ground off so that it was no longer of metal. Around his rather portly waist Achan wore a fine, long linen skirt topped by a white woolen robe with purple pomegranates embroidered on the sides. Over this the judge wore the ephod, a short vestlike garment, which was strapped to his body at the shoulders and tightened around the waist by a dazzling scarf of blue threaded with fine filaments of gold. Unlike the ephod worn by the high priests, Achan's was empty of the twelve jewels, three in a row that were symbolic of the twelve tribes.

Again and again Abinoam's curious gaze was drawn to Achan. The artisan knew little of the judge save that Achan had come to Kedesh from Shiloh, where the sanctuary of the Ark with its tablets of the Ten Commandments were kept, nearly two decades ago. Claiming himself a Levite, or servant of the priests, Achan—because he could read and write—had gradually assumed the role of judge, a position that had grown with his ascending power in Kedesh. A widower, apparently having no desire to remarry, Achan lived alone, seemingly content with his role as supreme authority for the domestic and religious problems of his people in the town.

Of middle years and of middle height, with a tendency to run to fat, Achan still was able to present a certain sturdy and solid appearance to all who faced him. His eyes were large and brown, almost liquid in their coloring, under great tufts of eyebrows that jutted outward. A tremendous spade beard, the color of dark honey, swept past the curiously triangular-shaped ears, hid the broad and sensuous lips, and skirted under the short, stubby nose. With some fascination Abinoam watched Achan's square-tipped fingers, amply covered with hair that even carpeted his wrists, play a soundless tune upon the shaft of the oxgoad.

Save for themselves, there were no others in the waiting room.

Abinoam, who had dressed simply in his gray robe and plain woolen skirt, leaned closer to Achan, who was also seated on the three-legged stool which had been provided for all petitioners seeking the king.

"There has been more contact between you and Jabin than with myself," Abinoam said. "Your affairs bring you often to him, while he has never seen me. What sort of man is the king?"

Achan whipped disturbed and worried eyes over the craftsman. "He is a man," he said irritatingly, "like other men. And like other men, who is to know what the state of his mind will this day be?" The judge pursed thick lips up with concern. "We should not have come here. It will only increase his anger. You should have obeyed his edict without coming here to protest it or question it." Achan shook his head with displeasure. "And the fact that your son struck down one of his soldiers will not make it an easier burden for us."

Abinoam's eye gleamed with sudden contempt. "*You* have fields, Achan," he said softly, "and you receive tithes from those who come to you. Your stomach," he added, his eyes sliding down over Achan's ample girth, "will not be drawn lean by hunger. But my son and I have nothing. And all we have saved and worked for has been taken away from us. As to Dael's striking the soldier—it was a defense of his life and"—Abinoam swallowed heavily—"mine."

"Nevertheless," Achan insisted primly, "we should not be here. Your request for a special dispensation to continue working in metal will never be granted. Indeed, perhaps the very sight of you will inflame Jabin's anger so that you will be lucky to escape punishment."

"How so?" Abinoam asked curiously, trying to keep the sudden pounding of his heart out of his voice. "The king has never beheld me. What knows he of me?"

"Enough to have you slain," Achan answered shortly. "Think you Jabin has no eyes nor ears to reveal to him what you do to his altars and his priests of Baal? Oh, while he has never seen you, Abinoam, your name is already marked in the records as a creator of trouble, as a dissenter, a mocker of the religion of Canaan. As often I have told you, you and those who follow you will someday meet their death at the hands of the king and the priests."

"I and those who follow me," Abinoam answered quickly, "follow the word of the one and only Jehovah, the God of Israel and"—the clay-colored eye flashed suddenly—"*your* God as well, Achan, since you are His judge."

"Of course, of course," Achan answered hastily. "I, too, believe in Jehovah. But must we always live in warfare because of the God? Can there not be peace between the followers of Baal and Jehovah in the land? Why cannot the two religions merge, the best taken from each——"

Abinoam's mouth set in firm lines. "There will never be an

assimilation between Jehovah and Baal. Never. And how can the spiritual worship be reconciled with that of statues, of human sacrifice, of bestial cults where women sacrifice their virginity to——"

He stopped as Achan held up a warning hand. "Wait," the judge whispered nervously. "I think we are about to be summoned. I think——" And suddenly he rose as the door opened and a little man, smooth-shaven and with alert blue eyes, entered the chamber and stood facing them.

Achan, tugging at Abinoam to rise with him, bowed his head and murmured, "Welcome and peace to you, Merobel, chamberlain to the great king, Jabin of Canaan."

Merobel nodded, his eyes resting coldly and almost insolently upon Abinoam. "And he with you?" the chamberlain asked. "Is he the one who comes to petition the king?"

"He so does, my lord," Achan murmured. "He is Abinoam ben Ebenezer, a craftsman and toolmaker of Kedesh."

Merobel nodded again, his gaze never leaving Abinoam. "A name not unfamiliar to the king," he murmured, and the frosted words sent their chill deeper into Abinoam's heart. As he saw the one-eyed man's reaction, Merobel's smile thinned. "However," he said, turning now to Achan, "this day must be edged with good fortune for the two of you. For not only will the king see you at once to hear your plea, but he is in a good mood. A very good mood," the chamberlain added.

"A new wife?" Achan ventured, attempting, for the first time, a weak smile.

"Better yet. Jabin's great champion, Og of Bashan, he who is known as the Bull, won a great victory in the arena yesterday. And you know how the king feels about his fighters and gladiators. In addition, a tremendous weight of metal and jewels fell into the king's lap as a result of the heavy wagers he made on Og. So—fortune smiles on you this day, Israelites."

Merobel nodded again and bade them follow him. "The king

visits the royal bakeries this morning," the court official informed them, "and has ordered I bring you there. . . ."

Both Achan and Abinoam relaxed immediately at this information. Jabin must surely be in a good mood to receive them, not in the cold and formal, imposing throne room, but in the warm informality of the bakeries. For a moment both men of Israel looked at each other; then, silently, they began to follow Merobel through the maze of corridors that led to the rear of the palace where were found the provision rooms, slaughter chambers, kitchens, wine cellars, and the bakeries.

Smiting their nostrils now was the tantalizing and humid odor of freshly baked bread. As Achan sniffed deeply, Merobel smiled tightly again. "Because of his love and concern for the gladiators and his champions, Jabin takes a personal interest in the food that is prepared for them. Hence, his presence in the bakeries is no uncommon thing." He paused before a wooden door, swung it open on the leather hinges, and entered the place of the baking of bread.

Abinoam's first confused gaze made him imagine he had blundered into a chamber full of giant beehives under which yellow-and-red flames danced. As far as the eye could see, these ovens stretched in endless rows, with the bakers, naked to the waist, hovering over them, tending to the fires or thrusting long shovels into the bellies of the hives and removing their treasures, long and oval-shaped loaves of bread. In the center, between the two rows of ovens, were the mixing tables, where other workers plied deft and busy hands into dough, shaping the loaves before having them speared above the gratings of the stoves. Still others, most of them women, Abinoam noticed, sat cross-legged on the floor against the wall, with pyramids of bread piled up near them, applying a glossy finish to the loaves, varnishing them with a mixture of egg yolk and water.

And standing before a laden table was Jabin, the King of All Canaan, his fingers busily tearing into the soft heart of a freshly baked loaf and bearing it to his mouth.

Although he was donned in no royal raiment, his head bare of crown or diadem and his hands carrying no scepter, there was no doubt that this man was a king and ruler. Naked to the waist like the others, clad only in a dirtied linen skirt that failed to hide the bulge of muscled leg or hard protuberance of the stomach, his still massive arms covered with a rug of red hair that ran over chest and abdomen as well, Jabin was the dominating and outstanding figure in the noisy, hot chamber.

As he neared the monarch, Abinoam observed him carefully in a long and scrutinizing manner, as if to memorize every feature. The toolmaker saw the cheeks, hung with little pillows of fat, that quivered as Jabin chewed the bread lustily. Neck and chin seemed encased in pinkish envelopes that bulged with blubber. Over this flesh loomed a round, short head, completely shaven to hide the increasing baldness. The neck was thick and muscular; the nose, short and tilted upward, exposed a generous amount of coral cartilage. The mouth, small and puckered almost like a snout, was busy with food. The arms still showed the remnants of the man Jabin once must have been, the famed warrior, charioteer, and fighter. The ruler's biceps still retained the burly, crushing strength that hundreds of rearing horses had been unable to break.

But the eyes, Abinoam wondered, the eyes—cold and light blue, small and cunning and without fear. In them shone the power and might and authority of the ruler of Canaan.

As Merobel neared the king and was about to throw himself to the ground in a prostrated bow, Jabin raised a careless hand and bid them stand. His voice, Abinoam perceived, was high and squeaking, a surprising sound to emerge from that massive torso.

"My lord king," Merobel was murmuring, "I bring thee the two Israelite petitioners—Achan ben Mahli, their local judge, and Abinoam ben Ebenezer, a toolmaker of Kedesh."

The little icy eyes passed briefly over Achan but lingered with deliberate intent over Abinoam's now impassive features. For a long time the single gaze of Abinoam and the piercing look of Jabin held, locked until both were broken at the same time. The king, rolling the soft pith of dough in his hands, looked around, found a honey jar, and dipped the bread into it. Almost in the same motion he popped the food into his mouth.

"Speak," he ordered, his mouth full, nodding at Achan.

"My lord, the king," Achan said quickly but with respect, "I appear before your countenance with this toolmaker who has come to seek your wisdom on a matter of state."

Jabin nodded, his jowls still working heavily with the effort of chewing. Then, wiping his hands on the skirt, he nodded at Abinoam.

"Say what you have come to say, Israelite."

Abinoam hesitated imperceptibly. What could he call this man, how should he address him? To call him lord or king would be false, for Jehovah was the only lord king of the universe. To call mere man king was not only false, Abinoam pondered, but close to blasphemy.

"Well?" The icy blue eyes were regarding him quizzically. "It seems to me, Israelite, that when you are away from me your tongue springs readily with words about me—words of slander and abuse and yes"—Jabin's face, grimmer now, darkened suddenly—"revolt." As he saw the startled look in the artisan's eyes the king nodded quickly. "Oh yes, Israelite. Your name has been made known to me as leader of those who would overthrow the throne of Canaan and set another upon it. One you call Jehovah . . ."

Achan, almost groaning audibly, bowed his head, but Abinoam remained erect, facing the monarch. Jabin blinked once, placed his hands on the table behind him, heaving his broad buttocks to the table top.

Since he was shorter than Abinoam, this seated position now made it possible for him to stare down upon the toolmaker.

"I still wait," Jabin said calmly.

"Ruler," Abinoam answered, finding his lips stiff and dry, "it is wrong to say I plot revolt or overthrow of your throne. I neither seek nor crave political upheavals. I am only a follower of the true God, Jehovah——"

"Whose followers mock my priests, destroy the altars of Baal, break up worship and prayer," Jabin finished for him. "All of which are acts of violence against the state. Against Canaan. For Baal is Canaan and Canaan is Baal. Therefore, you who lead can rightfully be called an instigator, a plotter and a rebel against the land, against me."

"I only——" Abinoam began to protest, but Jabin's uplifted palm was a wall against his words.

"*I* know only this, Israelite," Jabin answered, his voice still calm. "I know that you led a raid of your fanatics against my altars at Shimron, which you knocked down and destroyed by fire. Less than a month ago you and those who follow you had a pitched battle with my priests at Nahatol to the south, where three of the priesthood were slain. And who chopped down a new temple at Madon and smeared the idol of Baal with dung? Who extinguished the altar fires at Kitron while the women were worshiping Astarte?" The king's voice raised to a higher pitch. "Is this how civilized people act? And always the reports are brought back to me that a lean and red-bearded, gaunt, one-eyed man leads this rabble."

The king's hand found a lump of dough, and the stubby fingers closed around it tightly, sinking deeply into the pulp. "I could have crushed you as I do this dough," he said. "But I was lenient, for I do not like to spill blood needlessly. I am ruler of a civilized land and want to keep it thus. I waited, hoped you would see the error. But it was in vain."

"My lord king"—the quivering bass of Achan touched Jabin's ears now—"perhaps your words have burned some meaning into the mind of this man. I, too, have warned him that——"

"Silence . . ." The single word, chilled with contempt, was both an order and dismissal for Achan. "I speak to this one now, Achan, not you. And you, Israelite," the king went on, "have you nothing to say?"

"Only this, Ruler," Abinoam answered stiffiy. "I and those who believe with me worship only Jehovah, believe in only Him. Any other gods can be only an abomination in the land."

Jabin's mouth became a hard, tight line. "And what right have you to impose *your* God upon my people?" he demanded. "Who gave *you* the power to say that your Jehovah is better than Baal? It appears to me that Baal is a far more peaceful god than this one of war you profess to follow. Baal is the deity of the fields, of the crops. He brings peace, not everlasting warfare."

"And so will Jehovah," Abinoam answered confidently, "once all accept Him. Your Baal may be as you say, of peaceful and contented nature. Yet he is nothing but an idol, a bit of superstition cast into wood and stone before which your women prostitute themselves with strangers in the fertility rites and cast their seed before his fires. Not so with Jehovah. For Jehovah lies within the breasts and minds of all men and shows them the difference between right and wrong. No idols are needed for Jehovah. Each man has Him within himself and thus sees Him eternally."

Jabin's heavy fist crashed onto the table, sending the honey jar dancing, making the lumps of dough jump and scamper across the finely finished wood. For a moment Abinoam thought the great fists would descend to strike him. But Jabin controlled himself magnificently, taking a deep breath. Looking steadily again at Abinoam, he demanded:

"Speak of the reason you have come to see me, Israelite."

Abinoam leaned forward until his own hands rested on the table, just barely grazing the skirt of the king. "I have this day come to see you, ruler, to beg of you to allow my son and I to continue working in iron. To allow us to earn our bread. For all we possess lies in our hands. We own nothing else. All that we possessed was taken yesterday by your soldiers. Let us continue making our peaceful implements and tools. For neither my son nor I ever fashioned weapons to be used against Canaan."

Mirthlessly Jabin regarded him, shaking his head with a sort of helpless admiration. "Truly," he remarked, "you are either a fool or a man without fear. Do you know that by a single motion of my hand I could have you made prisoner or slave or end your life? Yet you stand before me and boldly demand that I make empty one of my own decrees! Wait," he added as he saw that Abinoam was about to reply. "You say you fashion no tools against Canaan. I say you do! Perhaps not of metal, but certainly of propaganda and slander and calumny and deeds. Therefore, I deny your request."

"Then for my son," Abinoam said, his voice lowered now. "Let him continue at least. I am old, and hunger is no stranger to me. But he——"

A flicker of sudden interest danced in the monarch's eyes. "Your son—was he the well-built one who struck down one of my soldiers at your forges?"

"In defense of his life, lord."

Jabin's glance bent downward. "I heard of that fight. Great skill and speed and strength." The cold blue eyes swept upward over Abinoam's face again. "Has your son any desire to become a gladiator and fight in the arenas?" Jabin stopped, staring, as he heard Achan's weak chuckle and saw the rueful smile being born on Abinoam's mouth.

"I am afraid my son has no interest in such pursuits," Abinoam said. "In fact, he regards Jehovah much in the same light as you do. He bears no love for Jehovah, seeks only to find peace and contentment in his work. That is why," he continued seriously, " I plead for him now. Give my son a special dispensation to continue work, at least until he has earned enough to continue his studies elsewhere or set up his own forges. I ask not for myself, only for him."

"Denied," Jabin said easily. "I have set my name and seal to an order, and it remains so. Work with iron, possess the metal, and you do so illegally and you will be killed for it," he continued, his gaze never leaving Abinoam.

"But why, why?" the toolmaker's tortured answer broke from his throat. "Why this sudden decree? Even if all the smiths and all the toolmakers in all of Canaan spent all their hours making nothing but weapons—could they fashion enough to strike down the king in warfare?"

"Why?" Jabin answered, almost murmuring. His eyes became

distant. "I will tell you why. Because I want peace in the land. More than anything, I want peace. But I cannot have this peace so long as there are factions of Israelites against me, men like yourself. Perhaps, as you say, you and your son fashioned no weapons of iron. But others have. I know that full well. My spies have eyes and ears. To the south, in Benjamin, that hotbed of discontent, the men *do* make weapons. I have seen their products." Jabin leaned forward earnestly. "Hear me, Israelite. Of Canaan am I, Canaan-born and bred, and with pride. Canaan can be rich and powerful and hold a mantle of peace all over the fringes of the Great Western Sea. Hazor can become the capital of the world, rivaling even Egypt's great cities. My people are merchants, traders, and they can bring wealth to the land. But how can this be accomplished if, within my midst, there are such as you who are seeking trouble? I must be rid of them before I can even begin to plan for the great peace."

As both Israelites looked at him in surprise, Jabin nodded again. "Such is my dream. To make Canaan the greatest of all nations. And it could be done. Easily so. And I will tell you more. Together, Israel *and* Canaan could make it so. Together, as brothers, we could build the land. But you and those like you would not have it thus. You selfishly seek your own gains. You forget that Canaan is surrounded by enemies at its borders—Egypt to the south, the new Assyria to the north. Ever must Canaan be vigilant. And this vigilance includes the enemy in its midst—Israel. Let Israel drop its religious warfare against Baal and I, King of Canaan, promise you equality and freedom. Together we can make of this land the greatest. But such a request is a dream, is it not?"

It was as if the king were pleading now, Abinoam thought. But at the question he dropped his eyes. There was only one answer to what Jabin had asked, and both of them knew what it was.

"Then you have all the answers," Jabin said heavily. "Yours—and mine. Now you know the reason for the monopoly on iron. I cannot have weapons fashioned against me in my own land, by my subject peoples, if I want Canaan to be great and to grow. Therefore, I repeat and warn again—cease and desist from all metalwork. Turn in any hidden stores of iron, for if they are found in your possession or on your property, there is nothing I can do to save your life. So have the priests demanded it, and so must I do."

Jabin gave a brief look at Abinoam. "Go now, Israelite," he said, not unkindly. "I know you have bravery, appearing unto me. And I respect that. But let us meet no more, save it be for a conclave of compromise and co-operation. Leave me now. . . ."

Almost wearily he waved his hand in dismissal. Then, as he remembered something, he called out, "Stay! There is one other matter I wish to reveal to you. So far I have been able to keep the priests from erecting an altar to Baal at Kedesh itself. Now I can no longer hold them back. Even this morning my workmen and the soldiers who guard them are building a new temple and altar for worship. I tell you this, Israelite, in warning. I want those altars to remain. Lead your followers against it, and . . ." The voice trailed off, pregnant with silent meaning.

Abinoam, who had been taking long strides toward the doorway of the bakery, halted suddenly. Stiff with surprise and shock, he wheeled to face Jabin.

"Do my ears hear right?" he demanded, his voice quivering. "You have ordered altars erected at Kedesh? Within sight of the people of Israel?"

"Within sight," Jabin answered evenly, "and make sure that those altars are not the last thing your followers behold."

"At Kedesh?" Abinoam asked again, his hands clenched, his face growing stern. A flame of anger licked upward at him, seeping through every sinew, sending him quivering with uncontrollable force. "My people will have to witness the abominations of Baal—this gross and obscene worship in which they might take part?"

"So have I ordered, and so shall it be."

"Then I shall——" Abinoam began. His breath came harshly and unevenly. The nostrils spread wide and the teeth bared in the whitened face. Almost panting with effort, he glared at Jabin, then without a word turned sharply and walked out of the room with stiff and angry steps. . . .

Jabin was silent for a long time, watching the doorway through which Abinoam had disappeared. It seemed to Achan as if a tiny sigh escaped from the broad chest. The king's eyes found the judge and looked at him. "There goes a man," Jabin said softly. "Would that he were with me instead of against me." Then, blinking quickly again as if by the act he could shuffle his thoughts back into a pattern, he turned to Merobel, who had been hovering respectfully near the three men all this time. "See that he leaves the palace grounds in safety," Jabin ordered, "and that no harm befalls him here. I want no extra uproars raised by his fanatics should he be hurt. If it were not for that, I would long have——" His mouth closed tightly and his fingers, flat now, slapped the surface of the table.

As Merobel bowed, nodded, and hurried off at Abinoam's heels, Jabin looked at Achan. The king's hands found another lump of dough and began rolling pellets aimlessly. As soon as Merobel had disappeared, Jabin jumped heavily down from the table and gestured toward the judge.

"Stay with me," he said, "and come into the flour storeroom with me yonder." Without waiting for a reply, the king slowly walked toward the other end of the bakery, pushing aside a curtained entrance which led to an empty little room where the finer flour of wheat and corn was kept for banquets. Now the place was devoid of sacks. Only a thin dust of white, shot through with golden specks that leaped from the single aperture, filled the chamber. As soon as Achan had entered, Jabin faced him.

"What reports of your spying do you bring me?" the monarch asked with no preliminaries. He smiled slightly as he caught the fear in the judge's eyes. Derision lengthened the king's lips. "No one will overhear us in this place," Jabin assured him. "You have been gone three weeks on your judging tours throughout Israel and you must have seen what I need to know. Speak, then. . . ."

Achan suddenly licked his lips, glanced around again, the brown eyes shifty and furtive now. With considerable distaste, moving away from the judge, Jabin asked curiously.

"How can the gold I give you for spying on your own people pay for a peace you never have? Do the shekels smooth and pave your way to slumber at night? Does a traitor's head rest easily on the sleeping pallet?" the king taunted.

"My lord king, I . . . I . . ."

Jabin rubbed the residue of honey from his fingertips, looking down upon them as he spoke. "Such is the way of the throne," he said, more to himself than to the uncomfortable man before him. "Forced to deal with all manner of men, even spies and traitors like yourself. I know such as you are necessary in political and martial intrigue. But I wonder," he continued, looking up now, his full glance sweeping with contempt over the judge's face, "I wonder if, had Israel fewer spies and traitors, he could not long ago have united his tribes and prevailed even over Canaan."

Once more Jabin saw the bowed head of Achan. "How really feels it," he asked with genuine curiosity now, "to be traitor, to live in fear of betrayal at any given moment?"

For a moment Achan made no reply. Then quickly—and almost proudly, the king marveled—the judge's head came up, the great half-moon of a beard rising with the chin, the shoulders heaving with an indifferent shrug.

"Like every profession, my king." Achan answered slowly, "it has its calculated risks. You ask how it feels to live as a traitor, and I can tell you, my lord, it is a better life than to live in poverty. . . ."

How can he know, how can he understand, Achan was wondering, what it means to be poor, to have nothing? The judge's palate soured with the old and familiar vinegar taste as he remembered his youth, he, the orphan, denied and wanting and finally becoming a Levite, an assistant to the priests, because his family stemmed from the tribe of Levi. The priests, the hated *kohanim*—he almost spat—how they exacted their tithes, tolls, and tributes from the stupid people, the superstitious ones who slaved for them! He thought of how the priesthood waxed fat on the compulsory offerings, how they threw only the lean and meager scraps of scorched meat and marrowless bones to their menial slaves, the Levites. The priests! Growing rich on a worship they secretly despised, stealing whenever they could, and hiding their loot under the guise of being the chosen ambassadors of Jehovah. The priests, with their fine robes and soft, perfumed palms, forcing the Levites to do all the filthy tasks at the sanctuaries, the making of fires, the hewing of wood, the carrying of water, the disemboweling of sacrifices, the backbreaking, sweat-soaking, humiliating labor, fit only for slaves, not men. And what was a Levite *but* a slave, serving the priests day and night, unable to own any land or property, forced to reside only in certain designated cities, to engage in neither trade nor commerce. No—the judge breathed deeply—he was glad he had left the ranks of the Levites and had used his cunning and wisdom to start reaping some of the golden kernels of fortune himself. Now he had fields and crops and flocks of his own; he dealt with the caravans; he bought and sold at a profit. He was already the richest man in Kedesh, even with the modest contributions given him by those for whom he judged. But the greatest bulk of his income came from the purses of Jabin, whose gold and silver poured into his palm for the spying that Achan did.

So be it, he vowed grimly. Better a spy than a servant or slave....

"So long as you pay me, my king, and pay well," Achan made answer now, a slight and mocking smile parting his beard, "I will traitor continue to be and work for you and Canaan. It matters not to me—so long as the hard metals fill my chests. Besides"—the smile grew bolder—"the risks are not as great as imagined. For who would suspect myself, Achan ben Mahli, a former Levite and now a judge of Israel, to be treacherous? What better cloak of camouflage could I don? As a journeying judge, traveling in all the districts of Israel, supposedly to dispense only justice and loving-kindness and mercy, my eyes have good opportunity to see all, my ears can overhear rumors and plots against Canaan. So I serve you, my lord, and, I think, serve you well. . . ."

"Then serve me now," Jabin said, still wiping his fingers on his skirt.

"And the gold, my lord?"

Jabin grimaced. "As always. Merobel will pay you. Now speak. . . ."

And Achan spoke of all he had beheld and overheard, how certain sections of Israel—especially the ever-dangerous and malcontent men of Benjamin, tough mountain fighters to the south, were openly showing tendencies of revolt against Canaan and of uniting under one leader of Israel.

"And is there such a leader in all of Israel?" Jabin asked quietly.

Achan smirked. "None, my lord, nor is there much likelihood of one ever being chosen."

"How so?"

Achan shrugged again. He thought of Israel, divided and helpless Israel. Torn in their loyalties and devotions to one another, jealously watching their allotted boundary lines, squabbling over the inheritance left to them by Moses, the clans and tribes were suspicious of and hostile to each other. And even their firmest pillar—the belief in Jehovah—was already shivering and tottering under the warm and seductive touch of the loving arms of Astarte, the female cult goddess, consort of the great Baal.

"Regard the temperament of the tribes," Achan said earnestly. "See mighty Judah, the most powerful of all to the far south, staying aloof and indifferent from any controversy with his blood kin, already marrying women of Canaan and becoming assimilated with Canaan. And across the Salt Sea glowers rich Reuben, sulking, while his enemies, Moab and Ammon, suck the strength from him. And there are little Dan and Asher, who want no part in any uprising and are content to seek the favors of the sea gods who will cast blessings upon their ships and trade. Parts of Manasseh and Gad, haughty and disdainful because of their half-Egyptian origin through Joseph, might attend a conclave of the tribes, but not much more."

"And the real troublemakers?" Jabin demanded thoughtfully.

Achan counted them on his fingers. "Only five, my lord king. Five out of twelve. Benjamin, of course. Ephraim; Naphtali, of which Kedesh and its leader, Abinoam, are the chief hotbeds of revolt and dissension; Zebulon, and Issachar. As you know, the Levites own no land or property and do not concern themselves with this."

Jabin was frowning, rubbing his palms together in reflective thought. "And what of food supplies and weapons?" he asked.

Achan's tone became stronger, more confident as he related he had seen illegal stores of iron and copper hidden by the smiths of Israel, had seen arrowheads and speartips gleaming white-hot in the fires, sword blades being flattened on the forges.

"Of that there will be an end now." Jabin smiled cruelly.

The judge nodded. "But in their food supplies, they also act in secret," he confided. "They use their wine presses to prepare—surreptitiously—wheat. In the troughs of the presses where should run the juice of the grape, there flow instead the kernels of wheat, there to be beaten and threshed. This I have seen with my own eyes. They hoard the wheat for their fighters. And more, my lord king. At night, to avoid your takers of the tolls, they use not the regular highways with their official tax booths, but smuggle what produce they can to the caravans, to sell to them without being taxed."

Jabin grimaced and slapped his hand against his thigh in annoyance. "And these," he said between clenched teeth," are the ones who profess to follow a god of peace! They conspire against me, prepare warfare against me—and yet scream it is for peaceful purposes. With cunning and craft they fashion warfare. Well, it shall be given them! So long as they foment revolt in the heart of Canaan, I will wipe them out, destroy them before they rot the whole land."

"My king has spoken," Achan murmured.

"And you keep speaking as well," Jabin answered sharply. "Prevent, at all costs, any attempt at unification. I want no leader to rise among this desert rabble to trouble me."

"I shall so attempt, my king."

Jabin's cold gaze swept over the judge's confident features. "And what words will you use to stop them from searching for a leader?" he asked.

Boldly again, Achan smiled at his ruler. "I will frighten them," he said easily. "Frighten them with words of what it will mean to have a king over them," he added, hoping that the mockery in his voice would not be too evident. "I will weigh down their hearts with suspicion and mistrust of what a king could do. I will reveal to them what deep wounds the hands of a ruler can scratch into their lives—that a king would take their sons for his wars, their daughters and wives and sisters to be cooks, perfumers, bakers, or sewers for *his* court. I will make known to them that a monarch will force labor upon them, taking them from their own work and their own fields. I will say to them that a king would make them plow *his* land and reap *his* harvests, while their own burned under the sun. I will show them how a monarch could confiscate their vineyards and flocks, if need be, or exact a tenth—for taxes—for his own pleasure. In short, I will tell them that with a king over them they will only be servants and not free men."

The slandering mockery in Achan's tone touched Jabin's cheeks with color, but he controlled himself, allowing only his eyes to show what he felt.

"So speak to them, then," Jabin said harshly. "And if your words are not enough, I have other means to silence their plotting tongues. Being fashioned for me in the royal smithies of Hazor is a new weapon that will astound and startle them and bring the fear and death to them so that——"

As he saw the surprised and calculating look in the shophet's eyes Jabin checked himself at once.

"A new secret weapon, my lord?" Achan asked softly. "Perhaps it should be granted me to know of this and to——"

"It is none of your concern," Jabin answered, a prick of annoyance lancing through him for having allowed the heat of his anger to melt the locks of his discretion. "Now depart from me, for I have much more this day to do."

"My lord king . . ." Achan cleared his throat and looked at Jabin for permission to speak again. As the king, showing visible annoyance again, nodded, Achan continued. He looked positively embarrassed now. What seethes in that traitor's mind of his? The king wondered.

"Speak—but quickly so," Jabin said.

Rubbing one hand against his wrist, Achan said, "There has but lately arrived to stay with me at my home, my lord, a kinswoman of mine, one Deborah bas Shillem. She is from Benjamin and is the daughter of my father's nephew. I know little about her save that——"

"Is she beautiful?" Jabin asked, a mocking light in his eyes now. It was known to all that Achan was a widower and had no woman of his own.

"She so is, my king. Of great beauty, with strange-colored hair. And of great wisdom and intelligence. For in Ramah, which is more than three days' journey to the south, from whence she comes, she has already carved a name for herself, a reputation——"

"As what?"

"As—as a judge, such as myself," Achan answered shamefacedly. "Only five and twenty, she nevertheless knows the meaning of the written words, is familiar with the laws, bears great influence among those she sees."

Jabin's grin was broad now. "A woman judging in Israel!" he commented. "You will have competition now, Achan."

"She comes only for a visit, my lord."

A little frown of worry creased the monarch's forehead. "Why has she not come before? What does she here? And from Benjamin too—that center of rebels and insurrectionists." He looked again at Achan. Almost with resentment he said, "How does it come to be that a woman is able to assume so much power and learning among your people? Women should not concern themselves with such matters." As he saw the judge shrug, Jabin, not without the touch of resentment again, said, "If such great knowledge and wisdom is hers, it could have come only through one way. She is a sorceress. . . ."

The monarch's eyes held those of Achan steadily until the bearded man shook his head slowly. "That I doubt, my lord," he said earnestly. "We allow no sorcery in Israel, and it is punishable by death. No. I think she picked up her learning from wherever she could, by herself, from those who were willing to teach, by listening and watching. At any rate, I judge her visit harmless here. It is our custom to keep track of our bloodkin and she——"

Jabin waved a weary hand. "Enough, enough," he said testily. "We waste too many words and burn too much time on a mere woman. Go you now from me and do what you have to do. Report again to me when you know something new and definite."

As Achan hesitated again, the king frowned once more. What troubles you now?" he demanded.

"My lord king—the gold?" Achan asked.

Rime hardened Jabin's eyes and he allowed his glance to press the judge with icy touch. But Achan kept his face before the king, who finally jerked his shaven head at the door. "Follow me," he ordered, the contempt thick in his words, "and I shall arrange it with Merobel."

3

ON THE MORNING that his father was appearing before Jabin, Dael was moodily striding toward the east, to the slight ridge of hill where, long ago as a boy, he had discovered a huge limestone cave and made it his own.

It was his study, retreat, and sanctuary, a place where he took his dreams and plans, where he had mastered the mysteries of reading and writing, aided by old Kner, an Egyptian hermit who had dwelled there. While Kner had been alive and had taught him, Dael had found a certain amount of happiness. When the lessons were over, Kner would tell him of the wonders of the world, especially of Egypt, and had instilled in the youth a desire to see for himself the great metropolis of Thebes or Memphis. From the aged and ailing Egyptian, Dael had heard of the smithies of the Nile, of the famous craftsmen, the jewel makers, who specialized in their arts, and it had become his flaming dream to pursue his studies in Mizraim as soon as he could. Old Kner also told Dael of histories, of the lives of men, of the ways of the world. When, five years before, Kner had finally fled the physical world, Dael had grieved for and missed him—missed the long, cool nights of study and argument, the flashing moments of revelation as some problem was made clearer to him, missed the grunting admiration for the articles of metal that Dael had created and brought for Kner's inspection.

But Kner had also left his heritage behind for Dael—scrolls and parchments and scraps of slate and pottery, upon which the written wisdom and lore had been enscribed, and over these the young toolmaker pored in lonely vigil after dark.

Now, as he neared the cave, his heart was heavy as he contemplated the future. For what now was there left to him? How could he earn his living? And what of his unfinished study and work? And Egypt? A dream, he told himself miserably, a dream blasted to shreds because of his father and that insane Jehovah worship of his. As so often before, he trod the familiar path that led to the mouth of the cave, stopping suddenly, aware that his place of retreat had this morning been usurped by a stranger. His private little kingdom had been invaded.

For one thing, instead of being black and forbidding, the mouth of the cave and its entire chamber were ablaze with lights, alive with color. Blinking with surprise and from the glare, Dael paused soundlessly before the entrance.

Lamps burned within the cave now, lamps of every conceivable size and shape. Clay lamps, with their squeezed brims to make a spout for the hemp that floated in olive oil; saucer-shaped givers of light that were flat-bottomed and delicately balanced on niches of rock; more ornate ones of copper, with their handles shaped in the form of animal heads; and even a tall footed lamp, with its punched-out holes, that had been thrust into a crude wooden stand. There were smaller lamps, all made of metal, with designs of flowers and birds and stars on them, of such fine workmanship that Dael's hands itched to touch and examine them.

But he paused at the entrance, silently watching the flickering tongues of light that ate away at the shadows, driving them, leaping, to the fartherest corners, where they lingered, crouching, ready to spring back upon the girl who was seated in the midst of the radiance.

Dael stared at her.

Stared not only at the woman but at what she was doing. Surrounded by bits of pottery upon which words had been written, hard-baked bricks, glossy covered tablets of beeswax, more precious animal hides, flat stones—all bearing writing—the stranger gave the immediate impression of being a scholar. For in her hand was a split-reed pen which she was using to write upon the soft inside of a sheepskin, the letters seeming to fall into neat and orderly rows, as if guided by their own intelligence, the cursive script dropping like grotesque rubies from the red-inked tip of the reed.

He took a closer step, still unseen and unheard by the woman, who was bent over her task. Dael sniffed softly and cautiously. The odor of burning oil and smoldering hemp lay as thickly in his nostrils as it did upon the walls of the cave.

Still closer he came, marveling at the beauty he beheld in her now. Even while sitting cross-legged and bent over her work, he sensed she was tall—perhaps not more than two handbreadths shorter than himself. But the greatest wonder of all—he took a deep breath—was her hair. Never before had he gazed upon such coloring. The color of butter, he thought, a pale, creamy hue. And he wondered whether it was as soft as butter as well. Straight and without waves or curls, it flowed down her back and, even at first glance, seemed to mark her a woman apart from the others of her sex. Honey and butter, he told himself, not knowing what made him think of the two ingredients now. Lady of the Lamps—*Ayshesh Lapidus*—the phrase bubbled in his mind and then broke over his tongue until he longed to repeat it aloud.

Carefully he studied her, his eyes solemn but scrutinizing carefully. She seemed light and lithe of movement, her fingers and hands supple as she moved pen or parchment. Maturity had touched her with exciting care in the deep swell of her breasts and the hidden lines of thigh under the long skirt she was wearing. Her lashes, long and fan-shaped upon the smooth cheeks, he noticed furtively, seemed to spread out like the shining rays of a tiny sun old Kner had once shown him on a tablet of Egyptian picture writing. The eyebrows were insect-shaped, rising like crooked wings on the forehead. He longed to see her eyes, to note their color, but could not, since her gaze was lowered upon her writing.

Still closer he stepped. The artist in him admired the flawless skin, the short, round nose ending in a tiny tilt, slightly spreading and pushing upward the triangular-fashioned nostrils.

Truly—he caught his breath again—such beauty had never been his to behold before. Almost without realizing it, he was close enough to see what she was writing, and before he could control himself he began to read, his voice sounding alarmingly loud in the silent cavern.

" 'In those days,' " Dael read, his eyes fastened upon the parchment, " 'there was no king in Israel, and every man did that which was right in his own eyes.' "

Even before the first words had rolled off his tongue she had dropped the pen, half rising in startled surprise, facing him now, her mouth opened slightly. As he took his glance from the script he saw the color of her eyes for the first time.

Gray. Deep, dove gray with little yellow flecks dancing in them, he observed. And I was right about her height, he thought, almost grinning, as she rose to face him. She is tall, far taller than any other woman of Kedesh.

For a moment both were silent, watching each other warily. And when speech came it was born of the woman first. "What do you here and who are you?" she asked, her voice low and pleasant despite the slight tremor in it.

He allowed himself a full smile at her, leaning idly against a wall, hooking his thumbs in the rough and unfinished cowskin belt around his waist.

"Since you be the intruder," he answered easily, "I think the question you ask should be mine to demand."

Her eyes blinked once. But a slight look of defiance cemented her face and hardened her chin. She was more composed now, bending to pick up the pen and replace it carefully on a niched wooden tray chiseled to hold writing instruments. When she had finished, her gaze was level and undisturbed.

"I saw no markers of ownership in this cave," she answered. "Yet you say it belongs to you. What proof have you?"

Still smiling, he shrugged. "There is proof. One, this place is mine by discovery and long use." As he saw the smile of derision starting to curl the long, thin upper lip he went on hastily: "Secondly, search that niche over there." He indicated with his head a depression in the stone wall. "You will find a stone tablet there. Since you know how to read, I will tell you what is enscribed there."

Still only half believing, her hands reached above her for the tablet, found it, scanned it quickly.

" 'The refining pot is for silver,' " Dael repeated from memory, " 'and the furnace for gold, but the gods try the heart.' " He was saddened as he remembered the time old Kner had told him the ancient proverb and he had written it down.

When he finished and looked at her, he caught her full surprised gaze upon him. Her eyes, he noticed, were even a deeper gray than he had imagined, and her mouth looked lovely in the lamplight. Just above the lips her fingers must have left a red stain from the ink, and he suddenly felt an overwhelming desire to approach her and, with a gentle finger, wipe off the crimson blur. But he controlled himself, still standing easily before her, a crooked half smile on his features.

The insect wings of her eyebrows lifted slightly in a gesture of quizzical surprise and disbelief as she continued to stare at him. Truly, she thought with a secret and quickened breath that both annoyed and yet somehow pleased her, this man was one of the most unusual she had ever met. Not just because he could read and write, an almost unheard-of thing for anyone not trained in the ways of scribe or priest. But his very physical appearance demanded attention and, yes, she admitted to herself, admiration.

It was not just his height alone, she told herself staunchly, even if he stood taller than most men she had seen, not the dark, almost olive skin and the small curling beard that shadowed his cheeks, chin, throat, and upper lip. The nose, she decided critically, was also not too unusual in its clean, straight sweep from the forehead, broad and unmarked, over which hung carelessly the uncombed locks of his dark hair. There were men in Israel with the same colorings and shades, but somehow, in this young stranger, they combined to form a face of singular masculine attraction. A face, she thought quickly, startled at herself, that must draw women to it. The voice was low-pitched and quiet, she approved silently, a sign of good inner control on thought and action. The straight, well-formed white teeth were a definite asset, as was the round heavy chin, showing determination and will of character. If such as he stood before me in judgment, she decided quickly, I would both believe him and respect him.

The lashes of his eyes were short and bristly and of a strangely colored reddish-black. But his eyes were what held her, seemed almost to lure her with a strange and compelling attraction against which, at this very moment, she found herself fighting. The irises, dark as a black olive, seemed alive and burning set against their strangely rimmed red halo. At times, she wondered, could that red flame in his eyes blaze into yellow when anger or other emotions stirred him? Or would they always be this color when peace and contentment honeyed his veins?

Nor was the rest of him to be quickly ignored, she reflected under suddenly lowered lashes, annoyed once more at the quick flow of warmth that seeped upward over her body and even tinged her cheeks. Physically this man was superbly gifted. The breadth of his shoulders spread the cloth of his short mantle almost to bursting. His arms, from massive shoulder socket to broad fingertip, were corded in hard, bunching knots of resilient power. A similar sheath of muscle rippled on his back, swelled his chest, and pinched the slim hips into tough strength. And he moved easily, too, she was aware; he seemed to ripple, glide, was lithe and fluid on his long legs, sturdily supported by the flat-muscled thighs and rolling-sinewed calves.

A man, she judged silently to herself, at least in outward appearances, powerful, determined, poised, with the face of a dreamer or scholar, the hands of a craftsman, and the body of a gladiator. But what of his heart, his mind, his emotions? True, he was educated, but was there more beyond that?

Silently she replaced the stone tablet in its niche. Then she smiled at him for the first time. "I admit," she said in her clear but not loud voice, "that I be the trespasser here. Clearly, you have proven your right to this cave. If so"—and she bent quickly and began picking up a scroll or two—"I will leave it to its rightful master."

He watched her for a moment as she continued gathering up her parchment rolls, slipped a hard wad of leather into the bottle of red ink and duller cakes of earth into a small horsehide bag.

"What is that?" he asked curiously, pointing to the flattened cakes.

She paused for a moment. "Of this I make my own ink," she explained. "It is red ocher of earth, which I mix with gum and then dissolve in water." Then she went on with her gathering.

He continued to watch her, mystified and yet musing about her, silently admiring the sheen and flow of her hair, feeling again that strange desire to rub off the red ink mark above her mouth. He could not let her depart like this, he decided quickly. Not until he knew more of her, whence she came, what she was doing here in Kedesh, who her people were, how she was named. Besides, he thought with a sinking heart, what good was the cave to him now? There would be little time left for study and dreaming for him. He might have to leave Kedesh anyway and seek his livelihood elsewhere.

"Stay," he said to her, his voice rising slightly, so that she looked up in surprise. "You need not leave. The cave is yours. I have no further use for it." He took a deep breath but fastened his grave eyes solemnly upon her.

She smoothed her fingers over a parchment. "How is it so?" she asked. "First your words and glance accuse me of being an interloper, and now you bid me not only welcome but allow me to stay?"

He shrugged. "I said I no longer have need of the cave. I"—he swallowed heavily—"might have to leave Kedesh soon, and I would rather entrust someone like you to this place than leave it to another." He saw the unvoiced question in her eyes and, before he realized it, he was bitterly pouring out the story of the previous day's evil events, of the destruction of the forges, of Jabin's edict on the monopoly of iron, of his own ruined plans and hopes of continued study in Egypt, of the poverty and the economic ruin that faced his father and himself now.

She listened silently through the flow of words, offering no comment, uttering no questions. When he had finished and was staring dumbly upon the ground, she touched his arm lightly with the rolled parchment.

"It is as I have written," she said softly. "In those days there was no king in Israel, and every man did that which was right in his own eyes." She looked at him and he wondered if there was a challenge or mockery in the gray depths of her eyes. "So what intend you now to do—ben—ben——" she asked, searching for his name.

"Ben Abinoam," he said. "Dael, the son of Abinoam of Naphtali."

Her smile was almost a mischievious grin, gleaming, the space between the two front teeth strangely tantalizing. "It is about time that we made known to each other our names," she said. "I am Deborah bas Shillem of Benjamin. I have come here to visit with a distant kinsman of mine, Achan ben Mahli, who is the judge of Kedesh." She paused imperceptibly. "I was born in Ramah."

They looked at each other, both smiling, both feeling the wariness and antagonism melting away in the heat of the lamps. Suddenly she thrust forward her hand and found and clasped his wrist in an impulsive gesture. "In peace, Dael ben Abinoam, I behold you," she said formally.

"And stay in peace and welcome, daughter of Shillem," he answered seriously. "And I repeat what I have said before. This cave is yours from now on."

She bowed her head, as if offering thanks to him, then looked up quickly. "And what do you now, Dael?" she asked. "For surely there is nothing left for you in Kedesh save to——" She stopped, her lips pressed together suddenly.

Impassively he shrugged. "I could hire myself out to be a servant unto others of Israel until the year of jubilee would free me of bondage. Or become a paid mercenary for Jabin. Or seek my fortune along the seacoast cities where dwell the brethren of Asher and Gad."

"And your father?" she asked quietly, not looking at him. "What of him?"

"My father," he said, so bitterly that she cast surprised eyes upon him. He was about to go on but stopped himself. He bent down, picked up a fragment of stone tablet, looked on it impatiently, and threw it away. "I know not what the future holds for me," he added.

"I see," she answered, and he knew that she did not see, could not understand at all. He watched her as she began to arrange a series of tiny phials, jars, and bottles on a wooden shelf he had erected along the wall. Liquids, red and purple and blue, shook and gurgled within the containers of copper and leather and rough opaque glass. He stretched out a curious hand to finger a tiny container of glass along which small mosaics of lapis blue and henna red ran in intricate fashion.

"Of this material I have heard," he said with ill-concealed interest. "Is it not made of salts and sands?"

"Yes." She nodded. "In Egypt they create many beautiful things of this, which is made of sand and salts blended together by fires." She watched him as with tender care he held the bottle and examined it. She heard him sigh.

"I, too, could work with this material if it were only given me to learn more in Egypt," he said, at first wistfully, then with a hardening of the lines of his mouth. "I shall probably never see it."

"And what could be taught you there, Dael?"

He still held the bottle in his hands. "All I want to know," he answered gravely. He tapped a finger against the glass. "How to work in this material. How to fashion wondrous jewels, earrings, bracelets, arm bands, rings. Oh, I am but a simple toolmaker now, taught by my father, but at the Nile I could . . ." His voice trailed away.

Gently she took the bottle from him and arranged it with the others. He continued to look at the paraphernalia she was setting out before her from cedarwood boxes and smaller bags and purses of leather and linen. Pots and containers of ointments and oils, greases and unguents were drawn from the throats of the bags and set carefully at her side.

As he watched, he frowned suddenly. Quickly he gestured at the large array of material at her feet. "What is all this?" he asked, his voice more severe now. He looked at her sharply. "You know that—sorcery is forbidden."

He had expected her to get angry, but her laugh, full and merry when it came, startled him. "I practice no sorcery," she smiled finally. "What you see here are but harmless ingredients. No sorceress I—just a woman of curiosity. True, I have learned a few tricks of magic, but for my own amusement only. Here—I will show you."

Deftly she took two phials, shook a few drops from each into her palm. "See," she laid, "both liquors are colorless. Now watch while I mix them." With pursed lips she poured the contents of both containers into a larger dipper, and Dael gasped as he saw the liquid turn crimson.

Deborah smiled at him. "For the foolish and the superstitious," she explained lightly, "I have turned water into blood. But you and I know," she confided, as one child with a secret to the other, "that the red color came from this." And she quickly opened her palm to show Dael a crushed pellet that lay there, still oozing little drops of crimson.

"Nothing but henna placed within a tiny fish bladder which I pierce with a nail," she revealed, "and allow the henna to fall into the water. The whole trick—and that is all it is," she continued, "is moving my hand so swiftly that your eye cannot follow it." As she saw the stupefied look on his face she laughed again. "Wait. I will show you another, even more astounding."

From another bag she withdrew what seemed to Dael a long rod made of hardened wood with a leather head on it fashioned after that of a serpent. Deborah's hands twinkled, and in the space it takes to draw a breath the rod had become alive, twisting and writhing on the stones of the cave's floor. So vivid and real was the action that Dael stepped back swiftly and looked around for a weapon to smite the crawling, shivering reptile on the floor.

"Stay, stay, Dael," Deborah said, amusement rich in her throat, "it is but another trick. Behold." She stopped, picked up the serpent in her bare hands, passed a palm along its quivering body, and suddenly the thing in her hand was a rod again.

She beckoned Dael to come closer and let him examine the magical rod. "It is a device of springs and mechanisms," she showed him, "where by just pressing my hand I can erect the rod or, with my thumb, release the springs which will send it writhing on the ground. Here—do it yourself."

With silent laughter she watched as Dael managed to stiffen the mechanism and then release it so that it appeared like a snake. When he had satisfied himself a few times, his grin was as broad as hers as he returned the apparatus to her. There was an added gleam of excitement in his eyes as he said:

"I, too, have a trick of magic which might be of interest to you." Before she could answer, he had walked over to a corner of the cave, ripping off a black cloth from something that appeared like a stone to Deborah. Dael placed a hand over a tiny lamp of iron—its base constructed in the form of two snakes intertwined—and extinguished the flame in it. Carefully he removed the wick, poured the oil into a basin, and then held out the small flame giver to her.

"Behold this," he said almost dramatically. He held the lamp close to the stone, then placed it almost perpendicular to the surface. Suddenly he released his grip.

The lamp, instead of falling to the ground, seemed to leap through the air in a straight line, like an arrow in flight, and then fasten itself against the stonelike object and remain, trembling slightly, clinging against the rough surface.

Deborah gasped, her eyes narrowing.

"Wait," Dael said triumphantly, almost like a little boy showing off a new-found treasure. His hands picked up a broken buckle of iron from the floor. Once again he held it to the side of the mysterious stone, and once again the metal was drawn unerringly to the surface and remained hanging against the side of the strange rock.

"Allow me," Deborah said, her brows still creased. She tugged both the lamp and the broken buckle from their resting places and then held them about an arm's length from the stone, releasing her grasp. At once both metal objects arched over to the target, again finding it and remaining against it.

With wide eyes the woman stared at Dael. "What manner of rock is this?" she inquired.

"I call it a stone from heaven," Dael explained. "For I actually saw it fall from the skies one night. It was blazing as it streaked through the darkness. It fell in a field not far from here. Later I chipped a part of it from the main body and brought it here." He flicked a nail over the gray creased and seamed surface. "It is hard and not unlike iron metal. I had planned to fashion some objects from it. Now, with the iron monoply declared, I do not know what to do with it."

"Others know of this?" Deborah asked, still staring at the meteoric, magnetized iron.

"None of whom I know," Dael answered. "I buried the biggest bulk of it, bringing only a fragment here for my own study and observation."

She ran a finger over the surface again, tracing the ridges, grooves, and valleys in the meteor. "Stone of heaven," she murmured. "I have seen the streaks of fire in the heavens and thought they were stars falling. But I never knew that it was like this."

"Why it should attract metal, I know not," Dael confessed. "I have tried it with iron and others—and the attraction still holds."

"Perhaps," Deborah said, concentrating, "there is something within the stone that gives it strength to pull metal unto it. But why? And how?" she pondered. Her eyes suddenly gleamed with curiosity. "Would you take me to the field where you have buried the rest of this stone?" she asked. "I would behold it."

He hesitated for a moment and, in her woman's instinct and with female intuition, she guessed at the delay. He had said no one else knew of the stone. It was his secret to keep. And now she, a stranger and a woman, was asking him to——

"I will so do," he answered slowly, and she was surprised at the sudden, tugging lift of her heart. She understood the compliment in his tone; he was willing to share his secret with her.

She smiled at him. "I wish to thank you," she said, liking the sudden warm light that appeared in his eyes. He looked away from her then. "Come," he said, almost harshly, afraid his voice might betray him, fearing that his fingers might reach out of their own volition and wipe off the red smudge that rested so close to her lips. . . .

Brilliant sunlight wrapped a gilded and warming cloak that both covered and embraced them as Dael and Deborah strode through the fields to find the buried stone of heaven.

The girl listened as Dael spoke of his work as toolmaker, of the things he dreamed of fashioning someday as a master jeweler in the land. As she matched his stride to fit his long steps, she told him that the Ark—which contained the tablets of the Ten Commandments—now at the holy sanctuary at Shiloh, had a broken cover and could use a good jewelmaker and craftsman.

"And who knows?" she said lightly. "Perhaps someday, Dael,

your hands will mend the Ark and bring the needed repairs to the gift of Jehovah to His people."

He glanced at her sharply. Was she, too, he wondered in an instant's bitter reflection, still another one of the fanatical followers of Jehovah? But he dismissed the thought as nonsense. An educated woman, wise in so many ways, could not possibly have any ties or entanglements with gods or religions. Like himself, she was interested in the things of the world, how they were fashioned and for what purpose and use.

She asked him about the various procedures he used in his work, and eagerly he responded, telling her of the right kinds of metal for various objects, of the heat required and its correct intensity, of the amount of air that should be bellow-blown, of the best way to make fires from camel-dung fuel, of how to burn out the dross from the metals and leave them pure, how to bend and shape into form.

Surprised at her intelligent questions, at her interest, he plunged on into matters of his work, stopping only when, almost ashamedly, he realized she had been probing him subtly, finding out things about him, while he had rushed on and on, wrapped up in his own knowledge and affairs.

And the woman was also wondering at the complete ease and relaxation with which she found herself talking to this man whom she had known for little more than an hour, a stranger and yet stranger no longer. She felt the growing affinity, like a bond tightening, drawing them closer and closer together. Was it because we seem to have common interests, share mutual curiosity, she marveled, or is it more than that? Whatever it is, she reasoned, it is stimulating and interesting.

And good.

As if from a great distance, she heard his voice saying: "I have been babbling too much of myself. And what of you, Deborah?" His smile was almost shy as he looked at her. "You know everything about me, but I know little of you."

"And little enough there is to know," she replied. "For I am but a woman in Israel, and that is little indeed."

"But you are not like other women!" he found himself objecting hotly. "You are learned, wise, educated, beautiful, with such beauty as has never before——"

He stopped, his face darkening with the rush of blood. She had also ceased her walking and was looking at him with mingled curiosity and pride and surprise.

Her head was swept back, her chin rising, the lovely, mobile mouth opened in surprise. In her eyes he could read an emotion that was half pleasure, half suspicion.

"You really think I am beautiful?" she asked, her voice lower than he had heard it up to now.

"I so do, Deborah," he answered quickly, finding his breath coming shorter suddenly. He took a step closer to her so that he could look directly down into her face. "Why, has no man before ever told you so?"

The gray eyes were lowered. If she made answer to him now, telling him that others had admired her beauty, it might make him resentful or even jealous. If she replied that no man had revealed his longing for her, it could make him scornful or even unbelieving. So, in the way of woman, she said nothing, merely smiling as she looked up at him again.

"But," she said quickly, shifting into the offensive now, "I know that the young women of Kedesh must be no strangers to you." Her smile was half serious, half teasing, but it disappeared when he shook his head solemnly. "No time for women had I," he answered gravely. "There was too much to do, too many tasks and work and study. Between the fires of the forges and the scrolls of learning, I had little time to——" He smiled wistfully at her. "And you?" he asked.

She nodded quickly. "I understand what you mean," she asserted with sympathy. "I, too, had little time. I—I"—and she looked down upon her hands—"I wanted to be the equal of any man in Ramah, because I knew the position of women in this world. So I studied to acquire knowledge, the only weapon left to me. I learned the meaning of the written words, mastering the five languages and their scripts. Then I pursued the study of the laws, aided by those who would help me, mostly the old men, who thought they were satisfying a mere woman's whim. Then"—her eyes had a faraway look in them—"I learned the laws and rituals, not only of Israel but of other lands, until I this day——" Her voice suddenly faltered. Should she tell him? Would it create a chasm, a difference between them at the start?

"Yes?" he prompted gently.

"Until I became the woman judge of Ramah," she concluded softly, swiftly scanning his face for any immediate reaction.

It came at once, a look of surprise, incredulity, and amazement, so naked, so revealed, that there could be no doubt of what he felt.

"A shophet—a woman judge?" He swallowed heavily, his eyes never leaving her face.

She laid her fingers on his wrist lightly. "You make it sound too important," she chided. "Actually, it is not a task as heavy as it might seem. I merely answer a few questions, interpret dreams, explain the domestic laws, offer advice and counsel to those who seek it. It is nothing. Certainly nothing," she added "of which to be in awe."

They were standing now in the great shadow of a box tree that loomed four times the size of a tall man. Sunlight, filtering through the branches, danced on her features, lingering on her cheeks and touching her mouth like a soft and golden veil. "After all," he heard her say, "I am just a woman with a little knowledge. But a woman . . ."

Dael felt his stomach muscles tighten, his heart tugging fiercely within him. Was she offering him a challenge, a dare to prove that she was more woman than judge? Before he realized it, he had stepped closer to her, had reached out for her, had swept her into his embrace, and, feeling her yielding and yet not yielding, he fastened his mouth and body against hers.

Time roared and pounded in his ears during the embrace, until she suddenly broke from him with a cry, fiercely pushing him away, averting her lips and her head. Instantly he freed her, stepping back, a cold tide of shame and regret chilling the heated blood in his veins. He stared at her, his breath harsh in his throat, as she held out her arms in a protective gesture before her.

"I beg of you, please it to be so," he heard her say. "I am still a maid and——"

"You need not fear," he apologized quickly and humbly. "Even if you were not what you say, I——" He turned away from her, leaning against the trunk of the tree.

Deborah dropped her hands, hoping their tremble would not be noticed. A tiny twinge of disappointment raced through her, and she wondered whether it was because he had given in so quickly, made no further attempt. On her lips the pressure of his kiss still seemed to linger. Inwardly she realized that perhaps she had deliberately invited his embrace, had wanted more. Deborah, Deborah, she thought to herself. You thought you knew all, of love and men and women, and yet one kiss, the single, fleeting embrace of a stranger—a man you have known but for a few hours—— could stir you so, could bring such delight as you have never known before. Greater even—her hammering heart pounded—more exciting than the discovery of new knowledge or the opening of unread scrolls or the dispensing of judgment. How came this to be? she wondered almost helplessly.

But to Dael she presented a hurt and angry countenance that very well masked the true fiber of her emotions as she looked at the young craftsman again. This time his gaze no longer slid ashamedly away from hers but met her eyes openly. And between them now and through them there existed a newborn and not unwanted intermingled feeling of confusion and bewilderment and longing. Both realized that not only was this new, but something they could not, at this moment, even attempt to define. Shyly, almost like children, they smiled at each other.

"I ask your forgiveness," she heard him say.

"If there was something for which to forgive, I would grant it," she answered lightly, her eyes still intent upon him. But her mind was already flashing ahead to find a subject that would lead them away from this new—if exciting—moment. She looked at the tree. "Is this where you have buried the stone from heaven?" she asked, trying to control her voice.

Relieved, he nodded. "Under this tree I did bury the stone after I discovered it. It was not large, but very heavy, so I merely took a chip off the main rock. Nor rests it deeply in the embrace of the sand," he added hurriedly, bending and picking up a flat rock with a triangular point. "I can dig it with this," he assured her.

Silently, still musing, she watched his serious and concentrated face, the sleek and supple movement of arms, back, and shoulders as he started to scrape and probe into the loose earth. Soon a sheen of perspiration silvered the olive skin as he labored. Faster and faster he dug into the soft loam, until at last the gray-black and seamed surface of the rock became visible.

Curiously Deborah stared at it, her mind again wondering at its origin, at its journey across the heavens until it had reached its destination here at the insignificant village of Kedesh. She watched as Dael, still breathing easily, lifted the stone—it just fit in the cradle of his arms—and placed it a little distance away from the freshly dug hole.

"Here," he said, pointing out a small, rectangular space in the meteorite, "is where I cut my piece away." She saw him pause, his eyes suddenly blank with surprise.

"What is it?" she asked, leaning forward.

Without speaking he gestured to the underside of the stone. There she saw another cut, larger than the first, that had been sliced into the rock. "There is another cut here," Dael was murmuring, "but one made not by my hand." He arose, licking his lips.

"Another must have found the rock and removed a piece of it," he said heavily.

4

THE SUN, slipping with desperate, crimson defeat into the western sea, was now sullenly hurling its last shafts of light against the unmarked trunk of the box tree against which Deborah and Dael had leaned for most of the morning and afternoon.

The passing of time had gone by without their knowledge, had sped past them on silent feet as they had talked of and to each other, learning more of their pasts, their interests, hopes, and plans. Between them the bond of affinity and understanding, which had been as tough and raw as a fresh hide thong in the early morning, had, by late afternoon, been hardened and yet made more flexible by the warmth of their words and the sun.

While the mystery of the missing chip of meteorite still troubled Dael, he tried to make light of it to the young woman. A hundred things might have happened to it, he explained to Deborah. A man owning a field and looking for a good marker with which to establish his boundary lines had perhaps discovered the stone and had cut it to use on his lands.

"Or," he had puzzled, "perhaps the soldiers of Jablin—who are erecting a new altar to Baal—might have found it and are making use of it."

Deborah's eyes flickered with sudden interest. "Where is this new altar to be built?" she inquired.

Dael shrugged. "On the outskirts of Kedesh. It is the first one so to be erected. I saw the soldiers and the masons this morning before coming to the cave and inquired of them." He frowned slightly. "It will not remain for long. My father will see to that."

"How so?" she asked, her gaze veiled now.

Dael grinned at her. "For most of his life my father has been destroying the altars of Baal. But never so close to home. By tomorrow he will have gathered up the other foolish fanatics who listen to him and will descend upon the high places."

"And you?" she prompted. "You take no part in these assaults against Baal and his priests?"

"I?" He laughed shortly. "Never. I have no interest in Baal or"—and he looked at her sharply—"any other gods. Including," he added bitterly, "the most infamous of them all, Jehovah."

She was silent, allowing her finger to trace aimlessly a queer design in the sand around her knees. Curiously he followed her moving finger and the pattern it left. "I have never seen such a figure as that," he declared, the artist in him aroused at once. "It appears like the inside of the lotus flower."

Silently she nodded, her hand finishing the outline of what appeared to Dael to be two triangles piercing each other. "A star?" he asked.

She nodded. "A six-pointed star, made of two triangles on each other. It is an ancient design, used by many people before us. It is said that it is also a symbol of love—and life—the two triangles of man and woman placed over each other. However, I like to imagine it to be a symbol of something else. Of the star of Israel, to be worn by its king someday."

Dael straightened his legs in a little gesture of annoyance. "And they talk of such things in Benjamin too?" he asked. "Has Jehovah corrupted everything in the land?" He slapped his thigh in irritation. "Why can't they understand that the only true godliness is to be found in work and in creation, in what a man fashions with his own hands? In beauty and in learning and not in following a war god. There is true religion to be found. Often so have I exchanged words with my father—but he will not listen. No wonder Jabin hates him and seeks to destroy him. And myself," he added bitterly.

Deborah's smile, when he beheld it, was quietly unnerving to him and he could not understand the reason. "But how can you face a foe, who is armed with a sword, with only books in your hand?" she demanded without harshness. "How ever will learning and knowledge and beauty prevail over an enemy who has spear and chariot and speaks with the voice of thunder? Oh no, Dael ben Abinoam. That cannot be. Sometimes you must have war before there can be peace. How could you, a peace-loving artisan, be able to work in security and safety and without fear if the dove of peace does not brush her wings against you? Even now, at this moment, your livelihood has been stripped from you, your fortune confiscated, and your plans cut to ribbons because of the power Jabin holds over you. If Israel were free, if Israel had fighting men who——" She paused as she saw the anger darken his face and draw tight his lips. With dismay she watched as he rose slowly to his feet and looked down upon her with bitterness.

"Since you came from Benjamin, a place of rebels," he said sarcastically, "I should have known better than to speak to you of how I feel about Jehovah."

"Dael, I only meant to——" she began, stopped by the snort of derision that came from him now.

"So you, too, are a follower of Jehovah," he accused. He bent over her, his eyes suddenly dulled, his face hardening. "You do not deny it?"

"I do not deny it," she answered in a low voice. "For how can I? I am a judge. A dedicated woman . . ."

"Dedicated to warfare and blood," he grated derisively. He took a deep breath. "So be it then. Perhaps," he almost sneered, "you would find more in common with my father than with me. Why do you not approach him? He will need help to knock down the altars of Baal."

He looked down upon the ground, where the six-pointed star was still etched in the sand. With a single motion he lifted his foot over the design and obliterated it with his sandaled toe. "And so will Jabin do with all who follow this symbol of Jehovah," he said darkly.

And swiftly now she, too, arose, facing him, her face drawn and defiant, her eyes shaded with quick and heated emotion. She felt like shouting at him, to scream out how wrong he was, how foolish and naïve—but caution stilled her tongue with a cool and restraining palm.

Unashamedly he grinned at her. "If you so desire," he taunted, "I will speak to my father of you."

He took a step forward, and for one blinding and fleeting moment, edged with a sort of wild hope, she thought he was going to kiss her again. But instead he merely stretched out a forefinger, touched her upper lip, and rubbed it.

"There was an ink smudge there," he said, half turning from her. Then he wheeled around and, without looking back, moved away from her, from the tree, and from the pleasant afternoon. On her mouth the touch of his hand still seemed to caress her. She thought it would be enough to silence her, but instead she heard herself calling after him:

"*Do* speak to your father of me, and perhaps I will see him."

But he made no reply.

And Abinoam and Deborah did meet that night, met under the same tree where the son had left her. Only this time the fields were veiled in the silver mantle of moonlight, and instead of Dael standing before her, it was the dour and one-eyed Abinoam.

"The cave would have been better for a meeting place," Abinoam was muttering, "but Dael is there this night, looking over some of the new scrolls you have brought. And," he added, leaning closer to her, "what else bring you from Benjamin?"

"News of the best," she replied quietly. "For the first time the tribes of Israel are prepared to unite and to join in combat against Canaan. That is the true purpose of my visit here, for I have been instructed to carry the news to all who follow Jehovah against Baal."

Abinoam straightened up, his gaunt frame thinly silhouetted against the horizon. "It has gone as far as that? The tribes are really in accordance? All of them?"

"Not all." She shook her head quickly. "Only the Benzi factions—Benjamin, Ephraim, Naphtali, of course, Zebulon, and Issachar, and perhaps the west of Manasseh. The others have definitely refused their aid."

Abinoam spat softly into the sand. "Someday they will plead with us to help them."

"Perhaps." She drew her light mantle over her shoulders. "I will be honest with you, Abinoam," she said after a pause. "Before Israel takes the field against Canaan, a leader must be chosen to head the ranks of the Lord. Frankly, your name was brought by the men at the council tables. And just as frankly, the elders of Israel felt that, while you did not lack fire nor initiative, you did not possess the necessary caution and coolheadedness that a leader must have. Stay and hear!" she went on, seeing that Abinoam was about to protest. "The elders know of the extent of your zeal in destroying the Baal altars at the high places and your unrelenting fight against the worship of Astarte. But the same elders also think that many times, and foolishly and hotheadedly so, you acted in careless anger when diplomacy or caution might have succeeded more. They feel that, needlessly, you have antagonized the priesthood of Canaan, have incurred the wrath of Jabin himself, where you should have kept your intent secret and sought to gain his friendship."

"In short," Abinoam growled, "to have acted like a spy?"

"Like a diplomat better." She smiled. Then her face became serious. "And speaking of spies, I reveal still another reason for my coming here. One, of course, is to be as close to Hazor, the capital, as possible. Rumors may reach me quicker here, plans might be made known faster this way. But also I must unfold to you that there are spies among the men of Israel itself. Men who, perhaps, are in high and trusted places."

Abinoam's one eye was staring unbelievingly at her. Visibly shocked, he said, "You mean there are men of Israel, those who profess to follow Jehovah and then act against Him for Canaan?"

She nodded curtly. "I so believe. There are those, and we have already found a few. Gershon of Ramah was one. Baruch of Zebulon another. And a few others . . ."

Utterly confused, Abinoam groaned. "But why, why? What prompts men to act thus?"

"Gold and power," she answered, trying not to smile. "Thus has it ever been and thus shall it be. And, knowing this, we have to search out those who are spies against us. I would not doubt that there are a few even in Kedesh."

"Never!"

She shook her head, almost in pity. "I hope you are right, Abinoam. But it would bring me no surprise to find one or two such men."

"Not at Kedesh," Abinoam answered fiercely. "I know the hearts and temperament of all those who follow me. And they are true to the will of Jehovah. You will find no traitors here, bas Shillem!"

"May it so be," she murmured. Then she placed a hand kindly on Abinoam's shoulder. "Of one thing we know. There is no doubt over the faith and fire of Abinoam of Naphtali. Else his name would never have been mouthed as a future leader of Israel. Remember that, Abinoam," she continued in a softer voice, glad to see that he was becoming mollified. "Control your temper, act with caution, think with a cool mind, and it may yet be given you to carry the standards of Israel into the field against Jabin."

He stood with a bowed head and moving lips, and she did not interrupt his prayer until he looked at her again. "How long stay you here?" he asked.

"For a time," she answered. "Until I have made sure there are no traitors here, that you are one qualified to lead and so will report to the elders, and to hear what I can what voices come out of the palace of Jabin." She paused, looking away from him suddenly. "Have you heard any rumors that Jabin is constructing a new and secret weapon to be used against Israel?" she asked.

Abinoam shrugged. "None," his answer came. Then his voice rose with curiosity. "Such a report has reached your ears? I have heard nothing."

He watched her shrug. "Perhaps it is but a rumor. At the moment it still is not of great importance. Tell me, Abinoam," she continued. "What intend you doing now that Jabin has forbidden work in iron or metals? How will you live?"

His face creased into heavy lines and the bony shoulders sagged. One hand tugged the eye band back into place around his head, while the other fingered the three-pronged beard uncertainly.

"*I* will have food and shelter from those who follow me," he answered. "But my son—Dael——" Abinoam sighed and looked down upon the ground.

"He will not stay and fight wtih you?"

"He? Dael?" Abinoam's laughter was salted with bitterness. "He prefers scrolls to the shield and spear, the forge to fighting, beauty to battle, and the jewelers' flame to freedom. Of no interest to him are matters of politics or religion. As to Jehovah"—Abinoam's voice caught in a sharp cough—"to my son He is just another god, of no meaning and even less purpose." Abinoam sighed again. "To every man his burden in life, and my son is mine. Why," he added, the single eye beginning to flash in the moonlight again, "he refused to come with me to see Jabin this day, as I already have informed you. And on the morrow, when I strike down the altars to Baal that are being built there"—he indicated the east—"I go alone, without my son."

Her chin lifted with instant and alerted suspicion. "Hold your anger, Abinoam," she cautioned, "and do not move against the altars of Baal on the morrow. Wait."

His hands had been clenched, palm within palm, as he had spoken of his son, but now her words seemed to sever them and cause them to drop heavily at his sides. "Have I heard rightly?" he asked, the beard beginning to come up in rising anger and stiff defiance. "You forbid me to smash the altars of Baal?"

"Not I," she replied evenly, in her heart telling herself that this man, fanatical and blind with the heat of his anger and righteousness, could never be a leader. "Not I—it is the wish of the elders that you be restrained from creating any disturbance against Jabin at this time."

Abinoam's face came closer to her, until the bristles on his chin were a fingerbreadth from her. "All my life I have fought for Jehovah against Baal," he said, almost snarling his words. "I have given an eye for that. And I shall give my life if necessary. And not you nor the elders can prevent me. Know that and remember that! When the altars are erected, I will abolish them, grind them into dust!"

"And the hopes of Israel with them," she commented acidly. "Now you lend ear to me, Abinoam. It is the elders' wish—and mine, too, if you must know—that we proceed with caution now. We need time. We need time to combine, to find a leader, to gather stores and create arms. We cannot have Jabin move against us quickly and suddenly because you have aroused his instant anger. Perhaps this edict of the erection of the altars, even that of the iron monoploy, is merely to test Israel—to see if Israel is ready to fight. And we are not prepared. We must have more time. And to gain this time we must placate Jabin as much as possible. You must not act against him nor instigate any move he might make against Israel. Let the altars remain. They can be smashed down another time."

The head of the gaunt craftsman rose higher. His eye closed and the beard pierced the sky. The scarred and knotted hands rose upward. "As Jehovah is now my witness," she heard his low vow, "I will destroy the altars of Baal, where they are built, and when they are built. And no man," he added, his fierce face pushed closer to her, "and no men, and certainly no *woman*, be she judge even, call tell me what to do. For I act according to Jehovah's will!"

"I warn you, Abinoam——" Deborah began, stopping as she saw the artisan's long figure, stooped and bent at the neck now, stride away from her, moving slowly until the moonlight no longer touched him and he was robed by the night.

For a long time she stared after him.

First the son, now the father, she thought unhappily. Truly, it had not been a good beginning in Kedesh.

Then she remembered the kiss, and her heart was somewhat lightened. . . .

5

ON THE flat rooftop of his two-storied home Achan tossed restlessly on his sweat-soaked pallet, seeking in vain a touch of breeze that might lay cooling fingers upon his body. For hours he had lain thus, unable to find slumber, staring sullenly at the sky through the latticed vines that formed a sieved wall for privacy. But it was the month of Elul—hot, dry, and dusty Elul, the last of the summer months before the rains. Elul, the fiercest of them all, he thought, the very breath of which seeemd tinged with fire and which spat the fine, harsh particles of sand, gathered from the eastern deserts, upon human and beast alike.

Groaning, he arose from his resting place, hitching up the loose loincloth over his hips as he walked to the low parapet and gazed moodily below, above, and around him. Kedesh, at this time of night, lay in great silence, the very buildings seeming more closely huddled together than by day. Only in the distances, where lonely shepherds kept their vigil by flickering campfires, was there any movement. Even the silver pins of the stars, fastening the canopy of darkness against the sky, gleamed coldly and aloofly from their great heights.

Rubbing the wetness from his chest, the judge sighed loudly. Truly, he pondered, things were not going too well for him. Etched deeply within him by the acid of Jabin's contempt of this morning was the premonition that his plans—his very life—were at stake.

There was no doubt about the way the monarch felt toward him, the shophet of Kedesh. Of course the Canaanite gold kept fattening his purse, but what was to stop Jabin, with one blow, from severing the leather thongs of his moneybags and this throat as well? The role of spy and traitor was not only a wearing one but edged with considerable danger at all times. One wrong move, a careless word, an intercepted message, and my life is ended, Achan thought miserably. For a wild moment he thought of giving up everything, leaving Kedesh and this whole turbulent, restless land, to retire to Egypt or Tyre or to the countries to the north, and there live in comparative safety and free from worry. He had accumulated enough wealth for such a move. But would there be enough for him to exist, once he departed from here? What could he do among strangers?

No, he decided, as he so often had in the past, he would remain, playing his double role until it would bring him what he sought, enough material wealth and gain to be able to retire permanently and safely without fear of what the future might bring. Another year, he thought with rising excitement, another year of spying for Jabin, and I will have enough to flee this accursed land and get the freedom and security for which I have so much longed. One more year, perhaps, one single turn of the seasons, and I will be able to draw breath without the fear choking me or the terror lying heavy and cold in my bowels.

As it is now, he thought bitterly, easing his elbows along the rough stone surface of the parapet, pushing a knee against it for support, and staring unseeingly into the darkness again.

He had no doubts as to the cause of his fear. The arrival of Deborah, totally unexpected and suddenly, had not been lightly taken by him. He was sickeningly confident that her visit was not merely one of courtesy or family or observing of kinship. Nobody —especially a woman—comes from Ramah, three days' travel away, after many years, just to pay her family obligations to a distant relative. Add to that that Deborah was a judge in her own right, with powerful influence and ambitious friends—and the motive for her arrival was clear. Nor did the fact that she stemmed from Benjamin itself, certainly the most fiery and revolutionary of all the tribal districts of Israel, cloud the purpose of her arrival.

It was plain that she had come for two reasons, had been sent here with a twin plan, to seek out a potential leader for Israel and —he shuddered suddenly—to reveal him, Achan, as a spy for Jabin.

Oh, he was not fooled by her honeyed phrases of thanks for the courtesy and care he was giving her. He was deeply suspicious of her, and what worried him most of all was what she could do to him if she ever unmasked him as a traitor. Despite the heat, the judge shivered again. He had seen the end of those who dared spy against Israel. He knew full well the end of all spies—the final miserable and bloody finish that culminated with the thrown rocks hammering against a skull, smashing the life out of a man.

But had she come to expose him or to find a new leader? Or for both reasons?

His mind, spurred heavily now by fear and unrest, began to race over the various possibilities, charging past them, turning and wheeling back to reconsider them at a slower pace, then galloping on. And with each new consideration it became clearer and clearer to him that, no matter what the woman's motives were, Abinoam was the focal point. In Achan's mind the face of Abinoam loomed larger and larger, getting more threatening with each passing moment.

Abinoam, Abinoam . . . So long as this man remained alive he represented a definite threat and danger, not only to Jabin himself, but most certainly to Achan. Any way it might be considered, Abinoam was the stumbling block.

Had Deborah come to investigate and search for a leader who might head the combined ranks of Israel against Canaan—was not Abinoam a likely candidate? Already the one-eyed fanatic had a large and loyal following in Naphtali. His name was mouthed all over restive Israel. It was very much in the realm of possibility that Deborah, instructed by the elders of the Benzi factions, had come to Kedesh to talk to the toolmaker and search his mind and ability as a leader. If such was the case, the quicker Abinoam was eradicated, the better. The death of Abinoam—and Achan was surprised to find himself already thinking in terms of murder—would be beneficial for Jabin and most certainly for himself. Already the judge could see himself standing humbly before Jabin, saying:

See, my lord king, with the death of Abinoam I have rid you of a potentially dangerous enemy, have removed the threat of a leader rising against you with a combined Israel, have so disrupted the rebellious tribes that they stand helpless before thee. And in addition, my lord, this death may well serve as a warning to all of Israel that similar fates await any man who dares rise before the wrath of Jabin. This act will hammer the fear into the hearts, shrivel their courage, and make dry and brittle their ambition.

And Jabin would reward him for that deed. Heavy and ample would be the weight of metal in Achan's purse. And better yet, perhaps the monarch would find less contempt for him and treat him more as an equal and not with the usual scorn and degradation.

And supposing that the rewards of Jabin would be so great that Achan need not wait for a year to have enough riches with which to retire and live in permanent security and ease? It was worth the gamble. It was worth the calculated risk. Upon Abinoam's death would rest the future fortunes of Achan.

With the excitement rising high in blood-tide, he began to pace the roof restlessly, his hand active in his beard, tugging gently.

There was one reason enough to have the life of Abinoam ended quickly. But the second reason—that of both Deborah and Abinoam looking for spies and traitors—was of greater worry and danger to him. What if Abinoam already suspected and had told Deborah to come here to help him unmask the shophet of Kedesh? What if they were already planning to trap him? He could afford no risk of waiting now. Either of his two fears was sufficient to have the one-eyed one taken from this earth.

So be it then! he vowed silently, his palms coming together in the moment of decision. So far as he was concerned, Abinoam was already dead. The woman did not matter; she would go back to Ramah and have to report her failure. As for the son—Achan grinned into the blackness—he was a nonentity, a dreamer, a weakling, and there was nothing to be feared from him.

What remained to be done now was to arrange the killing of Abinoam so that it would cast no suspicion upon himself. Later, when he talked privately with Jabin, he would make the monarch understand what had been done. The King of Canaan, not unversed in the secret arts of diplomacy that often used the implements of murder, would be pleased at the subtlety in which the matter had been handled.

But how was the killing to be arranged? It had to be done at once, this very night if possible, he realized suddenly. Strike now and swiftly and hotly so! He strode back to the parapet, again looking at the sky, his attention suddenly held by the flashing streak of a falling star whose slashing path across the heavens he followed until its brilliance had died out against the horizon.

And suddenly the heart of Achan hammered in fast strokes. Again the hairy fingers found the spadelike beard and dug savagely into it. The broad chest heaved with breath that parted his thick lips in a smile of triumph. By all the gods, he exalted, would he be a superstitious man he could regard that falling star as an omen of omens, a sign, a portent of good fortune to come.

For he remembered now another night when anxiety and fear had kept the clasp of sleep from him, another night when, from this same parapet, he had watched another falling star. Loosened from the firmament, it too had cut its way across the darkness but had not disappeared into the void. Instead, the blazing arc had swooped downward, pointing to the earth in a fiery bow that touched the nearby fields. Out of curiosity that same night, he had found the spot where the meteor had buried itself, its surface still warm to the touch. As it cooled, he had examined it, surprised at its weight and its resemblance to the metal of iron. Great had been his initial impulse to inform Abinoam, who knew of such things, but fortune had smiled upon him then when he decided to keep the secret to himself.

Many were the reasons for his so doing. If the stone was of iron, its worth was great, not only to the iron-hungry smiths of Israel—who would eagerly purchase it for a goodly sum—but also to the merchants and caravan leaders whose craving for heavy metal was as great as that of the smiths. A hundred buyers could easily be found for it.

He had wanted to remove the stone immediately, but its weight and the fact that dawn was already brushing the east with huge strokes of red and gold made him decide to wait for another time. He did not want to be observed struggling with the meteor as he staggered back to his house.

A few weeks later, upon his return from a circuit tour of judging, he went at once to the place where the stone had fallen, discovering that it had been removed to a new hiding place. It took him four nights of secret search until he found the meteor's new earthen cache under the boxwood tree. And the fact that the stone had been chipped verified his suspicions. In Achan's mind there was no doubt over the identity of the one, or ones, who had done this. Of all the men in Kedesh, only two, Abinoam and his son, had enough knowledge and curiosity about iron to have recognized the stone for what it was. And only these two had the tools for the cutting of the rock.

Achan's first reaction had been to approach Abinoam angrily and demand ownership of the stone by right of discovery. But caution had stilled his eagerness when he remembered that the iron-monopoly edict, already in effect throughout other sections of Israel, would undoubtedly touch Kedesh as well. Better not to have the forbidden metal in his possession now, he had reasoned. Let it remain where it was. For the time being, he had contented himself merely by cutting a piece from the rock, to have a sample to show those to whom he would want to sell the entire stone.

And so he had done, borrowing a chisel from Abinoam's own forge on the pretense that he had to sharpen his oxgoad. The bit of stone, now hidden under a pile of discarded mantles and animal skins, lay in his own chambers.

And that same chipped piece of ore would be the cause for Abinoam's death. . . .

The plan, once worked out in his mind, was so simple that it was bound to succeed, as most successful things in life are. He would surreptitiously bury the chipped piece of stone on the meager strip of worthless land in back of Abinoam's ruined forge rooms. The father and son did not sleep there; they lived in a modest small adobe home at the other end of the village. The fact that the forbidden metal would be found buried on Abinoam's property would be enough to convict.

And to sentence to death.

But how was the stone chip to be discovered and by whom? he worried for a time until the solution presented itself. It must be entirely accidental, so that no proof of guilt might throw its dangerous shadow upon him. No others must be part of the plot. Only he must participate in it. Again he tugged savagely on the beard, as if to force the details from it.

Yes! he gloated. It could be done. And in this way. The chip would be buried. Then, hurrying across the field, Achan would pretend to stumble over the lightly covered meteor. He would cry out aloud in pain. Nearby were the soldiers of Jabin, the guards who had been assigned to keep sentry duty over the materials to be used for the erection of the new Baal altars. Achan's cries would arouse the guards, would have them storming fiercely to investigate the cause of the uproar. The iron chip would be discovered and its presence would hurl the guilt into Abinoam's teeth and have him brought before the Canaanite justice.

Achan's hirsute fingers dropped from his beard. Let it be done so, he thought, walking swiftly over to the corner of the sleeping chamber. There he found the pile of dirtied and cast-off mantles and skins, dug into the heart of the rubbish, and found the piece of ore. He wiped his sticky hands once on his chest before he held the piece of iron against his hands. But the sweat still cloyed his palms and, in his fingers, the meteorite felt as if it were already covered with blood. . . .

Dargan, the sergeant in command of ten, spat on the dice again, rubbed a broad thumb over their surfaces, and cast once more. In the dimly lit sentry hut, erected hastily to provide shelter for the soldiers who were guarding the rocks and stones and pitch that would build the altar of Baal, a single lamp of clay flickered angrily against the dark corners. Its feeble light, however, was strong enough to pick out the dice, spun from Dargan's hand, as they tumbled against the earthen floor, thudded against the flimsy wall of hide, and then lay still. The three tiny playing pieces were beautifully ornate, each looking like squashed pyramids of onyx, with the four numerals deeply engraved on them.

Dargan's brown, piglike eyes peered at the exposed numbers.

"Twelve," he grunted triumphantly, looking at his two companions, who also wore the thin, blue ribbon of rank on their mailed collars. "The woman is mine."

As he stooped to pick up the dice before the faces of his two disgruntled colleagues, Dargan thought that at least this night had brought some compensation. And it was coming to him, his mind reflected bitterly, for surely these last two days had been laced with misfortune. First had been the summons to lead the raid upon the toolmaker, coming on a day when he had expected to spend his hours in the brothels of Hazor. Then had come that most humiliating scene of all, when that accursed *Yehuda,* the son of the artisan, had knocked him to the floor in sight of the grinning soldiers of Jabin. Finally, he remembered, the leader of a hundred, his own lieutenant, had ordered him to keep vigil last night before the altar place. There was no doubt that the lieutenant, one Harmish by name, a young fop who had bought his commission, had done this just as punishment.

So Dargan had resigned himself to hours of uneasy waiting and watching, knowing that danger loomed and threatened at any moment, because these men of Israel became crazed over the question of other gods and foreign altars and might strike, with fury and anger, in the darkness. In the beginning Dargan had heartily wished for an attack, to be led by that one-eyed one and his son. He had kept his spear ready, hoping to thrust it into the bowels of the son as he would come charging into the encampment to destroy the materials for the altars and drive off the soldiers.

But evidently there was to be no attack this night, and, to pass the long hours away, the dice game had been started, with the favors of one Basshema, who had once been a concubine at the court and now ran her own establishment, at stake. And now Dargan had won the right to be the first to visit her as soon as this business of guarding was over.

He picked up the dice, patting them lightly before opening the throat of the tiny goatskin bag in which he kept them. "Tomorrow night at this time," he taunted the losers, "I'll be casting these dice again—but with Basshema, to win certain pleasures from her." He tightened the thongs with his teeth, put the bag carefully into his waistband, and then yawned loudly. He peered outside, sniffing the cooler air. "An hour before Shamash brings the dawn," he muttered. He was about to turn back to the hut when the sight of a soldier running hastily toward the shelter stopped him. Dargan waited until the mercenary, one of those assigned as an outside guard near the fringe of the village, approached, bowed and saluted, and then waited for Dargan's permission to speak.

"Well?" the sergeant asked testily.

"My leader"—the soldier was still panting slightly—"there is a disturbance on the field."

The brown eyes narrowed instantly. "They come?" Dargan demanded, his hands already feeling for the dagger and sword around his waist, his eyes sweeping to the opposite wall where the tall spear leaned.

"No, my sergeant," the soldier reported. "There was just one of Israel. He who calls himself the shophet of the village. He had been crossing the fields, he said, to the usual morning worship of his god, when he fell and stumbled against a rock or obstruction in the field. He raised such a cry that we heard him and found him on the ground, moaning and groaning, and his head lightly wounded from that which he had struck."

Dargan's huge hand clenched into a fist and he began to move it up, as if to strike the messenger. "And for this, son of a she-dog," he grated, "you come and disturb me—because one of Israel has fallen and stumbled?"

The soldier stepped back, frightened by the raised hand and the cold, angry glint in the sergeant's eyes. "The shophet bade me rouse you," he said defensively, "and said this was a matter for the soldiery, since he has been hurt on the strip of land belonging to the toolmaker, Abinoam, whose forges were the day before yesterday destroyed by you."

Again Dargan was of a mind to strike the soldier, but the name of Abinoam stopped him. He recalled the old one, the father, and, more bitterly, the son. Perhaps, he mused, feeling a sudden and expectant excitement piercing through his loins, this might bear further investigation. He nodded curtly. "Return with me," he ordered the now-relieved soldier. Then he jerked his head at one of the other sergeants. "You also, Perbaam, come with me. And you, Konor," he said, "remain here and command!"

He strode over to the wall, picked up his spear, and then motioned with it for the messenger to lead them to the place from which he had come.

As they strode through the silent fields, Dargan saw that from several nearby houses lights were beginning to appear. And as they neared the scene of the accident, the sergeant beheld a small but rapidly growing knot of villagers already gathered there. In his ears came the sound of moaning and soft cries.

Shoving past the soldier, Dargan shouldered his way through the whispering, surprised, and still-sleepy men of Kedesh, until he had pierced the clump of watchers and looked down upon Achan, who was seated on the ground, groaning softly and holding his head. Even by the dim light of the torch that Perbaam was carrying Dargan could see that the Israelite's hands were smeared crimson from a cut he was trying to stem on his forehead.

"What has happened here, Israelite?" Dargan demanded harshly, looking sternly down at Achan, who continued to rock to and fro, still holding his head. When the judge refused to answer, Dargan prodded him with a toe. "Release your tongue and speak to me!" the sergeant ordered again.

For the first time Achan looked up at him, making an attempt to rise, and then falling weakly. "Sergeant of Jabin," he finally was able to say, "I have done nothing. I was on my way to worship the coming of the new day, according to our custom, when I stumbled and fell against something, hurting my head. If I cried out too loudly, I am sorry."

The judge case a swift, cunning glance at the darkened jowls of the sergeant. When he, Achan, had slashed the piece of ore across his forehead, he had been a little too enthusiastic; the blow had brought blood and an aching of the head. He had buried the piece of ore lightly and then had cried out, bringing the soldier to investigate. At first he had regretted making the calculated accident so real, but now, still reading the sneering doubt on Dargan's features, he was glad it looked so realistic.

"For a judge of the village, you must indeed be blind," Dargan was saying. "And even a child would have raised less of an outcry than you. Israelites," he added with contempt, "who are ready to weep when they bump their heads . . ."

Yet Dargan hesitated to leave. There seemed to be something more here than a mere simple accident. Achan was, after all, an important person in the village. And the sergeant—without knowing why but with the instinct of long training and battle—knew that there was more here than the mere surface indicated. He stared hard at Achan, saw the other's eyes regard him steadily, then shift and rest upon a darker object half buried in the ground. It is almost, Dargan thought, as if he wants me to pick up that object and examine it.

"Against what fell you?" he asked, his voice less harsh now.

Immediately he saw relief—and a look of something else—flicker in the judge's eyes. Achan indicated the buried object, which looked like a stone, to his right. "Against that, my sergeant," the judge muttered.

"Bring the torch closer," Dargan demanded tersely of Perbaam. As the latter hovered closer to the fallen Achan and the stonelike thing in the sands, Dargan stooped swiftly to pick it up, grunting loudly in surprise at its weight.

Curiously the sergeant stared at it, felt of its surface, again aware of its weight. A little pulse of excitement rippled through him. No ordinary rock was this, he thought suddenly, but something unusual. From its weight and texture it appeared very much like——

Like iron.

A savage grin parted his lips. He dropped the meteor at his feet. "To whom belongs this strip of land?" he demanded of Achan.

But the judge merely bent his head and refused to answer. Before the ever-increasing crowd his tongue could not bring accusation against Abinoam. He felt sure that one of the villagers would mouth the answer—a confidence which quickly bore fruit as he heard a hushed and awed voice from the crowd call out:

"This land belongs to Abinoam, the toolmaker, in the back of whose forge it stretches."

Dargan's grin became wider and fiercer. "Return to the sentry hut and bring five more soldiers here," he commanded the soldier. To Perbaam he said curtly, "Come with me. We'll pay another visit to the one-eyed one."

"There is no need, my sergeant," the soldier was saying, "for he must have been aroused and already approaches."

Dargan's head jerked up quickly, his nostrils spreading and

flattening against his cheeks in excitement as he saw Abinoam approaching in long strides, hastily tying the roped belt of his shoulder-seamed *simlah,* the mantle made of camel's hair and wool, while his cowhide sandals, their straps still untied around his ankles, flapped against his soles. Behind him, Dargan noticed with hard satisfaction, loomed the taller figure of the son.

The sergeant's hand tightened on his spear shaft.

Looking neither to the right nor the left, Abinoam strode up to Dargan. Rigidly, his arms hanging stiffly at his sides, he faced the Canaanite. "Why do you disturb the night?" the toolmaker demanded. "And why do you return? Was not the destruction of my forges enough evil for one week?"

Dargan leaned a little on his spear. His eyes, alert and knowing now, flashed from Abinoam to Dael, who stood at his father's side. Then he smiled grimly. Without looking again at Abinoam, he called out tersely to Perbaam.

"Arrest this Israelite and have the other soldiers bring him before Jabin."

Abinoam took a step backward; then, stiffening in quick anger, strode forward, until his face was but a handbreadth from that of Dargan. The latter, relieved to see the five other soldiers coming at a trot from the sentry hut, smiled again, facing Abinoam.

"No king yet of Canaan be you," Abinoam said thickly, "to arrest at will and without charge or cause."

"There," Dargan said, his tone dangerously low, "lies the charge and cause." His booted toe indicated the fallen piece of ore. "Iron. Iron found hidden on your land, Israelite, and illegally possessed. Two days ago I informed you of the penalty for keeping the metal secretly."

Abinoam's startled eyes anchored to the ground, swept over the stone, lifted themselves—heavier now—to the smirking sergeant's face.

"I know of no iron in my possession," the toolmaker said firmly. "All I had you confiscated."

"All that was openly seen," Dargan reminded him smoothly. "I had not the time to look for hidden and unlawful caches of the hard metal." He lifted the spear a little from the ground as he saw Dael make a movement and then check himself. Let that son of the toolmaker say one word, Dargan's thoughts raged, and my spear will tear his throat of speech forever.

Again Abinoam's eyes rested on the bit of meteorite. Swiftly he bent to examine the ore closely, fingering it, lifting it, and then dropping it. Before he could arise, Dargan's voice again smote their ears.

"Have you satisfied yourself that it is iron?" the sergeant mocked. He laughed, shortly and harshly. "I admire your calmness," he continued. "It will well serve you when Jabin's swords sever your head."

There was a rising, shocked murmur of the onlookers, one that became louder as another figure pushed through the crowd and came steadily to the center of the circle. Dargan stared as the woman—for there was no doubt she was one, and of great and startling beauty—stopped before him and at Abinoam's side.

"What means this breaking of the night?" the sergeant's amazed mind heard her voice. It was rich with authority, hard with command, so much so that long training and discipline caused him to answer as he would one of his superiors. "Iron has been found secretly in the possession of the toolmaker," Dargan said, already annoyed and flushing with hot anger that he had to make reply to a woman. He tapped the meteor with the point of the spear, making a small, metallic ringing.

Deborah's cool gaze brushed disdainfully over Dargan, swept down to the iron, then stopped as she beheld the seated figure of Achan. "Kinsman," she uttered in surprise, "what has befallen you?" She took a step closer, her face concerned. "He is hurt," she announced, "and in pain."

"Caused by the iron stone against which he fell," Dargan finished for her. "A truly unlucky fall—for the one-eyed one," he added, the gloating unconcealed in his voice.

"Was that how it happened, kinsman?" Deborah asked sharply.

But Achan still made no reply, merely groaning loudly and shaking his head.

By now the five extra soldiers had formed a protective square around Abinoam and Dargan. The sergeant, suddenly tiring of the game, shivering slightly from the cold, gestured to his men. "Take him," he said almost wearily, "and he will be brought before Jabin in the morning."

As the soldiers began to close in around Abinoam, the toolmaker suddenly backed away. His beard quivered and his hands raised high. "As Jehovah has witnessed," he cried, "I secreted no iron and know nothing of it." Wildly he looked around him, as if seeking help or allies. But nobody stirred.

He took a step forward, his hands outstretched in a pleading gesture that was blocked by the stony visages of Dargan and the guards. Seeing that it was hopeless now, the toolmaker wheeled back. "Dael," he said, his voice breaking suddenly, "Dael, I——"

This was the moment for which Dargan had been waiting. "Unsheathe your swords against the son," he commanded loudly, "and if he makes one move, slay him." Inwardly the Canaanite hoped that the son would make the move. Even before the soldiers' swords might act, Dargan's own spear would be hurtling upon the helpless body of Dael.

There was the slight hissing sound of steel against leather as two swords were slid out of the scabbards, their blades pressed against Dael's breast and throat.

For a long moment the weird and unreal tableau was indelibly etched on the minds of the participants and onlookers alike, the silent, unmoving figures, the naked blades whose burnished surfaces were already catching the first reflections of gold, gray, and red from the dawn, which also placed its hands upon the hard features of the men.

Then, as if squeezed by the silence from the crowd, a voice cried out, choking in excitement and fear and not yet cleared of sleep:

"Flee, Abinoam! Flee for your life!"

The toolmaker started. Already in his mind he knew that flight was the only thing left to him now. Faced with the evidence of the chip of ore, with the savagery of Dargan and his mercenaries, with the edict, with the dozens of witnesses— not the least among them the shophet of Kedesh himself—the one-eyed leader knew that only death awaited him should he be brought before the throne of Jabin. And he would not face so humiliating an end, his knee would not bend before the King of Canaan for mercy.

For a brief moment the head of Abinoam went up proudly, the three-pronged beard piercing the ever-increasing light.

"Into Your hands, my lord Jehovah," they heard him say, the voice increasing in power with every syllable, "I entrust myself. For You are the one God, the only God, and whatever You do is blessed and with reason." Abinoam was fairly shouting now, moving forward. As if fascinated, the guards parted a little before the thrust of his body. Then, lowering his head but still shouting, Abinoam lurched forward, the impetus of his rush bowling over one of the soldiers. His elbows held high and pumping hard, the long, lean legs lengthening their stride, the toolmaker plunged through the protective circle of watchers and began to run, a mad, headlong dash away from his tormentors.

Guided more by fear and shame than intuition, Abinoam took flight past the spot where Achan was still crouched. And what happened then—there were few who were able to recount with certainty the order of events. Some said that Achan, attempting to rise suddenly, accidentally bumped into the rushing flight of Abinoam. Others claimed that the craftsman stumbled suddenly. Deborah, watching closely, was sure that the judge deliberately lifted himself just as Abinoam came past him—shoving out a long foot, over which the artisan tripped.

As he tried to retain his balance, his arms spread wide and high, Abinoam's body weaved and danced in a queer ballet. Against the lightening horizon the whole gaunt frame was revealed—the flapping simlah and sandals, the thin body, the fierce points of the beard outlined clearly and sharply.

For Dargan, the figure made a perfect target.

In the flicker of an eyelash the spear was cupped solidly against the mercenary's palm, the fingers sure but holding the shaft loosely. Almost effortlessly Dargan cast—cast in an expert, looping underhand throw. Even at a greater distance he could not have missed; here, at only forty-five feet, or thirty cubits the result was inevitable.

In a low arc the spear rose, then dipped sharply downward, catching the fleeing Abinoam between the shoulders, the cruel, barbed point burrowing into skin and tissue, digging deeper. The toolmaker stumbled, weaved, uttered a frightening cry, and then fell on his knees. He tried to roll over, but the shaft of the spear was in his way and he fell sideways. Once or twice his legs kicked out wildly, the lean body shuddered.

And then lay still. . . .

Along with the others, Deborah rushed forward, screaming, her voice lost in the awed and angry shouts of the others. Only Dael and the two who held their steel against him remained immobile. Then, as if stopped by a force unknown to her, the young woman turned swiftly to look at the piece of meteorite that now lay at her feet. Swiftly she stooped and picked it up. The wide gray eyes inspected the piece of stone expertly. In weight and texture it resembled perfectly that which Dael had shown her the day before. In her mind there was no doubt that this piece of the stone from heaven had come from the same meteorite Dael had found. Against her fingers the chiseled side rose to a rough triangular point that scratched the skin of her palms. For a wild moment she debated the possibility of taking the chip and hiding it. Then she discarded the thought; Dargan and Achan would no doubt take the piece of meteoric iron to Jabin as proof of Abinoam's guilt and as the cause of his death.

Quickly she dropped the stone and hurried forward, pressed by the rush of the crowd, to where Abinoam lay in death. . . .

"Are you convinced now?" Deborah was asking quietly, looking directly at Dael. In the sanctuary of the cave, the sunshine of the afternoon could not reach them, and the memory of what had happened at dawn—the father's death, the burial, the parting of Achan and Dargan to appear before Jabin with the incriminating piece of evidence—seemed locked out. Immediately after the burial of Abinoam, Deborah had taken Dael to the resting place of the main body of the meteor, had shown him the second cut made in the stone, had explained that the piece she had examined could have come only from the original rock.

"Do you recall," she asked, "whether Achan ever borrowed an instrument that might have been used for the cutting of the rock?"

Dael took a deep breath. "Once," he answered heavily, "the shophet demanded a chisel which he said he would need for the sharpening of his oxgoad. My father gave it to him. And it was returned several days later."

Deborah nodded quickly. "And with that chisel Achan chipped off the piece of stone. There can be no doubt."

Dael's palms slammed together in frustrated rage. "But why, why!" he stormed. "Why should Achan want my father's life?"

She turned away from him, facing a lamp, poking a finger into the pool of oil and stirring it absently. "Because," she murmured, "Achan is traitor and spy against Israel. Because Abinoam represented a threat to the gold and security he was seeking from Jabin. Because perhaps he suspected my coming here to make a leader of your father." She turned back to Dael, her eyes pleading now. "Dael, Dael," she cried out. "Think you the guilt of your father's death weighs not on me? Perhaps had I not arrived here he still would be living."

He shrugged. "It matters not now," he answered. "If what you say is true—Achan wanted my father dead—it would have been arranged sooner or later. With or without you," he finished, trying a weak smile but failing as sorrow pulled down the corners of his mouth. Then his broad shoulders straightened. His head lifted and the red rim around the black iris gleamed hotly. "But the death of my father shall not go unavenged. In his teachings," Dael went on grimly, "he often told me that the god Jehovah demands a tooth for a tooth, an eye for an eye. That is one part of my father's creed I shall obey."

The woman looked at his set face, white now, at the half-closed eyes. Then impulsively she moved toward him, letting her hand rest lightly on his shoulder.

"No, Dael," she said, her voice very low. "You will get vengeance—but not at once. You must wait. It cannot now be done."

"It must!"

"No," she repeated, still softly, and when he looked into her eyes he was surprised at the infinite tenderness and, yes, wisdom that glowed in them. Again she shook her head so that the butter-colored hair seemed to ripple and move with a life of its own in the light of the lamps.

"How reason you thus?" he finally demanded, his voice harsh, but knowing he was already prepared to listen to her and, even if he protested, to accept her decision.

"For three reasons," came her swift answer. Her fingers spread and pointed with each word now. "First, the evidence against Achan is far too meager. For what, actually, have you for proof, should you take this before the judges and elders of Israel? A piece of chipped rock? Achan stumbling in the field? Or his deliberate tripping of your father when he tried to flee? Use that and you will see what little weight it would have in a sitting of judgment. Secondly"—he watched as she began to rock back and forth as if she were reciting—"remember this. Should you reveal that the piece of stone that Achan took from the original which fell from heaven was also known to you, would not the judgment be against you? For would it not be said to you, 'Why did you not reveal the presence of the stone of iron? You knew it was illegal to possess metal or even have knowledge where it might be found.' If you knew about the stone and did not so report it, would that not make you as guilty, in the eyes of the elders and those of Jabin, as your father? Would you not then be liable yourself to arrest and punishment?"

Dael bent his head, acknowledging the logic of her words. In the first flaming heat of anger and desire for revenge there had been no protective cloak of caution to throw over his emotions. Now the voice of this strange woman was tempering his reaction with cold wisdom and reflection.

"And thirdly," he heard her say, "you have your own life now to consider."

His head shot up, jerked high with surprise. "*My* life?" he demanded.

Smiling slightly, she nodded. "Your life, Dael. For, having destroyed the tree, how long think you Achan will deliberate before he chops down the branch—you—as well? He knows the laws of revenge, what you yourself cited, the eye for the eye, the tooth for the tooth. Think you that Achan will want to live with this fear? Do not underestimate the man. He will remember that you know he borrowed the chisel—that you must have seen that cut in the stone and known that only Achan could have made it. For who else has enough wisdom here in the village to know of iron and its ways? Having rid himself of the father, would not Achan want the son eliminated as well?"

Dael stared at her defiantly. "But if Achan felt that the iron might also implicate him, why did he so use it? Why did he not find another way to betray my father?"

Her bee-shaped eyebrows rose eloquently. "That, too, has puzzled me. But perhaps there is reason for it. Remember that there was no other iron—save the stone—which Achan could have used. It was the easiest way. And perhaps also——" She hesitated, bit her lips, and looked away from the young craftsman.

"And also?" he prompted.

"And also," she murmured, still not looking at him, "it may be that Achan reasoned you would make no effort for revenge. That you were a peace lover, unwilling to fight, wanting only your studies and your work—and that you would flee from Kedesh once your father was placed in the grave."

He placed his hands on his hips. "In short," he said mirthlessly, "Achan considered me coward?"

She made no answer. When the silence thickened between them, she finally looked up quickly, her worried eyes sweeping over him. "*I* said not that," she said swiftly. "But it may be that was what Achan thought. Also, consider this. Even if he thought you might revenge him, Achan would be prepared to have you slain, with the excuse that this was done to protect himself against the blood-avenging for your father. He would be justified in having you killed."

He was about to reply, but, breathlessly now, she gave him no chance. "There is nothing left for you but flight—and at once," she urged. "If you stay here much longer, nothing awaits you but perhaps the assassin's noose or the knife in the back from a hired killer of Achan's. Go to Golan, Dael," she went on. "Golan, the city of refuge . . ."

He listened dully as she explained that Golan was one of the six cities of refuge, so designated by the laws of Israel to give sanctuary to all men whose lives were in danger and who had to flee from death. Once in Golan, Deborah pointed out, Dael would be safe.

"In addition," she continued, "there is in Golan a kinsman of mine, one Ard of Benjamin, who served Jabin as a mercenary at one time and then fled for his life from Hazor. Reveal to Ard that I have sent you to Golan and he will help and befriend you. You will not be alone. What say you, Dael? You will heed my words?"

"No," came his stubborn answer. "If I flee here, I do so in shame and disgrace, without having avenged my father. And am I not entitled to revenge? For does not the law say that——"

"An eye for an eye, a tooth for a tooth," she finished mockingly. A tiny smile, half of derision, half of pity, trembled on the full lower lip. "Can this be Dael ben Abinoam talking?" she asked bitterly, more to herself than to him. "Dael the scholar, the aloof one, the pacifist, the hater of wars and bloodshed, Dael the artist who longs for the security of Egypt?"

That her words had stung him, she was sure, beholding the sudden shadowing of blood over his cheeks and the tightening of his lips. As she smiled, almost taunting him now, her head cocked slightly to one side, he was finally moved to speech.

"And is it so wrong to wish for Egypt," he said sullenly, "although you are wrong if you think I seek security there?"

He tensed, waiting for her reply, which, he was sure, would be barbed and sharp with insult. But to his surprise she looked at him, her eyes cool, the smile slowly vanishing from her features. Amazed, he watched her nod her head.

"Egypt," she was saying. "It might yet be given you to reach the Nile."

"How?" he demanded bitterly. "As a corpse for their embalming houses?"

"No." Her gaze was level again. "No, Dael. Perhaps you can go to Egypt and, by reaching the Nile, perform a great deed for all of Israel as well. Wait!" she cautioned with uplifted palm as she saw he was about to break in upon her words. "I speak not in idle fancy or in dreams. Hear me and heed my speech and remember my words."

She watched his face again as she told him of the true reasons for her coming to Kedesh, of wanting to be closer to Hazor and Jabin, of desiring to search out the heart of Abinoam to see if he was the one to lead a united Israel, to keep her eyes and ears open for spies and traitors, such as was Achan. And with each revelation of her plans, his face underwent a corresponding change, moving from open sarcasm to doubt, swinging to surprise, to incredulity, to sheer amazement, and finally, she noticed with relief, to respect.

"Nor are these all the reasons," she went on, speaking swiftly now, to keep her advantage. "There is another, one I have not even revealed to your father."

"But the son?" he asked, a weak smile hovering around his mouth.

"The son may learn," she answered, shaking her head. "No, hear me. In Benjamin, through a rumor from an escaped Israelite mercenary who served Jabin, there reached my ears that Jabin is constructing a new and terrible secret weapon which he hopes to use against Israel, to slay the Israelites and keep them from Canaan forever. Indeed, I had hoped your father might have heard of this—but he had not."

Dael's face worked with shocked concern. "A new weapon?" he managed to ask, feeling ashamed because he seemed like a child before a tutor.

She nodded again. "Jabin is in the process of fashioning this secret weapon of destruction, with his smiths and engineers hard at work on it."

"But a rumor—word from other mouths who heard from other lips," he began lamely.

"No mere rumor this, Dael. The soldier to whom I spoke was sure. Into my ears spoke he, saying he had been one of the very soldiers assigned to guard the house in which this terrible weapon was being created. And from this same man I know the exact place of the house, which is located just outside the gates of Hazor to the east. Before it, it has a well with the images of two entwined doves on it. It should be easy for us to find."

Unbelievingly he stared at her. "Us?" he repeated dully.

"We. Tonight." The ring of command was in her voice. "Together we can make our way unseen to this place where is kept the weapon. You can make a picture drawing of it. Then you will take that same drawing to Pharaoh Merenptah in Egypt. You will show him the drawing, make your report to him. He might be persuaded that Jabin is plotting an uprising against Egypt, and planning to use this very secret weapon against the might of the Nile. For who is to know?" She smiled faintly. "Perhaps that *is* Jabin's plan—to try out the weapon first against Israel, correct its faults, and then hurl its full power against Egypt. For Jabin would like nothing better than to be free of the fist of the pharaoh, whose forts still dot the land and whose lords and officers still exact tolls."

Dael felt the inner muscles of his thighs start to tremble, and he eased himself against the wall of the cave. "You mouth madness!" he whispered. "What part can we, a humble toolmaker and a woman, play in such great events?"

"Smaller events, created by lesser people," she reminded him, "have changed the history of the world. "It can be done. It is bold enough. And think what it would mean to Israel. Convinced that Jabin is planning war against Egypt, the pharaoh could strike first. And heavily so. And while Egypt and Canaan are locked in combat, and each drawing the blood and strength from one another, Israel will have its chance to draw breath, to gather its strength, to unite, and then be ready to strike against Canaan. And once the men of Israel are combined and powerful enough, when they have the weapons and the food and"—she paused for the briefest of moments, not looking at him—"a leader, there will be victory for us. What matters it who wins between Canaan and Egypt? Both will be so weakened by their struggle with each other that perhaps it will not even be necessary to engage the victor in battle. Israel might negotiate a peace without bloodshed. And all this," she finished, "being done to enable you to get to Egypt."

She had been speaking rapidly, the heat of excitement propelling her words and bringing the color to her cheeks. As he tried to absorb all she had said, as he sought to digest and understand her meaning, he was also painfully aware of her last statement, the gibe she could not refrain from giving him.

He cleared his throat noisily. "And how do I reach the Nile?" he demanded. "You know I have no fortune, no metal, no property, nothing I can sell. And from no one to borrow."

"I know that full well," she answered. "But we have time. Time, which is as good as heavy metal or fortune. You will have to reside in Golan for an interval. Perhaps there it will be given you to make your way to Egypt somehow."

"Somehow," he echoed mockingly.

"Somehow," she said crisply and with confidence. "But remember this. Jabin cannot be ready to move against Egypt for at least another two years. He has to get the other princes of Canaan to support him. He has to gather supplies and weapons, train men. And, in addition, there is no information that his secret weapon has as yet been completed. Certainly it has not been tried out in the field. That, too, will devour time—time to be of advantage to us. We can afford to wait"—she pursed her lips in thought—"two years, if necessary."

Suddenly she was staring at him, a new light in her eyes. *Two years,* she thought.

Two years of not seeing *him.* And what guarantee was there of ever seeing him, once he reached the Nile? Two years. The weight of time, of the days, the weeks, the months, churned heavily in her breast and laid its cold pressure upon her heart, clamping it so it could hardly beat.

In sudden and bewildered shock it came to her now that this young craftsman meant more to her than she had been ready—or willing—to admit or to realize. Coldly and angrily she tried to deny this to herself, telling her reason that, with the certain dangers he faced, it was only his safety with which she was concerned.

Liar! her heart accused her mind. Not concern for him, not his danger, not his security troubles you as much as his absence from you. For you will have to live without him.

But how can this be? she marveled as she had before, at his kiss. He is still stranger to me. And I am dedicated, not to man, but to knowledge and science and study. Never before have I desired man. What magic is this? What sorcery bewilders my mind and makes my heart tug toward him the way the stone from heaven pulls the metal to it? What——

"And Achan?" she heard Dael's voice coming as if through a

distant fog, thick and swirling and cold around her senses.

"Achan?" She fought for time to rearrange her thoughts, to set them in familiar and known patterns which she could trace into words. "For the time there is nothing to be done about the false shophet. He will be watched. I will warn others of him. And in time his own guilt and deeds will trap him. His evil will be as exposed as the rope from which he will hang."

Two years . . .Two long, uncertain years . . .

Dael looked at the woman carefully. She truly believes all this, he thought, for see how her breath moves her, how the redness stains her cheeks, how veiled her eyes are with her dreams. But were they dreams alone? Inwardly he realized that, on the surface, things could be worse. Bad as the situation might be, it still offered him one thing—his trip to Egypt, a chance to reach the Nile and to continue his studying there. At least, he reasoned, it was a start, even if it might be by shameful flight. But flight from what? he asked himself with rising anger. What, after all, have I here in Kedesh to keep me rooted to the land? Why should I remain? Is my father alive? Have I lands or property? May I practice my craft? With my trade and livelihood at an end, my very life in danger at any moment, why should I remain? What ties stretch me to Kedesh?

None.

None, he decided, almost with a feeling of relief, with final decision. So let it be then. I will go. If *she* so desires it and so thinks it good, I will go. But I go only because she has shown me the wisdom of her thinking, and for no other reason.

Once again their eyes met. This time Deborah did not press him, seeing he was about to answer. And when she heard his words, her heart tugged fiercely and joyously within her.

"I will go," he said solemnly, "but I go not because of Israel or because of Jehovah. I go—because I want to reach Egypt and because—because——" He stopped, fumbling for words, wanting to and yet afraid to explain a new emotion that moved him.

"Because?" Her voice was no more than a whisper, no louder than the sigh of burning oil in the lamps.

"Because," he answered gravely, his eyes intent upon hers now, "thou hast so asked of me." He flushed again as he realized that without his knowing it he had spoken to her in the personal, intimate way. "It is a debt I owe for all you have done me. For your exposure and warning that Achan wants my life."

She made no answer. She could not reply to him; there was no response that would express the overflooding fullness of her heart now. Embraced by the silence between them, they remained speechless until she looked up.

"Let us then go to the well of the two doves where the place of the secret weapon is," she said. "No, not now," she added hastily as she saw him rise. "We wait until dark. I will bring parchment and ink for your sketch." Her eyes swept over him. "And you had best arm yourself. For," she went on, her voice suddenly faint with anxiety, "there will be guards there who have orders to kill. . . ."

6

SIDE BY SIDE they lay, their heads just visible over the sandy brow of the hilly bank that sloped downward to the guarded area where the large shed had been erected. To their left, below, was the well Deborah had mentioned, its statue of the entwined doves quite visible in the bright starlight. In the cleared area before the building, three fires blazed, silhouetting the figures of the soldiers who guarded Jabin's secret.

"There seem to be no more than five," she whispered anxiously to Dael, whose long form was stretched out on the sand. He moved uncomfortably; the bronze dagger in its sheath at his right side kept pressing against him and reminding him of the danger he was yet to face.

He turned to look at the woman, amazed at her calm. She had garbed herself in a simple simlah, with a horseskin bag, supported by a single strap, over her shoulder. In that receptacle, he knew, she had brought parchment and red ink for the sketch he was to make of the secret weapon, plus several small phials and her mechanical rod that could be turned into a serpent. When his questioning eyes had met hers, she had smiled. "To beguile the sentries while you are within the shed," she had explained.

He still could not understand her coolness. He himself felt frightened, unsure. The dagger at his side reminded him that he might have to use it and that, for the first time in his life, he was bearing arms. Yet she considered this whole episode as an adventure, almost a lark, confident of his success. Does she not fear also? he wondered. Does she not realize that we are playing with our lives this night?

As he looked at her again, she touched the back of his hand, as if in understanding. "Fear not," she whispered. "It will go well. I know that this day has been full of trial for you. Yet I have not seen you weep for your father, and I know the sorrow you bear within you."

It was true, he thought grimly. He had shed no tears over his father when Abinoam had been returned to the clay from which he had come. Sorrow and anger and the desire for revenge had smoldered in him, but the only outward sign he had borne was the reddening of his eyes. No more. But she had known and, in knowing, had understood.

He felt her grow tense suddenly and he followed her jabbing forefinger. "There—to the right," she was saying. "Is not that Dargan, the sergeant of ten?"

He also stiffened. No matter what part Achan, the betrayer, had played in his father's death, it had been Dargan's spear that had felled Abinoam and had pierced the life from him. And if Dargan were here now . . . Dael's hand slid over the sheath, feeling the hard shaft of the knife. The tough fibers of muscle around his stomach seemed to contract and grow stiff—whether from fear or anger, he had no way of knowing. His eyes narrowed as they concentrated on the figure Deborah had pointed out.

He nodded quickly, realizing that only the clearness and brightness of the night made identification possible. But there was no doubt about it. It was Dargan, evidently appearing at the shed for an inspection tour. Both the man and woman watched as Dargan made his way from fire to fire, stopping at each one, and then proceeding into the shed, remaining there for a time and finally emerging from it. They saw his figure stop at the nearest flame, kneel down, and receive some food one of the other soldiers started to give him.

Deborah touched Dael again. "They are feeding now," she

whispered, "and it is the best time for us. You know the plan?"

Once again he nodded. Deborah was to proceed in plain sight toward the guards, making no effort at secrecy. There she would pause, half flirting, half serious, finally showing them her tricks of pseudo-magic which would occupy them while Dael—from the rear—would make his way into the back of the shed, hoping to be unseen. There he would find the back door, go into the building, find the secret weapon, sketch it quickly if there was enough light, and then make his way out again while Deborah still held the rapt attention of the soldiers. A signal—the yelp of a wild night animal, the jackal—would tell Deborah that Dael's mission had been completed. Only then would she leave the soldiers and return to this place where they now were hidden.

It was a plan fraught with danger, not only for Dael but for her. There was no guarantee that she could control the soldiers by her tricks alone; as the men were alone and wild for women, perhaps, she knew she faced possible assault. And as for Dael, he had only the dagger. But it was the only plan feasible for so short a time. The sketch had to be made and Dael would have to depart to Golan, to the northeast, this very night.

"It is time," she said again. Her hands fumbled with the bag, withdrew the small piece of parchment, the phial of red ink, and the split-reed pen. These she handed in silence to Dael. Gravely he tucked the bottle and pen into his waist, wrapping the parchment carefully around them at first.

"I go now," she was saying, rising to her knees. For a moment she turned to look at him, the gray eyes wide under the hood of the simlah. Then, impulsively, she leaned forward, her lips brushing his cheeks. Her mouth was cold and did not linger. . . .

"May Jehovah guard your way, Dael," she said quickly, and then, without further word, arose and began walking down to the fires.

For a long time he watched her, saw her approach the guards, saw them huddle around her, bring her to the fire. He observed that she seated herself well in the center of the light, heard voices coming dimly to him, laughter now as she opened the bag. The soldiers crowded closer, calling to each other. And from the other fires the men, curious, strolled over.

Dael swallowed the hard, taut ball of fear in his throat. When earlier in the day she had outlined her plan, he had objected to it hotly, pointing out that she was taking an unnecessary risk, even if calculated. He said he could make his way, alone and unaided, to the secret-weapon hiding place. But she had laughed at his protests, saying that the only way for Dael to meet the minimum of danger was for her to draw the attention of the guards away from the shed.

"Fear not," she had reassured him, "they will not harm me. For I will appear to them as a vendor of magical potions, selling love powders and amulets to increase their strength with women." She patted the bag. "The packets and phials are with me. In addition, because of my magical tricks, I will also strike fear into their hearts. They will be in awe of what I will reveal to them and think me sorceress, capable of doing evil to them should they want to assault me. In addition, I will inform them I have come from an Egyptian caravan—the one camped near the wells at Hazor. The soldiers will respect me even more, knowing they cannot afford the wrath of Jabin should they harm me."

And now, he thought with a secret, grudging sort of admiration, her words were bearing fruit. There seemed to be no harm befalling her. He watched her bending over the bag, showing her wares, caught the brief glitter of the phials, heard the low exclamations of awe. Not one of the men seemed even to touch her, standing well away from her as she began her sleight of hand and clouded their bewildered minds.

Dael's eyes searched anxiously for Dargan, wondering if the sergeant would recognize her as one of Kedesh. But Dargan, after having snatched at some food, had disappeared.

When Dael had counted five figures huddled around the fire before which Deborah sat, he moved silently, rising lithely to his knees, sliding down the bank, and starting a fast crawl to the rear of the shed. From time to time he paused, raising his head to see if he had been observed. But evidently the woman had the attention and interest of the soldiers well within the grasp of her clever hands.

Cubit by cubit Dael neared the building, until he could see the poles and rough cow-leather canopies and walls above him. Once more he paused, his eyes seeking an opening, finding it in a space between two pegs in the skirts of the tent skin. With the dagger in his mouth now, he moved sinuously, wriggling over the last spans of distance, squirming under the opening, for a moment lying on his back while his eyes adjusted themselves to the darkness.

He lay there, resting, his breath coming easier now between his clenched teeth. The blade of the dagger tasted metallic and salty against his tongue. Softly he withdrew the weapon from his mouth but kept it in his right hand. Slowly he rolled over, first on his stomach, then rising to his knees, every sense alert and throbbing.

He saw at once that he was in a single large chamber, in the center of which loomed something that appeared like a chariot. Crawling toward it, his hands clawing at the dirt floor and his toes scraping softly, he was finally able to touch the spokes of the object.

A chariot indeed, he thought swiftly, a war wagon. But what was unusual about that? He lifted himself higher, his hands before him, to touch and feel and explore.

The light seemed to be better now, coming weakly through the tent walls from several slits in the roof and from under the skirts of the hide. His free hand groped, fumbled, and then settled around something cold and hard and sharp.

He stared now—stared as the form of the chariot became fully visible.

He sucked in his breath with shocked surprise. Chariot was this, of no doubt, but of a kind he had never beheld before. What his fingers had felt was steel, and he could see now that this metal, in the form of long, wicked scythes, was attached not only to the hub of the chariot, but also along the panels as well. Three of the wicked blades extended from each hub, and three more from the long harness pole.

Expertly his craftsman's hands went over the vehicle. The chariot was extremely well built, with a high, protecting panel that would hover well above the driver's waist, thus making it impossible for him to be hurled out when in the shock of combat. In fact, the rim of the panel was almost as high as the shoulders of the horses that would pull it over the field of battle. His fingers swooped over the straps hanging from the inner rim, which were used by the guards or spearmen to support themselves against the lurching roll of the war wagon. The floor of the chariot was about a yard in width, large enough to hold two extra guards to protect the driver and spearmen. The wheels were high, well placed in the rear for easy riding and maneuvering. Hard leather quivers for the arrows and spears of the archers and spear throwers were built in diagonally against the shielded and armored sides of the panel.

Once more the artisan's fingers traveled along the innovation—the real secret of the war wagon—the swordlike, bladed scythes. They were of steel, made of good iron, hardened by fires of camels' dung, he knew. Now he could understand the purpose of Jabin's iron monopoly. With hundreds, perhaps even a thousand such chariots to build, the monarch of Canaan would need every bit of metal he could find.

And what a weapon—he shuddered suddenly. So far as he knew, he had never heard of blades being used on hubs and poles. What a terrible and devastating instrument of destruction this was, he marveled, a revolutionary concept of mobile warfare never, so far as his knowledge went, used before by any conqueror. With a thousand such wagons, Dael realized, his fingers running along the sharp, razorlike edges of the naked scythes, Jabin would be invincible. For what defense was there against chariots like these? In the open field, what might could stand before such bladed vehicles? Those knives, flashing and whirling on the wheels, could cut their way through rank after rank of the enemy.

Oh, she was right, she was right, his mind repeated. Not for Israel alone was Jabin constructing these weapons. True, he might try them out against the wild and untrained and undisciplined tribesmen of Israel, but their real worth would be proved against the cavalry and infantry and unarmored chariots of the pharaoh himself. No small wonder that Deborah wanted Merenptah to see a sketch of the chariot. The pharaoh would have to be a fool not to recognize at once that such a weapon—still secret—was meant for his destruction alone.

Quickly he dug into his waistband for the ink, pen, and parchment and, squatting near the wagon, where the starlight came through an opening in the roof, began his sketch. He worked surely and with skill, the ink moving in full, bold strokes. The light was too dim to make a detailed sketch, but this rough outline would do for now. Later he could fill in the details from memory.

When he had finished, he waited for the ink to dry, flapping the parchment to and fro. Then, satisfied that the drawing could not be smudged, he folded it carefully, placed it securely within the waistband. The ink and pen he thrust into his sheath. Then, making sure he had disturbed nothing, he began making his way back to the space from which he had entered. He was just about to crawl under when the front canopy parted and, in the flickering glimmer of light, he recognized Dargan.

The Canaanite paused on seeing the crawling figure on the floor. Then, before Dael could bounce to his knees, the sergeant was upon him, the full weight of his hurtling body knocking the toolmaker flat.

In a single moment Dargan's hand had reached for and found Dael's throat and began, with the thumbs pressing and boring inward, a numbing, painful pressure. The impetus of Dargan's body had forced the dagger from the artisan's hands, and it clattered away under a chariot wheel.

Dael was aware of the weight of the Canaanite, of the blinding, cruel grind of fingers on his throat, of a suffocating odor of oil, garlic, and leather from Dargan, whose breath fanned hotly over his face. Dael's tongue was like softened metal, propelled from his mouth by the force of the mercenary's hands. Little lights, swirling swiftly into colored arcs of blue and orange, spun before him as the pressure increased.

There was no sound in the shed other than that of Dael's labored and choking breath and the harsh grinding of Dargan's teeth and his frantic panting. Harder and harder the toughened hands of the soldier dug, and a nausea swept over the Israelite as he squirmed and writhed, flopping his body around the floor. Weakly his hands sought a grip of their own, clawing at the leather and chained mail around Dargan's shoulders and chest—only to fall away.

Dael tried to bring up his knees, hoping to snap them into Dargan's groin, but the strength was flowing out of him rapidly and he had no power behind his kick.

With the last of his strength Dael heaved again, hoping to bridge his body and hurl his enemy away. In so doing, he managed somehow to slither on his side, his right hand suddenly flung sharply against the dagger sheath that Dargan was wearing at his waist.

In an instant Dael's fingertips ran across the tooled leather, sliding upward until they touched the ivoried hilt. With a sob he flicked the dagger from its cover, moving its blade along Dargan's side, and then slowly—oh, so slowly, it seemed to him—raised it, higher and higher and back and back. Then, his mouth working silently, he let his right hand come down, the knife pointed directly at Dargan's left side.

Dael put all the strength he could summon from his nearly paralyzed muscles and quivering sinews into the blow. He felt the steel strike flesh, and he pushed down harder and harder, his whole body shaking.

There was no outcry from the Canaanite.

Suddenly, it seemed to Dael, the weight slipped off him as Dargan toppled to one side, freeing a hand to slap it against the wound. A little astonished gurgle bubbled between his lips as he sprawled over the man from Israel, and Dael could feel the great spasms that shook the soldier, fierce and long at first, wild, and then growing softer, weaker, and finally ending in a little quiver.

Freed of the choking pressure, Dael lay still, the brilliant, flashing lights before him diminishing, the breath coming back to him. He gasped, swallowed, felt the pain in his throat. His tongue seemed bloated and swollen, and when he sucked for air it was as if sparks of fire were searing his palate and throat.

Wearily and yet cautiously he moved to one side, getting on hands and knees, shaking his head free of the broken cobwebs that still wound around his mind. He stared at Dargan in the dim light, but there was no movement from the mercenary.

Dael rose to his feet, weaving, seeking support against the panel of the chariot. As his breath evened and his vision cleared entirely, he examined himself for wounds, finding none. Curiously he looked at his hands, surprised to find them clean and clear of blood.

Silently he bent and retrieved his own dagger, which he sheathed. Unable to help himself, he stared once more at the body at his feet.

He had killed. This was the first man he had ever slain. And with vengeance, too, for this Canaanite had taken the life of his father.

And as he looked, as the sickness and dizziness ebbed away, a new flood of feeling powered his blood and leaped through him. With my strength, I slew him, he thought, almost with a feeling of exultation. I have fought for my life for the first time and prevailed. He felt his lungs and chest fill with breath. Despite everything that had happened, he could look upon a slain enemy with a feeling of pride and power. I took this man's life, he thought; my hands alone brought his end.

It was a new emotion, heady, exciting, something he had never sensed before. It gave him a feeling of confidence that warmed his blood and raced through him like wine. And as he stared again, he wondered why he felt no guilt, no remorse. Indeed, as his strength and his reasoning returned to him, he could almost look compassionately upon the corpse of Dargan.

Shrugging, he turned away, stooping low over the tent curtain, sniffing gratefully at the night air before he began the low, crouched, half-running, half-crawling pace back to the sandy hiding place.

When he reached it, he lay on his back for a moment, still resting. Then, cupping a hand to his mouth, he uttered the signal—the yelp of the jackal. High and thin it swept through the night air. From his position he saw Deborah look up and then drop her head to her tricks again.

Calmly now, he waited—waited until he heard her return to him, sensed more than felt her drop beside him. She was breathing quickly. "You are unharmed?" she was asking, her hands already roving his body to search for wounds.

"Unharmed," he answered. "And thee?"

She chuckled. "I left them in awe and fear. Not one so much as even dared look me in the eyes." She paused. "You had trouble."

"Dargan." He nodded.

Her mouth opened, but no words came, and he said, so simply that it still surprised him, "I slew him with his own dagger. . . ."

He saw her bite her lips. "No one heard nor saw this?" she asked, and he shook his head.

"Then," she said hastily, "we must flee here instantly. The body will be soon discovered. Your flight must be immediate. The danger is great—for both of us."

He nodded again, rising slowly.

"Come, then," she said. "You have the sketch?"

"I have," he informed her. "And it is as you say. A secret weapon indeed. Chariots with blades on them. Big, fast war wagons, armored and bladed . . ."

Her soft intake of breath was answer enough for him. With her hand in his they ran toward the safety of the buildings of Kedesh, finally pausing before the walls of Abinoam's house.

There she turned to him. Silently he gave the pen and ink to her, showed her the rough sketch, over which she pondered for a few moments. Then, as she returned the piece of folded parchment to him, she said, "Keep this and guard it well, for the fate of Israel may depend upon it. And now you must flee."

Soberly he looked down at her face. "Parting," he said sadly, "when we met only yesterday."

"We will meet again, Dael," she said, her voice low. "So I swear it. I will have contact with you in Golan. But go now," she added worriedly, looking around for fear they might be discovered. Then she faced him again.

"It will be given us to meet again," she said, hoping her voice sounded confident and that her sorrow had not warped it. "So I know and so I feel. It was a fate that tied us together and its bonds will never be broken. Oh, Dael, never, never!" she cried out now, unable to help herself, pressing against him, bringing her arms around his neck and his mouth upon hers. "Never, never," she murmured against his kiss, feeling the lightness and tenderness of it, the first kiss of lovers who have just discovered each other, only to lose one another.

She heard his deep breath. Then his voice, low and full of wonder at what had happened between them. "Go then, Deborah," he said heavily. "I will watch thee. But turn not back to behold me. When you next see me——" He stopped himself.

Half nodding, she wheeled and turned and began to run from him. For a long time he watched her, staring, peering until she disappeared from his sight.

And not once did she look back. . . .

PART TWO

THE ARENA

7

UNKEMPT, dirty, his beard caked with sweat and sand, Dael finally made his way slowly to the Refuge Gate of Golan after four days of travel through the wilderness of Bashan. Before him stood the city, almost as if mocking him with its shape of a fist, the thumb jabbing sarcastically to the heavens. This projection was the *migdal,* or armored tower, piercing its way to the sky. It stood, as was usual in all Canaanite towns of that time, at the northwest corner of the community, guarding the precious wells. With sand-reddened eyes Dael noticed the notched slits for the defending archers, the hooks for slings and spears on the rear walls, the boards used to slide the great kettles of pitch on attackers. Around the whole city was a cleared space of some forty-five hundred feet outside the walls, which Dael knew was a sort of exercise yard for refugees, beyond which they did not dare venture on risk of their lives. Thick walls of sun-hardened mud and strengthening stones for buttresses girded the city of refuge.

A nonchalant sentry lounging against the wall of the Refuge Gate, squinting curiously against the sun at Dael, demanded the toolmaker's business, the nature of his flight, nodding when Dael said he was fleeing from Hazor because of having—against his will—slain a Canaanite mercenary. The sentry in a friendly fashion nodded to Dael to follow him and ushered him into a small sentry room just inside the gates. There a fussy, harassed little Levite with a yellow-white beard and stained skirt of linen and tired brown eyes told the artisan to sit down and began questioning him, his hands restlessly moving the pens and scrolls on the small table before him.

When Dael had finished, the Levite shook his head with slight annoyance. "There have been so many of you lately," he complained bitterly. "What times are these in Israel that men must flee here for sanctuary? You come here and it is our duty to maintain you. Of course we cannot send you away—but how to feed and clothe you remains a constant problem." He puffed out his lips and stared at some of the symbols he had scratched on yellow, cracked papyrus. "However, I see you have a craft. There will be some work for you." He sighed again and then looked curiously at Dael. "You slew one of Jabin's men?"

"I so did."

The Levite nodded. "You will find much company here then," he smirked. "There are others here with the same crime staining them. Of course they all claim it was done in self-defense. And we do not probe," he finished. He yawned suddenly, stretching his arms over his head.

"Here, then, are the rules you must obey," the Levite began rapidly. Reciting as if by rote, he said, "Food, clothing, and shelter will be provided you from the regular tithes of the priesthood. If you want more, you work at it. Forbidden you is entry into the regular part of Golan, where dwell the law-abiding citizens. Forbidden you is the company of woman. You will be assigned to a refuge barracks with the others. You may not venture further than the extent of the cleared space around the walls. When in time your priest or judge dies in Kedesh, you may appeal to the elders there for a new trial and, if acquitted, return home."

"I have committed no crime in Kedesh against Israel," Dael reminded him stiffly. "I fear the vengeance of Jabin instead."

"Well—I just am repeating the laws to you," the Levite muttered. He shuffled the papyrus rolls again. "It is unfortunate, perhaps, that your own town of Kedesh is no longer a city of refuge. Once it was, you know."

Dael shook his head. "Even if it so were now, I could not stay there. Jabin is too close and too powerful."

The Levite grunted something under his breath, and the moody eyes swept over Dael again. "One thing more," he advised. "The men here are of a strange temperament. They practically rule themselves and have their own standards. You will have to undergo some sort of initiation, an ordeal by combat, before being accepted as one of them."

Dael loked up sharply. "Combat?" he repeated dully. "I thought that the manslayers here who seek sanctuary against the kin of those they have slain are forbidden arms."

The Levite's palms waved easily. "Oh, you will use no weapons as such. Clubs or fists or flaming torches or wrestling. It is a rule fashioned by the men themselves, the better to gauge and judge a newcomer and thus assign him to his proper place in the refuge center. It furnishes them with excitement, relieves the dull monotony of their lives, releases their pent-up emotions. All newcomers have to go through this. We tolerate it"—he shrugged—"because seldom is real harm done, and it quiets their restless and bitter spirits." His eyes swept over the powerful frame of the toolmaker again. "You need not worry, Naphtalite." He grinned. "You have already prevailed in a death combat, and your body is strong and hard."

He bent his head, assigning Dael to a barracks, telling him where he would eat and where he might wash and find cleaner garments. Sticking his head outside the door, the Levite called to someone to guide Dael to his new home. Just before he was ready to leave, Dael nervously asked, "Is there one here called Ard of Benjamin?"

The Levite looked up with sudden interest. "You know him?"

"Only of him," Dael explained wearily. "I bring greetings to him from one of his family."

"He is here," the Levite said, "and I will so inform him of your message. He will undoubtedly see you. Like you, he is a fugitive from Jabin."

"How so?" Dael asked.

The Levite smiled. "When he sees you, he will tell you. Now, go with this man and refresh yourself, for within a day or two you will be challenged to the combat ordeal."

Cleaner, somewhat heartened after the midday meal of lentil soup and bread, Dael lay on his narrow pallet—one of forty within the low-beamed barracks—and stared unseeingly at the roof of rolled mud and twigs above him. As he heard someone enter the building Dael sat up quickly and watched the stranger who approached him.

The man, walking with a rolling, peculiar gait, was short but solidly built, with long, powerful arms that hung almost to his knees. As the stranger came closer, Dael could see the red face, the keen blue eyes, the nose that looked as if some great hand had been smashed against it, spreading it over the high cheekbones in indiscriminate fashion. A huge wart over the left eye and two tremendous tufts of orange-red hair, topped with silver, that sprang from the temples and uselessly tried to hide the balding pate gave the man the appearance of some semi-comic horned creature, pugnacious and burly.

Yet as he came closer to Dael the stranger smiled suddenly, his face warming as if by some inner kindness. The smile remained on his features as he stood before Dael, who arose slowly from his pallet.

"I am Ard of Benjamin," the arrival said, his voice deceptively soft and low. He stretched out both arms in the gesture of peace, and Dael grasped them in return, marveling at the feel of strength in them. The quick, clever eyes scrutinized the toolmaker swiftly but with care.

"And I am Dael ben Abinoam of Kedesh in Naphtali," Dael answered. He gestured at the pallet. "I have little to offer you in hospitality save this pallet. Rest there, Ard of Benjamin."

The tufted one nodded and seated himself carefully. Dael remained standing. "The Levite brought me news of your coming." Ard explained, "and related that you knew of me from one of my family. It would be a kindness to know who sends me greetings."

"Deborah bas Shillem," Dael informed him, feeling her name sing against his lips. "Deborah," he repeated, just to hear the sound again.

Ard's eyes crinkled with pleasure. "Deborah!" he repeated, slapping a huge fist on his thigh. "It must be five years since I last beheld her—but she still lives in my mind."

Ard's enthusiasm was so warm that Dael looked at him. "What is the relationship of kin between you and Deborah?" he asked stiffly, hoping the suspicion in his voice was not too evident.

For a moment Ard's shrewd gaze bored past and through him. If the little man thought anything, he gave no sign. "Her father and mine were brothers," he explained. Ard leaned forward again. "Is her beauty undiminished?"

"Even more perfect that it could have been," Dael agreed solemnly. He felt a rush of words flood his tongue, a need to talk about her, to bring her closer to him this way, but he stilled the turbulent phrases.

"And her wisdom still abides?" Ard was asking. "For truly there was a girl who thought of little else but knowledge and reading and learning. There were times when I thought she knew more than the priests or judges."

"She is judge now, of Ramah," Dael said proudly.

Ard slapped both hands together in delight. "So I knew it, so I knew it would be!" he exclaimed, grinning. "She has done it, then. Hear me, Dael. Someday she will be a leader in Israel. Wait and behold this for yourself," he added with sureness. "She is rare, and only once in a lifetime does a woman such as she appear unto men." He paused for a moment. "How came she to mention me?" he asked.

"Before I left for Golan," Dael replied, "she told me you, too, resided here and might offer me friendship."

"Which I do," Ard said gravely. "And there is no need for you to repeat to me what brought you here. The Levite informed me. And, strangely enough, I too, came here, because of Jabin."

As Dael looked at him, Ard nodded grimly. "At one time I served the King of Canaan well and with honor. I was gladiator for him and then trained other fighters for his schools. And trained them well, too, for many of them brought great fame and fortune to Jabin. And the king was pleased because I believe he loves his gladiators more than he does gold, woman, or wine. Yet when Jabin insisted that I worship Baal instead of Jehovah, when he pursued me relentlessly to forsake the God of my fathers, I——"

Ard saw the question in Dael's eyes and answered it before the craftsman could utter the words. "Why did it make so much difference to Jabin whether I worshiped one god or the other?" Ard shrugged. "Perhaps it was of little matter and concern to *him*. But his fighters, the men I trained, insisted that I follow Baal instead of the unseen deity of Israel. The fighters were superstitious, claiming that evil would befall them in the arenas if I made not the proper sacrifices to Baal nor beseeched him. So when the clamor grew great and Jabin commanded me to worship at the altars of Canaan, I refused. As punishment, Jabin deprived me of my rank and privileges—I held the scarf of an officer in his army—and threatened to send me back as an ordinary mercenary to the army. I still refused. When the monarch's men finally came for me, I fled —to Golan. But I slew no one. Here I am safe."

"Cannot Jabin go after all those who reside in Golan and the other cities of refuge?" Dael asked.

Ard shrugged. "And what would it avail him? Few of the men in the cities have committed crimes against Canaan itself. The cities are poor and of no significance, produce little and have meager trade. Jabin has much more to do than to concentrate on leveling the sanctuary places. Besides, the cities are of a religious nature, and Jabin is cautious about arousing a religious conflict with Israel. Certainly it would not be worth it to do it for the cities of refuge alone."

Dael was looking curiously at Ard. "And you gave all this up, faced danger and perhaps death just because of Jehovah?"

For a moment the eyes of both men clashed, and it was the artisan's gaze that gave way first. "Just for Jehovah?" Ard repeated. "What mean you? Is not Jehovah the God of Israel and are you not a man of Israel? Take Jehovah from Israel, and what is there left? Where remains the identification, the integrity—the very being of men at Israel? However"—he broke off, his smile weak now, seeing that Dael was getting both confused and annoyed—"we must not pass words between us of such matters. Now," he added, leaning forward and tapping a finger on Dael's knee, "the Levite has informed you of the ordeal by combat you must achieve?"

As Dael nodded, the trainer continued. "It is nothing to fear. There will be no death. But you must go through with it. Already the lots have been cast and it has been decided that you will fight with the flaming torches. One Gibeah, a mighty man of valor here, will be your opponent."

Dael licked his lips. "I know nothing of such combat," he began uncertainly, stopping as Ard waved his fears aside. "Surely it will be less of a trial than to kill an armed offcer of Canaan. Flaming torches are provided you. You will maneuver them as you would a sword. When your opponent's torch is knocked out of his hand or when he thinks he has had enough, you are the victor. And," Ard contined thoughtfully, his eyes again taking inventory of Dael's body, "when I wager—I shall wager on you. And get the heavy odds." He grinned.

Dael smiled back nervously. "I should thank you for the confidence."

"You will win," Ard said indifferently. "Gibeah—he who is known as the Hill because of his strength—will be no match for you, I know." He nodded wisely. "You have the body of a fighter. There is strength and speed in you," he continued, thinking as he talked that truly this young man had been blessed. The long, tapering, well-muscled legs spoke of speed, the arms and shoulders bulged with power, and the chest and stomach—heavily muscled—would act like shields against any blows.

With his eyes half closed Ard asked lazily, almost indifferently, "Have you ever wanted to fight in the arenas as a gladiator?" When he popped his eyes open again, he smiled at the surprised incredulity on Dael's face. "No, then? Well, it could be, it could well be," he murmured. "There is a new method of fighting in the islands of the Great Western Sea, where I, too, fought. It could happen that——" Then he shrugged and stood up. "More of this later," he promised. "In the meantime, fear not and rest. You will be informed when your time of ordeal will come. And," he added as an afterthought, "if you so desire, I could show you the basic moves of a torch fight. If you so prefer."

"I so prefer," Dael said quickly.

Ard's hand slapped Dael's shoulder lightly, dug faintly into skin and muscles. "So be it then. Meet me at sundown outside the barracks. I will have two mock torches and we will see what you can do with them. Who knows," He grinned in his friendly fashion again. "Perhaps this is but the start of many lessons I shall give you." He winked broadly at Dael, nodded his head as if in confirmation, and then, on his queer, rocking gait, walked rapidly out of the room.

How many men there were around the fighting area reserved for the fugitives of Golan, Dael had no way of knowing. But from the rise and fall of the deep, masculine voices he was aware that many hundreds had come to see him, the stranger, have the mark of authority—and perhaps that of approval—stamped upon him by Gibeah, who would seal it in the flaming heat of the torches.

There were no other lights in the circle of combat now save for the two torches in the hands of Dael and Gibeah. Looking down at the seasoned olivewood in his grasp, its smooth, finished grain feeling like polished leather, Dael was glad that Ard had given him some brief and introductory instruction with the brands. He stared downward, looking at the amber color of the wood and the blazing knobbed end, which had been dipped in bitumen pitch. His face grew grim and tight and he lifted his eyes to behold Ard's worried features outlined against the smoky glare of the torch.

"You remember the rules of torch battle?" the squat trainer asked, his voice no more than a whisper. With bent head Dael nodded, feeling a surge of anger seethe through him. Rules, always the rules and regulations, he thought bitterly. The rules of Israel, of the shophet, of the priests, of Jabin, of Canaan.

And Jehovah's rules, for which his father had died.

"Repeat them after me, then," Ard was insisting. Dael, his hands running aimlessly up and down the unlighted part of the torch, licked dry lips and began the recitation, taught to him by the trainer, which he had memorized:

"Not as a club must the torch be used, nor is it to be held in both hands and swung like an ax. Only one arm holds the torch, which must be used to stab and to thrust and to defend. The free hand must not be used as a weapon at all, and kept extended only for balance. Once your opponent falls to both knees, both touching the ground at the same time, the contest has ended."

"Good," Ard breathed. "Remember this. Be quick. Move swiftly. Keep him off balance. Bewilder him. Use your torch as you would a sword, as I showed you. But with care," he cautioned, "for in your zeal you may overlunge and trip and fall. And remember that the flames can blind you. Be aware of that."

As Dael nodded again, a tall man advanced slowly into the circle of light thrown by the blazing brands. Sharply he clapped his hands, the dry, brittle, staccato sound instantly spurting silence over the multitude.

"With Jehovah, go," Ard breathed, shoving Dael gently to the middle of the area, where Gibeah, looming large and sinister against the shadows, was already waiting. In the giant Hill's fists, the cubit-long torch seemed like a puny candle.

The tall man, evidently the referee, motioned both men closer to him. "Hold your torches in your right hand," he ordered.

"Hold!" Ard cried out from the darkness. "The stranger's strong hand is his left, not his right."

There was a rising murmur of sound from the expectant crowd which died away as soon as the official ordered Dael to hold his torch in his left hand. "Remember the rules and obey my commands!" the referee called out with sharpness and warning. "I will bring shame to and declare loser the man who uses as a club his torch, or his free hand to strike, gouge, or choke. To begin!"

He pounded his palms together and nimbly skipped away from the fighters, starting to circle them, watching alertly and craftily.

For a moment Gibeah stood still, the torch high in his hand, grinning broadly and almost arrogantly as the man from Naphtali. Then with the swiftness of the leaping light of the torch itself, Gibeah lunged forward, the flaming tip bowing a fiery arch across the blackness. Pivoting sharply on his heel, Deal met the thrust with the handle of his own torch, coughing lightly from the smoke, feeling the shower of sparks settling and burning briefly on his naked chest. Like the Hill, Deal was clad only in a loincloth.

The crowd expressed its approval of Dael's defense by a collective roar in which the sudden snarl of Gibeah's disappointed rage was muffled. Once more the Hill jerked forward and once again the sound of wood meeting wood cracked sharply through the darkness. Sparks blossomed on tiny lighted wings, falling and scattering on the sands.

Gibeah withdrew, more cautious now, the torch held low, his left arm spread out wide for balance. Once he sneered, making a derisive motion with his free fingers for Dael to go on the offensive. But the Naphtalite waited quietly, his right arm swinging easily at his side, the brand raised high in his left. Breathing was important here, he told himself. Let the Hill expend his breath until it would come in torture through throat and nostril.

As Dael waited, as Gibeah circled like a cat, the onlookers became impatient. Sporadic hand clapping clacked in the ears of the fighters, and there was the restless shuffle of hundreds of feet against the earth. From the rear, somebody bayed like a jackal;

another voiced mocked with the crow of a cock, bringing a derisive howl from the throat of the giant, unseen audience.

A raucous voice rasped from the dark, directed obviously at Dael, "How well he dances, this mighty hero, this strong *gibbor*. Let us strike the drums and sound the pipes for him."

In quick and sardonic response, dozens of voices were raised in whistles, snatches of song, and obscene bellowings, all in cadence to the rhythm of pounding palms and feet.

As if spurred by the taunts, which were not meant for him, however, Gibeah rushed forward, weaving his torch to and fro, suddenly thrusting it forward. Easily Dael met the obvious lunge again, but this time the handles of the brands met, clashed and gripped, and refused to slide off each other. Straining and grunting, the olivewoods laid between them like a fiery cross, the two men strove together. Gibeah's face was already streaked with soot, through which the perspiration traced winding rivulets. To Dael's satisfaction, the Hill's corded chest was already starting to heave with shortened breath and effort. The Naphtalite, however, drew air easily and cleanly through unblocked passages.

If I could taunt him, flame him into careless anger, Dael thought, twisting and turning, trying not to be the first to let the torch slip. But Gibeah, the grin hardening into a grimace of frustrated anger, pressed down harder on the stock of olivewood.

"Why shame me thus?" Gibeah hissed, his face close to Dael's. "Make combat with me . . ."

"I am not used to fighting with boys," Dael said softly, saving his breath. He saw the Hill's eyes narrow with insult, watched the grin evaporate from the spread lips and bared teeth, heard the sucking intake of labored breath. With a desperate heave Gibeah slipped his torch away from Dael's. The licking tongue of fire hotly caressed Dael's abdomen.

He winced with sudden pain, aware of the stomach muscles tightening protectively against the seared flesh. His lips caught against his teeth as he rocked back on his feet, stumbling badly.

Instantly Gibeah was upon him with the fierce swiftness of a striking leopard, the torch winking like that great cat's eyes in the dark. Back and back Dael continued to stumble, his right hand now desperately clutching the air for balance, his left hand, slippery with sweat, feeling the grip on the torch loosen.

And in the night, madness reigned among the watchers, who screamed and yowled and cursed and prayed and exhorted. Gibeah was still moving forward like the wind, the firebrand in his hand slashing like livid lightning. Dael's toes, gripping the loose earth, finally found anchor, and he stopped still, his body weaving and bobbing to avoid the jabbing, darting fires before him.

With a howl of triumph Gibeah bounded toward him, but the Naphtalite, his balance fully recovered now, acted with quick cunning, still pretending he was slipping.

As Gibeah, in one great leap, thrust the blazing olivewood at him, Dael pivoted, slipped under the lunge, and writhed aside suddenly. Hurling forward under his own speed and push, Gibeah's torch met only the night air. As he himself lurched now, sliding on the sands, he looked around wildly for his opponent, who was no longer in front of him.

And at that moment Dael, using the reserve strength and breath which he had so carefully hoarded, was upon Gibeah with blinding speed.

Later it was said, by those who had watched and still remembered, that it had been impossible to determine where the torch ended and the body of Dael began. For they seemed to be as one now, fiber of the same fiber, each part of the other. A jabbing, thrusting, leaping Dael danced around the confused Hill. On the left side and on the right, from behind and in front, that devilish torch kept taunting Gibeah, its yellowed tongue of flame bending and mocking with insolent taunts. As the crowd beheld this dazzling exhibition of speed, they roared their approval and delight. Turning, pirouetting the man from Kedesh, not still for a moment, broke through Gibeah's guard and flicked his fire closer and closer to the local hero's body. Gibeah, sobbing from weariness and gasping for breath, the perspiration gleaming in a gilded patina upon his shoulders and chest, gritted his teeth and kept moving backward. Clumsy were his motions now, feeble his defensive thrusts as he tried to parry the jabs and lunges of the evernearing flame.

Bent low, Deal moved forward again, his head tucked in a natural fighting way between his shoulders, his right hand spread wide, the fingers open, the left hand moving the fiery circles closer and closer to Gibeah's eyes. Nearer and nearer the flame danced and whirled, the heat already close enough to singe Gibeah's eyebrows, the giant wick flicking at eyelashes blinding him momentarily. Dael rushed forward again, his torch moving in steady, concentric circles of light, finally passing swiftly before Gibeah's eyes. With a cry of anguish the Golan fighter dropped his torch, putting up both fists before his eyes, dropping to his knees in surrender.

Delirium rocked the night.

The referee stepped in quickly, holding Dael aside, peering into Gibeah's tearing face. "Has the newcomer prevailed over thee?" the official asked, and Gibeah, slowly shaking his head, answered:

"He has prevailed . . ."

The referee took Dael's torch from his hand, swung it thrice over his head in the victory sign, and then cast it away. Then he gestured to some men at the edge of the circle. "Bring oil of olive and unguents for Gibeah," he commanded.

Dael, hardly hearing the applause and shouts, hurried to the fallen Gibeah, bending over him solicitously. "Your sight——" he began, feeling easier as the Hill grinned up at him. "I will see," Gibeah said. "Fear not." Impulsively he extended his arm upward, and Dael grasped the hot and still-sweating palm.

"I would have your friendship, Naphtalite," Gibeah said, the smile still alive on his face despite the pain he must have felt. "Is it given me?"

Dael nodded. "Henceforth I am your brother," he said formally, suddenly pleased at the pressure of response against his hand.

"But now the brothers must part," a new voice said, and Dael turned around to see Ard hovering closely to him. "The Hill will be in good spirits," he assured Dael, starting to lead him away. "Tomorrow you will see him and listen to his excuses. But now—you are to come with me. For there is much I have to say to you, and at once."

Ard threw a robe over Dael and then, shouldering his way through the excited crowd, led him toward a building that cast its shadows not far from the barracks of the refugees of Golan.

8

STILL without speaking Ard hurried Dael along to the structure. Passing through the gateways of the building, the Naphtalite observed that they were large enough to admit horses and chariots. As Ard saw Dael pause, the trainer hesitated for the first time. "Behold," he said with a broken grin and waving his arm at the ruins around him, "the wonder of what once had been the ancient power of Canaan. I am leading you into the 'Great House'—once the palace of the rulers of Golan, but now nothing but crumbling walls and faded glory."

To their left now lay the old and smoothly worn watering troughs for the animals, while the space to their right boasted feebly of hitching posts of stone and the cracked tiled floors of old stables for the war horses of the chariots.

The palace itself had the usual five-room ground floor, Ard explained, two chambers for the chargers, two for storage purposes, and an anteroom. The two upper floors had been reserved for the exclusive use of the royal family itself. Stone walls supported the ceilings of the lower rooms, while those higher up were constructed of adobe. As they moved up the cracked stairway, Dael stopped to admire the still-brilliant frescoes on the walls and the oval-shaped pillars. With professional and curious interest he examined closely the vivid coloring—black, yellow, red, and white were reflected at them; the exquisitely formed birds, suns, and eight-pointed stars still seemed to gleam with life.

Along carved niches stood the ivory and stone statuettes of the gods and goddesses of Canaan, with the figures of Hadad—the weather god, more familiarly known as Baal—and the serpent goddess of fertility prominently displayed.

Dael stopped before the statue of Baal, staring with narrowed eyes at the horned cap on the deity, the right hand holding the thunderbolt, the left clasping the forked lightning. Because of this god, he mused bitterly, men were dying or would soon be locked in mortal combat. Jehovah, too, had thunder and lightning, he reflected. What, then, was the difference between the two gods? Why should men redden their swords with each other's blood because of these two? Over a name? Simply because one was called Baal, the other Jehovah?

Dael also examined an ivory statue of the serpent goddess, nodding over the intricate workmanship, one finger tracing the slim lines of ivory that were the goddess's swelling thighs merging into the head of the serpent, whose tail came from the earth itself and whose head rested against the body.

A limestone altar with its four projections, or "horns," dominated the second floor. More nude goddesses, whose identity was unknown to both Ard and Dael, danced in mute stone around the place of worship. All these female figures, Dael noticed curiously, had their navels ringed by ten magic marks.

Near the altar loomed the life-sized sculpted creation of Astarte herself, who wore her lyre-shaped headdress with the two horns at the base. Donned in a long, loose, flowing robe, she held the cross of life in her right hand, while in the left she grasped the scepter of authority.

Stone benches adorned the walls, and on these Dael saw more statuettes and figurines of lesser gods and their consorts. He stopped to touch gently the disks, game pieces, boxes, spoons, and rings that were scattered along the benches, lying undisturbed there through the years since long-dead hands had placed them there. Bowls, fashioned in the form of seashells and covered with gold leaf under the ivory, held the artisan's rapt attention for many long moments. Ard found a cosmetic jar with gold leaf over mouth and neck, shook it, and sniffed delicately at it.

Next to the cosmetic container rested a dice game, ten blue pieces in the shape of lions prowling fiercely over the ebony-inlaid board. Ard picked up a miniature lioness and threw her gently against the board, pleased to see her roll to her feet and remain standing. "A good omen." He grinned.

Then he motioned for Dael to come closer and to seat himself on one of the benches. From his girdle Ard withdrew a tiny bag that contained oil, and with this he anointed the Naphtalite's slight burns on chest and abdomen, daubing carefully with the soft woolskin in which the bag had been wrapped.

"I brought you here so we could be alone and make words and meanings between us without interruption," Ard began. Looking away from Dael as he stuffed the bag back into his girdle, Ard continued:

"I want your mind to hear what I am to say, to.weigh and consider. Wait!" he cautioned as he saw Dael about to say something. "Hear me first. I think I know men. And remember, I have trained men and fighters for Jabin. Many of them, but not one did I ever see such as you."

Ard nodded again, tugged at his wart for a moment, and continued: "sometimes a man is born with natural abilities. He can learn faster than other men, or perhaps his hands are gifted such as yours are for work with brush, ink, wood, or metal. But another gift has also been awarded you. You are born to the arenas as a gladiator."

As he saw Dael start to smile, Ard's face grew thoughtful and serious. "No, mock me not!" he cried out. "I know whereof I speak. I watched you this night. You move with great speed; you have cunning and heart and a strong body. Only to a few men is this gift of natural ability in combat ever given, and such a one are you. I think"—and again he looked away from Dael—"that, with the proper training, I could make a gladiator out of you. For surely I have made such with lesser material."

The trainer looked away again, his eyes distant. He was not sure whether he had done the right thing, revealing everything to Dael at once. But there could be no doubt. In this young toolmaker lay the seeds—seeds? no, already the blossoms!—of a great fighter. The torch fight had proven that, and proven it well and with stunning force.

How can I tell him what it means? the trainer pondered. The long and endless hours of training, the hard work, the patience, the waiting, the expectancy. And yes, the fear, the fear of the first combat, the fear of losing. But the gains were tremendous, he sighed. Not only fame and riches and women. But more. Self-respect. Confidence. And as his trainer, I could——

He allowed his mind to dwell on the pleasant possibilities. In his desire to make a fighter of Dael a little hidden motive churned hotly. For, ever since his flight from Hazor, life had palled for Ard of Benjamin. He missed the excitement of the life with the fighters, the strategy and the planning, the times of combat. In addition, and he was honest enough to admit it, there would be new wealth to be made from Dael, heavy metals, gifts, tripods of gold and silver, favors to be won on fights and wagers. At the moment Ard had nothing. Ahead of him, if he remained at Golan, there extended only a gray and dreary parade of monotonous, empty days. But with Dael—— Ard drew a deep breath. The glory would come again; the banners would fly for him once more. They would travel the broad shores of the Western Sea to the Grecian islands, fighting in the great stadia there. And as fame and fortune would come to Dael, it would also garb Ard of Benjamin again.

Why not, why not? he asked himself hotly. He felt this had to be. In a way he was sure now that Deborah had deliberately told Dael to seek him, Ard, knowing that her kinsman, a trainer of fighters, would see the potential in the Naphtalite. For she was clever, knowing the ways of men, realizing that if *she* told Dael what she wanted he might resent it. But in this way——

"I am sure," Ard said, "that you could be a champion of all gladiators. I myself will train you, teach you all the lore and cunning there is to know. It will take time—but you will be repaid. Not only in fame and prestige, but with fortune as well." He peered at Dael under the shaggy tufts of eyebrows. "What say you, Dael ben Abinoam?" he asked softly.

Dael looked down at his hands, clenched and unclenched his fingers. When finally he looked up, there was a whimsical but set and determined smile on his face. "These hands," he said, lifting them before Ard's face, "are the hands of a craftsman—not a gladiator. I thank you for your confidence in me, and it prides me deeply that you think I could be worthy of the arenas. But I make things with these hands, Ard, not destroy them."

"You could destroy your entire life here with these hands," Ard answered stiffly. He stood up suddenly, brushing a restless palm over the bald pate, running the fingers over the upright tufts. "Think, Dael, think!" he said. "What I offer you is no mere dream but reality. What awaits you here in Golan? What is there for you in this city of refuge? Like the others, you will stagnate, rot away in your own idleness, be eaten up by the acid of unfulfilled dreams until your bones and your very soul become brittle. At best"—Ard shrugged—"you will have to wait until your judge or priest dies and a new one appointed before you can even appeal your case. And, as was told to me by the Levite, this is not a matter of Israel even. The man you slew and for whom you fled is of Canaan. Thus you might be doomed to stay here forever."

Anxiously the trainer scrutinized the toolmaker's face. Had his words enough force to be driven home? Was his meaning clear enough? Ard decided that he would have to apply harder vises of persuasion.

But stay! he cautioned himself. Perhaps there was something in the past of this young athlete that could also be used. What, after all, did he know about the Naphtalite? Surely there must be more, he told himself, else his kinswoman, Deborah, would not have planned so carefully to have Ard meet the stranger.

"Dael"—the trainer's voice was soft again—"you need not reveal this if you do not so desire. But I have told you of my past. Now I would hear your story. The Levite said you had spilled Canaanite blood. But I know not why. Sometimes it eases the mind and soul to mouth what has happened to another. Tell me—if you want so to do."

And from the look on Dael's face, Ard knew his strategy had been full-born and powerful, edged with guile and touched with success. Why, he marveled, the young man *wants* to tell me! "Speak and fear not," Ard said persuasively, "and remember that I, too, am a fugitive from Jabin."

In a torrent of phrases that surprised him with their force and abundance as they rushed from his lips, Dael found himself revealing all that had happened to him, all that had befallen him, from the destruction of the forges, to the discovery of Deborah in the cave, the secret of the stone of heaven, the rigid enforcement of the iron monopoly, his father's death, and Deborah's part in the revelation of Achan as the betrayer. As he mouthed the events of the near past, corresponding emotions swept over his face, dark with memory now—anger over the decree and his father's stubbornness, sorrow over the death of Abinoam, hatred at the mention of Achan's name, a sort of reluctant pride over the killing of Dargan, a hesitation when the secret of the scythed chariot was revealed. Only when it came to Deborah, Ard noticed at once with a growing understanding, did Dael try to mask what he felt.

So it *is* the woman, Ard thought.

And as he listened, nodding with sympathy or understanding, Ard again marveled at the mind of woman, especially that of his cousin. For surely her intention was plain now, as he had suspected. She had wanted Dael to meet him, sure that Ard might persuade him to go on to better things than to remain a fugitive in Golan. There could be no other reason. Else why had she urged Golan as the place for refuge? There were other cities of refuge, all of them more distant—and hence safer—than Golan, to which he might have fled. But Golan had been chosen, he was confident now, because she had wanted Ard to meet him.

Finally, when Dael had finished, Ard for a long time sat still, his shoulders heavily rounded under the burden of silence that now draped him. Then he looked up, smiling, his eyes bright and warm. He rose to his feet and laid light hands on Dael's back.

"It is good you have spoken and lightened your heart," he said kindly. "Now we are strangers no longer. No secrets thrive between us."

"The scythed chariot," Dael began to say uncomfortably. "Perhaps that should not have been revealed. For it was to be secret between Deborah and myself until I reached Egypt."

The trainer's old fighting instinct asserted itself with sudden awareness. *Now,* he thought swiftly, now is the time. The opening has been made. Now the moment has arrived, riding hard on Dael's words of confession.

"Egypt?" Ard said craftily, shrugging. "It is a long way. And certainly few refugees have the means to reach it." He shook his head mournfully. "I doubt if you ever will come to the Nile." He lowered his lashes and let them shroud his eyes. His face loosened into a melancholy droop.

And he waited.

"But I must reach Egypt!" Dael said sharply, also rising to his feet. "Not only have I promised Deborah so to do, but I want to study there and learn their craft and——"

Ard's seamed and callused palms raised themselves upward in a gesture of defeat. "But Egypt is so distant," he complained, shrugging. "It will take several silver talents or at least one gold talent of weight to reach there. And just *how,*" he went on, his voice becoming sharp with scorn and hard with derision, "do you plan to arrive there? To be carried in the lap of your dreams? To be borne to the Nile in the arms of hope? You said your intention was to stay here. So be it, then. Remain. And you will, Dael, for years and years."

The blow was a telling one, Ard saw with rising satisfaction. Bewilderment, reluctance, not unmixed with a newborn despair, were highly evident on the toolmaker's face. Strike and quickly so, Ard's instinct screamed at him. Give him no quarter. He is confused and, while he so remains, with his feelings fluid and flowing without purpose or direction, stagger him more but guide him as well.

"However," Ard continued, "a way is open to you. Follow my words. Let me train you as a gladiator for the arenas. Only then will you be free. Only then will you obtain the riches needed to go to Egypt. You will never have to worry about iron or craft, for your fists will take the place of both wherever you go."

Dael was staring at him, his lips compressed and his face turning pale. His fingers locked and opened again. Quick to seize his advantage, Ard unmercifully went on: "Once in Egypt, you can fulfill your promise to Deborah and show the pharaoh what you have discovered. Beyond that your duty need not extend. What the pharaoh does or does not do will be of no concern to you. You will have your chance to study and, after your period of learning, become your own master, free to set up your forges where you please. You will by then have the means to do it."

Ard closed his eyes. "In the Grecian islands they have such craftsmen as you wish to become. Their work is a wonder, for I have seen it. You could settle there," he continued, "with the woman of your choice, she who will be your wife."

Ard heard Dael's quickly indrawn breath.

The trainer shot a quick glance at the younger man, trying to probe the thoughts that must be in turbulent riot within him. With lowered face Dael was thinking, *He is right*. There is honor in being a gladiator. For a moment he felt the same rising excitement as when he had slain Dargan and had conquered Gibeah.

"Tell me," Dael was saying, his eyes suddenly serious and intent upon Ard. "*If* I so decide to train—and I make no promise now—but if I follow your counsel and become what you think I may become, how will the money be found for the journey to Egypt?"

Ard rubbed the smile of victory from his face by pretending to pull thoughtfully at his mouth. "How?" he asked almost indignantly. "By wagers, of course. Wagers which we shall win with you. Many caravans stop here for water before proceeding on through the wilderness. They are filled with restless and bored men—men who will be glad to find excitement in a bout with one of their own heroes, upon whom they will place their metal. Indeed, many of the caravan captains would be glad to have a gladiator along with them on a journey, to relieve the monotony, and give us free passage for mock bouts. By the time we reach the port of Tyre"—and Ard's eyes closed in speculation—"there will be enough for the ship's voyage to the Nile as well. If not, we can linger in the Purple City to fight there and earn what we need."

"And"—Dael's voice was low and very tired in surrender,—"you are certain I have the fiber of a gladiator? That I can fight and prevail? You make no error?"

Ard regarded him steadily. "If you will obey me, follow my instructions, if you will not stray from the paths of training I lay out for you—then I am certain. So I swear it. For I have trained men who became future gladiators, and only two had as much as you already possess. But," he added almost harshly, "it will not be easy. It will be, for many months, your whole life. You will think of nothing else. In fact, you will not think at all, save what *I* tell you to think. You will be my prisoner, I your master. You will work and work. As a slave works. But if you obey me, you will be a champion of champions. So I now promise you."

For a long moment the eyes of the two men were locked against each other. Dael's breath was deep in his throat and his mouth worked with effort. Then he held out his hand, which Ard gripped at once.

"Then please to begin, Ard!" Dael said quickly. "Tell me what is to be done."

Still looking at him, Ard smiled and shook his head over the unseen but powerful influences that a woman can have over the mind and feeling of a man. . . .

9

"THIS is how it will be," Ard said a few moments later, as they were sitting side by side on the stone bench. "Hear me and hear me well, Dael ben Abinoam. Hard and rough and cruel will be your life for the next six months. Yes, as long as that, because before you begin the training for a gladiator I want you to know the life of a soldier as well. Military training will not harm you, and who knows"—he paused—"but someday it will be of great value to you. It is good to know the arts of war. There are in Golan many men who will aid me; men who have been soldiers. Besides, as I will later show you, we have weapons of a sort here, even"—he grinned—"a few broken and discarded chariots and old horses to pull them. But they will suffice. In addition, you will learn to lead men, a wonderous thing in itself. For who knows? It is no secret that Israel can use military leaders. But hold!" he cautioned as he saw Dael about to begin an annoyed protest. "It is all part of your training. And one more thing. What I have in mind for you is not to be the ordinary sort of gladiator."

"What mean you?"

"I mean that I have other plans for you," Ard replied. In a way, Dael was making a dream come true for him as well. The two tufts of hair nodded and the trainer's breath was loud in the maimed nostrils. "A gladiator's life is short indeed if he fights with weapons or against animals. But such will not be your fate. Oh, gladiator you will be, *but you will never enter the arena with weapons.*"

Ard sat back and smiled at the surprise on the younger man's face.

"You will fight, Dael, Fight with blood and with pain. But your life will not be at stake. There is a new method of fighting, one born in the islands and rapidly gaining favor, where men meet each other *with their fists only.*"

"A *gamor?* A fist fighter?" Dael asked.

"Yes," Ard said. "Think of it, Dael. Something wonderful and exciting has been perfected in the islands. Man fighting man, only without weapons, just with the hands the gods gave you. Fighting only with your wits and your strength. With cunning and grace and swiftness and beauty. Oh, Dael, Dael—wait until you see what I have beheld. Two men, splendid athletes, approaching each other, their arms and hands thong-wound, striking at each other, moving away and toward each other in calculated steps, dodging and ducking and striking—suddenly and swiftly like the serpent."

"And you so fought as well?" Dael asked curiously.

"So fought I"—Ard nodded energetically—"else would I be here now to teach you? For with weapons a normal gladiator's life is of short years. Too early does he spill out his life on the sands. But in this new way, combat with the fists only, a fighter can go on and on. Behold me, in the fortieth year of my life—yet I could still stand toe by toe and fight. And you are not yet three times ten in years. You can trod the arenas for a long time to come. And retire, with your health intact and your limbs whole to enjoy the great fame and vast riches which will be heaped upon you. Oh," he went on, shaking his head, "you will bear scars. That is inevitable, for the hard fists can cut, and cruelly so. Behold me," he said, touching his smashed nose. "Or there may be wounds under your eyes that will never heal properly, or your ears may curl back from the blows. But if you are careful and train well, you might even avoid such disfigurement. At any rate, as a gamor you need not fear an early death. That is the best thing of all. But," he said, suddenly standing up, "let what I have told you be the first lesson. For it will be some time yet before we are ready to wind the leather strips upon you. In the meantime, you will learn the life of a soldier. And because of that I would show you what your new tools will be, toolmaker." He grinned fondly. "Come. . . ."

Dael followed Ard down the staircase to a small corridor that led into a gloomy chamber in which a single wall torch cast a fitful light over the room. And Dael gaped at the accumulated armament his eyes beheld.

Double-edged daggers of flint and iron shone dully against the shadows, while barbed, bronzed spears huddled onimously near them. On the floor, to their left, rose a great mound of slings, their leather thongs just touching the pile of clay and stone slingballs heaped near them. Battle bows, long and curved and powerful, made of wood and ivory and horn, festooned the walls in martial patterns. Swords of every description, long and short, curved or straight, single and double-edged, plain and ornately hilted, stood thrust stiffly into their wooden uprights, their sheaths standing silent guard beside them. Round or curved or shaped like the body of a woman were the shields of iron, leather, bronze, or wood, while the shining heads of the battle-axes cut through the dimness in fierce and slashing manner. Row upon row of wooden-carved boomerangs lay neatly arrayed on the floor next to the studded maces and hammers and hatchets and clubs. A giant double-edged scimitar, its blade winking wickedly in the feeble light, its inlaid ivory handle curved with figures of warriors, rested in solitary splendor at one side. Quivers of arrows, some feathered, others less adorned, hung against the back wall.

"From whence came all this?" Dael whistled in surprise.

Ard chuckled. "Some have been here for a long time. Others were brought by the refugees. Some have been purchased. Or stolen from the shops where the civilians live." Ard winked. "But it will be enough for our needs. On the morrow, you start. Behold these weapons well, son of Abinoam, for they will become as familiar to you as your own strong left hand."

And so it came to pass that Dael ben Abinoam of Kedesh in Naphtali went before the Levite physicians of Golan and knelt before them while they examined his body, searching his skin for the white dots of leprosy, turning back his eyelids and peering within for the diseases brought on by sun and sand and heat, prodded indelicately at all the openings of his body, and then pronounced him firm and sound. An apprentice physician, upon Ard's insistence, had Dael shaved of his beard and his head cropped of hair, leaving only a stiff brush covering the skull.

"Now you look more like a man." Ard grinned, running a hand through the upright bristles left on Dael's head. He scanned the artisan's face. With the beard removed, there was more character to Dael's face, Ard thought. The chin, plainly visible now, showed strength and stubborn determination; the mouth was sensitive, yet masculine.

"The reason for removal of the hair is obvious," Ard explained. "In combat, whether as a soldier or a gladiator, why give your opponent an advantage to grasp you by head or beard? This way —your enemy's fingers will find little to seize."

And in the days in which the sun was born in blazing glory and the nights that shrouded its death, Dael began to learn the skill and lore and technique of the weapons of warfare.

His teachers were many and eager and experienced. Made restless and bored by idleness, the former mercenaries and soldiers of Jabin or other rulers volunteered to teach Dael all they knew. With the weapons from the armory at their disposal, these men—headed by the eager Gibeah—plunged into the task with enthusiasm, teaching and explaining, enforcing a rigid life of discipline upon the Naphtalite, as stern and unrelenting as that within the ranks of Jabin's cohorts.

With sling and slingball, with crude dagger of wood, then stone, then bronze, he was taught the rudiments and principles of small-weapon fighting, and then the refinements of attack with these instruments of death. Then followed days of training with stone mace and poleax, with spear, both bronze and iron-tipped, of Egyptian and Minoan origin and creation.

In the hot, shifting sands of the training pits he learned the spectacular footwork of shield defense, using shields of all sizes and shapes and understanding their purpose—the triangular shield, the round, the long, the barrel-formed, the long Grecian shield which was feminine in shape.

The third week of training saw him start the use of the sword, working first with a wooden weapon for practice and then—with Gibeah, his instructor, pleased at his progress—moving on swiftly to bronzed scimitar and the famous double-edged weapons of iron.

By the end of the sixth week he was mastering the bow and arrow, taking part in a competitive match with veteran archers. Dael's stone-tipped shafts did six times quiver into the heart of the skin of sand that was used as a target.

The final stages of the training were the hardest for him, for he was taught how to ride, how to manage a horse and drive a chariot. As Ard had said, there were several run-down and broken old war wagons, which Dael himself repaired for use. Three horses were obtained for him, and with these he overcame the Israelite's natural fear of that animal, learned how to clasp thigh and heel against heaving flank, how to wheel and turn and charge and block, how to use sling, bow, boomerang, sword, and javelin from the back of a charging mount or the floor of a lurching vehicle. He was taught how to brace himself against the rocking pitch of the chariot in full motion; how—with one hand—to grasp the strap that hung from the panel and to use sword, spear, or ax with the other. He served on all three positions of chariot fighting, as driver, as bowman, and as shieldman, offering protection to archer and driver. He spent long, backbreaking, perspiring days under the melting sun of Golan with the two-wheeled and the four-wheeled vehicles of war, with those of leather-covered wheels and those of wood.

And he smiled when he thought that, safe in his waistbelt, were the plans of a still newer and more awesome weapon—the scythed chariot.

Turning, wheeling, charging, lurching, stopping within a small circle, spinning expertly around marked routes, the chariots—four in number—plunged through the dust, with the roaring hum of wheels, the neighing that blasted from the red-rimmed mouths and nostrils of the complaining and weary old horses. The curses and shouts of drivers and instructors shattered the brittle blanket of heat that wrapped the plain.

When Dael's teachers confided to Ard that they had taught him all they could, the trainer nodded and revealed to Dael that the next phase of his training—that of the gladiator itself—would start immediately.

"There will be days"—Ard smiled grimly—"when you will wish you were back on the chariots again. For this new learning will be harder and more exacting of your strength and skill. You will have to forget everything, all wishes, all dreams, all desires. Even of women," he added, his eyes swift upon the other's face, then dropping away as he saw no response. "Oh, there will be one mistress to whom you will be most faithful, who will never leave you. She will be good to you if you so are to her. But she is also very demanding, possessive, jealous and fierce in her love, and you will have to give her all your strength and wits and cunning. You will find you will have no time nor thought for her sisters."

As Dael looked at him, wondering if the trainer was serious or jesting, Ard slapped him hard across the buttocks. "Fear not!" he cried out. "She is truly the best of all mistresses. She will never desert you for another."

"And the name of this most virtuous of women, Ard?"

The trainer winked. "Work, Dael ben Abinoam. Work. . . ."

Nor was Ard jesting, as Dael discovered the next day. Even before the sun's ruddy face, flushed with early desire, had pushed aside the robes of night, Ard had wakened the toolmaker from Kedesh and brought him, still sleepy-eyed and complaining, to the shores of the small lake that fringed the northern sector of Golan and whose waters made it a favorite oasis for the caravans. "Four times around the lakeside," Ard ordered, and now his voice was no longer soft with gentleness but carried a whiplike edge that knifed Dael into instant obedience, "then return you here. And take long strides, for I will be watching you."

"From the shade, no doubt," Dael sneered, wriggling out of his simlah and shivering in the cool of dawn.

"From your side," Ard snapped, "for I run with you and pace you, great gamor!"

Dael grinned happily. "Then I will lead you a chase, old man!" he said. "See if you can keep up with me. Perhaps," he added, "I should call someone to watch because you will need help when I am through."

"Worry for yourself only," Ard said grimly. "Come now, and see who is the better man!"

And by the time he was circling the lake for the fourth time, Dael was willing to admit that Ard's still-tough and well-trained body made him the better man. While Dael's steps were faltering and his breath labored hotly and painfully in his throat, Ard seemed to job along carelessly and indifferently, almost joyously, talking loudly, declaiming lewd poems at times, or singing at the full power of his lungs. From time to time he would cast a sly glance at Dael's tortured face, hearing the sobbing gasp for breath, the snuffing of air in nostril, the heavy pad of leaden feet in the dust. Once, as Dael caught himself from stumbling, it was Ard's steady arm that kept him upright.

"Military training has its merits"—Ard flashed a hard smile at him—"but it cannot compare with fight training. You think this is hard?"

"I yield, I yield." Dael was panting. "You are the better man. How much more of this?"

"Much." Ard grinned. "Tomorrow, when we run again, there will be a pebble in your mouth and, at the height of your voice, you will serenade me—loudly and clearly—with soothing songs."

"I'll sing—with curses for you," Dael's tortured voice complained.

"Make them long ones then!" Ard said happily, and then, as if to humiliate him even more, sprinted away in a burst of speed that left the Naphtalite far behind.

When the running for the day was finally over, Ard led the panting Dael to one of the larger training pits. There he bade the young man rest while he picked up two sets of what appeared to Dael to be long, leather thongs.

"These," Ard said, waving them in front of Dael's sweat-streaked face, "are the tools of your new trade. These and the strength and cunning within you. Now behold me as I don them."

Flipping the leather bands open expertly, Ard began to wind them carefully, first over his left-hand knuckles, over the four fingers, making the thongs snug and secure around the second joint, and then passing them over the palm.

"Always leave the thumb free," Ard grunted, "for it will be useful to thrust into an eye or into the throat of your opponent." He passed the soft strips, soaked with oil to make them pliable and yielding, over the palm again, working the leather diagonally across his hand now. Then Ard began to move the strip upward, over wrist and forearm, binding it tightly in overlapping circles, until they formed a leather cuff, winding high up to the muscles of the arm. With his teeth Ard tightened the thongs. "The leather protects the knuckles and skin from swelling," he pointed out.

With considerable interest Dael watched as the trainer began winding the bands around his right arm. "How many windings does it take?" he asked.

"As many as there are tribes of Israel." Ard grinned at him.

"Twelve for each arm. Sometimes more, depending upon the length of the arm of the fighter." He gave a final tug at the tightened leather. Holding up his arms now, Ard showed Dael that they did indeed form an oddly fashioned glove over the fingers.

"This will be your first task, to learn the method of winding the thongs and doing them quickly and with great skill. And you will be watched when it is done, at times by the trainers of your opponents, for sometimes a fighter will slip a rock or metal between the strips, to strike a harder and deadlier blow. The thongs are long," Ard continued, bending down to a little cedarwood box that had lain at his feet all this time. Opening the hinged cover, he pulled out two more sets of thongs and handed them to Dael. "These are of cowhide," Ard revealed patiently, whipping the leather open. "They are long and must be wound correctly lest they slip off during combat."

Awkwardly Dael held the thongs, eight full cubits, or nearly twelve feet in length, feeling their soft pliability and the film of oil that still covered the dark brown leather. As Ard aided him with the initial windings, the little trainer's voice never stopped. "The thongs not only protect your hands," he explained crisply, "but also, at the same time, form a cutting edge. Actually, when you do fight, you will be permitted to slide a crescent-shaped piece of even harder leather—made of the hide of river horse from Egypt—between the windings around your knuckles. This harder leather will give you the added power to stun your opponent with a single blow if you break through his guard."

Concentrating on the tautening of the strips of cowhide, Dael merely nodded. When the winding had been completed, Ard looked at them, snorted in disgust, ripped the bands off, and made Dael do it over. Three more times did the man from Naphtali circle his hands and arms with leather before Ard gave any sort of grudging approval. When he had tested the strips for tightness and firmness, he grunted, nodded, and stepped away. "It will do for the first time," he admitted gruffly, "although I have seen inexperienced and callow youths do better than have you as a start. Now, remove the thongs and sit down. Every day at this time, when the mid sun is too hot, we shall have a talking period, where you will ask questions of me and I shall answer."

"How are the days of training going," Dael asked, "and how long will the period be?"

"I will answer the last part of your question first," Ard said, carefully placing the rolled thongs back into the box. "You will train with me for six weeks. Then I think you will be ready. We shall engage in a mock bout before the men of Golan—and," he added sharply, "before any caravan leaders who are interested in wagers. I say six weeks, Dael, because in that time I know of a caravan that goes to Tyre, from where Egypt may be reached. I go with you, of course, as your trainer. Unless you would rather——" The blue eyes searched Dael's face carefully, warming as Dael nodded and replied: "I would you come with me."

"Perhaps it is not enough time," Ard went on, as if arguing with himself. "But your body is good and the training will have been hard. Briefly, our schedule of work will run in cycles of five days. That is how they do it in the Grecian islands. On the first day I will teach you movements of hand and foot that will be light and quick, and you will fight against your own shadow as if he were your opponent. On the second day I will subject you to great feats of strength, much running and the lifting of heavy weights and the bending and twisting to strengthen the muscles all over your body. The third day will be the best—for you—for you will relax then with milder exercise, and I will teach you the strategy of the arenas. On the fourth day you will learn methods of defense, while on the fifth day"—and the grin turned up the flattened nostrils—"you and I will engage in actual combat. And your blood will flow, Dael—of that be sure. So it will go. And above all, you must obey me and do as I command."

Ard looked at the other. The trainer knew he was rushing Dael through much faster than ordinarily, but there were two reasons for this. One was the arrival of the caravan. The other, more important perhaps, was that Ard wanted Dael to have no time to think or brood over himself, his future, or the woman Deborah. Whipped by constant action during the day, by exercise and work, his mind occupied with new things to learn and memorize and remember, Dael would have little time for moody reflections. When the day was over and the artisan had been fed, he would go straight to bed, to be fresh and ready when dawn came. Relentlessly Ard drove him, but with a purpose behind it.

"Now remember this," he was saying, tapping Dael's knee with one finger for emphasis. "Remember and obey. These are the things I forbid you to do while you prepare your body for the arenas.

"You will embrace no women.

"You will not touch wine.

"You will arrange your hours with the sun, arising with Shamash, and then be on your pallet when he sinks into the sea.

"Figs and cheese and as much meat as possible will be your sustenance. You will abstain from too much bread and take little of honey or sweetmeats.

"Above all, you will obey me. And you will live for one purpose only. To work and perfect yourself. Remember that in order to win victories—and to have the money for Egypt—you must labor to achieve that. Is all understood?"

A tight little smile quivered on Dael's mouth. "Truly," he said, "you sound like Jehovah, with all his 'thou shalts' and 'thou shalt nots.' "

The trainer's eyes swept over the other's face quizzically. He was about to make reply, then thought better of it. Least of all did he want to engage Dael now in theological argument. If he wanted to sneer at the gods or Jehovah, let him. For the time being, only the training counted. And then the victories.

"Go now," he said to Dael. "The sun rides high and we have much to do. Feed yourself lightly and return to me within the hour."

In the days that followed one another like links in the chain of time, Dael discovered that Ard had neither exaggerated nor underrated the grueling, sweating, torturous schedule of training. In groups of five the cycle of daylight hours wheeled over Dael, blasted at him, burned into his body and mind with flaming lessons that could not be forgotten.

Wearing either the leather earcaps or the tightly fitting helmet to protect his ears and face, Dael went through the drills and exercises that Ard so ruthlessly enforced upon him. In the mornings, after his three or four circlings of the lake shore, Dael bent and twisted and writhed his muscles of abdomen and thigh, rolled on the ground, sat up and down, lifted himself by his arms and toes from a prone position.

And when the sun's rays lengthened, Ard watched him wind the leather strips—with Dael doing it swiftly and expertly now. Then the trainer would command once more, his voice barking the orders that sent Dael, like a string-jerked puppet, dancing and bobbing and weaving, ducking against the movements of his own shadow. Fleeter and more lithe grew his movements, his legs flying on the sands, gripping with power and moving with swiftness. His arms snaked out with strength and agility as he jabbed and probed and smashed his fists into the mocking black shadow that always danced before him in rhythm to his own movements.

At noontime, after a light repast of fruits and goat cheese, both men rested, with Ard spinning the great tales of famous fights and fighters, pointing out where and how each hero had erred, making sure that Dael understood the nature of the mistakes that had been committed in the arena.

And later, in the shade now, behind the barracks building, Ard continued to watch and teach as Dael, grunting and perspiring, thundered his thonged fists again and again into a boarskin bag filled with a mixture of fig seeds and sand. Mercilessly Ard would hover near Dael at those times, his dry, sharp comments driving Dael on until his wrists moved like streaks of light against the bag and the slapping rhythm cracked out in steady staccato bursts of sound. From time to time Ard would have some of the idle watchers swing the stuffed skin with Dael moving closer to it, rushing it, weaving and sliding away from its momentum, and then hammering his fists against it from the side.

'Faster, faster." Ard would urge. "Move around. Remain not quiet. Your greatest asset so far, O Tremendous Hero, is your speed. Avail yourself of it."

On the days of the heavier exercises, a jaunty Ard would stand by as Dael, with bronze-tipped pick and shovel of wood, dug into the earth, lifting the sands of wetter and heavier clay from one pile to the other, filling pit after endless pit. For hours Dael's back would be bent and raised with this constant digging and shoveling, until he cried out in complaint. But Ard merely grunted something, quipped words to the onlookers, who grinned and drove Dael on with fury. Settled back comfortably against the wall of the barracks, Ard had his eyes closed, as if napping. But Dael knew better—after a time—than to take advantage and relax and lean on the shovel or pick. One second of hesitation, and Ard's rasping voice was sure to lash out at him.

"Are you training for a bridegroom's task, Dael ben Abinoam? Remember this. No bride but a brawny brute will embrace you on the sands. Therefore, prepare your muscles, gamor! Dig—dig—deeper and harder, but dig!"

Or when they both had the thonged gloves on Ard would instruct gently, "Like myself, you are left-handed. That is the arm of your strength. Use it only to strike for the telling blows. Save your right hand to confuse or block a blow."

Once, as Ard was showing him how to block and parry with elbow, forearm, and shoulder, the trainer suddenly chuckled. "The islanders, good as they are, still make one mistake they have not learned to correct. They lean all the way back and bend their right knee. Do this, Dael, and watch what I can make happen to you!"

As Dael obeyed, realizing he was off balance at once, Ard slammed hard at his stomach. Trying to protect himself, Dael ducked and immediately swayed, finding himself falling. Even before he reached the ground, Ard's gloved hand had found his chin and had tapped him lightly on it.

"See?" the trainer taunted gleefully, as a shamefaced Dael scrambled back to his knees and feet. "In actual combat you would be stretched out on the sands now, deep in the sleep of a blow. Another thing the islanders are fond of," Ard went on, rubbing the bottom of his nose against the leather, "is that they prefer placing blows to the head only. But *we* shall do otherwise. Smashing to the abdomen and the rib bones can hurt and take the breath away. So we shall concentrate on both head *and* body. Although," he added thoughtfully, "in some island arenas a blow to the stomach is considered to be illegal and will disqualify you."

Dael, wanting a brief rest, placed both gloved fists on his hardened, slim hips. "What do you mean—we shall do this and do that? Why, you old he-goat, while I am in the arena fighting, you will be too busy making your winning wagers on me to even behold me. *We*——" he scoffed, but his teeth shone in a smile.

Ard turned around and nodded at the men who were watching. "Hear him talk," he said. "Already he considers himself good enough to win wagers. Why, you ox, you lumbering, stupid river horse, you clumsy elephant," he said, shouting now, "what would you be without the skill and cunning from me you bring into the arena? And continue now before I knock you to the earth for all to see." And the trainer began throwing his fists in furious slashes at Dael, who laughed, backed away, and easily blocked the blows.

He was getting better, improving with every day, and he knew it. A new feeling of power and confidence seemed to be born within him each time he donned the thongs. His breath came evenly and calmly, even after hours of work; his legs bounded lightly with muscle. He felt strong and sure and, sensing this, much of the moodiness had left him, and he smiled and joked more easily.

And Ard, watching him, also smiled secretly and told himself: Dael is merging into real manhood.

Once, as they stood in the sun, Ard cautioned him, "Take advantage of everything—even the very elements. If the ground be wet after a rain, move quickly and try and set your opponent off balance as much as possible. Or watch the sun at all times. Look at old Shamash up there." He gestured with his free thumb. "Some morning as the sun rises you will win the choice as to which direction you wish to face. Now—how would you reply?"

"I would place Shamash at my back," Dael answered at once.

Ard peered at him. "Why so?"

"Because in that way the sun would be in my opponent's eyes and thus would blind him when he moved against me."

Ard's eyes opened in a burlesque of surprise. "So something *has* seeped into that shaven pate of yours," he said, but he was grinning. "You are right. I once won a fight that way in——"

"I've heard the story," Dael answered, flicking out his wrist and touching Ard on the nose. "That's where you probably obtained that beaten-up face of yours, looking at the sun instead of the other man."

Ard started to say something, changed his mind, and took another position. "Now. Watch me again. When you strike, remember to do so with all the force of your shoulder muscles, not that of arm and wrist alone. That's why you dig, champion," Ard sniffed. "But also remember to follow the forward movement of your shoulder with that of your arm and wrist. In this way you strike with triple strength. Let us try it."

As Ard faced him, Dael smiled and then lowered his head carefully, as he had been taught to do, the left arm cocked close and protectively to the chin, the right extended, ready for blow, push, or block. Ard skipped a little closer, flickering out his right hand, dancing back with little short steps, circling Dael warily. Dael, head still lowered, his eyes never leaving Ard's fists, also moved swiftly, stopping as Ard suddenly dropped his guard and looked disgustedly at him.

"Truly you have a skull of iron," the trainer growled. "How you ever taught yourself to read and write remains a mystery for the ages. How often must I reveal this to you—that when you move away from your enemy you do so away from his strong hand. Since most of the men you will face will be right-handed, keep away from that arm. Move always to his weaker side—from right to left, right to left. Now, let us again try."

So in the silence of the long afternoons they practiced, fought with snorting, rasping breath, with the sounds of the shuffling of naked feet on the sand, or blows striking flesh, or grunts or curses or hoots of derision and yells of triumph.

"No—not so. Watch me, Dael!" Ard would command. "Snap the wrist. And bear that right hand higher. Do not let it droop, lest you lose its protection. It is your shield, remember. . . . That is better. Once more. . . . Now again. . . . Good! Fine. . . . Once again and——"

And Ard was suddenly sprawled on the sand, a surprised look on his face, grinning ruefully as he saw Dael above him, a hand stretched out to help the trainer rise.

"I—I meant not to strike so hard, Ard," Dael was saying, his eyes searching Ard for any hurt. But the doughty little Benjamite, after getting to his feet again, rubbed his chin and looked thoughtfully at his pupil.

Pupil, he thought. Dael was that no longer. Ard had taught the man from Kedesh all he knew. And that last blow had proven it. So swift had it been, he had not seen it coming. And the force within it, although reined and checked by Dael, had been strong enough to send him to the ground. What if Dael had used his entire strength? Ard drew deep breath. Well, Dael was ready, but he could not let the craftsman know that, lest it bolster his confidence too much and make him too sure of himself. But soon—soon, Ard reflected, they would have to leave. And there was so much to be done before—arrange the mock combat, the wagers, plead with the Tyre-bound caravan leader for passage, then to—— He stopped himself, aware of Dael's curious gaze upon him.

"I have not hurt thee?" Dael was asking solicitously.

Ard's lips rolled back in a sneer. "Hurt me?" he asked indignantly. "With what? That little fleabite of a blow? I tripped, that is all. Come now, and watch a master at work, fledgling one. Like this. . . . No, no, *no!* Bring the right hand up higher and faster. And slip your head and neck aside when you see the blow coming. Because if you intend to duck that short blow, you'll run right into it."

Then there were the twilights, the best time of all for Dael, short but sweetened with the breeze and honeyed smoothly with relaxation, when Ard forbade Dael to move. Under the trainer's gentle and wise hands, every muscle in the toolmaker's body was soothed and caressed into comfortable looseness as Ard knelt over him, oiling and massaging his body, then raking off the sweat, dirt, and grime with a curved, wooden scraper. And when Dael's body was fresh and clean again, Ard would knead it and anoint it with sweet-odored oils and croon gently under his breath.

Then and then only, Dael allowed himself to be lost in memory and think of Deborah. Then and only then, coming to him as if curtained in the gentle mists of time, the image of Deborah would rise before his eyes. She had promised to keep in touch with him, but so far silence had been his only reward for waiting. Was she ill? Had Achan discovered her and harmed her? Or had Jabin——

Unhappily he turned over on his back. "Enough," he told Ard. "Enough. I will feed and then rest." He stared unseeingly up at the walls.

And Ard, watching and sensing, thought: I must act now. And quickly, for the time has come. . . .

"Dael."

Ard's voice had the old, beloved softness and kindness within it now. "Dael, hear me now. I plan to leave you for a time. When I return, the caravan to Tyre will be here. Then we will arrange the mock combat, the wagers, and the passage to the Purple City. In the meantime you wait for me, continue your schedule, but lightly so. Gibeah will take my place."

Dael stared at him. For the first time in weeks, in the long days of training, Ard would not be with him.

"Where go you?" Dael demanded.

Ard waved his arms vaguely. "Oh," he said uncertainly, "there is much to arrange for the trip. Men I must see. Affairs to——"He paused lamely.

Dael continued to gaze at him. "For how long will you be gone?"

"Three days. No more, Dael."

The son of Abinoam nodded to himself. Three days. With a mount, a three-day journey could account for a trip to Kedesh and back easily. For surely there was no other place for Ard to go. Nor any other reason but to——

"Ard," the toolmaker said. "Ard. When you arrive there—ask her——" He swallowed, dropping his head.

"Oh, Ard, bring her back to me before I leave!"

10

WHEN at twilight of the third day of Ard's departure the trainer returned to the barracks and called Dael's name, the latter rose from his pallet, his eyes searching anxiously behind the squat figure.

"She could not come—you have not brought her?" Dael asked, aware that his tone was half accusing, half bitter.

Ard shook his head, and for a moment Dael thought his question had been answered in the negative. But the smile on the mashed features caused his heart to leap suddenly.

"Contain yourself, hold!" Ard said, relieving himself of several packages. "She is here."

"Where?" Dael's eagerness shot him forward at the trainer's side, and he seized his arm. "I would see her. And at once! Where is she?'

Ard removed the clutching fingers from around his forearm. Ruefully he shook his head. "Love," he grunted. "It can addle a man's brain. Love—the emotion which none can defy and which all seek so fervently. Love, which——"

"Give me no philosophy now!" Dael shouted. "Where is she? Why has she not come with you?"

Ard placed both hands on his hips, eased against a wall, grunting with satisfaction as he scratched his back against it. "Dael," he said calmly, "she is no woman of the streets nor harlot to seek you out here. She is dedicated. And a judge. When she arrives, honor must be paid her first. She is at the home of a Levite, preparing," he added with emphasis, "to meet *you.* At the lake shore. For where else is there? She cannot come here, and you cannot enter that part of Golan which is for non-refugees only. So calm your emotions. I have brought her, she is here, and you will see her."

"When?"

"Soon, soon," Ard assured him. He shook his head again. "How little you know of women," he chided. "You would have my kinswoman, dirtied and grimed after the journey, to appear unto you unbathed and uncleansed. And unadorned. No woman would ever appear like that before *any* man, let along one who calls himself lover to her. Nor," he went on, the shaggy eyebrows raised in admonition, "should you appear plainly clad to her. For that reason I have brought you something for the occasion."

The trainer bent, as if to pick up what he had brought, then thought better of it. "Even I am befuddled by all this matchmaking," he muttered. He gestured to Dael. "Get on the bench. I would prepare you. You have washed?"

Dael nodded, stretching out on the wooden bench that served as a rubdown and powdering table. At Ard's command he stripped the loincloth from him, and the trainer began to rub him with the fine, grated yellow and black powders of earth, giving the Naphtalite's body a supple, gleaming sheen. Dael had always admired the technique the trainer used—the way he dug his arm to the elbow into the large vase of powdered earth and then, with great skill, flipped wrist and forearm so that the powders settled like gilded and ebonied dust upon his body.

"And how are affairs in Kedesh?" Dael asked, sighing a little under Ard's expert fingers.

"If you mean Achan, he is away on his circuit. If you mean Jabin, the monarch has no suspicion that you have slain Dargan. No one knows who is responsible for the crime. As for your leaving, all think you fled to find your fortune elsewhere. So you see, you have nothing to fear. All is as well as can be."

"And she—Deborah?"

Ard slapped the side of the vase. "By all the Asherahs!" he burst out. "I have just told you. She is here. Could she have come if she were unwell? Of a truth, great hero, the fates have been kind to you. She, too, must leave for her period of judging around the district of Naphtali. Indeed, had I come a day later, she would not have been able to be here. As it is, she must leave tonight—as soon as she sees you."

Burning disappointment cast its ashes heavily through his body, and he sagged in every muscle. "So soon must she leave?" he murmured. "I had thought she would remain to see us in the mock combat, and then——"

"She cannot remain—not even for overnight. Her guards from Kedesh will escort her back before dawn. As for the mock combat," Ard continued, "that, too, this day I have arranged. The caravan is here and will remain for two more days, sufficient time for us. And"—he grinned happily—"there will be wagers made."

"But why," Dael murmured, almost to himself, "must it be so between us? To meet only to part?"

"So has it ever been between lovers," Ard commented. "There is a saying, you know, that he who loves must suffer."

"You need not remind me," Dael answered shortly. As he continued to stare moodily at Ard, the trainer flicked powder-stained fingers into the fighter's face. "It could have been worse," Ard reminded him. "Suppose she could not have come at all? And it was close, I tell you. This way, at least you will say your farewells before leaving."

Then, before Dael could lapse into disappointed melancholy, Ard walked over to the corner of the chamber, shoved aside a heap of unwound and used thongs, half-emptied jars and vases of oil and unguents, and finally found what he had been searching for, one of the packets he had brought with him. It was wrapped in a square of lacquered papyrus, neatly tied with a ribbon of purple linen. Ard loosened the knot with a careless finger and then, more gently now, lifted the contents from the box for Dael to see.

Never before, Dael told himself with indrawn breath of stunned wonder, had he beheld so splendid a garment. It was made of the sheerest, lightest, and whitest of linen—a triangular-shaped kilt that bore along each edge of its closely cut hipline three little bell-like tassels of gold, crimson, and purple. As Ard, smiling shyly, held it out for Dael, the latter turned his eyes upon the Benjamite.

"For you, for you—take it and wear it tonight for her," Ard was saying, his face getting red with embarrassment. "You have deserved it. You have worked hard, and this is a gift for——Oh, put it on!" he snapped, unable to watch Dael's face any longer. "I had a few coins left from my wealth in Hazor," the trainer grumbled. "It was nothing. A trifle. Someday you'll repay me if you wish." He rubbed the bottom of his nose furiously and winked his eyes sharply.

"But where—from whom——" Dael was asking, his hands smoothing the fine cloth.

"From a trader in Kedesh, and who else could have brought it for me but from the islands? It is what they wear there—the Shardana, those who live far beyond Caphtor, near that land which sticks like a foot into the Western Sea. Someday we shall visit there and fight their champions and you shall see for yourself. But for now, hurry and don it, for you have little time."

When Dael was dressed and impatient to be off, Ard again quieted him. "She is not yet ready," the trainer pointed out. "There will be time for you to eat."

"Eat? Now?" Dael's black eyes burned with scorn. "How can I feed now? I have no hunger to——"

"Nevertheless," Ard said calmly, "you must eat. You are a gladiator now, remember? I have asked Nagar of the cooks to prepare us a special repast. After all, Dael, this is your graduation night. Were you now at Hazor in the barracks of the fighters, there would be a feast for all the former students. So come. You need food, even if your soul denies it."

Firmly he led Dael into the barracks kitchen, where a grinning Nagar was waiting. Although the thought of food was secondary now in Dael's mind and he ate almost automatically, he could not help being aware that Nagar had outdone himself this time. The wine was light and golden, made from the white grape, and delicious when the square, nutted fig cakes were nibbled with it. The flat and delectable fish from the lake swam again, not in water, but in a sauce of honey and butter, which Ard greedily scooped up the hard-baked flat bread, so bent into halves as to form spoons. Melons and nuts completed the meal.

As Dael moved restlessly and would have stood up from the low table, Ard again shook his head. "There still is time," he cautioned.

"Time—time——" Dael snorted. "She leaves before dawn, and the moon is already out, and you say——"

"There is time," Ard finished smoothly. "Besides," he went on, his fingers reaching into the broad sash at his waist, "I secured this for you while at Kedesh." Almost indifferently his fingers held something that gleamed white as he tossed it to Dael.

The man from Kedesh took the object and examined it curiously. It was a slim, narrow strip of pure ivory, and it had, he perceived at once, his name engraved upon it in beautifully etched script. At one end of the plaque there was a star-shaped hole.

" 'Dael ben Abinoam,' " he read slowly, " 'of Canaan. Graduate of the Soldiers School, the Chariot School, and the Gladiators School.' " He lifted his eyes and fastened them upon Ard, who shrugged.

"Upon graduation from the schools at Hazor," the Benjamite said, "such amulets are given to all. I felt you deserved it as well. The hole is for the chain which will hold the plaque around your neck." He smiled whimsically. "Usually the chain is of gold or silver. I—I had not the means to purchase one for you. But another has. According to the custom of Canaanite women, she will fasten the chain and then slip the amulet around your neck. You will wear it, I suppose, at all times. They all do. Next to the red-fringed skirts of the army and the laminated helmet that all graduates get, this is the most sought-after award of all."

Dael fingered the ivory, turning it around and around in his fingers, his heart too full to say anything. Once again he looked at the inscription. " 'Dael ben Abinoam of *Canaan,*' " He formed the words with his lips again, glancing up sharply at Ard. "Why of Canaan? Why not of Israel?"

Although Ard's face assumed an instant look of bland innocence, he could not face the Naphtalite's gaze. "What differs it?" the trainer finally asked softly. "Canaan or Israel? Surely it is not important to you? You worship neither Baal nor Jehovah, so why should it matter?"

Then the keen blue eyes lifted and scanned the younger man's face with penetrating scrutiny.

"I—I only thought——" Dael began, aware of the heat rising to his cheeks, and an uncomfortable feeling raced up to his chest. He took a deep breath, waiting for further words, unable to find any.

"I had thought of that too"—Ard nodded—"and finally decided that it would be better for you to gain your fame as one of Canaan rather than of Israel. For what is Israel this day? Who has heard of it? But Canaan"—he spread his hands—"Canaan is known. Besides," he added in a softer tone, "who knows but that your victories will please Jabin, since it will be rumored you are from Canaan. You know how he feels about his gladiators. Who is to tell but that, fighting as a man of Canaan, you will earn Jabin's pleasure and his friendship." Ard looked away again. "Jabin can be a powerful friend—when needed."

"But in Egypt——" Dael began, stopping only as Ard replied, "Egypt, too. Think you your welcome would be warm in the Nile land if it was known you are of Israel instead of Canaan? Recall that not so long ago Israel was slave there. Men of Jehovah caused much trouble, and the stench of their deeds still lies cloyed in the nostrils of the Egyptians and their pharaohs. Now hear me. About Egypt. It is true that I have made wagers with the Tyre-bound caravan. But unfortunately, even if we win heavily, it would not be enough for a ship's passage to Mizraim. And you cannot, after all, arrive there like a pauper. You must have funds—money with which to live, to entertain if need be, to bribe, to pay for your studies."

Dael was looking intently at him now. "And what is your plan now, Ard?" he demanded. "To delay the trip?"

Ard nodded. "To delay—and yet not delay. We can earn money and your fame while on the route to Egypt. We need not fly there at once. Instead, we can make our way slowly from Tyre—then northward and westward to the land of the Hittites and then swing southward to the Grecian islands. All along the way you will fight and earn the metal and fame. Thus, by the time you arrive in Egypt, you will do so as a rich man, one with honor and prestige, not as a begger or a humble gladiator seeking a fight desperately to pay his servants and for his food. Worry not about the transportation. There are many caravans going that way. Besides," he went on, "there are rumors that there is a plague in Egypt at this time. Better to wait."

"For how long?" Dael moistened his lips.

Ard shrugged again. "Eighteen months. Two years at the most, if need be——"

"But——" Dael protested.

"But——I have talked with Deborah. She sees the wisdom of it. In addition, two years is not too long. The tribes of Israel need time to unite and gather their armament. It will take that long."

Dael's hands bunched together. "But what if Jabin decides to strike out against Israel before that time? You know what his scythed chariots could do to the tribes."

Ard nodded again. "I know," he said glumly, "but it is a risk we must take. However"—a smile lightened his features now—"you have seen the secret weapon itself. As a craftsman in such matters, you know how long it takes to build even a single one.

And, so far as we know, there is only one—and untried as yet. Jabin probably is planning to construct perhaps five hundred of these to add to his famous nine hundred chariots of fame. Think how long that work will take. Remember, he has to purchase the iron, find the smiths, prepare, and try. It will easily take two years' time. And by then . . ." His voice trailed off.

Dael sat back, his lips pursed, his forehead creased in concentration. "Tell me," he finally said, "is this Ard talking—or Deborah?"

Ard, a huge grin splitting his face, arose rather unsteadily. Dael wondered if the trainer had not taken more wine than he thought he could hold. "So we are back to my kinswoman again," he said. "So be it. Of course I speak with her thoughts. What know I of military strategy? I am a soldier, yes, but I plan not the schemes of battle. I merely obey." He hiccuped politely and smiled again.

Dael kept sitting at the table, not knowing whether to be amused or annoyed. Clearly, both Deborah and Ard had talked his future over well. And the woman was still intent upon using him in her plans. He had little doubts now that she had arranged the flight to Golan instead of another city so that he might meet Ard.

And the future? He sighed restlessly. What did it matter so long as he reached Egypt, finished his studying, became his own master with his own forges? Then he would ask her to marry him and take her, as Ard had suggested, to one of the islands and live there in peace, untroubled by religion or the gods or Baal or Jabin or revolts and plotting. Keep your goal in mind, he told himself, never deviate from the path that leads toward it. Let the others scheme as they may—but you will do as you so desire to do.

He arose, surprised when Ard seated himself again, his hand reaching out once more for the wineskin. Lazily the trainer waved a languid hand. "You may go now," he said. "She will meet you at the lake shore."

"And you?" Dael demanded.

"I?" Ard's fingers curled fondly around the wineskin. "I remain here, or would you have me, like an extra hand, along? No, I stay here." He tapped the bulging skin. "I, too, have a mistress here, and we shall pleasure each other. Go now, for time is short."

Dael paused a moment, then turned on his heel and strode out into the night.

The highly polished surface of the bronze mirror before her cast back Deborah's reflection as she paused in her combing, still holding the oval-shaped comb of ivory idly between her fingers. In the large chambers of the Levite women's quarters, where she was now a guest, she was dressing carefully for her meeting with Dael.

Impatience, anticipation, and excitement made her hands tremble at the thought of this first encounter with the Naphtalite since his flight. But at the same time she was aware of a caution and withdrawal that calmed her emotions. For she still knew not fully how he felt, what he felt. It had been months since they had last seen each other. Perhaps he had become embittered, indifferent. In meeting him she was afraid of exposing her heart too quickly lest it be hurt, and yet not wanting to hurt or disappoint him should he still bear love for her. A man changes, she mused, but a woman in love remains constant, driving toward the desired object with all the strength and guile and planning necessary. A man's world was composed of two parts, his ambition and his work, and his love for a woman. But a woman had only one world —her man.

Deborah smiled slightly. To think that her thoughts would be ranging thus, she, the dedicated one, the learned woman of Ramah who never before had dwelled long upon the desire between man and woman. But regard me now! she thought. As a schoolgirl. And what is more, she marveled, I am happy doing what I have done, preparing myself for him.

It had been a close call, she thought as she slipped the purple bands which ran through a bone support, decorated with the ankh sign of life, under her breasts. The brassière, of the latest Egyptian styling, tied in front, the knot just covering the heart-shaped design of the ivory. She had planned to get in touch with Dael sooner, or had hoped that Ard would make the first move. But her own busy schedule, plus a caution made necessary by Achan's presence, had prevented her from sending any message. Indeed, she had been on the verge of going out under the palms of judgment throughout the district when Ard had made his surprise visit and had prevailed upon her to return with him, if only for a few hours, to see Dael.

And for him, she smiled, she had taken her boxes and phials, the paint mills and the henna flasks. For him she had ground the paint which now rouged her cheeks. From the uncovered alabaster ointment boxes had come the brown cinammon powder which she had dusted liberally over herself. A haze of powder-dust, diffused with the light of the wall lamps, still hovered over the room, and its faint but sharp tang hung over her. A blue headband swept back the butter-light hair, and an ankle-length skirt, cleverly embroidered down the hips with red-and-gold pomegranates, both revealed and hid the outlines of her body. With the tiny camel's-hair brush she had stained toe and fingernails and then, using an even smaller bristle, she had carmined her lips with a deep, crimson blush that gleamed smooth and velvety before her critical inspection. Her last task had been to draw—carefully—the heavy lines of kohl under the eyes and over the lids, extending in a line that ran to her temples.

Under her left ear lobe dangled an exquisitely formed *nefer*—the Egyptian lute of happiness—of silver, its miniature body and tiny strings of woven, silvered threads quivering with each movement of her head. Her wrists and forearms were sheathed with heavy bronze bracelets that reached, like metallic cuffs, nearly up to her elbows. But her fingers were bare of adornment; no rings glittered on her hands.

She gave herself final and serious inspection, running the comb lightly over her hair again, wetting her lips and eyebrows, which she smoothed back with a finger. The dove gray of her eyes looked quizzically back at her from the mirror, and the full lower lip dragged downward in a satisfied smile of approval. Only the tiny space between the white front teeth seemed to mar her appraisal and she mocked herself, like a little girl, by flicking the tip of her tongue in and out of the cavity.

Then she arose, walking to the canopied door of her chamber. There two of the guards who had accompanied her from Kedesh, who had been sitting cross-legged on the carpets, also rose silently and followed at her signal. Trailing her watchfully and respectfully as she left the room, descended the low flight of the stairs, and stepped into the quiet street, already silenced by night, the two men kept their distance, their eyes roving alertly around her. Without further incident she was led to the walls that girded the city, emerging between them at the Gate of the Wells into the open space, heading for the tiny lake glimmering like a pearl in the darkness. There, Ard had solemnly promised her, Dael would be waiting.

With the guards trailing discreetly behind her, she sniffed deeply at the cool air, her eyes lifting to the heavens, beholding the moon, which was shaped like an axhead, chopping its way into the ebony of the blackness, the stars flying like sparks from the impact.

Before her now was the lake. And at the shore stood Dael. The two men dropped back into the shadows while she advanced unsteadily, aware of the quick hammering of her heart. Her hands clenched and unclenched, and she felt the sudden wetness on the palms. To dry them she slipped her fingers into the sash that bound her waist, searching for the small linen-wrapped package she had brought for him.

He *has* altered, she was at once aware. The physical change was very apparent; he looked taller, leaner, harder. But there was more. The shaven head and face, now coming nearer to her, seemed masculine and commanding. He moved with a stride of confidence and sureness as he approached her. She felt a surprising little chill tap with cold fingers up and down her spine, and it seemed to her as if the hair on the back of her neck suddenly bristled. The brass-studded red leather sandals shuffled roughly in the sand for a moment as she took quicker steps toward him.

"Dael . . ."

Moved by an impulse she did not want to define, her hands sought his, sought and found, fingers slipping over his palm and thumb, clasp tightening and gripping with pressure. She felt the overpowering tide of his strength sweep her close to him. He was trembling as she folded herself against him, her eyes half closed, her mouth uplifted.

His own lips found hers, lingered, caressing and demanding at the same time, moving up to her cheeks, her eyes, swooping back to the corners of her mouth, finding the pulse that throbbed in her throat. Her hands were locked around him and her kiss was as fervent as the swirling fires within her now. Her fingers curled into the bristle of hair, pulling sharply, relaxing and holding at the same time. And it seemed to her she could never stop drinking of the sweetness, the strength, the security that his arms around her gave.

But it was the woman who broke away first, smiling tremulously, a little breathlessly, as she stepped away. "Was it not worth it, Dael?" she heard herself saying, surprised to find she had the power of words. "The waiting—and the uncertainty and the loneliness?"

The only answer he could give was to nod dumbly. As he reached out for her again, she shook her head. "Wait," she whispered. "There is so little of time left to us, and so much to be said. But first"—and her hands found the packet and extended it to him—"this is what I have brought you."

Soberly he opened the papyrus, seeing the finely linked and hammered gold chain leap with quivering life against his palm. When he held it up, the metal gleamed with the same softness as the small moon above.

"Your amulet," she was saying. "Allow me to slip the chain through it and then hang it around you."

Silently he stood as her fingers ran the links through the ivory plaque, as she reached upward with both arms and placed the chain around him so that the ivory hung, shining like a luminous white rectangle, against the mahagony of his chest. "Thus," she said, "do all the maidens of Canaan when their men finish with their training."

Gravely he thanked her, unable to say more, afraid that any speech between them now would shatter this moment, rob it of its tenderness, chill it with the cold of reason. Had she so demanded of him then, he would have willingly offered her anything and everything; he would have promised her all she could ask, forget his dreams of Egypt, go back with her to Ramah, anywhere—so long as she would be there. But as she led him to a rock that was half buried along the beach, his mind and passion cooled. What, after all, he asked himself savagely, had he to offer her now?

Together they seated themselves on the broad face of the rock, staring out at the lake. Over them the silent night suddenly seemed to come alive with sound and movement. The water, its surface disturbed by the caresses of a rising breeze, broke into rippling motion that careened the reflection of stars and moon into weaving pin points of light. Tiny wavelets rushed with soft, excited whispers of their own as they tumbled over and over against the beach, like white-frothed tongues licking at the sands and then retreating, Deborah thought idly. From the barracks came a solitary voice singing off key, while from Golan itself the muted sounds of the city beat against the stillness with a steady but soft rhythm.

"Dael," she said again, not relinquishing her hold on his hand, "there is much for you to know before you leave. Will you listen?"

He nodded, and in a rapid pace, as if afraid time would snatch the words from her mouth before she could utter them, she told him of the events in Kedesh, which Ard had already briefly outlined to him.

No suspicion, she said, was directed against Dael for the murder of Dargan. The other soldiers, the guards whom she had beguiled with her charms and magic, upon questioning, had remained adamant, saying no one had lured them from their posts. "And what else could they have said?" She smiled slowly. "For to admit I had been there would have meant their own lives. As for Dargan, he had many enemies, and it is thought one of them slew him. The fact that he was killed in the secret shed is of little significance. Nothing was disturbed, the chariot remained intact, and many have been the guards already assigned to watch that place."

As for Dael's departure, she went on, that, too, was considered with logic and unmarred by suspicion or hysteria. It was rumored that the son of Abinoam had left Kedesh to seek his fortune elsewhere.

"And the stone from heaven?" Dael asked.

She giggled. "I had it dug up from its hiding place. So far, Achan does not know, for he has been away for weeks. Fear not—the stone is already in Benjamin and will be molten down to make weapons, *if*," she added, a slight, bitter tinge to her voice, "the tribes ever unite and combine in their choice for a leader. None has yet been found. Your father's name had been mentioned, but now . . ." Her voice faded, but her eyes remained upon him. "There will be a gathering, a conclave of the men of Israel," she confided anxiously, "within two months or so. Perhaps then something will be achieved." She squeezed his hand. "And now, Dael, how goes it with you? Tell me of your training."

He told her of his days with the weapons and in the training pits, leaving out only what he thought was needless. Intently she listened, asking intelligent questions about the weapons, their use and technique, nodding her head over the field tactics of chariot warfare, looking sympathetic when he told her of the ordeal in the torch fight and of his harder training as a gladiator.

"Now," he finished, "Ard thinks I am ready. There will be a mock combat, a sort of practice bout, in which we hope to win enough wagers to pay for the passage to Egypt." Suddenly, remembering, he looked at her warily. "From what Ard has revealed to me, you would not be averse to a longer period of waiting before Merenptah sees the sketch I have made of the scythed chariot?"

She took her time in answering, her fingers stroking aimlessly the back of his hand. "No," she finally admitted. "I have talked to Ard—and even a delay of two years would not harm us. It would take that long to——" And she looked down upon her hands that were entwined in his. It was easy to say "two years," but how long, how empty and void the days could be during that time.

He told her of Ard's plan to strike north from Tyre, work through the ancient Hittite empire, then downward to the Aegean until Egypt was reached. And she nodded and agreed it was the best plan. "Nor should you forget," she reminded him, "that there is plague on the Nile now. . . . Actually, we have time. Remember, there is no guarantee that the pharaoh will rush into instant warfare merely because you bring him a report of a secret weapon that Jabin *might* be planning to use against Egypt. In fact, I doubt whether that is the monarch's design—for the moment," she continued thoughtfully. "He is in no position as yet to wage a full-scale war against the pharaoh, and neither is Egypt—recovering from invasions by the islanders and those from Libya, prepared for combat. But," she went on, "if we can plant the seed of suspicion in the pharaoh's mind, if your warning to him will serve to increase the garrison strength in Canaan, then will Jabin act cautiously and refrain from using the chariots against us so quickly. For I have no doubt he means to hurl the vehicles against Israel first and, once and for all, drive us from the land. If we can delay that attack by making the pharaoh suspicious, then your journey to Egypt will have fulfilled its purpose."

Ironically he thought of the ways of fate. Here was he, a simple toolmaker, suddenly hurled into great events of international proportions. And because of the times, he was not even free to remain in his own land or take the woman of his choice. Why should this be so? he pondered. Was there a definite pattern? Had something been established at his birth to combine his life with Deborah and Jabin and even the mighty godhead of Egypt?

He sighed, looking at Deborah again. In him struggled two wills—one to take her now, possess the sweetness she could offer. And why not? he argued with himself fiercely. When would he again see her?

But instantly the other part of his mind objected. But Deborah was not merely *a* woman. She was apart, different, exciting, not like the others. But how do you know that? the taunting objector asked within him.

You cannot destroy what you have found, the alter reasoning told him calmly. Between you and Deborah now has been born something tender and ever-growing, something infinitely sweet and eternal. Force her now, and you will lose this. Lose it for all time to come. Take her with violence, or even with surrender, and it will stain the relationship between you forever. Better leave it this way. At best, you have little to offer her save your love. Later, perhaps, when you will be your own master, you can give her more. Besides, you are not sure. Perhaps only friendship or sympathy drives her to you. Or her own dreams and plans of seeing a united Israel, in which you will be the instrument. There was no sure way of knowing her mind and, until he knew, he told himself, he would not have her as a man possesses woman.

Once again he sighed and, hearing it, she nestled closer to him. "Are you, too, thinking of the time we shall be apart?" he asked.

Gravely he nodded. "I hope," he said slowly, "that it matters as much to you as it does to me."

She lifted her hands from his, swept them over his face, her fingers searching every line, every cavity. A fingertip ran over his lips and he kissed it gently.

"It matters, Dael—it matters a good deal; more, perhaps, than you realize. Oh, I wanted this not," she rushed on. "I sought it not, neither did I think of it. But in the cave, and later at the stone from heaven, when my eyes rested upon you, I——"

He silenced her words with his lips.

Bent over her, he saw two little moons reflected in her eyes. Wanly she smiled at him. "I know," she said softly, "I know what you feel. We are at the verge of parting, perhaps never to see each other again, and we are man and woman. And the night is around us. So I know. But I also know that you think as I do. That it is better this way. We shall have more to remember."

"And less to forget?"

"And less to forget." Her lips opened and closed and she quickly turned her head away. He peered suspiciously at her face, at the corners of her eyes, which seemed to gleam with sudden and moist silver.

"Tears?" he asked kindly, wiping a finger softly over the edges of her lids.

"Tears. I am not ashamed of it. I think of the weeks, the months yet to come——" She broke off, then looked at him again. "One thing, Dael—one thing I ask of you. If you tire of Egypt, if you find it is not what you want, if your dream is an empty one—you will return? You can so promise me?"

At that moment he would have promised her the moon above. And what indeed would Egypt be if he had to live without her afterward?

"I so promise thee, Deborah," he answered, and his words were again blanketed by her mouth. For a long time they clung to each other, fighting the rising tide of passion within them, refusing to be borne along on its tumultuous waves. As if understanding, it was he who broke away now.

"I never thought," he said slowly, "that such feeling could exist. Never."

Her laugh was low and almost contented. "What we have discovered, others have done so often in the past and will continue to do in the future. It is nothing new—except to its discoverers."

From the distance an owl sounded its frightening call. She shivered once and murmured, "Even the birds are melancholy this night. And, since we speak of birds, I have written you a poem for a going-away gift."

He was almost incredulous with surprise. "Poetry?" He smiled.

"Poetry, and I am also writing a history of our days in Israel. And perhaps," she went on dreamily, "I shall describe someday a great battle where the cohorts of Israel overcome the chariots of Jabin."

"The poem, Deborah?" he urged gently.

She smiled, righted herself in his arms, and began:

"The voice of the swallow speaks and says
Thou shalt not, O bird, disturb me.
I have found my brother in his bed.
And my heart is still more glad.
When he says to me—
'I shall not go far off.
My hand is in thy hand.
I shall stroll about
And be with thee in every pleasant place.'
He makes me the foremost of maidens.
He . . injures . . . not . . my heart . . ."

Her voice faltered and broke and she began to weep unashamedly. "*I shall not go far off . . . and I will be with thee in every pleasant place* . . . Oh, Dael, Dael——"

He tried to swallow the stinging saltiness that bittered his own throat now. Silently he sat there, caressing her hair, staring at the lake, unable to move or speak or even think.

Sounds of footsteps on the sand roused him from his acid reverie, and he looked up just in time to hear Ard's voice coming at him.

"A very pretty picture indeed. Alas, however, that I must end this."

Deborah raised her face sharply. "How so?" she demanded. "It is still far from dawn."

"But the dawn must not find you here," Ard said. "There arrived but an hour ago a courier from Kedesh, bearing with him certain orders from the priesthood. With him he also brought the news that Achan is expected back earlier than you anticipated, kinswoman mine. Therefore, if you would be in Kedesh when the shophet returns, you cannot wait for dawn but must leave immediately. That way, Achan will have no suspicion about you.

Should you be absent when he comes——" Ard shrugged apologetically. "I need not put the words into your mouth."

"I am a judge and can be where I want," she flared. "I need not make explanations to Achan. I go where I please——"

"But not to Golan," Ard said softly. "For you have no business there, and Achan's mind will burn with suspicion at once, and you will be forced to lie to him." He looked down upon her soberly. "I do think it is best, Deborah. For your sake and for Dael's. Besides, the caravan wants the mock fight in the morning, shortly after dawn, and my fighter needs strength and sleep."

"But what of the guards who brought her here?" Dael asked. "Would they not reveal that Deborah came here to me and——"

"No," she said thoughtfully. "No. They will say nothing. They are my own men from Ramah and care little for Achan. No," she sighed, rising reluctantly. "I think your words bear truth and safety. I will go."

"Deborah!" Dael cried as he rose to his feet.

She passed her hand over his face. "I know," she murmured, "I know full well. But it must be so. However, fear not. Strengthen your heart. I will keep contact with you by runners or couriers, who will bring messages to you wherever you are."

"Not from Kedesh?" he asked hastily. "If Achan ever intercepted one of the letters and knew that you were in correspondence with me——"

"No, no," she answered swiftly. "I will have them sent from Ramah instead. There we have no enemies. Dael . . ."

She was standing close to him and he wondered if she would reach out her arms for him again. But instead, with a strangled little sob, she turned, fleeing from him, not looking back once. Behind her the shadows of the two guards melted after her running form.

11

DAEL hawked the clotted blood from nose and throat and looked at Ard. Still panting and ruefully trying to smile between his puffed lips, the trainer rockily faced the three men who were standing before him.

Gibeah, who with Perbaal, the caravan leader, had watched the practice bout, shook his head slowly as he stared at the defeated Ard. "For a fighter who six times tasted sand this morning," the Hill remarked sourly, "you seem very pleased. As," he continued, looking at the still-gesticulating, vociferous crowd that was melting away, "do the watchers. What pleases you so in defeat?" he asked wryly.

Curiously he stared at the huge yellow-and-purple bruise that, like some rapidly blossoming flower, was spreading over Ard's left cheek. The trainer's eye was also cut, and the mouth still bled a little.

Ard's painful grin spread slowly over the battered features of his face. "Have you ever seen such a one as this Naphtalite?" he asked, his voice hoarse but rising in delighted admiration. "This is the first time in my life, either in active combat or in retirement, that any fighter could six times down me. And so swiftly too."

Perbaal nodded. "I have beheld many fist fighters in the course of my journeys," the tall, bearded merchant remarked slowly, "but this one surpasses them all."

"You hear, Dael?" Ard smiled happily, turning to the man from Kedesh, who was unwinding his thongs. "This is professional opinion now. What say you?"

Dael remained silent, busily wrapping the leather into a roll. In silence the men stared at him. Dael was unmarked after the fight, save for a slight swelling on the bridge of his nose where one of Ard's blows had driven him backward. Otherwise, he bore no signs of blows. The fist fighter, clad only in the protector wound around his hips with a papyrus thong, seemed like a bronze statue etched with gold against the shadows and the sun.

"He is the very lightning itself," Perbaal added. "But," he cautioned, seeing a new glint in Ard's eyes, "he still lacks experience."

"A child would know that," Ard cried out, "for was not this his first combat?"

"Still," the merchant continued, his fingers deep in his beard, "it would be interesting to see what this man would be like two or three years from now."

"You will see, you will see and hear and remember that you first saw him fight,"Ard asserted vehemently. "And you will also remember who trained him."

"And that, too, you could have done better," Perbaal taunted. "He is fast—true. Terribly so. But he still carries his shield hand, his right, far too high to be effective. That must be remedied. You feinted him cleverly and thus gave him that rocking blow on the nose because of that mistake. And he also forgets to move to his left at times. But——"

"But you will take us to Tyre?" Ard asked.

Perbaal nodded glumly. "I have so wagered and, having lost, I keep my part of the bargain. Be ready by sundown, when we depart," he added, turning away. "We travel by night, when it is cooler."

Gibeah and Ard watched the leader walk back to his pitched tents. Ard then ordered Dael to don his mantle and keep the perspiration from drying too quickly. The trainer looked at the sand where the losers had throw their belts. Here and there some slivers of metal glinted, a few semi-precious jewels winked in the sunlight, and a single battered cup of bronze lay half buried against the heaped grains. Pieces of clothing, a holed mantle, a worn pair of sandals, a belt of leather lay scattered haphazardly.

Ard kicked at the winnings with disgust. "They are hardly worth the effort to pick up," he said. "Had not Perbaal wagered against you, Dael, it is doubtful whether we could even have reached Tyre. You see now the truth of my words—that we will need bigger and fatter wagers before we can even begin to earn the expenses of what it will cost us?"

Dael, starting to walk toward the barracks, nodded. "You need not pick up what the others have lost," he said over his shoulder. "The men are poor, like myself, and refugees, and have little with what to wager. Return their losses to them."

"Are you maddened by the sun?" Ard almost squeaked in indignation. He stooped and, with his thonged hands, began hurriedly to retrieve the meager winnings from the ground. "Never return the wagers, slight as they are. Go to the barracks and wash, and I will be with you. We will rest and then depart at evening."

And thus a new life began for Dael ben Abinoam.

Tyre, the Purple City, was easily reached and without mishap. From there, luck favored them and, upon promise of sharing the first winnings of Dael's next fight, another caravan leader was found, who promised to give the trainer and his fighter escort and passage.

So the caravan started north from Tyre, finally passing Halap and Carchemish and piercing the forbidding crags and cliffs of the Taurus Mountains. There was little for Dael to do during this phase of the journey, and he spent most of his time marveling at the products the merchants were bringing into Asia Minor, hoping to exchange them for hides and iron, the most precious commodity of all.

As the asses were unburdened of their packs and the traders

opened them to see whether the jogging, bouncing hours had caused damage, Dael hovered over them, his eyes widening at the wonders he beheld. The usual products—the kernels of golden-white Canaanite wheat, the purple wines in their rough skins, the heavy layers of combed wool, the closely packed and sticky rows of figs and dates, the clear yellow honey in the hide flasks, the bags of barley, the bundles of linen, the bunches of dried leeks and garlic—did not excite his interest as much as the less familiar goods.

His craftsman's attention was immediately drawn to the curiously wrought jars of metal and ivory and clay from Egypt. Some were fashioned in the shape of human or animal figures and contained, the traders explained grinning at him, rare and wonderful perfumes and ointments with which the women who purchased them hoped to make themselves beautiful for their lovers. Flashing Phoenician gemwork and gold inlay, delicately hammered bracelets and amulets, sandals with silver soles, pins for scarfs, ivory scarabs with incredibly minute details made him catch his breath in wonder and admiration at the skill of their manufacture.

Best of all he loved the little statuettes of bone or ivory—also from Egypt, where the elephant tusks were in abundance—which were created in the shapes of procupines or women. There were the little monkeys of metal or bone with puffed cheeks, who held musical instruments between their tiny paws, which made him smile in genuine admiration. He was surprised when he was informed that salt made up nearly an eighth of the caravan's entire list of goods for sale. The salt was abundant in Canaan and Israel, the merchants explained, because it was so easily evaporated from the sea in the sun, with the dried, white crystals left thick in the huge pans.

So, Dael spent the bulk of his time. Several times a week Ard had his fighter dismount from his ass and jog along with the caravan on foot. Occasionally, either with Ard or some daring and eager soldier of the escort cavalry, Dael would have a mock fight, with the merchants cheering both men and making careless—if small—wagers on the gladiators.

Thus, by the time the caravan reached Marash, Dael had tapered off into fine physical condition, not trained to too fine an edge but roughened to Ard's satisfaction.

Once the city was entered, Ard established quarters in the fighters' barracks for Dael and then disappeared for a few hours to make the arrangements for a bout. When he returned that evening, looking more pensive than usual, Dael questioned him, demanding to know what terms had been set and whom he would meet. But all that Ard would reveal was that Dael's opponent was called Sharma, named after the son of the two great local gods.

"Now this Sharma," Ard finally went on, unable to stand Dael's constant spurring of questions upon him, "bears more years than you. He is about eight and twenty and has fought for six years. But he is also weary with age and moves not as swiftly as you. He is clever, and you will have to watch him because of his experience."

"He has a wife—children?" Dael asked, feeling an insatiable curiosity to know more about this first professional fist fighter he would face. He wondered what this Sharma looked like and who had been the men he had fought before.

Ard looked intently at him. "One thing learn, and learn now quickly and without fail," he said severely. "The personal life of your opponent should never matter to you. Never, at any time. It will so happen that you will meet your opponent before a fight in the rooms for dressing and bathing. Anywhere. It may so happen that words will be exchanged between you, and you will admire the man for what he is. But once on the sands, forget him. Think not of him as a person. Look not even at him, but keep your face lowered."

"But—is he—I mean does he have a ——" Dael insisted, unable to help himself.

"This one time, and this single time only, I will tell you," Ard said, not unkindly. "Yes, he is married. He has four children, all sons. He earns his living as a hewer of wood, which he sells. Actually," Ard said with more confidence, "I think you will prevail easily over him if you remember what you have been taught and fight with head and strength. This Sharma is only a local hero. He has never fought outside of Marash and thus could not have met many of great skill. He certainly has not had your training, Dael. I so chose him deliberately from among three others because I think you will be able to learn from him without paying too high a toll for the experience."

Dael nodded thoughtfully. "And the stadium?" he asked.

Ard hooted with scorn and derision. "Stadium?" he asked mockingly. "There is no such structure here. The watchers gather at the side of the grassy slope of the hill. They stand. There are no benches for sitting. Below them lies the sanded arena. That is all. But wait until we reach the Grecian islands, Dael. *There* you will see what is meant by an arena and stadium. Thousands of people, banners, parades, a roaring crowd, sufficient dressing rooms with water and oil and attendants. Wait, and all this will be given you for your own eyes to see and to marvel."

Ard carefully tightened the last winding of the thongs on Dael's arm, running a thumb and forefinger over the tautly spiraled leather, and then grunted his satisfaction. Dael, who had been seated on the short, three-legged stool, his head bent and his body relaxed under Ard's touch, looked up.

"Stand," the trainer commanded, watching as the gamor rose to his full height.

"You are now ready for your first combat," Ard remarked carefully, his experienced eyes seeing that no detail had been left undone. The oil of olive lay smooth on the massive shoulders and chest and gleamed on the face and in even, thicker layers was ribboned around the edges of his eyes. As Ard carefully smeared more oil over the cheekbones, he asked, "How feel you?"

Dael's grin was halfhearted. "If this Sharma is only half as filled with fear as I am, then victory is mine."

"Then it is good," Ard replied soberly, nodding to emphasize the words. "It is nothing to have fear. It is to be expected. All fighters have it. But to carry this fear and *still* fight—that is the mark of a man. The fear will gnaw at you before each combat, but it will be so familiar by then that you will almost welcome it as an old acquaintance."

To calm his fighter, Ard went into a long and already repeated tale of his first time in the arenas, knowing that Dael would hardly listen but wanting to let the gamor relax with the quiet rise and fall of words.

And Dael hardly did hear what Ard was saying. In his mind ran the single thought that this was the day for which he had been trained, a day upon which his entire future and fortune might hinge. In the hot sun of the fighting circles he would meet his first opponent. And it would not be sufficient merely to win—but how he won. Perhaps Ard had been mistaken, perhaps he was not fibered to be a fighter. If so, then all was lost—his dreams, Egypt, and the return to Deborah.

The thought of the woman steadied him and determined him. He could not lose this day. He must rise as the victor, to go on and on. He would not even allow the thought of defeat to shadow his hopes. Far too much was at stake. Because of this day, the caravan had led him from Kedesh to Tyre, then to the long wilderness routes to Marash, on the border of the Hurri lands of the Khatti those who had been known as the Hittites. Once the Hittite empire had been of the greatest, but the invasions of the islanders from the Aegean to the west had conquered them, weakened them until their power was as dust. Perhaps as Canaan itself would someday be. When Canaan was conquered and——

Startled at the weave of his thoughts, he looked up, hoping that Ard had noticed nothing. A hard, almost rueful smile stretched Dael's lips. For the first time he had thought of Canaan in terms of the military and political. Had someone told him a few months ago that he would be concerned with the future of the Canaanites, his laughter would have been harsh indeed. But now? He shook his head just as a figure blocked out the light from the doorway. With annoyance, Ard stopped his talk, recognizing the fat man in the entrance as one of the official messengers of the arena whose task it was to summon the fighters.

"Canaanites," the courier said sharply, "the time has come. You are awaited."

"Is Sharma already in the circle?" Ard demanded quickly.

The messenger's eyes were cold with contempt. "Champion of Marash is Sharma," he said quietly but indignantly, "and he enters only after the challenger."

Ard's finger strayed to the wart, caressing it absent-mindedly with soft strokes. His eyes, however, remained level and cool upon the fat one. "It is the custom of the local champion to be the host and welcome the stranger to the sands," the trainer said gently, but his voice was icy and firm. If Dael, Ard thought, goes first into the arena and is there forced to wait for Sharma, he will be knifed by a thousand blades of anxiety and worry before the local fighter appears. It was an old trick, he well knew—to make the newcomer wait—but he was not going to allow it to happen to Dael in his first combat.

The messenger paused uncertainly, rubbing his cheek with a finger. Finally he shrugged. "I will inform Sharma of your words," he said, more respect in his tone now. "Is it really so, this custom of the Grecian islands, to have the visitor be welcomed?"

Ard nodded soberly. "It is the very latest manner of etiquette among gladiators," he assured the other. "And I am sure that the great Sharma will be proud to follow this custom." Dael, who had been listening in silence, saw Ard turn his head quickly toward him, barely perceiving the lightning wink that flickered over an eyelash and then skipped away.

Muttering to himself, the courier plodded away. Both Ard and Dael remained waiting quietly until, within moments, the fat man was back, his face beaming now.

"Sharma says that if such is the island way he will abide by it. He already waits."

Ard nodded at Dael, who arose and stood near the trainer. Ard picked up the extra set of thongs and held them out for Dael to grasp in his left hand when he stood before the audience and judges. In his own hands the trainer carried the round, leather cap which the fighter would wear in the arena and the smaller strip of soft deerskin which would be inserted over the Naphtalite's teeth to prevent them from being knocked out by the blows.

As they strode out into the sun, Ard began talking to Dael in low, quick phrases. "Now hear me," he said intensely. "We fight according to the island laws. If the combat lasts more than three hours and neither of you have prevailed, then shall you each be given the privilege of casting lots for a free blow, the winner of the cast allowed to strike at the loser without defense. If you will be knocked down on the sands for many times and no longer have the strength to rise again, you can hold up a forefinger as a sign of defeat. Once you give this signal of surrender, you will have lost the fight and your opponent may not strike at you again. But," he added, slipping an arm over Dael's shoulders, "I think not that the bitter acid of defeat will this day tarnish your palate. Move quickly and think coolly at all times. Fend off his blows and then use your longer reach to strike. Fortune is with us today also, because you may hit at other parts of the body as well as the head. It will be no foul if you throw your blows to the body. Hammer, then, at his ribs, his stomach, his heart. It will weaken him. Then, reach your fists at his jaw or his head. Now, do you remember where the vulnerable parts on the head are?"

"The chin, the left side of the temple, the back of the neck, and under the ear," Dael recited from memory.

"And the throat, do not forget the throat," Ard urged.

They stopped as they reached the sloping hill that formed the natural amphitheater, below which the small, sanded area looked like a yellow drop of perspiration that had fallen from the grassy brow of the incline. Ard stared, shaking his head with disgust.

"This they call an arena," he sneered. "Behold it. No benches. Only a tattered purple awning under which sit the leaders of the town upon their broken stools." He pointed in derision at the canopy, then swung his arm to encompass the rest of the onlookers. There were about a thousand of them, either standing or lying on the grass, eating fruit or gossiping. Smaller knots of the audience were gathered around a short man with broad, sloping shoulders and thick, hairy legs.

"Sharma," Ard said.

A pulse suddenly tripped into beating life in the back of Dael's head as he stared curiously at the man whom he was to meet. He felt stomach muscles contract with so sharp and swift a motion that it was almost painful, and he shivered suddenly. Ard's wise blue eyes did not fail to notice the reaction.

"Have no fear of what you feel," he said kindly. "Thus it will always be so with you, no matter how many times you fight. But soon you will accept it as part of your task. It is nothing for which to bear shame. Come now, for we must approach the canopy and take the vow."

Before Dael could ask what Ard meant, he was standing before the purple awning, staring into the grim-visaged, hook-nosed Hittite ruler of Marash and the four dignitaries with him.

"Make your vow," Ard was whispering. "Sharma has already done so. Just do as I do," Ard added quickly, dropping to his knees, his head bent.

"By Baal and El, the great gods of Canaan, I give this vow," Ard was chanting in a loud voice, "to serve well my fighter and to plead for his victory. As Baal gives fruit to the fields and quickens the wombs of women, so will I serve my fighter." Casting a side glance at Dael, Ard started to tug the fist fighter to his knees. "Make the vow and fall to the ground," the trainer whispered urgently.

But Dael remained standing, his shoulders held back in stiff stubbornness, his chin raised defiantly.

"The vow, Canaanite," one of the men under the canopy called out. From the staff of pine cones in his hand Dael reasoned he was a priest or some religious authority.

As Dael remained standing and a little murmur arose from the crowd, Ard scrambled quickly to his feet again. "My lords," he said, bowing to the men under the awning. "My fighter is young and as yet untried in combat. Give me leave to counsel him privately, for he has vowed to so many of the gods that he knows not to which one to dedicate his strength for this fight."

The priest with the pine cones nodded gravely, and Ard turned to Dael, placing his mouth close to the Naphtalite's ear. "Now hear me!" His hot breath fanned Dael's cheek. "You must go through with this avowal. It means nothing, I tell you. It is a mere formal ritual. You saw me, a man of Benjamin, fall to my knees, although it is Jehovah I worship. But it is an empty gesture and meaningless, and so I consider it and so must you. It matters not to which god you mouth your vow. *But say something.* Touch your knees to the ground and utter the first thing that comes to your head. Otherwise you will win only disfavor here at the start. They will think you are without the protection of any gods at all and therefore you are evil and cannot win. Or else, fearing revenge or retribution from their own deities, they might not even permit you to fight Sharma. Now, use your head and do as I command. And quickly so!"

Dael grimaced, then nodded and fell to his knees. Ard was right, of that there was no doubt. It mattered not about the vow. The fight was the important thing. But the man from Kedesh was adamantly determined, even in farce or mockery, to give no obeisance either to Baal or Jehovah, the only two gods he knew. What was Baal to him? Dael asked indignantly in his silent mind. And Jehovah? Should he plead to this bloody war god who had taken his father and fortune and had cast him adrift upon the world?

But to whom?

Astotte, the goddess of love? True, he knew of love but not of her carnal delights. But still she was a female goddess, and gentle and loving in the way of women, as Deborah was, as Deborah might be, as——

Deborah...

Even before the thought had sprung alive in his mind, it was being cast out in the words on his tongue.

"I vow to the goddess"—he paused—"Ayshesh Lapidus, the goddess of the lamps, to whom I dedicate my strength and whom I beseech for victory."

He raised his head, then his body, getting to his feet again, unable to meet Ard's knowing look and nod of approval. Only the priest, when he turned to face him again, looked puzzled. "Goddess of the lamps?" he was asking. "Of Canaan? I know of no such——"

"My lords"—it was Ard, speaking quickly again, the guttural Canaanite accent thick in his throat—"she is not well known, a local goddess under whose sign my fighter was born." He spread his hands in apology. "A minor goddess, my lords, but one he worships. The goddess of the lamps which kindle knowledge and love." Ard looked at the priest, who finally nodded and shook his head wisely.

"I have heard of her," he said with dignity. He raised the pinecone staff, passed it in three circles before Dael, then bowed to the ruler. "They may now begin, my prince," he said formally.

At the words, the referee, who had been standing behind the canopy, emerged at once, striding with important steps to both fighters. In his hands he carried a short wand of wood with which to tap the fighters or thrust between them to separate them if they should be locked together or tend to wrestle with each other.

On the opposite side of the arena Sharma's trainer had already adjusted the leather helmet and the mouthpiece. Ard also quickly slipped Dael's equipment into place, tightened the thongs for the last time. Dael noticed that in his waistband the trainer carried a little pouch, much like a tiny wine sack, with a linen pad thrust through it. He was about to ask its purpose when Ard roughly shoved him into the fighting area. Walking up to him, almost lazily and indifferently, was Sharma, a powerful figure of a man, with tremendous arms and biceps and with chest and stomach appearing as if they had been woven out of thick corded bands of bronze. Like Dael, the local fist fighter was barefoot.

Remembering Ard's instructions never to think of his opponent in personal terms, Dael kept his face lowered. But as the referee took his place between the two fighters, Dael was unable to help himself, raising his eyes to Sharma's face for one quick and curious glance.

Sharma, too, was looking at him, the brown eyes kindly, the mouth smiling. The Hittite winked at him in a friendly fashion, then looked away, almost indifferently.

"Assume the first position," the official ordered, his voice flat and toneless but his eyes hard and alert as he placed the rod of wood between them, holding them apart with it.

Both Sharma and Dael nodded and, as if propelled by the same instinct, went onto the initial position of the arena. His left heel raised slightly, the right elbow hoisting his forearm so that the knuckles were turned outward to Sharma, Dael at the same time lowered his left shoulder, tucking his chin protectively against it. His left hand, the striking one, was coiled at the center of his chest, while the right hand, held very high, acted as his shield. Opposite Dael, Sharma had crouched into the stance of the regular right-handed fighter.

"Commence!"

The dry tone of the official and the withdrawal of the wand came simultaneously.

Dael at once moved swiftly to his left, his right hand darting out at Sharma's body, only to have the blow blocked by the Hittite's solid elbow. Suddenly, with lowered head, the smaller man rushed in at Dael, both arms flailing furiously, thrusting aside the startled Naphtalite's guard. Without thinking, Dael took a protective step backward, his right hand lowering for an instant.

It was enough for Sharma.

Once inside Dael's guard, the Hittite drove two hard blows, snapped from the wrist and whipped straight from the shoulder, at Dael's mouth and chin.

A curtain of flame enveloped Dael's vision. For an instant the earth reeled for him and shook and came up to meet him. He tasted the sands of the arena, sand that was salted with his own blood that flowed copiously from his cut lips. In confusion he stared down, seeing the crimson spatter dripping from him, surprised to find himself on hands and knees, sagging lower and lower, with the thunder of great drums beating in his ears. For long spasms of tortured time he heard only the vibrating sound of the beating skins, then he began to be aware of another noise—the rising, almost hysterical pitch of the cry of the crowd. His right knee trembled and was unable to support him, and he fell prone to the ground, sprawling awkwardly. Sharma, intent upon the kill now, pounced upon him and began beating a merciless and rapid tattoo upon his ribs and neck and head.

The new pain helped clear his mind. Shaking the blood from his lips, Dael drew the stiff knee upward, his forearms quivering with effort as he tried to rise. Infuriated, Sharma stepped closer, practically straddling Dael now, the tremendous arms moving like the tongue of a cat lapping milk. Under the barrage of blows Dael sagged again, his whole body bending and arching, like an inverted bow of mahagony, back to the embrace of the ground.

Sharma was above him and at his side, breathing heavily through his nose as he sought to strike at a vital spot. Dael lowered his head, shook it, taking the blows as they came, remembering Ard's words to rest at such times, even if the opponent was unrelenting and the pain fierce. His neck and shoulder muscles bunched up now and, for the first time, he heard Sharma snarl with rage as the Marash hero was unable to down him completely.

Slowly the strength and vision were returned to Dael ben Abinoam, with a sudden surge he straightened his knees and arms and sprang upright. Weaving and blinking, his hands up instinctively now, he moved forward unsteadily.

The referee touched the wand on his shoulder and ordered Sharma to step back.

"Canaanite," the referee called to Ard, the dry tones whipping over Dael, "succor your fighter."

According to the island rules of fist fighting which governed this bout, each time a man was knocked down was considered a time for a brief rest. At such moments the fighter's trainer was allowed to help him, provided the battler was able to get to his feet unaided. Even as he remembered this, Ard was already bounding toward him, the tiny little sack which Dael had seen in the waistband now open in his hand. From it Ard poured a clear, yellow liquid onto a linen cloth in his hand. Dael felt the trainer's palm support the back of his neck, gently massaging the muscles there. At the same time, the moistened cloth was whisked again and again over his bruised mouth. Dael tasted the flavor of the honey, lemon, and wine that filmed his lips, and he licked thirstily at it.

"God of a thousand thunders!" Ard was whispering harshly at him. "Have you forgotten everything I taught you? You allowed the Hittite to knock aside your defense and reach you from the inside—as I warned you. He will kill you that way. Stay away from him until your head clears. Then use your greater arm's length. Can you hear me?"

Dael nodded. His tongue still sought the nectar.

"Again, to commence!" The referee, with impassive look, raised the staff, touched the two fighters. Sharma, on his toes now, the brown eyes narrowed with caution, shuffled forward swiftly, his left hand jutting out, the right held very low, the palm upward for delivery.

Warily Dael moved away, dancing lightly on the balls of his feet, circling constantly to his left. Sharma, snarling again, the saliva-moistened mouthpiece brown against his mouth, rushed in. Again Dael danced away. Sharma stopped suddenly, his face twisted with rage. In exasperation he dropped his arms and held them lightly at his sides.

"Are you dancer or fighter?" Sharma rasped.

Dael made no answer.

Sharma turned in desperation to the official. "He shames me," the Hittite complained, "skipping like a lamb around me. Force him to close with me in combat!"

"Put up your hands," the official told Sharma, "and save your breath for the fight."

Almost sobbing, Sharma coiled into his crouch again, his arms held high, and, once more with lowered head, started his charge toward the Naphtalite.

And this time Dael moved—moved with the glittering speed of sunlight on the bronzed head of a spear. In one motion he seemed to be moving away from Sharma and, almost at the same time, he had side-stepped, pivoted quickly, and struck three times with such swiftness and savagery that only two blows were seen. Twice his right hand shot forward, catching Sharma on the chin, snapping the head back so that the helmet was shaken loose. The Hittite's mouth opened and the mouthpiece, freed from the clench of the lips, dropped to the sands. As he reeled backward, Dael bored in once more, his left arm, with all its strength, spearing deeply into the exposed and heaving abdomen of Sharma. The crack of flesh meeting leather whipped through the air.

As Dael stepped away, Sharma began to fall gracefully in a half circle, his hands clutching at his stomach, his eyes already glazed and unseeing. Almost gently his body touched earth, turned over lazily, quivered, then straightened out, with only one knee raised. The Hittite's arms were helplessly outflung from his shoulders. His lips opened, closed, opened again, but no sound escaped them. Only a thin ribbon of crimsoned saliva streaked his chin.

Dael, lowering his arm, waited quietly. So did the referee. The crowd was hushed in silence. Overhead the sun beat down upon the three motionless figures in the arena, but Sharma did not move. The official, carefully placing his staff on the ground, kneeled beside the senseless Sharma, rolling back the fighter's right eyelid and peering within. The referee grunted, rose to his feet, and then beckoned solemnly at Sharma's trainer, who with lowered head and sagging chin walked disconsolately up to the fallen body of the hero of Marash.

"See for yourself," the referee said. His eyes moved from Sharma back to the trainer. "Do you agree that your man will not this day fight again, and that the Canaanite has prevailed?"

With saddened eyes the trainer nodded dumbly. "I so agree," he said in an almost inaudible voice. Once he looked at Dael, then removed his glance. He kneeled before Sharma and began slapping his face gently and rubbing the Hittite's lips with wine and vinegar from his own little goatskin bag.

His face cracking into the widest and most beaming of grins, Ard ran up to Dael, throwing his arms over his shoulders, hugging the victor furiously, pounding him with joy.

"Lightning—that was what it was, by all the Asheras!" Ard was shouting hoarsely. "From this day hence, you will be called Barak. Barak, the Lightning. So shall you be known to all men. I do not think that all your blows were seen. There were three, were there not?" he asked delightedly.

"I—so think," Dael answered uncertainly. He felt very weary; his arms seemed weighted with metal, and there was an uncomfortable throbbing in his temples.

"What matters it?" Ard said, releasing Dael and rubbing the upright tufts of hair excitedly until they were ruffled into little horns. Between them, the bald pate gleamed a bright pink. "Truly, I could wager that such a combat they never could have witnessed before. For look you, Dael, already come the first fruits of your victory."

From the audience there came the glitter of jewels and metal as the gifts were thrown to the conqueror. Fruits, bags of wine, a few mantles trimmed with fur landed around Dael.

At the canopy the priest was calling to the fighter, who approached slowly with Ard. In the hands of the ruler of Marash was an immense tripod of iron, while a smaller one of silver rested at his feet. Both of these gifts the king silently handed to the kneeling men before him.

It was Ard, rising again, who took the tripods and examined their triangular structures carefully, a thumb running along the metal. He hefted the awards expertly in his hands, realizing that the smaller of the trophies was of solid silver and of great value. He bowed in thanks and appreciation, with Dael following the cue and uttering his vocal expression of gratitude.

Dismissed now, the two men walked back to the arena, where Dael, with curious eyes, watched Sharma being led away from the circle of combat. With faltering steps, hardly hearing the gentle voice of his trainer, the defeated hero of Marash stumbled to the dressing rooms. Dael could see the hurt he had inflicted upon his opponent; the crushed mass of flesh that was the mouth, the chin swollen, the darkening bruises upon the abdomen. When they had passed, Dael took a deep breath. "Will such ever happen to me?" he wondered out loud.

The sharp blue eyes of the Benjamite regarded him carefully. The tufted head nodded solemnly. "It will so happen," he promised. "Not often, I hope, but it will occur. You cannot win all the conflicts. And the sooner you remember that, the better it will ease your spirit. But"—and he slapped the fighter's broad back—"enough of this melancholy prophecy. It will be a long time before I lead you off the sands in defeat. Barak." He grinned. He shook his head in mock admiration. "My problem will not be with defeats." He smiled.

"With what, then, Ard?"

The trainer's eyes were calm and quiet upon Dael's. "With her——"

Dael's face was the look of surprised innocence which he hoped masked what he felt. "She?" he asked. "Who?"

"Your goddess of the lamps," Ard replied, the smile thinner on his lips now.

12

AND NOW, in the weeks and months that followed, it seemed to Ard that Fortune, who had merely winked and beckoned at them invitingly at Marash, now openly invited them to enjoy her full favors.

After his victory over Sharma, another followed quickly when Dael prevailed easily over the chosen gladiator of Kanish, striking the local hero to the earth twelve times before the finger of defeat was raised. There the fighter from Naphtali was showered with lavish gifts for the first time, coins, tripods, jars and cups of silver and bronze, some of them filled with oil of olive or perfumes.

Northward Ard and his man continued, battling the elements, the cold harsh winds that blasted with frozen breath from the icy mountain crags and seemed to thicken the blood with a film of frost. By now the rapidly accumulating wealth of the two Israelites enabled Ard to purchase an ass of their own to carry their winnings and prizes, then another, and two more, until the trainer boasted he had his own private little caravan, all laden with gifts, awards, prizes, and trophies. In addition, Ard was shrewd enough to wager and win and also do a little trading on the side, with the result that when they swung northwestward to Ankara and then Salapa, he also hired two burly guards to watch over and protect their treasures.

They were trekking the wilderness between Salapa and their next destination—a place called Troia, where, Ard said, there had once been fabulous kings and queens and fighters—when the first courier caught up with them, bearing a message from Deborah.

Wrapping himself in the thick camel's-hair robe—a gift from an unknown lady after his victories at Ankara—Dael huddled close to the campfire and, with shaking hands—whether from the cold or emotion he could not tell—opened the creased and dirtied roll of parchment. In the feeble light Deborah's bold but still feminine strokes of script writing leaped before his vision. For a moment the letters seemed to dance and merge and he had to blink his eyes to see them better. Swiftly he looked up to see if Ard was watching him, but the trainer was dozing at the other side of the campground; the two guards were sitting close together and casting dice, while the runner, one of the professional island men, nodded drowsily with his own dreams.

Deborah began her first letter to him with neither greeting nor salutation. "Of these things I now write," her missive started. "I am well and I hope that health flourishes within you and that you are victorious wherever you go. Around Kedesh there hovers a sort of uneasy peace. There have been no more raids. The shed which we visited is still guarded, its secret still untried. Achan himself comes and goes on mysterious errands of his own, no doubt continuing his role as spy and traitor. He leaves most of the local judging to me, for which I am glad, because it offers the excuse for my remaining here instead of returning to Ramah, from where this message is being sent.

"However, I have prevailed upon the elders of all the tribes to meet in conclave at Shiloh, there to discuss the problem of unity and a choice of a leader. It is to be hoped that such a gathering will take place within the next half year. The hand of Canaan, outside of Kedesh, lies heavily upon the rest of Israel, thus forcing the elders to realize that some action must be taken if peace is to be secured. I know you think it strange that peace can be found only after warfare—but such are the times. We will sheath our swords only when there is no further use for them.

"You, too, are winning fame in Canaan, although you are far

and distant from there. The praise of your victories has already reached the ear of Jabin and lies all over Canaan. Barak the Lightning of Canaan is known here, the reports of your fights coming here from wanderers and merchants and caravan leaders who have beheld you. Jabin is pleased to think a Canaanite is bringing such fame to his land. Indeed, it is being said that already the monarch talks of bringing you back to meet his own great champion, the terrible Og of Bashan, the Bull of Bashan, as he is more popularly known.

"My heart beats ever with a prayer to Jehovah that no sickness comes upon you and that your strength will remain with you in all your ordeals of combat. I still remember that time at the lake when I thought I——" And here Dael noticed that the words had been darkly and heavily inked and scratched out. Try as he might, holding the parchment so close to the fire that the edges were singed, he could not make out the phrases she had inked out. Instead, the next sentence closed the letter in an almost aloof, impersonal way, saying she would continue to write to him from time to time. She warned him, however, not to make answer to her with the courier, who would not be sure where his letters to her might be sent. "Let this correspondence be from me only," she advised. "There is no need to point out the danger to you if a letter—either from me or from you—should by Achan be intercepted."

Dael rolled the parchment back into its clay cylinder envelope. Then, rising heavily, he opened the bottom of his sack, where he kept his most private and valued possession, and there buried it.

And all that night he sat before the fire, unable to sleep, his eyes unseeing, his mind back at a lake shore in Canaan. . . .

And it so happened that at Troia, in the great ruins of the stadium, fickle Fortune finally turned her face from Dael, and he met his first defeat at the hands of one Phaistos, who fought with foot and tooth and nail, finally driving Dael unconscious to the ground with a kick in the groin. An infuriated Ard, who had been screaming warnings over Phaistos' illegal method of fighting—the butting and kicking and gouging and choking—had to be pulled off the back of the referee. The crowd, wild-eyed and hotly prejudiced in favor of the local fighter, began to show their displeasure by hurling everything within their reach—fruits, stools, food, stones, and rocks. Before this onslaught Ard had barely been able to drag his nauseated champion out of danger, fleeing from the place that very night.

They spent several more weeks in idleness on the island of Tenedos, waiting for a ship to take them to Lesbos. There, Ard said importantly, Dael would see his first real and genuine stadium, built according to the latest and best manner of island architecture.

Nor was Ard wrong, Dael realized, when he first beheld the stadium, a magnificently fashioned amphitheater set in perpendicular lines of stone and marble against the slope of a hill. Benches ran from end to end of the arena, while deeper seats, carved out of wood and ivory and cushioned with wool, graced the very center of the structure.

These, Ard pointed out, were for the very rich and influential, the rulers of the island and their honored guests, not a few of which would be ex-gladiators themselves. Gilded and purple canopies fluttered protectively over the benches. The arena itself was vast—seven hundred and fifty feet in length and nearly one hundred and thirty five feet in width. A brilliant carpet of green, marked with white starting lines for the foot, torch, and ball races, blazed in emerald glory between the circular running track where the chariot races were held. The arena itself lay directly in the center of the grassy area, a golden oval of fine, hard-packed sand.

As they strolled on the turf, Ard showed Dael the marked circles where the discus, stone, and spear throwers stood when they heaved their weapons for distance. "Also, they have here great acrobats who leap on and off the backs of running bulls," Ard said. "We shall not be given to see all this, since the great athletic festivals are held only at certain times of the year. And the prizes offered are wondrous indeed. If you should win your fights here, you may have a gold coin, with your image engraved on it, struck for you. Or some beautiful poetess may compose a hymn of love for you. Golden or silver bowls will be offered you, as well as oil. Who knows—" he smiled—"but that a likeness of you may be fashioned from stone. These people here are gifted artists and greatly skilled in statuary work."

When Ard showed him the dressing rooms, Dael was even more impressed. There were private baths for the competing athletes. In every room the walls bristled with outthrust shelves containing flasks of oil, sponges, extra thongs, long-necked jars of ointment. Scrapers made of wood or bone or ivory or bronze, and bearing the names of their owners burned into the handles, hung from tiny hooks on the doors. Attendants by the tens stood ready to massage and oil the body, to scrape off sweat and lather from perspiring skins with the instruments known as "strigils" in the island tongue. Lute players, mouths and fingers ever ready to improvise words and music about a fighter or athlete, wandered in and out, playing for the champions who dashed into the cold plunge-baths or lay on tables as they were being massaged or powdered. Curiously Dael examined some of the powders, black, yellow, red, and tan, which were kept in intricately woven baskets of reed.

Watching him, Ard was amused. "Some of the powders serve good purpose. They close the bodily openings to prevent sweating and keep a fighter dry and cool. The others"—Ard shrugged—"are merely for purposes of vanity. When a fighter strolls into the arena, the colored powders make his body appear more sleek and powerful. It pleases the women and makes them pick favorites upon whom to wager."

A former pugilist, to judge from his splayed nostrils and puffed and broken ears, offered in his hoarse voice to help attend Dael and prepare him for the fight. Good-naturedly Ard accepted the offer, promising to pay him two coins of silver if Dael should win or two of copper if he lost. Then the trainer bade the ex-fighter explain the meaning of the many signs and messages which were scratched or daubed on the walls of the dressing rooms. This former gladiator and boxer, who called himself Themos, said that the majority of the notices were warnings that all fighters must bring their own oils to use, and that no scraper bearing the initials or name of the owner branded on the handle could be used, save by the man whose name it bore.

Themos promised to watch over their private athletic equipment, the thongs, punching bags, and the oils. Then the two Israelites strolled back to the empty stadium. They climbed up on the stone benches, surveying the scene below them. Again Ard explained that the science of fist fighting had progressed far in this place.

"Both fist fighters and wrestlers must belong to their own guilds here," Ard explained, "before they can enter the arena. Of course visiting strangers like ourselves are given honorary memberships. Still, there is much of dishonor here as well. A fighter who is rich enough but who desperately needs to win a fight for prestige may do so by purchase or bribe, either from his poorer opponent or from a greedy official."

Noticing Dael's slowly spreading smile, Ard whirled upon him. "And what amuses my mighty champion so?" Ard growled.

"I am thinking that now I know how you earned your fame and fortune as a fighter," Dael made answer, ducking the mock blow that Ard swung at him.

"Not I!" the trainer answered hotly and not without indignation. "True, I was often approached to let another prevail over me for a price. But I never agreed."

"Why?" Dael teased. "Because the offer was not large enough for you?" And again the Naphtalite escaped the wave of Ard's fists under his nose.

The trainer waved his arm around him. "And these seats are all purchased as well. On the days of the great events of competition, much wealth is passed to secure the best benches. Only rulers and honored officials can watch without paying for their seats."

Dael looked around him, to the left and right and below and above him, at the rows and rows and tiers of seats and benches that lined the stadium. "And all these are filled?" he asked in wonder.

Ard nodded soberly. "And more than filled. They even stand to watch the contests. This one at Lesbos can bulge with eighteen thousand spectators. Wait, and you will see. Perhaps the stadium will not be filled as it would be on a festival day—but there will be enough. Faces, mouths, a mass of screaming features. Sometimes," he added, his own voice getting softer with recollection, "it seems like one face, open and hideous and shrieking for your blood."

And screaming and ugly was the giant, multiple-featured face of the audience as Dael danced and pivoted and darted around the champion of Lesbos, confusing him, outmaneuvering him, and bewildering him with dazzling feints and thrusts, with the flashing speed that had never been seen here before, with the lightning-like blows that sent the fighter from Lesbos to the ground. Before he fell for the last time, the island champion had been blinded with cuts over both eyes, his body hammered so that it gleamed a dull red under the blows that finally—and mercilessly—cracked him into unconsciousness.

The fighter from Canaan was literally that day showered with gifts, with jewels and coins and silver wedges and gold rings, perfumes, wine, oil, flowers, fruit, garlands—anything the crazed onlookers had with them to cast at Dael's feet. Messengers bearing invitations from ladies hovered around him as Ard threw a mantle over his shoulders and began to escort him back to the dressing room. They even tried to crowd into the chamber itself until Ard, cynical and curt, drove all away save Themos and began removing the grime and sweat from Dael, sending him to the baths, then rubbing him down with the oil again. "It is always so," Ard said bitterly as his hands kneeded the fighter's muscles. "Win—and they all clamor for you. Lose—and you are scorned and forgotten. Just remember that, my champion."

Made drowsy from the massage, tired from the fight, Dael looked lazily at the Benjamite. "A fortune must have been hurled at us this day—and you yourself must have won heavily on wagers."

"I did," Ard answered shortly, "but if you think it is enough to get you to Egypt—you are wrong. We still have a long way to travel. And we still need more. Let patience calm you, Dael. Because patience brings the best rewards of all. Hear my words and remember that I am older and wiser than thee," he finished kindly, using the familiar, personal tone now.

Ard noticed that Dael had not escaped unscathed from this combat; the lobe of his right ear had been torn. As Ard gently applied the healing lotions to it, he joked that now Dael would have trouble wearing the earrings the ladies had been sending him in admiration.

"Now, look you," Ard said roughly, "You will not be able to fight again for about a week, until your ear heals. During that time, if you want to avail yourself of the invitations from your women admirers, you may——" Ard paused, feeling a little embarrassed, suddenly relieved when he noticed Dael's eyes crinkling with laughter.

"You little Benjamite bull, you!" Dael grinned. "If *you* want women so keenly, why not ask of me outright to take you along?"

Ard grew fiery red with shame. "I—I meant not that," he muttered. "What want I with women?"

"Or I?" Dael echoed slowly. He closed his eyes. Ard, his hands fragrant with perfumed oil, looked at the younger man and lightly touched his shoulder. "I know, and I think I understand," he said. "So let there be no more jesting of this sort between us." To Dael's surprise a great sigh heaved from Ard's breast. As the fighter stared, Ard nodded unhappily. "What is true of you is true of me. I need no woman, because I want only one."

"Ard!"

"True." The trainer nodded glumly. "She still waits for me in Ramah. But—enough of this. For the time being, we serve only another woman, and her name I have already revealed to you."

"I know." Dael turned over on his back. "My mistress—work."

And now, for Dael ben Abinoam, it was as if time itself had become timeless, until he lost count of the days, the weeks, the months, the very seasons themselves. Stadium replaced stadium, arena gave way to other arenas, dressing rooms soon all became familiar although they were thousands of leagues apart. From Lesbos the two Israelites proceeded southward over the blue seas of the Aegean, to Skyros, then to Chios, where Dael twice fought, losing first to the champion Micus, and then winning the second bout when that brave and wonderful fighter was unable to rise from the sands.

Island after island passed for Dael, until it seemed to him that time itself was a whirling spindle of months in which webs of stone and sand and blood and sun and leather and gleaming bodies were woven in endless fashion. Southeast to Samos, then to Naxos, where Dael won four fights in a row.

It was not until the two men from Israel had touched the mainland again, in Salamis of Boetia, that the second courier from Deborah found him. He came just before Dael's initial bout at the great stadium. Refusing to allow his fighter to have his mind disturbed by any news—either good or bad—Ard prevented Dael from reading the message until after his fight. As a result, the Salamis sportsmen witnessed one of the shortest fights in their records—with only three savage and powerful blows Dael had stretched the favorite in the arena. And he ran from his admirers even before the shower of gifts began to descend upon him from the benches.

Deborah's message was this time buried in the bottom of an oil jar, presumably containing the oil of pressed olive but actually bearing only a cup or so of the fluid. The script was on sheepskin, fat and soft from contact with the oil, written in heavy black ink. As usual, she began her missive without preliminaries.

"Evil days have fallen upon Israel," she wrote. "Jabin is now openly determined to rid the land of our people once and for all time—to drive them back over the River Jordan and into the deserts again. The secret chariot has been removed from its shed, and rumor has it that Jabin is trying it out in the field. His smiths and forges work by day and by night, fashioning the war wagons with which he hopes to cut Israel to ribbons. And attacks upon Israelite settlements continue to grow in force and in blood. Fallen to the Canaanites are Achshaph, Shimron, and Kitron, all utterly destroyed, the men sold as slaves or mercenaries, the women and children meeting worse fates. Even the Ark of the Tablets at the holy sanctuary of Shiloh may be threatened. And still Israel waits, turns the other cheek for more blows, unable to decide upon unification or to choose a leader. Now is the time for a leader of Israel to arise! However, with the help of Jehovah, I have persuaded the elders to meet within two or three months to gather for the purpose of making plans to combat Jabin and to choose one who will lead. Even the most hard-necked of the elders of the tribes realize that something has to be done.

"Only Kedesh still remains untouched because, many say, of Achan's having won favor with Jabin. But for the rest of the land, the taxes are heavy, and the rope of liberty which binds us together is being shredded by Jabin's sword.

"Still, strange to say, Jabin becomes more and more pleased as news of your great victories in the islands reaches his ears. There is little talk of anything among the men of the kind save of the day of your return and a bout with Jabin's champion, Og of Bashan. Indeed—although I am not sure of this—a court rumor has it that Jabin is going to send his personal representative to bring you letters and seals of safe-conduct and an invitation to return to Canaan, where you may meet his Og.

"I, too, would like to see your return—but not because of combat in the arena. I realize that it is more than a year since we parted—and the time past seems so long, and that ahead of us even longer."

There the message ended.

Dael read it again, and then once more, before putting it away with the other he had received from the woman of Ramah. . . .

He began to fight mechanically now, bringing Ard's wrath down upon him. He seemed merely to go through the motions of fighting, bringing sharp and stinging words of rebuke and warning from the trainer. But each time, Dael rallied enough to gather his strength and wits and weave them into a net of defeat which he flung over the bloody heads of his adversaries.

Athens beheld the fighter from Canaan with wonder and applause as he won his first two fights, and demanded that he remain to meet the best of their champions. Ard eagerly signed the contracts with the guild, providing for a long series of bouts for Dael. For two months they remained at the great city, while the mighty ones of the island challenged their strength, were downed in defeat. But three times during that period Dael himself was crumbled in losses, although he won over two of his victors later with hammering fists.

When the contracts with the guild at Athens had been fulfilled, Ard took his fighter westward. Dael, shining with great fame as Barak the Lightning, was also laden with wealth. His prizes and wagers had accumulated now so that it took thirteen asses to bear their burden and four burly guards to protect the metal, coins, cups, tripods, jewels, furs, and oil from marauding brigands, bandits, or raiders.

In Chairobes and Nanpaktos, Dael had an easy time of it, disposing of several sensational local heroes with a speed and skill that left the exhausted crowds gaping in wonder. But when the two Israelites turned southward again, Dael became restless and moody and made a miserable showing in both Corinth and Mycenae, going down to defeat in the latter city at the hands of a much slower and older—but more wily—opponent, who sensed that the Canaanite's mind was not on his task. Although Ard's words were bitter and harsh that night, the trainer wondered if he had not driven his fighter too hard and whether Dael should have a long rest. Still, Ard knew they were not yet ready for Egypt, despite the wealth which was theirs. First of all, it would take a large fortune to set up residence in Memphis as befitted a great champion. And, while he learned at the smithies of the Nile, Dael would need more money. Secondly, Ard well realized, his fighter had to enter the land of Egypt with a certain amount of flourish and publicity. True, his fame was probably known—but what Ard wanted was to have the assurance of some Egyptian official, some ambassador who would see him fight in the islands, that a welcome worthy of a hero would be given him. In this way, Ard told himself, Dael would have an easier means of approaching the pharaoh himself.

Thus he spoke nothing at all of Egypt to Dael, but continued the journeying. However, Dael made up for his defeats in the tremendous stadium of Sparta, where nearly forty thousand people, already satiated with seeing the best of fighters, saw the man from Canaan challenge and then knock into senselessness ten of their finest fist fighters. It was a deed unheard of and unseen up to now, and Dael fought—literally—from dawn to sunset, with only short rests in between.

Ard rested his champion for three weeks after this exhibition of fighting skill before boarding a ship that would sail eastward to Rhodes and then Cyprus.

When Dael expressed his surprise at Ard's decision to press eastward—to Canaan—instead of to the south, where lay Egypt, the little Benjamite merely chuckled. "When the time comes, I will reveal you the purpose," he said. "Meanwhile, relax and rest."

The sea voyage was good for Dael. He seemed more at ease with himself, smiled and joked with Ard as before, and only reread Deborah's letters once during the trip.

As they edged close to Crete, Ard pointed at the ruins along the shore. "Once there, in Caphtor that you now see," he explained, "they had the mightiest of fighters and men of sport in the famous stadium at Knossos. But the land fell before invasions, the tremendous palace and buildings were razed to the ground. Earthquakes finished what human hands could not accomplish. True, they still have festivals there for athletes, but the people are poor and the rewards would be small. Hence, we do not fight there."

At Rhodes, Dael fought but once and, as a disgusted Ard later pointed out, it was fortunate that only one fight had been arranged. Dael's effort in the arena was listless and almost aloof, and he made only halfhearted attempts at meeting his opponent. The latter, a lithe and blond, blue-eyed young pugilist, moved into action swiftly. For an hour, however, he fought warily, afraid of the reputation of the Lightning from Canaan. But when the lightning failed to strike, the young Rhodesian became more confident—especially when the audience began to show its disgusted disapproval in the accustomed way. Fruits and stools and stones and assorted hats, caps, and robes came fluttering from the benches. Loud were the insults, the catcalls, the whistles of derision, the cockcrows of mockery that assailed the ears and shame of both fighters. The superb fighter from Rhodes, afraid that his own newly won reputation was being sullied by the hoots and insults, became reckless, spurred by humiliation into incautious haste. He moved too carelessly against Dael, who finally took advantage of the youth's inexperience, stopping him with a great, chopping blow to the chin. The Rhodesian never saw the fist that circled up at him. Even before he fell, face upward into the sands, Dael had struck three more times at him.

Little was spoken between the fighter and his trainer during the last stages of the sea voyage to Salamis in Cyprus. As they neared the shore, with Dael gazing toward the east, Ard walked up to him, also staring at the nearing port and the sea beyond that.

"I would be the son of a son of a fool unto the seventh generation," Ard remarked softly, "if I knew not what you think at this moment. That there, to the east, lies Canaan and Israel and your woman. But hear me now"—Ard smiled tightly—"for I think I can cheer you. This series of fights at Salamis will be the last before we go southward to Egypt, to the Nile, which will lead us to Memphis." He nodded energetically as Dael turned surprised eyes upon him. "The reason I chose Salamis is because Kanak, the representative of pharaoh and rumored to be a close friend, is ambassador here. Kanak will see you in the arena. Therefore, you must make the best fight of your career before his eyes. After you win I will approach Kanak and reveal to him our intention to visit his land. Unless I am mistaken—when we reach Memphis you will be welcomed as a hero should. Even the pharaoh will know of your coming, and thus it will be easier to see him on your errand. Do you understand now why I brought you here? You cannot enter Egypt as an unknown, unheralded. The whole city of Memphis must know of your coming and make its welcome to you and thus pave an easy way to the ramp of the pharaoh's throne."

"I see," Dael answered, "and I approve."

"Good." Ard's voice was hearty and businesslike. "See you, then, that you fight—and fight well before Kanak. If you are victorious, I am confident he will spread the news of your coming to his pharaoh and to all of Egypt."

And it came to pass that all Ard had planned bore rich fruit. Dael won all his three fights at Salamis, won them in a dazzling, sensational way, downing the first two champions after three hours of combat, almost losing the third, but staggering back from defeat to knock the third adversary to the ground, breaking his jaw. With Dael himself reeling in a semi-conscious state, bleeding heavily from his nose and mouth, weaving on his feet, Ard brought his conqueror before the official benches. There a hoarse and excited ruler placed a golden necklace over Dael's head, and Kanak, Egyptian ambassador, took off his own ring and handed it to a half-blinded Dael.

Ard asked permission to talk with Kanak later—permission that was eagerly granted—and Dael was led back to the dressing room by Themos, who revived him, washed, oiled, and powdered him. By the time Ard returned, Dael was himself again.

"For a time you need fight no longer." Ard smiled enthusiastically. "I have spoken with Kanak, and he is delighted that we go to Egypt. Already he has sent runners to Memphis to inform that city of your coming. And no doubt the pharaoh will hear as well. So rest yourself and calm your spirit."

"When do we leave?" Dael asked, excitement rising swiftly within him.

"In a week." Ard grinned. "I need the time to convert our wealth into coins and metal wedges only, to sell the animals, rid ourselves of the guards. Themos will come with us to help me." He patted Dael's shoulder. "How feels it," he asked kindly, "to start taking the first long step backward?"

And he nodded toward the east, and Dael did not have to ask what he meant. . . .

PART THREE

THE BATTLE

13

MEMPHIS, when they first beheld it from their ship, seemed as if a great handful of square dice had been cast indiscriminately against the right shore of the Nile. As far as the eye could see, the small, rectangular houses of sun-dried brick and wood dotted the area. Only in the center rose a few structures of more than two stories, among them the palace of the pharaoh, which was punctuated to the heavens by the great alabaster sphinx that dominated the Avenue of the Temple of Ptah.

It was the noisy, turbulent harbor that drew Dael's chief attention, for he had never seen such a place before. Set against a background of date palms, among which slothful and yet powerful water buffalo pulled plows or worked the irrigation-ditch pumps, the port quivered with life, bustled with energy, and bubbled with noise. The cacophony of a dozen tongues mingled in shouts, commands, and curses. The soft, slurring Egyptian tones ran a steady rhythm under the harsher bark of Babylonian traders, moved quietly under the guttural of Canaanite merchants, strove in vain to compete with the epithets of Phoenician sailors, was lost again the sharp commands of Grecian overseers.

On the waters of the harbor itself, the importance of Egypt as a sea power was manifest. Proud war galleys, more than one hundred feet in width and breadth, pushed their pitch-smeared prows haughtily against the smaller but more trim Phoenician vessels. One such Nile ship passed close enough for Dael to marvel at the tiers of the rowers, counting thirty oars on each side. This same ship also boasted the gilded figure of a lioness on the bow. Pleasure barques, shaped like a pair of fat sausages bound together, rubbed their sleek and gilded sides against the larger boats carrying huge obelisks on their twelve-hundred-foot hulls. Here and there tiny boats of papyrus and wood bobbed insolently before the snubbed and upturned prows of pleasure ships.

And on the docks the activity seemed more intense. Sweating slaves hauled, carried or tugged at jars of perfume, sacks of gold dust, huge rolls of dried papyrus, great boxes that were filled with instruments and tools of metal—all of which would be taken to the seaports of Canaan. And from the Egyptian ships that had just come from Canaan there were being unloaded logs of cedar-wood, jar after jar of oils to be used on the mummies, wheat, honey, oil of olive, glistening wineskins, and mounds of the pith of papyrus—from Byblos, the paper city—which would be dried and rolled into the writing scrolls.

A rich and cloying odor of spices and perfumes hung over the entire harbor district but failed to eliminate the heavier smell of mud and sweat and dung.

Ard, sniffing with disgust, said, "Truly, it stinks here, of man and beast, and the air is heavy. What I would give now for one mountain breeze of Benjamin."

As they left their ship, they saw that a small caravan was waiting for them along the narrow dockway. In crude Egyptian picture writing a ragged linen sign was held up for all to see.

"Memphis welcomes the great Barak the Lightning, champion of champions, from Canaan," the sign roared in its slashing crimson lettering. Dael stared as pipers struck up a tune and small boys with ebony skins began to beat pink palms upon the stretched hides of hand drums. One of the men in the group, who had been standing near a covered sedan chair, ran up to Dael and Ard, bowed, and, in accented tongue, bid them welcome.

"For you, my lords," he explained, his hand waving at the chair, the musicians, and the crowd of admirers.

Ard nodded, waited for Dael to climb into the chair, then closed the canopy around him quickly. He looked into Dael's puzzled face and laughed.

"It is all arranged," Ard said. "I told you that Memphis would open her arms to you."

"And for how much?" Dael asked.

Ard winked at him. "Kanak, the Egyptian ambassador at Salamis, asked for two silver talents. I settled with one of silver. It will take care of this and the house he promised to rent for us."

Dael sagged against the seat of the chair. "Three thousand shekels?" he murmured. "A fortune . . ."

But Ard merely shrugged. "I told you what it would cost us to come here so that all would know we had arrived. Fear not. It is an old trick and often used."

As they swung through the streets, Dael could hear the pipes and flutes, the rattle of the hand drums, and a mighty voice shouting:

"Make way! Make way for Barak the Lightning from Canaan, who comes to stay in Memphis. Make way!"

Ard rubbed a playful hand on Dael's closely cropped hair. "By nightfall," he promised, "even the pharaoh will know of your arrival." He paused to listen attentively and critically to the bellowing voice outside their chair.

"A leather throat has that one," Ard commented, looking pleased. "He is earning his silver."

"If there will be any left," Dael murmured innocently.

But if their arrival was made known to the pharaoh that night, Merenptah gave no sign of interest—nor for the many days while they waited to secure audience with him. As soon as they had been established in their new home, a comfortable if slightly crowded structure of brick and adobe of two stories, Ard used more of the prize money to bribe court officials to allow him to see the ruler of Egypt. Although the promises were many and profuse, the results were meager. A week passed, then another, and still a third, and there was no word from the court of the pharaoh.

Dael, in the meantime, spent his time roaming the city, always with Ard and Themos at his sides as guards. For it was dangerous to venture alone, especially after dark, into the winding, dark alleyways of Memphis with their stenches of refuse, garbage, roasting meats, onions, and garlic. They examined all they could—the broader avenues, ribbons of brick that pointed straight at the heart of the palace, the huge sphinx with its four-clawed paws resting on a block of alabaster and its beard reaching down to the great chest, the irrigation ditches, the streets of ships. There Dael would pause often to examine the work of the smiths and craftsmen, admiring the skill with which these articles had been wrought. From time to time he would venture forth to the northern part of town where these artisans dwelled, with their forges and smithies, but he never stopped to speak to them or enter their places of labor.

They visited the market squares, full of wonder at the variety of foods and goods to be found there, skirted the streets of the houses of pleasure cautiously, paused to listen to a group of the pharaoh's own musicians on a square, watched a troupe of pantomimists retell an ancient fable of a god being found in the rushes of the river, examined scrolls of laws and stories. Several of these Dael purchased, hoping to save them for Deborah when he again would see her.

But as the time grew heavy as the air around them, Dael became impatient, chiding Ard for the inactivity. But that trainer stubbornly refused to make another move. "The pharaoh will see us when he is ready, and there is little we can do about it," he said time and time again.

At the end of their third week a panting runner came to their home, bearing with him a papyrus scroll which invited them to appear at once at the Court of Scribes. Dael, excited, wanted to dress in his formal best for the occasion, but Ard chilled his enthusiasm with a careless wave of his hand. "It is not a summons from the pharaoh," he explained. Merenptah does not see his subjects, or those who come to him, at the Court of Scribes. It is perhaps some other matter—probably a lord wanting to arrange a bout for you. But we must go," he added thoughtfully, peering at the seal on the bottom of the message.

"Canaanite," he murmured, holding Dael's glance with his own. "Come, let us find out what is wanted of us."

Bent under the heat of the brilliant sunlight, they made their way to the Court of Scribes, inquiring where a Canaanite official might be found. They were directed to a low, squat building that blazed white against their narrowed eyes. Ard knocked politely on the doorpost and motioned for Dael to follow him as a voice within bade them enter.

The chamber, blessedly cool and dim after the outside glare, revealed only a single figure waiting for them beside a table and two stools. The stranger was garbed in a pleated kilt of white linen with crimson stripes around the borders. He was of medium height, brown-eyed and brown-haired, his appearance giving no clue to his origin. But when he spoke, it was in the familiar tongue of Canaan.

"Welcome, great Barak the Lightning and his trainer, Ard," the man said, inclining his head somewhat at the greeting. "I am Anash, who has come here to speak to you with the tongue of Jabin. Seat yourselves," he said politely, indicating the stools. Anash himself remained standing.

As they murmured their thanks, trying to keep the surprise and anxiety from their faces, Anash smiled at them. "You need not fear," he assured the two men from Israel. "The tidings from the King of Canaan that I bear you are good. In short," he continued, his voice becoming more crisp, "I have been sent here personally by Jabin to meet you. It was from our representative at Salamis—

who spoke with Kanak, the Egyptian ambassador, that King Jabin knew you would come to Memphis. And hither he sent me forth to say this to you:

"Jabin desires Barak the Lightning to return to Canaan, there to engage in a bout with his own great champion, Og of Bashan." As he saw Ard about to protest, Anash raised jeweled fingers. "It need not be immediately. There is time, the great king has ordered. But, to insure your coming back to Canaan, he has instructed me to give you these."

Anash plunged a hand deep into the kilted waist and drew forth two rolled documents. These he carefully leveled and smoothed out on the table before handing them to Dael. "They are passes of safe-conduct through Canaan," Anash pointed out, "and a promise of diplomatic immunity to both you and your trainer when you return. With these in your possession, no harm may ever befall you in Canaan. For they are the word of the king, and he speaks with honor. See his seal and signature," he added, pointing to the bottom of the scrolls.

Dael, reading rapidly, nodded, while Ard peered anxiously over his shoulder. "Is it genuine?" the Benjamite asked.

The fighter nodded. "It is. The impression of Jabin's own seal is here. And it is as Anash says. We are welcome in Canaan any time we so desire to return."

"But what does Jabin say?"

Dael began to read out loud for Ard to hear the words himself—words that told of the king's great pleasure in Dael's victories, of his having won fame for Canaan as a fighter, of Jabin's desire to see a match between Og and Dael. " 'And if you win,' " Dael read, " 'you may ask what you like of me. And I will honor your request if you are victorious. For I speak as Jabin, King of All Canaan, and seal this before the temple of the god Baal, who witnesses my oath.' "

Dael folded the documents carefully and tucked them into his waistband. Anash, who had been watching and listening silently, smiled and stroked a pleat on his kilt slowly. "You are indeed honored," the Canaanite said, "for Jabin rarely issues such invitations. Do not underestimate his keen desire to have you return and meet the Bull of Bashan. In fact—Anash coughed discreetly—"it is said that Jabin is more enthusiastic about this than he is about any other matter. Therefore, I would advise you to give this serious thought and, after your stay here is over, return at once to Hazor."

Rising now, the two men thanked Anash for his service; then, leaving greetings to Jabin, they departed. Once outside again in the fierce glare of the Egyptian sun, Ard turned around to face Dael. "Did I not tell you that it would be better for you to win fame as a man of *Canaan*—and not one of Israel? See what this has done? Now, any time you wish, you may return with honor to Canaan. And," he added more seriously, "in safety as well. Evidently Jabin does not connect you at all with the killing of Dargan."

"But," Dael protested, "the king knows I am of Israel. Why, then, should he——"

"To Jabin," Ard remarked soberly, "it is the same thing. As an Israelite, you are merely one of the many of Canaan. For so he believes and so wants he it. Remember this, Dael. Jabin is indeed a man of high honor. I know, for I have served him. His word is as proud and worthy as the man himself. He will keep any promises made to you." The trainer blinked his eyes, shook his head, and bent forward. "Let us hurry back," he growled, "because this heat and sun are enough to melt my marrow."

But when they reached home, it was a thoughtful Dael who turned to demand of Ard:

"The presence of Anash worries me," he confided. "For if he knew that I carried the sketch of the secret and scythed chariot to show to the pharaoh, and thus act as a traitor to Jabin . . ." His voice dropped off.

Ard, flicking a thumb over his nose, nodded in agreement. "So it has also occurred to me. There is a Canaanite ambassador at the court of Merenptah. What if we reveal the secret to the pharaoh and he, in turn, informs the Canaanite ambassador? We could be sent back in chains to Jabin. Moreover," he added, "remember this. Egyptians look not kindly upon Israel."

Dael, running his hands through his hair, nodded. Then, his face still creased with thought, he looked up. "Of course we take chances in revealing the secret to the pharaoh. But perhaps the chance may be lessened."

"How so?" Ard grunted, untying the straps from his sandals. He inspected his foot carefully, wriggled the toes for a moment.

"Hear me," Dael said earnestly. "When we are summoned before Merenptah, I will show him the sketch and picture I made of the chariot. But," he added with emphasis, "I will not reveal that *I* saw the weapon, nor that I made the sketch. Rather will I say that, before we departed on the journey, the picture of the scythed wagon was given to me by an officer——"

"An Egyptian!" Ard cried out at once.

"An Egyptian whose name I knew not and who begged me for secrecy and paid me to take this picture sketch to the pharaoh, to show Merenptah what Jabin was planning. I will merely inform the pharaoh that I did what I was paid to do—to bring the picture of the new war wagon to him. I will pretend innocence of the whole matter."

Ard grinned with relief and enthusiasm. "And in that way, no suspicion against us as spies will be directed. *If* the pharaoh would want to inform the Canaanite ambassador of such a matter, which I doubt." He slapped Dael on the knee. "I see that your head is good for more than stopping blows," he said affectionately.

"And if it were not so"—Dael smiled in return—"you still would be back in Golan, watching the torch fights." And he moved away from the doubled-up but harmless fist that the trainer flicked at his chin.

As if the summons by Anash had broken the dam of their days of waiting, another message reached Ard and Dael now in two days, commanding them to make their appearance before Merenptah, pharaoh of Upper and Lower Egypt, the thirteenth son of the great Rameses II.

Dressed in their very best—Ard in his Canaanite officer's robe, with the scarlet fringes and red scarf, the laminated helmet and the amulet of honorable service glistening around his neck; Dael in the rare kilt which the trainer had purchased for him after his training at Golan—they entered the vast vestibule of the throne room. There, fully armed and armored house guards inspected the summons and then opened the huge bronzed doors to the royal room itself.

Even Ard had to catch his breath in awe when he beheld the splendor and space of the tremendous chamber, which, at this time of early afternoon, was empty save for the figure on the throne itself and the two stony-faced palace guards beside it.

With its white limestone columns, nearly thirty feet high, thrusting their gleaming roundness into the roof of wood, the chamber seemed to assume amazing dimensions of breadth and height and depth. The six columns were arranged in two parallel rows, between which a low ramp rose slowly until it led upward to the throne. Purple and gold flowers splashed their colors brilliantly against the rounded bases, while the stems of longer lotus blossoms wound high up toward the roof. The brick walls, shining with yellow and blue and red, were lined with panels of ivory, three tiers of them, each as high as a man, with the famous ankh sign of life and more lotus patterns intricately engraved and painted on them.

And on the throne, which was shaped in the form of a lion of gold, Merenptah himself was seated quietly, his jeweled hands resting lightly on the metal mane of the carved beast.

Bowing, then falling to their knees, both men of Israel waited until Merenptah's voice, as dry as the rustling of the water weeds in the wind, reached their ears.

"Arise, men of Canaan."

When Dael, bringing his gaze up, finally beheld the pharaoh, his first reaction was of some disappointment. Surely, he reasoned, the monarch was of slight stature—the crimson leathered sandals, with their gilded bands, hardly reached the ivory block of the dais. The hands and arms were frail and scrawny, thrust out like slim limbs from the simple white tunic. The head, rounded and small, seemed hardly able to support the heavy, gilded headcloth which was circled by a diadem of glittering jewels. But when Dael looked into the brownish-red eyes, beheld the stubborn chin, the set and firm line of mouth, he knew he was looking into a face of strength and purpose.

"Arise and be made welcome, men of Canaan, mighty Barak the Lightning and Ard, his trainer," Merenptah said, a slight smile breaking across the stern features. The ruler of the Nile spoke in perfect, unaccented Canaanite. "In the name of the gods of Egypt, I bid you welcome and offer you the hospitality of my land. Word of your arrival had been brought to me weeks before, but I could not summon you until this day." The pharaoh leaned back slightly, his hands lifting for a moment then falling back in repose. "Now"—he smiled again—"reveal to me your plans."

"My lord pharaoh," Ard said quietly and respectfully, "we have no plans save those of rest. Barak is fatigued from combat and journey and chose your beautiful land to regain his strength. Also, he is desirous of study here."

"So?" The monarch's eyes swept curiously over Dael. "A gladiator studying? In what?"

"I am a craftsman in metal, my lord," Dael answered, "and it has been both hope and dream for me to reach Egypt and learn more from your masters of the forge. For I have seen their handicraft, which is known the world over." He paused, waiting, seeing the pharaoh nod.

"If that is what you wish," Menephthah said, "it shall be granted. We have the finest smiths in the world. But we can always use more. Egypt needs——" he began, then stopped quickly. "If it is your desire, Barak of Canaan, I can have it arranged that you work with Khi——"

Dael stiffened suddenly.

"Khi?" he said, almost stammering. "The greatest master of them all?"

Again the fleeting smile swept over the brown, lined face. "I see Khi's name is known all over. If that is what you wish, you may work and study and learn from him. I am sure he will be content to have you. But," Merenptah went on, a tinge of regret shading his voice, "I had hoped I would see you in the arena. You plan to fight no more?"

"My lord"—Ard's voice was brisk—"you will see Barak. I will this day arrange a match for the god of the Nile. But after that, my pharaoh, Barak will return to the forge."

Merenptah, his eyes closing for a moment, nodded. "We have not the champions you must have met, but there will be thousands glad to witness the might of Barak." Then the brown gaze fell upon Dael again. "You may have your choice, champion. You may continue as a fighter for Egypt, or teach in our own gladiator schools. Or, as I strongly suspect, you will work with Khi."

Dael took a deep breath. "I will do all three," he promised. "Ard will arrange a match. I will also help instruct in the schools whenever Khi spares me from his fires. For, as much as the arena calls to me, the pull of work in metal is stronger."

"And I, my lord," Ard broke in, "ask permission to teach in the gladiator schools while Barak gains in his craft. Idleness is not for such as I." He smiled wanly.

The pharaoh nodded, looking pleased. "And so it is granted," he said. "You are welcome to our gladiator schools, and may your stay there be in health and in vigor."

Merenptah stirred restlessly, giving sign that the interview was over. Ard looked warningly at Dael, whose hands reached into his waistband and found the rolled-up plan of the scythed chariot.

"My lord pharaoh," the Naphtalite said quickly, "there was another reason why we hoped our coming here would be blessed by your presence." He tapped the sketch. "This I would show you.

It was given to me by an officer who, when he heard we would make our way to Egypt, pleaded with me to take it to the mighty pharaoh to behold. I was paid for the task."

The thin hands reached out for the drawing but did not unfold it. The brown eyes, suddenly brighter and narrowing, looked at Dael.

"And the nationality of this officer?" he asked.

"Egyptian, my lord. He could not give his name. But he said the information you now hold in your royal hand is of vital intelligence to the pharaoh. Indeed, the officer swore that, should he be found with the scroll in his possession, it meant death to him by Jabin."

"Jabin? Of Canaan?" Merenptah frowned suddenly.

"Yes, my own lord. This officer was at Hazor when he secretly bade me carry the message to you."

Merenptah gravely unfolded the sketch, looked at it for a long time, studied it carefully from all angles. Then he let it drop on his lap. His eyes searched Dael's face diligently. "You have seen this drawing? You know what it is?"

"I have seen it, my lord," Dael replied. "And also was told by the officer that it was a new and secret weapon being fashioned by Jabin. It looks like a chariot."

"It is," Merenptah said gravely. "But what was the officer's fear?"

"That Jabin perhaps was constructing more of these war wagons to use against Egypt. To surprise Egypt and arise against the Nile in revolt."

The fingers tapped sharply on the parchment. The thin lips clamped together. When the pharaoh looked up again, there was a grim amusement on his face. "I believe not a word of your story," he said, almost lightly, smiling as he saw the quick pallor sweep over Dael's face. "There was no officer. Moreover, I believe you drew this sketch yourself and brought it to me as a warning that Jabin intends rising against me." He leaned forward, the mouth open a little now. "Nor are you Canaanites," he added softly, "because you would not betray your king." His gaze bored into them shrewdly, and the hands clasped together and then unclasped. "Israelites, of course." He nodded. "It has to be. Otherwise why should you bring me warning against Jabin?"

"My lord pharaoh——" Dael began helplessly, stopped only by the raised hand of the monarch.

"Stay!" the pharaoh ordered sharply. "And hear my words. You are foolhardy men to come here, knowing I could summon the ambassador from Canaan and have you sent back in chains, as slaves, to Jabin, who would execute you as traitors. But," he added, the rustle of his voice getting softer, "I admire courage. And," he went on slowly, thoughtfully, "I appreciate your bringing this drawing to me. It is the first inkling I've had of Jabin's restlessness. Not even my own spies had knowledge of such a weapon. Because of that, you need not fear I will betray you to Canaan." He smiled again as he saw both men sag with relief.

"Israelites," Merenptah murmured, staring at them. "There are few left in the land now. My father and grandfather knew your people as troublemakers, and it seems as if the third generation has not changed. Jabin is welcome to you, and will soon learn that you can be as a boil upon the body of the land. However"—he tapped the scroll and then circled it with his fingers—"much as I thank you for this service and warning, I must inform you that this weapon is neither secret nor dangerous, and Egypt fears it not."

As Dael's and Ard's faces showed their surprise, Merenptah went on easily. "I fear no danger from Jabin. He is not strong enough—either with or without scythed chariots—to rise against the might and wrath of Egypt. Moreover—hark now—the scythed chariot is no secret to Egypt at all." The pharaoh's voice was almost kind in tone now. "Nor is such a weapon anything new. The Nile knew of it years ago. When the Hyksos—the wild tribesmen from the northeast regions—invaded the Nile, they brought with them not only horses and weapons of iron, but such bladed vehicles as you have drawn for me. Needless to say, the armored wagons were of little use, especially in the mud. And the blades were brittle and easily broken off. In fact, although my own engineers and smiths have often talked of building a host of these scythed chariots, I have set my mind against it. They are too heavy, too cumbersome. They need too many horses to draw them. And they are easily mired. Therefore, you can understand what little use they could be for Jabin in Canaan, especially if he plans to use them in the hilly or mountain districts. And he would be forced to do so because any leader of any imagination would arrange his armies in the mountains, thus making Jabin's chariots useless. No" —the pharaoh smiled—"I fear that this information you have borne to me is of little value." As he saw their crestfallen faces, his smile broadened a little. "That is not to say I do not thank you for your interest and concern. I shall not forget it. Because of what you have done, the freedom of the land is yours. And as for Jabin, I shall indeed increase my garrison forces in Canaan and keep a stricter watch on him. But I fear him not. He can do nothing against Egypt."

Merenptah sighed, stirred restlessly. "Now I bid you leave me," he said as both men bowed. "Arrange the match as quickly as you can," he instructed Ard, "so that your fighter may soon go to Khi for learning. And may your stay here be in health and good fortune."

He raised his hands in dismissal, and Dael and Ard slowly backed away from the great throne and the thin-lipped ruler who was watching them. . . .

14

CAREFULLY Dael stirred the molten metal in the huge iron pot that hung from a tripod over the steady fire. The copper, already liquid, simmered slowly, with an occasional bubble breaking through the reddening surface. Bending closer to watch Dael, Ard wrinkled his nose from the heat. Dael looked at him quizzically.

"Bend a little closer, great trainer"—he smiled—"and you will have new nostrils, copper-lined, so that you will not have to wear nose rings at all." Then he carefully looked at the shelves of Khi's workshop, finding what he sought—a long piece of green wood. This he placed carefully on the floor while he continued stirring the pot and, from time to time, scooping off the scum of slag that dirtied the surface. Seeing Ard's puzzled look, Dael smiled again. "It is now I who teaches the teacher." He grinned. "Behold you," he said, pointing at the molten metal. "In the pot is copper, made liquid by the hot fire. But it is not pure. That is our biggest problem, to drive out the impurities from the metal. Otherwise the copper will be brittle and rough, with huge blisters of air in it. Someday"—he paused thoughtfully—"men will devise cleverer ways to clean the metal. But right now this is a method I have found and which has pleased Khi mightily."

He thrust the green piece of wood into the pot. Instantly flames enveloped the wand, licking swiftly up its surface. It burned slowly, a slight wisp of blue smoke curling along the staff. In silence both men watched it for a time.

"Somehow," Dael mused, "I have discovered that the burning green wood, when thrust into the molten copper, reduces the impurities. Perhaps the fire burns out the gases—I know not," he finished, wrinkling his brow in concentration. "But my method works. Khi has so told me that he has never seen as pure a copper as I make with this green piece of wood. However," he cautioned, "too great a piece of wood must not be used either, for that, too, will make the copper full of holes." He stared at the still-crimsoning but smoother surface of the metal. Then he walked over to the box of charcoal, digging a palm deeply into it and scattering its dust lightly over the liquid copper. "This keeps the metal molten," he pointed out, "and also somehow prevents the brittleness from forming." Absently he rubbed a hand over his face, leaving it streaked with black.

Musing, Ard looked at him. For five months now—shortly after the victorious matches which the pharaoh had witnessed—Dael had gone to work for the great master and smith, famed old Khi. Day after day Dael had labored—apparently happily—leaving the forges only for food or sleep or for his daily exercises in the great gymnasium where Ard now taught. The trainer had been adamant about Dael's continuing some form of athletic training. "Who knows when you will need to fight again?" he had urged, and Dael, seeing the wisdom of his words, had agreed to do some slight sparring, jumping, and running, and a few rounds of mock combat with Ard or the more skilled of the gladiator students.

Thus, Ard knew, the days had run their course, evenly, smoothly, without incident, dropping as mutely and as swiftly as the crushed flour from between the massive stone mill wheels. But was Dael really happy in his work? Did he long to return to Canaan and Deborah? Of that, Ard had no knowledge, for the gamor said little—if anything at all—about his future plans.

That he was learning and that he had pleased old Khi there was no doubt. Already he had perfected a means of copper smelting, and his products—bracelets, mirror handles, amulets, rings, and earrings—were already being sought after in the markets. Khi, pleased with his student, had taught him more of his skill and cunning, and Dael had been quick to grasp the theory and technique of the designs and fashions. He had spent nights poring over scrolls about metals, had talked long with the famous smith, asking questions and receiving the answers he needed.

But was this enough? Ard continued to think. Was this what Dael really wanted—after the exciting life of travel and fighting as a champion? Dael *seemed* to be satisfied, humming slightly as he continued to stir the bubbling copper. The fighter ran one hand absently over his chin, smearing his face with charcoal dust. His apron was stained and filthy, his hands grimed, sweat ribboned his neck and shoulders. Look at him, Ard wondered again, laboring as a slave, in the heat and dirt, when he could be donned in the best of clothes and enjoying the favors of countless multitudes, living as a prince of the land. Cummin-spiced wine could sooth his parched throat instead of the tepid water he was gulping now from a clay cup.

"Dael?" The trainer's voice was hesitant. As the Naphtalite looked up, the smaller man waved his hand over the room, including the forges, the tools, the piles of metal scraps, and shelves in one embracing motion. "Is this what you really want?"

Dael let the green-wood stick remain in the pot. Then, with a half-smile lifting one corner of his mouth, he pointed at the liquid copper. "You see this?" he asked. "You know what will be fashioned of it? Look." From a shelf overhead he took down a clay cast of a cup, handing it to Ard. Staring at it, secretly admiring it, Ard ran a finger over the brim of the vessel, the edge of which was so fashioned as to represent the waves of the sea.

"For the pharaoh himself," Dael announced. "A full twelve he wants for his banquet tables," he said, snapping a thumb against the fat belly of the cup. "I will mold the copper on this, then inlay it with gold leaf. And here too," Dael added, pointing to a shelf at his left. "More of the pharaoh's wishes." He indicated a heap of handles for bronze mirrors, all created in the shape of a nude woman with lovely rounded arms thrust upward to hold the mirror. "And this, too, for the pharaoh's women. All designed and made by myself. It is what I have wanted to do."

"Is it so?" Ard asked dryly, watching as Dael's gaze dropped from his, as the craftsman picked up a copper bowl and, with a piece of wool, began polishing it absently.

"Of course," Ard went on easily, "I can understand the satisfaction you feel. But is it enough? True, the world is yours now. You have the favor of Merenptah, either as a fighter or an artist. And old Khi is pleased with your work. And more," Ard continued, his eyes narrowing slightly. "And what of Perse, his daughter?"

Dael looked up, his eyes incredulous.

"A child!" he burst out. "Ard—surely you do not think that she——"

"Loves you?" Ard nodded solemnly. "She does. Nor makes she secret of it. Coming here day after day to stare at you when you work, those big, black sloe eyes never leaving you, watching every moment, each gesture, all you——"

"But," Dael challenged, his voice not so loud as before. His hands rubbed harder against the metal. "She is a child, Ard."

"She is sixteen, Dael, and has been a woman for at least four years. In this land——" Ard shrugged. "You yourself know what she must feel. You yourself know that Khi would be delighted to have you as a son-in-law. And," the trainer went on significantly, "after the old one passes to his fathers, all this—his forges, his metals, his house, all his property—could be yours. Why, you would be a lord in the land if you took her to wife."

He watched, seeing Dael's set face, smiling wanly as the Naphtalite suddenly nodded. "It is so, Ard," Dael admitted reluctantly. "I would have been ten times a fool and a son of a fool not to know. In fact"—he placed the polished vessel back on the shelf—"old Khi has already spoken for her to me. He said that Perse loves me, wants me in marriage, but was too shy to admit it to any save her father. And he made the gesture too," Dael continued. "All this could be mine after his death."

"But?" Ard prompted.

Dael sighed. "I know not. I know not the answer."

The blue of Ard's eyes met the black of the gamor, met and held. "You love her?" Ard finally asked.

The crooked smile appeared again on Dael's face. Rather stiffly he bent to a cedarwood box, lifted its fragrant cover, and found something that was carefully wrapped in another piece of oiled woolskin. This he held out tenderly to Ard. "Take this and behold it," he said softly.

Carefully the Benjamite unwrapped the package, his face exploding into instant awe and admiration as he saw what it contained. In his fingers the thin, fragile gold chain looked weak enough to snap with a flick of the thumb. And the tiny charms on it—all in the shape of miniature lamps—jingled as he held the bracelet up for inspection.

It was truly a work of art, a creation that proudly revealed the masterpiece of fashioning that had gone into it. The lamps, of divers sizes and shapes, were no larger than almonds out of the shell. Each one was an exact replica of a true giver of light, with hinged covers and cups where a teardrop of oil might be dropped. Turning it over and over in his hand, Ard could not take his eyes away from the golden string and the lamps upon it.

"For her." It was not a question but a statement, and he did not even look up to see Dael nod.

"I made it in secret," Dael confessed.

Silently the trainer handed the bracelet back to its designer. "And when," Ard asked, his voice slightly tinged with salt, "will she receive this gift?"

Again the twisted smile lifted a side of Dael's mouth as he replaced the jewelry back into the box. "I know not," he said. "Once I had hoped I could bring her here to me and we could go back to the islands. But I know she will not come. Not until she has done what she feels must be done."

"You have not heard from her?"

Dael shook his head. "Not since our journey to Egypt," he said. His face grew stony and cold. He rubbed the palms of his hands together to ease off the charcoal powder on them. "I vowed to return to her," he confessed. "But I had hoped and dreamed she might change her mind and come to me," he finished stubbornly. When Ard made no answer he went on almost defensively. "Besides, I cannot leave on an instant's notice. Old Khi has befriended me. He is a friend of the pharaoh himself. I cannot flee into the night like a thief." He sighed. "I have thought of her. She never leaves me, either by day or by night. Still——" He broke off just as the curtained doorway of the smithy parted and the figure of Khi appeared in the entrance.

There were those who whispered that Khi had already passed his ninth decade of life, perhaps more. But there was no way of counting the Egyptian smith's years. His step was still alert, his body—although gnomelike and twisted in one shoulder—moved with wiry strength. His eyes, as black as the ebony, were clear and unclouded.

In a deep, warm voice he greeted both Dael and Ard and then strode over to stare at the bubbling pot. For a long time he gazed into the cooling depths and then turned briskly to Dael.

"The metal looks good for fashioning." He nodded with satisfaction. "Tomorrow we can start the work."

"The pharaoh will be pleased with the cups, master," Dael murmured.

Khi looked sharply at him and, to Dael's amazement, shook his head. "Not for cups will this metal be used. The mind of the pharaoh has changed. He wants sword handles to be made of this for his officers."

Standing stock-still, Dael stared at him. "Sword handles?" he burst out. "For weapons?"

Khi nodded. "The pharaoh has ordered all work by smiths and craftsmen stopped if they labor on jewels or works of art. From this day hence all the craftsmen will make weapons—and weapons only. Swords, spears, lances, pikes, chariots, daggers." He shrugged when he saw Dael's face. "It is not my wish," he said shortly, "but the command of the pharaoh. The god fears continued invasions from the sea and has ordered arms to be created in abundance by all who work in metals." Almost kindly he looked at Dael. "I know the torment of your spirit, Dael," the old smith said, sympathy oiling his voice. "But it is the pharaoh's command. And we must obey. I like it not either, but what can I do? Like the others, I must bow and obey the wishes of the ruler of Egypt." He laid a quiet hand on Dael's shoulder, nodded curtly at Ard, and then walked out swiftly. They heard his voice rising in command to the other workers, smiths, toolmakers, and their apprentices.

For a moment Dael stared at Ard and then, as if the anger in him could no longer be stemmed, he took the green-wood stock out of the pot and hurled it against the opposite wall. His right fist clenched, the knuckles white, as he smashed it into the palm of his left.

"Always the war!" he said dully, his face working, a muscle along his neck swelling and throbbing with unspent emotion. "Always I must serve the gods of war, whether they are of Egypt, Canaan, or"—he almost rasped the word—"of Israel. Always must the tools of peace be put aside and the instruments that fashion warfare be picked up. Even here in Egypt——" He began striding the room. "All my life I have dreamed of coming here, to learn and study, to make things of beauty and not things that kill. Now again a king orders the fashioning of tools of death and I must create them. Even in Egypt—in Egypt!" he repeated bitterly.

Watching him carefully, Ard asked, "Is Egypt, then, so different?"

Dael whirled upon him, his eyes stormy. "Egypt is—*Egypt!*" he almost shouted. "The capital of the world. The seat of knowledge, the center of fashion and ideas and beauty and culture. Egypt is——" He broke off suddenly as he beheld the knowing, almost mocking smile on the Benjamite's face. Dael's head went down in a bow of defeat. "Of course," he murmured. "You are right, Ard. Whyfor should Egypt be different? Its very economic foundation is based on warfare, like the rest of the lands." He nodded, as if to himself. "I can understand now the pharaoh's reluctance to consider the idea of Jabin's scythed chariots as no threat to the Nile. Of course. The pharaoh knew it all the time.

Egypt, bled white by continual invasions and warfare, has neither the money, men, armaments, nor metal to go to war against Jabin—or any other king. Why," he went on, his voice rising in wonder, "Merenptah was probably frightened at the news of the secret weapon I brought him but pretended to be unexcited about it. The pharaoh knew he could rearm only with defensive purposes in mind. And now that he knows and fears Jabin's threat, perhaps, he has started to rearm frantically. That must be the reason for the new decree that Khi just uttered to us. Our arrival caused more concern than we were led to believe, Ard." He smiled weakly.

Ard nodded glumly. "And what do you now?" he asked. "Remain here—to make weapons for the pharaoh, or——" Deliberately he allowed his voice to trail away. "Think, Dael," Ard cautioned. "It is not as bad as it appears. The weapon-making will not last forever. In the meantime, you can be your own master here and have Perse as your wife and the great dowry of Khi that goes with it. In a year—perhaps two—you might forget this and——"

Ard stopped as another shadow darkened the doorway and as a voice, in Canaanite, called out if Dael the craftsman lived and worked here. When Dael answered, the room was entered by a stranger, still wrapped in a dust-dotted simlah, the turban stained and dirty, the beard unkempt. The arrival bowed politely and then cleared his throat importantly.

"I am Kohar, caravan owner of Memphis," the stranger revealed. "And I bear a message given me by one I met while at Ramah."

Ramah . . .

Dael's heart tugged sharply. He watched as Kohar's hands reached into his turban, removed a piece of papyrus from within the cloth wrappings. He gave it to Dael, who held it with suddenly deadened and unfeeling fingers.

"One Obed instructed me to deliver this to you," Kohar said. He coughed gently. "Although Obed paid me with a hundred shekels of silver, he said——"

"Here." Ard was fumbling at his belt, opening the small purse there, counting out four wedges of silver. He fairly threw them at Kohar, who grinned a yellow-toothed smile, bowed, murmured his thanks.

"How long since the message was given you?" Ard demanded sharply. Kohar shrugged. "I remember not the number of days. But not too long, since our journey was swift and uneventful." Once more he bowed, excused himself, and left the chamber.

"Read, read," Ard demanded as Dael continued to stare after the departing merchant. As if brought back by the sharpness of the trainer's voice, Dael slowly unfolded and uncreased the stiff document, his eyes leaping at the words. Ard saw him take a deep breath, saw the papyrus drop to the ground.

"Well?"

Dael moistened his lips. As if in great pain and from a greater distance, he whispered:

"Deborah has been arrested and taken captive by Jabin, with charges of sorcery directed against her. . . ."

"Think—and hear me," Ard was saying a few moments later, looking at his fighter, who, with bent head, was seated on a bench. "True—the message was signed with the name of Obed. And I know Obed, for he is the leader, the elder of the tribe of Benjamin. But *is* that his signature? How know you it was Obed who gave the message to the merchant?"

"I will ask of this Kohar and have him describe the man who placed the papyrus in his hands, and then——"

Ard shook his head. "Suppose Obed sent the message by another? Suppose that this same Kohar is in the pay of Jabin or Achan, with instructions to deliver the message to you in order to lure you back to Canaan, there to be trapped. No. That is no solution."

Dael looked up fiercely. "Can you not understand? She is prisoner now, and with a charge of sorcery against her. You know what that means? It is death—and I may already be too late."

"You are not late," Ard answered grimly. "This whole thing is a scheme to have you come back to Canaan, where both you *and* Deborah will be killed. Are you blind not to see through this plan?" Ard urged heatedly. "It is all Achan's doing. Having rid himself of the father as a potential leader of Israel, he now fears the son. Perhaps you have been chosen at the conclave at Shiloh to carry the standard of Israel into the field against Canaan. If so, what better way to end your career and life, along with her who instigated the rebellion, than to have you come back and fall into the pit so cunningly dug for you? Hear me. Let caution cool you. Wait. Rush not back. Learn more. Send your own messengers. If need be, you can always ransom her. You have the wealth now. Approach the pharaoh, if necessary, and he will——"

"The pharaoh, who is friend of Khi, who wants his daughter in marriage to me?" Dael asked indignantly. "No. This cannot be. Besides," he went on, his voice dropping, "she would not return, even if I did ransom her. She would not come to me in ransom." Again the cropped head shook stubbornly. "I must go to her and save her. And at once."

"Then you are mad indeed," Ard said quietly. "Perhaps you have received too many blows in the head." The trainer's voice thickened with anger and frustration. "Let us suppose you return. What will you do? Approach Jabin and demand that he give up Deborah at once to you? And," he continued bitterly, "the monarch will bow politely and return the woman? Fool, thousand kinds of fool!" he shouted now, one foot stamping on the floor. "The moment you trod on Canaanite soil again, you will be bound by Jabin's chains. And yet you say, like a child, that Jabin will listen to you. What will make him so do? Your smile? Your wealth?"

Dael looked right into Ard's livid face, and the Benjamite was struck with the calm determination he saw there. "No," Dael answered, "neither my smile nor my wealth will impress or influence Jabin. But the letter of safe-conduct and welcome and invitation and immunity will. Those that Anash handed me."

Ard spat in disgust. "Letters—scraps of papyrus and parchment—not worth living for. Or," he added darkly, "dying for."

"You yourself told me that Jabin is a man of honor, that he will keep his word. So said you, Ard. And Jabin's seal, sworn with the gods, is on the royal summons."

From the way Ard looked away, Dael knew he had scored. But not completely. "True, Jabin might keep his word," Ard muttered. "But how are we to know? Perhaps he already considers Israel at war with Canaan and will not honor the immunity he has promised you."

"Then we take that chance," Dael said grimly. "Forget not that I, as well as Jabin, am a man of honor. I vowed to Deborah I would return. And now she needs me."

"And," Ard asked again, but not so bitterly as before, "when you stand safely before Jabin, how will you bargain with him?"

"In this way. I will offer to fight his champion, the Bull of Bashan. I will wager my wealth and body against his promise to release Deborah unto me—if I win. . . ."

For the longest of moments Ard stared at his fighter. Then the trainer sighed and shook his head.

"You are mad," he decided again, "and, since there is no reasoning with a madman, I will return with you to Canaan." His shoulders lifted and then dropped in a great sigh. "Truly, this kinswoman of mine is a sorceress to so influence two men, so far distant and on so dangerous a venture. . . ."

15

NOW the way and manner of Deborah's betrayal by Achan and her arrest by Jabin occurred in this fashion:

It had begun long before the conclave of the tribes of Israel had gathered at Shiloh, the holy sanctuary city, to consider unification and a choice of a leader. Achan, restless because of Deborah's continued stay at Kedesh, fearing that in some way she was still in communication with the fugitive Dael, had—with bribes or threats —prevailed upon all the caravan leaders, or those who traveled to distant lands, to report to him if Deborah should try to have them carry messages to Dael for her.

But as the days and the weeks and then the months had gone and there was no interception of any message, nor, indeed, any news of a message at all, Achan had become somewhat eased. He had no way of knowing, at that time, that Deborah was writing to Dael and sending her letters from Ramah and not Kedesh. And after all, she had but twice communicated with the fighter.

So, Achan's suspicions were calmed for a time until the great meeting at Shiloh.

Before the black-and-brown tent of Benjamin over which flew the pennant of the ravenous wolf, the totem of the tribe, Deborah stood in the early sunlight, watching the scene around her.

For days now, the inhabitants of Shiloh, the sanctuary town in the territory of the rich and powerful tribe of Ephraim, had been watching with awe as the representatives of the might of Israel streamed over the two hills that sheltered the capital, where were kept the holy tablets of the Ten Commandments in their Ark.

How long had it taken to have the tribes gather finally and to vote for warfare against Jabin, to fight for their liberty and to choose one who might lead them? She closed her eyes against the sun. She herself, by writing and working and plotting and meeting in secret, by threats, promises, cajoling, explaining, speaking until she was hoarse, had spent more than a year in preparation for this day. And even then all the tribes were not united, she knew. Only Benjamin, Ephraim, Naphtali, Zebulon, Issachar, and certain portions of Western Manasseh had finally become convinced that there could be no peace for Israel, no freedom until the yoke of Canaan was removed. But the others? Haughty Reuben, proud Judah, doughty little Dan, burly Simeon, indifferent Gad and Asher—would they join the Benzi tribes? She doubted it, even if they had sent their representatives to this meeting. But she was aware that even in the magnificent tent of Ephraim, whose hexagon shape was held up by thirty-six poles, the aloof tribes had arranged their seats so that they were together, forming the opposition. And in the tent over which flew the unicorned goat of Ephraim, the dissension would rise loud and strong.

In her mind she reviewed the men whose decisions might change the destiny of Israel. Most important of all was old Nun of Ephraim—he who bore the honored name of the father of the greatest Ephraimite of all—the general Joshua. Nun's wisdom, shrewdness, wealth, and power would be a tremendous influence upon the others, and she breathed a little sigh of relief that Nun favored unification. Far too long, and with too much blood and flame, had Canaan reaped its harvest from the protesting men of Ephraim.

Then there was Jair, the chief representative and elder of the tribe of Issachar. Older, more feeble than Nun, Jair was also, however, the scribe of the tribes, the honored historian. He would follow Nun, no matter what the Ephraimite said.

Obed of Benjamin, short, powerfully built, outspoken in his opinion, a soldier and a fighter? Of him there was no doubt. Obed and Benjamin had fought Canaan all the time and were eager to end the days of Jabin's rule. Shimeon of Zebulon, a grave-faced and quiet scholar, would follow the advice of Nun. And Gershon of Naphtali—he was with her, since Naphtali lay so close to Canaan and was virtually a prisoner of Hazor, Jabin's capital. Of course, she mused, the dandified Heshbon of Reuben, he with the perfumed beard and the oiled and curled locks, might be persuaded to join the others if there was anything to be gained in the form of additional wealth or produce.

Of the other representatives—those who were certain to oppose any plan of unification or rebellion—she knew but little. She frowned and shook her head.

The sunlight caught the yellow-white shimmer of her hair and threw its rays back blindingly from it, spattering light against the sheer little veil of blue that covered her nose and mouth. Shamash also scattered his arrows over the dark blue gown that hung straight from her shoulders to ankles, caught only at the waist by a white belt of horse leather, buckled at the front with three horizontal hooks of brass. On her arms she wore elbow-length cuffs of lightly beaten brass embossed with silver designs of flowers and bees. She knew she made a dazzling appearance, one calculated to impress, with the combination of colors, the purple, the near gold, the white and silver.

From the center of the encampment a shofar blasted thickly, repeating its three notes over and over again. She straightened herself, knowing it was the signal for the start of the conclave, and began to walk toward the entrance of the large tent of Ephraim. Pulling the veil closer against her face, she made her way through the canopy.

Although sunlight streamed weakly through the dark brown

goatskin tent roof, it was not enough to light even part of the interior. Great lamps, blazing contentedly from the deep pools of oil on their bottoms, threw light into every corner of the immense skin dwelling. Additional lamps, attached by thongs to the poles, licked golden tongues against the shadows of the billowing skin walls. Under her feet Deborah could feel the rich carpeting as she approached the semicircle of silent men, each seated on his individual mat. Slowly Deborah neared the central figure, the blue-eyed, pink-cheeked Nun of Ephraim.

Jair, the scribe of Issachar, with the tired and sagging beard of gray and the half-closed eyes, intoned gently, "Deborah bas Shillem, the woman shophet of Ramah."

Deborah bowed her head, turned to face the others, who arose as their names were called—not in respect to her—but for purposes of formal recognition.

As she seated herself, somewhat in back of the men—because she was a woman and considered inferior—she watched as one by one the rest of the representatives arose to acknowledge their presence.

Jair, who as scribe carried on the tradition of the men of Issachar, barely lifted his head above the small leather scroll on his knees as he called out the names. He spoke softly, concentrating on the script, separating each word, she noticed with admiration, with the proper red stroke.

"Obed of Benjamin," said Jair.

Deborah smiled slightly at her kinsman. There was no doubt that Obed was both fighter and soldier. Small but built with bullish-like strength, boasting a fierce red beard that was unable to hide a stubborn jaw, and pale gray eyes, Obed had the hands of a man of war and the bearing of an officer.

"Shimeon of Zebulon . . ."

A tall gray-haired man with a straight nose, solemn dark eyes, and a tiny spade beard arose. He gravely inclined his head in greeting and then quietly seated himself again.

"Gershon of Naphtali . . ."

Smiling, his bulging belly quivering under his mantle as he stood up, Gershon looked as if he were about to wave in a friendly fashion at the others, then remembered where he was and seated himself quickly.

"Heshbon of Reuben . . ."

All eyes turned upon the tall, lean figure of the representative from the southeast. He was donned in a glittering robe of crimson, yellow, and blue that was wound tightly around him. Silver sandals sparkled on his feet, and the sweet-smelling odor of perfume from the long, upswept beard and mustaches reached Deborah's nostrils. As Heshbon bowed his head in greeting, a necklace of gold glistened for a moment against the pale white throat.

"Joseph from Western Manasseh."

A man of medium height and undistinguished features rose swiftly, bobbed his head, and sat down again so suddenly that few had a chance to study him.

"Jesse of Judah . . ."

All eyes were upon the tall, stately figure as he arose with dignity and, almost with aloofness, looked coldly at the others. There was a strength about the man that Deborah was instantly aware of, a feeling of superiority and derision, the cause of which she could not fathom. Heavily tanned, which made his green eyes look startlingly brilliant, his was a face heavy with arrogant handsomeness. Unlike the others, he was cleanly shaven, his hair cut short, hardly reaching down to his neck. His hands were also brown, Deborah noticed, looking strong and able. The nails were trimmed and cleaned to rims of white. Here, she decided at once, was a man of power, a leader, strong and confident. If only he were with Israel! she commented bitterly to herself.

"Peleg of Simeon . . ."

For a moment, startled, Deborah thought that Achan himself had arisen to face the others. For surely this man from Simeon could have been the shophet's twin. The same great black beard dominated the face, the eyes were as bold and cunning, the figure as burly and thick. Only the lips were thinner and more commanding than those of Achan.

In rapid order the others followed, the leaders of Gad, Asher, and Dan. The first two made no impression upon her, although Reba of Dan was interesting to watch because of his deeply lined and weather-beaten face, showing clearly his trade as a sailor, and the small, bowlegged stance, used more to the deck of a ship than the fine rugs of Ephraim. It was this Reba, in a very loud and booming voice, who said to Nun:

"My lord, as was decided among the leaders of Judah, Reuben, Simeon, Asher, Gad, and myself, only Jesse of Judah will speak for us. For we are together and of one opinion—Jesse will speak for us with our tongue . ."

As Nun nodded and Jair recorded swiftly, Deborah grimaced to herself. It was as she had feared—nay, had known all along. Outside of the Benzi factions, none of the tribes favored unification and rebellion. For by making Jesse their spokesman, they had come here with set ideas and adamant purpose.

Nun, leaning forward, smiling slightly, said: "And I am Nun of Ephraim, and the scribe here is Jair of Issachar." Other smiles were turned on him; all knew the two men, and Nun's introduction was to be taken as a polite and light jest.

But now Nun's smile was gone, and he sat up straighter, his face serious. "We are this day met and gathered to consider rebellion against Canaan," he began, "and, if so agreed, to choose one to lead us into battle. Now. Who speaks first? And for which cause?"

It was Obed of Benjamin who arose swiftly, leaning back on his heels once, then thrusting both hands into his belt. His gaze passed over the other men, pausing briefly at Jesse's slightly cynical smile.

"I make no secret of how Benjamin feels," Obed said. "For two generations we have battled Canaan. Of all the tribes, perhaps Benjamin has suffered most at the hands of the Canaanites. We are forced to worship their gods, while our Jehovah is scorned. We must bend our necks under their whips and swords, pay them a tenth of what we produce, or else face their raids with fire and sword. Far too long has this gone on. There can be no freedom for Benjamin—or Israel—so long as Canaan is mighty alongside us. The land cannot hold two rulers, cannot abide two different gods, two separate ways of worship. Therefore, I urge that the tribes unite, send their manpower against Jabin and his general, Sisera, and conquer them. I speak as a soldier, and bluntly so. But I also warn—Canaan and Israel cannot exist on the same land together in peace."

Almost glaring around him, Obed seated himself, to be followed by Gershon of Naphtali and Shimeon of Zebulon, all urging unification and repeating, more or less, what Obed had so hotly stated. Calmer voices were heard when Jair spoke, agreeing that unification was for the best, but urging caution and time; and Nun, himself, also admitted that he was for unification but added that so far no leader had been found for Israel.

It was then that Deborah wanted to arise and speak, stopping only when she saw the suave and confident Jesse of Judah get slowly to his feet. With an amused, almost pitying gaze he looked at his colleagues.

"For nearly two hours now," he began, his voice, although low-pitched, carrying easily to all, his speech refined and educated, "I have been listening to the talk—rather careless mouthing of words, it seems to me—of rebellion and battle. Obed, here, has spoken of the 'manpower' of Israel." Jesse's smile broadened sarcastically. "And just where is this manpower to be found? Where are our fighters?"

Instantly Obed, his face reddening, was on his feet. "Benjamin stands ready with five hundred warriors!" he cried out.

Jesse waited until Obed had seated himself. Then he smiled again. "Five hundred warriors," he repeated softly, mockingly. "And"—his voice become sharper—"do you know how many men Jabin can raise? A hundred times your five hundred warriors, Obed. More, perhaps. And forget not that Sisera also commands nine hundred chariots. Nine times a hundred," he echoed with emphasis. "Where has Israel the might to meet the challenge of such power? Where are *our* vehicles of war, our horses, our weapons? Our smiths are forbidden to touch iron. We have no trained men, no army. And"—he smiled sarcastically—"no weapons. Bows and arrows, yes; slings, yes—but swords, spears, axes, armor—— Would we go out against Jabin with a sling and a stone? No, my colleagues, to call for warfare against Jabin is madness. We would be hurled back over the River Jordan, so wounded as never to return. We cannot fight iron with naked fists."

Dramatically he paused, his hands outstretched, and Deborah, fascinated despite herself, could not take her eyes from the man. "Now hear me," Jesse said, his voice lower now, urging, soft and persuasive. "It is said we cannot live with Canaan on the land. But is this strengthened with truth? Why can we not live with Canaan? What or who is to stop us? Our tongues are similar. Our ways of life are alike, since we, too, have become tillers of the soil and depend upon the earth and sun for the crops. Already some of the great agricultural festivals have become part of ours. Why should we spill blood over nothing at all? In years to come"—and the smile became wise and knowing—"who will care whether there was a Canaan or an Israel? For they will both be the same, one land, one tongue, one tradition. And"—he paused briefly again —"one religion. For there is little difference between Baal and Jehovah. Both are gods, warlike or peaceful, as the occasion demands. Should we exterminate ourselves over the name of a deity? Behold the tribe of Judah. We have lived in peace with Canaan. We have absorbed part of their culture, and they have been steeped with some of ours. We live in peace together. Our men have married their women, and our women have borne children to Canaanite fathers. And is this so terrible? Is it worse than going to war and killing or be killed? No! say I. Better peace at any price— and this price is cheaply wrought—than warfare. Canaan and Israel can live in peace until the day they merge and become one people. Such is the opinion of Judah and of those who have agreed to have me speak for them."

As the officials of Gad and Dan and Asher and Reuben and Smeon nodded, Jesse, his voice clearer and more confident now, swept over them in impassioned and eloquent plea. "Hear me, brothers in Israel! Drive from your hearts this burning for war with Canaan, for it will bring you nothing but ashes. Live in peace with Canaan. Jabin is no monster. He longs for peace, too, wants Canaan to become great in the family of nations, and he will protect Israel and guide him and make his peace with him. Thus I, Jesse of Judah, and those for whom I speak think." He was about to seat himself when another thought struck him, and he remained standing.

"And you mouth hasty and careless words about a leader of Israel leading you into battle." His smile was rolled back by mockery now. "And where," he taunted, "is such a leader to be found, one who knows men and battle and weapons, who can instill confidence, who is brave and cunning and wise? And once, having been made leader, what is to stop him from making himself *king* over you, and ruling you in harsher ways than would Jabin?" he finished.

Jesse looked at them in triumph. He felt he had struck heavy blows on his behalf, especially by reviving the old fear among the tribes that their treasured independence would be taken away by a leader who might make himself king over them.

In silence Jesse seated himself, flashing a triumphant glance at the hulking Peleg and the gaudily gowned Heshbon of Reuben.

Almost unnoticed, her face, which was visible under the veil, pale and concentrated, Deborah arose.

"My lords!"

Her woman's voice, low but distinct, came as a surprise after the lower basses, baritones, and tenors of the males who had preceded her. Jesse's eyebrows went up in a sophisticated frown, while Peleg stared curiously at her. Heshbon, stroking his curled beard, entwined one finger in a strand slowly.

"Deborah bas Shillem, shophet of Ramah in Benjamin, rises to speak," Jair said.

Nun nodded. "Let her so do."

Deborah tried to steady her breath, wished she could wipe the perspiration that suddenly filmed her palms. Her breath was deep in her throat as she turned to face the men. Yet it was not without a feeling of triumph that she, a mere woman, who could be considered at times as no more than chattel, was to speak before the great elders of Israel. What other woman could boast this? she asked herself in order to fortify her trembling body.

"My lords"—her voice was steadier now—"it has been said that there could be found no man to lead Israel. But I tell you there is such a one. For I have seen this man, have talked to him and know he is the one."

As she saw their sudden, knowing looks, realizing what was going on in their masculine minds, already sensing the smirks and innuendoes, she turned to Nun. That old man, wise in the ways of his sex, called out sharply:

"This woman, Deborah bas Shillem, is a shophet for Jehovah and therefore dedicated. Let no man here think of her in other terms but those." His grave face brushed over their features in warning. Only Jesse's eyes retained their mocking challenge.

"It is not so much with a leader that we are concerned," he called out to her, "but the danger of going, weaponless and unarmed, to war against Jabin. How answer you that in your judgment, Shophet?"

Standing straighter, her eyes fixed upon the handsome features of the Judahite, Deborah said: "You lose your battles even before they begin, Jesse of Judah. For hear me now. Perhaps, as you say, *is there a shield or spear seen among forty thousand in Israel?* But forget not this, especially *ye that ride on white asses, ye that sit on rich cloths, and ye that walk by the way and tell of it—tell of it louder than the voice of archers,*" she needled Jesse, knowing he was one of the merchants who dealt with Canaan.

As her gaze flashed over the others, she added scornfully, "And you, Reuben, why are there great investigations of your heart to see which side to join in victory? Oh, Reuben—*why sittest thou among thy sheep? To hear the pipings for the flocks?* And you, Dan"—she indicated the seaman with a finger—"*why do you sojourn by the ships? And you, Asher, who dwells at the shore of the sea, and abideth by its bays?* No wonder you are aloof and indifferent. Not your blood is being spilled by Canaan, not your homes burned, your crops taken. But will you stand away while your brothers die under the double-edged blades of Jabin? What, think you, will happen to you, who believe Canaan is your friend, after the other tribes are destroyed? Will your women, your children be safe, then? Know you what the mother of Sisera, the general of Jabin, sings? I know, for I have heard. She cannot wait for her son to conquer Israel. '*Are they not finding, are they not dividing the spoil?*' asks this woman in joy of triumph over Israel. '*A damsel . . . two . . . damsels to every man.*' Is that what you want to happen to your wives and daughters and beloved ones? To feed Sisera's lust? For they will feed it unless you rise against Canaan."

She stopped, looking at their faces for some reaction. Nun and Jair appeared thoughtful, worried; Obed was beaming and nodding his head, while Gershon looked solemn. Only the non-Benzi leaders had faces of masks, all except Jesse, whose sardonic little smile never left his sensuous lips.

"You, Jesse of Judah," she went on, speaking directly to him, "speak of living in peace with Canaan. But how can this be when Jabin is determined to force *his* way of life upon us, *his* gods, *his* rules and laws and not ours. True—he bothers you not, because you trade with him and because you marry his women. But why does he tolerate this? Because he wants Israel divided. Because he wants to see Israelite brother fighting brother or perhaps not aiding him at all when he is attacked. It is Jabin's way of separating Israel by dissension, dividing it into little pieces, and then, one by one, swallowing them! Can you not see this, understand this, know it for the truth?"

Jesse finally looked down, waited politely for Deboah to finish. When she had seated herself, the man from Judah arose slowly.

"For a woman," he said, one hand squeezing his nostrils together briefly, "you have a most eloquent tongue. I see now how you came to be a shophet. Perhaps if more of our judges wore dresses——" He left the rest unsaid. "However, you have not succeeded in swaying me toward war with Jabin. On the contrary. It is people like yourself, fiery, hotheaded, incendiary, and fanatical, who will ruin Israel. And not what you call the indifference or indecisions of Judah or Reuben. No. I still hold that there be no rebellion and no unification. And you mentioned a leader. Would you reveal his name to us?"

Again Deborah stood up, swiftly and proudly now. "He is Dael ben Abinoam of Kedesh in Naphtali—he whose father was slain by Jabin and whose forges were destroyed."

Jesse delicately pinched his nostrils together. "Dael ben Abinoam?" he asked, turning to the representatives of Reuben and Simeon. "It seems I have never heard of this man who is——"

It was Nun who interrupted wearily. "Play us no scenes now, Jesse. You have heard of him, as has all of Canaan. He is the champion fist fighter whose exploits have excited even Jabin."

Jesse rubbed a finger along the ridge of his aquiline nose. Then he nodded. "It does seem to me that I have heard the name bruited about in taverns and on the streets." His mocking gaze rested on Deborah again. "And what has he done to interest Jabin so?"

Deborah was about to reply, but, catching a warning nod from Obed, she remained silent while the leader of the Benjamites faced Jesse. "You have indeed heard his name, and will hear of it more often. For this Dael ben Abinoam is a champion of champions, and Jabin had sent his personal representative to invite Dael to return to Canaan for a fight. This is common knowledge that even the children know," he finished indignantly.

Jesse looked surprised, grimaced, turned unbelievingly to the colleagues at his side. "A gamor?" he asked insidiously, insultingly of them. "A *fist fighter* to lead the hosts of the Lord? Surely, what nonsense is this?"

Propelled by the burning anger within her now, Deborah sprang swiftly to her feet. She tossed the lock of hair away from her forehead, and the gray in her eyes was burning black as she faced Jesse. "Yes, a fist fighter, Jesse," she said quietly. "A man who has fought in many lands and before many kings. A strong man, well versed in all the arts of war. If he is good enough to draw Jabin's interest, he surely is qualified to lead."

Jesse, rocking a bit on his heels, smiled and then asked softly, "This training in warfare you boast about—where did the son of Abinoam receive it?"

She was too angry to sense the trap. "At Golan," she snapped, "where there are many of mercenaries and professional soldiers to have taught him. Where——" She stopped when she saw Jesse's slow, triumphant grin revealing his very white teeth.

"At *Golan*?" he murmured, turning again to the men of Gad, Asher, and Dan, who also murmured displeasure. "This man, then, whom you tout as a leader is a refugee, a manslayer?" The jeweled hands were held high in protest. "My brothers in Israel, this is ridiculous. How can such a killer, a fugitive from justice, ever lead the hosts of the Lord?" Once more he turned to Deborah and, speaking as he would to a backward child, he asked: "And this hero of yours? He is still at Golan?"

"No." Although her voice faltered somewhat, she was still standing straight, her fists clenched, her shoulders thrust back defiantly. "He is at the pharaoh's court in Egypt. This was learned when Anash, the personal messenger for the king, returned after bearing Jabin's invitation to Dael to return to Canaan. At the moment"—she closed her eyes briefly and then opened them—"he works at the forges and smithy of one Khi, a master smith. So Anash revealed to Jabin."

Jesse made a helpless, magnificent gesture with his hands, bringing them high into the air and then slapping them against his sides. "My brothers!" he cried out finally. "This whole idea is madness. A manslayer and refugee, now in Egypt, to lead Israel? A fist fighter?" He turned to face Nun and Jair, his hands seeking his belt and hooking the thumbs into it. "No!" he said. "I see no merit neither in this man as a leader nor in the whole plan of combining and rising against Jabin. It is madness. It will ruin Israel. I, for one, do not agree. Nor will I rise against Canaan. We live in peace now with Jabin; we trade with him. And Gad and Asher and Dan do the same in their ships. Why should we disturb our way of life to satisfy the war lust of Benjamin or of Naphtali? No," he went on again. "And I think my colleagues concur." He turned to face the three others with him, who nodded solemnly.

"We do not fight against Jabin," the official from Dan echoed.

Nun looked at Heshbon of Reuben. "And you?" the old man asked. "How stand you?"

"With Jesse," Heshbon said without hesitation, not even rising, but gazing down at his rings.

Nun nodded, his face becoming grimmer. "And you, Peleg of Simeon?"

"Also with Jesse."

Nun looked at Jair, who was still crouched, writing on the leather scroll. "How stand the tribes?" he asked, and it seemed to Deborah that his voice was very tired.

"Against a leader and rebellion are," Jair intoned, "Jesse of Judah, Peleg of Simeon, Heshbon of Reuben, Reba of Dan, as well as Gad and Asher."

Nun looked at Joseph, from the western part of Manasseh. "And you?" he asked.

Joseph's answer was quick. "I favor the uprising against Jabin."

Nun nodded once more. "And so does Ephraim, of which I am the head."

"And Issachar," Jair murmured from his task.

"And Benjamin," echoed Obed proudly.

"And Naphtali," the fat Gershon said in a loud voice.

"And Zebulon," the melancholy Shimeon finished.

Nun nodded again. "So stand the vote then. Six for the rebellion, six against. . . . Israel is divided evenly."

But Jesse, still smiling, shook his head. "There are more against the rebellion than for it, Nun," he said. "Only half of Manasseh is with you. And forget not that three of the largest and most powerful of the tribes, in men and territory, join you not. I speak of Judah and Reuben and Simeon. Without their manpower and wealth, you cannot win. Think. Do you still want this war?"

"It so shall be," Nun said crisply. "But if Judah still wants to join——"

He stared as Jesse almost nonchalantly arose, beckoning for the other insurgents to follow him. "Judah and the others want no part of this," Jesse said calmly. "If the other six tribes want to annihilate themselves, there is nothing we can do. Come, brothers."

And one by one the six began to walk out of the tent. When Jesse passed Deborah, he stopped for a moment. Almost impudently he flicked a finger under her veil, lifted the cloth, and scanned her face. He stared for a moment, then let the veil drop.

"Beautiful as well," he murmured to her. "Wisdon and beauty in one woman. Any time"—he showed his dazzling teeth—"you want to visit Judah, do so. For there you will find real men, not these weaklings and dreamers of Naphtali or Issachar or the work horses of Zebulon." He tapped her playfully on the arm and then, without a single look backward, strolled out of the tent.

Nun's sigh was heard in the silence that followed. His eyes met those of the scribe's. "And so it is," Nun said heavily, "as before. Israel is divided. Only this time it is official. And what do we plan now?"

He looked from one to the other, stopping at Deborah, smiling at her. "Feel not too harshly about Jesse's manner," he said kindly. "The men of Judah are ever arrogant. I and the others know what great part you have played here, how you worked to have this gathering, and what your interests are. Perhaps," he said, his eyes closing in thought, "Jehovah means it for a woman to help in the salvation of Israel. And why not? The sons of Israel have ever honored their women, from the mother Sarah on, and shall so continue to do." Then his eyes opened and their blueness touched the gray in the woman's look. "But we must plan now, and quickly so. News of this conclave will certainly be brought to Jabin, who will prepare warfare against us. And we must gather our own men, dig out their secretly hidden weapons and supplies, and be prepared to fight."

He leaned forward again. "This Dael ben Abinoam. How soon can you reach him? And will he return to Kedesh to take over the leadership?"

Deborah looked down. What could she answer the old man? She had sent only two letters to Dael; he had answered none of them. Suppose he refused to return? What if the life in Egypt was too rich and full for him now? And, she thought with an empty, sinking feeling, suppose he had met some other woman by now?

"My lord," she finally said, "all I can promise you is that I will get in touch with him at once. I have so done twice before, with special runners and couriers sent from Ramah. Now I will try again. That is all I can promise."

Nun looked at her, biting his beard, rubbing a hand on his throat. "Let it so be, then," he said heavily. "We will wait. And while we wait, we shall prepare. But hasten to make contact with him and bid him answer now whether he returns to Israel to lead." He rubbed at his neck again. "One word of caution. Do not use runners now, for they will be too slow. Find, instead, a caravan from Kedesh which will take your message to the son of Abinoam by camel or ass and then by sea. It will be faster than going overland."

Deborah thought of the precautions she had taken not to communicate with Dael from Kedesh—because she feared Achan's treachery—then decided that the old man's counsel was the wisest. A runner or courier would take far too long. A message, borne by beast and ship, would cut the time in half. It was risky—she bit her lips—but it had to be done.

"I will so do," she promised, "and with haste."

Nun smiled gently at her. "Fear not," he said, "that you are a woman. For the lord Jehovah is with all of Israel, no matter what their sex. However, would it not be better—safer, perhaps—to send such a message from Ramah instead of Kedesh, which lies so close to Jabin's Hazor?"

"It would indeed, my lord"—she nodded—"and that is why—fearing traitors—I have sent messages from there. But Ramah lies far to the south from Shiloh here. Were this a place where caravans stops, I would send the message from here. But it is a risk we take. Daily, caravans leave for the coast from Kedesh. And I know a few of the merchant leaders now. Better I communicate with Dael from Kedesh than Ramah—because it will be faster."

And much more dangerous, she worried, although there was no inclination of the fear she felt as she looked upon old Nun.

And thus, by circumstance of necessity, the betrayal began.

Once back in Kedesh, Deborah immediately wrote out her message to Dael, addressing it in care of Khi's smithy in Memphis. The letter was unadorned by poetic wording. In simple, graphic terms it told Dael of the meeting at Shiloh, of the walking out of the six tribes, of the six who remained faithful, of their desire to have Dael return to lead Israel. "This is no indication that you will be chosen to lead," she wrote carefully, "but the elders of the Benzi would want to exchange words with you in person. There will be no danger for you when you return. You have the letters of safe-conduct and immunity that Anash granted you from Jabin."

She paused. Should she remind him that he had vowed unto her that he would return to her when and if she asked him? Her fingers trembled on the pen, were about to press downward to remind him of his promise. Then they stopped. No. She would not force him. If he came, it would be because he wanted to come and not because she had a hold over him because of a vow.

Carefully she sealed the message, rolled it into the clay container, brushed Dael's name over the dried surface, and then walked out to the wells to find Jeboash, a caravan merchant of Tyre she had known in Ramah and with whom she had done business before. Jeboash's train of camels and asses had visited

Kedesh and Hazor regularly, and—from the reports of the villagers—she knew the seller of goods was already encamped nearby.

When she found Jeboash and spoke to him and paid him for his services, giving him the message, she was confident it would reach Dael in faster time than had she sent it by regular courier. This was no time, she told herself staunchly, to use discretion and caution; haste was the paramount factor involved.

No sooner had she left Jeboash than that gaunt and lean merchant immediately sought out Achan. For he was one of the many caravan leaders whom Achan had seen, had warned to be on the watch for a message from Deborah. The silver that had been exchanged so often between the shophet of Kedesh and those in his pay now rang with victorious clangor. More wedges of the metal were slipped into Jeboash's hand, while those of Achan held the message that Deborah had intended for Dael.

Achan read it only twice before he picked up his oxgoad and practically ran to demand audience with Jabin, King of All Canaan. . . .

Jabin's private bedchamber, Achan thought disdainfully, hardly reflected the might and power of the Canaanite ruler. The room was austere, bare save for the bed matting in one corner, the huge bronze sword that was hung on a copper spike thrust through the wall, and the single woolen rug, dyed red and gold, that spread its colors up to the lip of the bed mat. Otherwise there was no indication that a king slept here.

When Jabin finished reading Deborah's message to Dael, he placed the parchment on the floor. His full, short length remained stretched out on the mat, the eyes staring at the ceiling. For a long time he uttered no sound. Indeed, save for the gentle heaving of his pondrous stomach, there was no movement of the king at all. Achan, knowing that Jabin had to speak first, stirred restlessly.

His hand rubbing his chest absently, Jabin finally spoke, still not looking at the judge. "I understand not your excitement in this matter, Achan," he said. "That the six Benzi tribes will revolt is no secret. I knew it long before. Nor was the conclave at Shiloh held in secrecy. All knew of it, and I did not even need my spies to inform me what had happened there. Why, then, is your spirit so agitated in this matter that you must see me at rest, in my own chamber?"

"But, my lord!" Achan protested, his beard quivering with indignation. "You have read the message sent by the woman. It is an open call for revolt against you, and asks that this Dael return as a leader. What could be more incriminating than that?"

"And just what," Jabin asked, his eyes still fastened on the roof above him, "would you have me do now?"

"Two things, my lord king," Achan said quickly, "and both of which may, as two stones from one sling, harm them. One—arrest the woman Deborah immediately on a charge of sorcery, which is punishable by death. Thus you remove the chief plotter and instigator against you. Secondly," he rushed on, afraid that Jabin might halt the flow of his words, "allow the news of Deborah's arrest to trickle through to Dael in Egypt. Let it be used as a lure to draw him back here in the vain hope of saving the woman. Thus you will have both of them as your prisoners, to be put to death. Dael and Deborah. In one blow you kill the main plotter against you and remove a potential leader."

Now Jabin sat up, slowly, grunting, still rubbing his chest until the flesh quivered and jumped. He yawned loudly and shook his bald head. "I greatly fear you read too much into all this," he said. "And hear me!" he added, his voice harder now as he saw Achan was about to protest. "There will be no talk of killing and bloodshed for the moment." The sharp blue eyes grew cold as they stared at the discomfited shophet.

"You speak of betrayal," the king went on harshly, "but you forget that I sent Dael letters of safe-conduct and immunity by my personal representative, Anash. Dael will undoubtedly use these *if* he returns. I need not place any snares for him. Indeed, I would not," he continued, the voice becoming flinty now, "because I have given my word and my honor in those letters, and have sworn to the gods and priests that no harm shall befall Dael when he returns. And I keep my word! I will not make my honor an empty thing."

"But it is no longer a question of honor, my lord king," Achan pointed out. "Israel is at war with Canaan, and Dael and the woman should be treated as enemies."

Jabin sat back, leaning against the wall, his feet thrust out. "Canaan is—as yet—at war with no people," he said. "What if a few of the tribes met and built up their courage by talking of rebellion against me? Is that an act of war? How little you know, Achan. . . . Besides, suppose I have them killed, as you lust after. What good would it do? *Good*?" Jabin continued with contempt. "It would create more harm than good. It might make martyrs out of both, heat the anger of the Israelites to so great a pitch that they would rise without a leader. And I do not want that now—not while Egypt still plagues us. Think you I want *two* enemies at my back and flank—Israel *and* Egypt both?"

Achan's smoldering eyes dropped to the carpet and his hands bunched together in helpless and frustrated rage.

"No," Jabin said firmly, shaking his head until the great pink dewlap flapped emphatically. "Your plan bears no weight with me, Achan. "And there are other reasons I do not want to see Dael destroyed. He is also, forget you not, a master smith now—and I can use him. And use him well indeed," he murmured, his eyes distant for a second. Then they flew open again and their icy cold touched Achan. "And you forget the most important thing of all. Why I sent Dael my invitation to return here. I want him to fight my champion, the Bull of Bashan. I want that more than you realize. Think of what a combat that would be! Dael against Og! Why, great princes and rulers for hundreds of miles away would come and see such a fight. And the wagers to be made! Nor need they fight only once. A series of three or five bouts could be arranged, along with a whole athletic festival, to show the rest of the world what Canaan is and what Canaan will be!" The king's breath drew in sharply and his eyes gleamed with inner excitement. "I have long planned and dreamed of this—and it shall so happen if Dael returns."

He stared at the crestfallen Achan and his face softened somewhat. "However," he said in a kinder tone, "think not that I am unaware of what you have brought me. I will agree to this much."

"Yes, my lord?" Achan looked up with revived hope and quickening interest.

"Let the news reach Dael in Egypt that this woman, Deborah, has been arrested by myself on a charge of sorcery." He smiled grimly as he noticed the lines around Achan's mouth relax.

"She will be arrested—but," he warned, one stubby finger lifted, "no harm shall come to her. Let it serve as a warning to the others that I know of their plans and can act at any time I so wish. As for Dael—if he wishes to return to save this woman"—Jabin smiled mirthlessly—"let him so do. The safe-conduct passes will be honored by my border guards. He will be treated here as a conquering hero. And if he wants the woman"—Jabin grinned widely —"*he will have to fight for her!* Now, is that not a better plan? Does that not insure two things? Dael's return and the certainty of a bout with Og?"

Glumly Achan nodded. The plan had merit. Deborah would be in chains, Dael would return and be forced to meet Og. But still——

"And after the fight?" Achan argued softly. "What if Dael should win?"

Jabin shrugged. "If he wins, I honor the victory. Whatever the stakes will be, he shall have earned them."

"Even if he wants the woman's freedom?"

"Even so," Jabin answered firmly, his eyes cynical as he heard Achan's low snarl of rage.

While Deborah's principal places of judgment were ordinarily at Ramah or Bethel, she also—from time to time—judged locally at Kedesh itself whenever Achan was absent or had other assignments. She had chosen to judge at Kedesh deliberately, to encourage the people of the town to regard her with favor and consider her one of their own. Besides, at Kedesh—unlike the two other seats of justice—she could meet those who beseeched her in a more relaxed and informal manner under the palm tree, just outside the fringe of dwellings.

On this day, as she approached the palm, she noticed that the crowd was larger than usual, with a heavy sprinkling of Canaanite civilians and soldiers. Nearing the place of judgment, she wondered which of the two cases before her today had drawn the larger than usual gathering.

The problem of Zalmon and his wife Miriam and the harlot Libnah? There was really nothing at all unusual in the situation. It had been Miriam who had brought the bitter complaint and charge against her husband Zalmon, who had embraced the flesh of Libnah. But more that that, Miriam had wept, while she herself was childless, her womb barren, the lusty Libnah had borne a son to Zalmon—and now Zalmon wanted not only to provide the harlot and her baby with oil, grain, and clothing, but to take them into his own home with Miriam. And this the wife would not tolerate.

The legal decision here would not be difficult, Deborah knew. There were ample precedents in Egyptian court scrolls dealing with similar cases.

The second case? It was hardly a matter for her at all, she mused, since it involved dream interpretation. She had wanted to refuse the request of the woman, Sarah, who wanted her dreams explained, but did not have the heart to disappoint her. Of course other cases might come along of which she did not know—and perhaps that accounted for the larger gathering.

Nodding briefly to those whom she knew, Deborah seated herself on the reed mat at the base of the palm. So simple were the cases before her today that she had not bothered to bring writing materials or scrolls to record the decisions or to substantiate her verdicts.

She called for Libnah, Miriam, and Zalmon to rise and stand before her. When the trio appeared—Miriam red-eyed and weeping, Libnah defiant, and Zalmon cocky and strutting—she looked at each in turn.

Deborah cleared her throat. "Miriam, the wife of Zalmon, comes to petition against the will of her husband, who wants to provide for the child of Libnah, the harlot, and Libnah herself, and to bring them both to reside under his roof. Hear, then, the decision, for so has it been written: Should a man's wife remain unfruitful and bear him no sons, and should another woman—even if she be known as a harlot—bear him a son, then the man must provide for the child and the mother. Grain and oil and cloth and shelter for both are the man's responsibility. So is the law rendered. But," she added as she saw Zalmon's triumphant look, "the law also says that there cannot be two mistresses in the same house. Therefore, Zalmon, you will not have Libnah share the same house with your wife Miriam, but will find other shelter for her. For this is the law and the word of Jehovah which must be obeyed."

She watched as the three shuffled back to the crowd. Deborah scanned the people for Sarah, who wanted the dreams explained. But so far the woman had not made her appearance. Instead, a short, fat woman of middle years—one Basemath—pushed close to Deborah and in a low tone so that none could hear said:

"Is it true that a potion of the pollen of the lotus flower, mixed with milk and honey and given my husband to drink, will increase the powers of his embrace?"

Sternly Deborah let her gaze fall upon the eager, warted face before her. "I know not," she answered, "and I do not deal in love or magic potions."

"I know not and deal not in such matters," Deborah repeated firmly, looking beyond the woman and glad to see Sarah approaching at last. Basemath, muttering under her breath, departed swiftly.

Now Sarah's thin, tall form stood before Deborah, her hands nervously twining together by the fingers. Nodding at her and smiling, Deborah said she had already been informed of the type of Sarah's dream but wanted the woman to repeat the images of her slumber for all to hear. "Now, what did you behold in your dream?"

"A large cat," Sarah's dry voice was heard.

"Then it is good. Your husband will have a rich harvest," Deborah answered. "And what else was revealed to you in the night?"

"The moon was shining on my husband's face," Sarah said, staring intently at the woman judge.

Deborah leaned back and closed her eyes. "That, too, is good and blessed, for it means that your husband has been forgiven by Jehovah."

"But as the moon was shining on his countenance," Sarah went on worriedly, "he was also staring into a mirror."

"And the reflection he saw in there," Deborah asked quickly, "was it his face he beheld in the mirror or that of another—woman?"

"I—I know not, I remember not," Sarah faltered, going pale.

Deborah nodded. "Usually," she said, "looking into a mirror is a bad omen—especially if another's face shines from it. However, since no image was cast from the mirror, be assured that you have nothing to fear." Deborah smiled softly. The idea that old Noach, Sarah's husband, might have another woman was ridiculous. The entire dream sequence, she decided, was a residue of Sarah's fear of losing her man.

Sarah, smiling with relief now, bobbed her head up and down with thanks. "My spirit is eased now that I know what my dreams meant," she began, "and it is good to have someone explain them to me——"

She stopped, looking with surprise as three Canaanite soldiers, an officer and two sergeants, brushed past her and stood before Deborah.

"Deborah bas Shillem of Ramah?" the officer asked. His right hand rested on his sword handle.

"I am so called," Deborah answered, rising to face the three. "What would you have of me?"

"You interpret dreams?" the officer demanded again.

Smiling slightly, Deborah nodded. "If people come to me and so ask of me, I give them interpretations, yes."

At a signal from the officer, the two sergeants stepped quickly at Deborah's side, seizing her arms and holding her tightly. She struggled indignantly, her face flushed with sudden anger and fright.

"What means this?" she cried out.

The officer spread his palms out mockingly. "It means you are disobeying the law of Jabin and Canaan by interpreting dreams. According to our laws, that is sorcery, and Jabin, King of All Canaan, has ordered your arrest." His eyes were hard now. "As a sorceress."

She was so stunned that she hardly heard the great murmur that arose from the crowd as the three men pushed her through it and began taking her to Hazor.

16

"CLEAR the throne room of all save the fighter and his trainer," Jabin ordered testily, the sausage-like fingers tapping restlessly against the arms of the ivory-and-wood throne. He watched as the guards gradually moved the scribes, the officials of the fighters' guilds, and the trainers of the school out into the courtyard, leaving only Dael and Ard to face him. From the throne he gestured to them to approach him. Although he had met the fighter earlier—when the contracts had been signed and the wagers made—there had been little time for the monarch to inspect Dael closely. Now, as the gamor approached him, Jabin's frosted glance carefully swept over every physical detail of the athlete.

Despite the inactive stay in Egypt, Jabin reluctantly admitted, Dael still appeared to be in fine fighting condition. Of course, he calculated, his trainer would ask for an additional three or four weeks of training to get Dael into a physical peak for the fight with Og—and I shall grant it to him, Jabin sighed to himself. For truly this fight between Og and Dael will be the battle of a century. The monarch glowed as he thought of that day.

To be sure, Jabin mused, the Israelite fist fighter was a fool. What man would wager all he possessed, all his wealth—what had it been?—Jabin's brow wrinkled in thought—twenty-five full gold talents?—and his freedom just over a woman? The terms had been specific and hard and written down and witnessed. Twenty-five gold talents and Dael's voluntary surrender to Jabin, to serve him in any matter the monarch saw fit, if he lost, against the woman and freedom if he won. Ridiculous terms, of course, Jabin sighed. But yet there was something to be admired in a man who would risk all. To Jabin it was sportsmanship of the highest type, something he understood and advocated. And, indeed, were I not a sportsman, and did not Dael's courage appeal to my sporting blood, I would not have honored the passes of safe-conduct and immunity that brought the two Israelites here to me. And even if Dael should win, Jabin told himself, what have I to lose? Nothing. Let Dael go back to the Israelites with his woman, let them lead the tribes into battle against him. What of it? What good would it do? Suppose the Israelites have their leader in Dael? What could such a leader do against an experienced general like Sisera, against the nine hundred scythed chariots which are ready for battle? What armament has Israel? Where are its weapons? In fact—Jabin grinned to himself—with Dael released as a leader, perhaps the Israelites might make a better battle of it than it promised to be!

The king's toes, clad in high white boots of white horse skin, wriggled in pleasure. He drew his woolen robe closer around him, however, because the throne room was cool. It was the latter part of the month of Marchesvan—October—a few short weeks before the cold and rainy season of Kislev began.

He waited until Dael and Ard, both standing straight before him, nodded in a quick bow. They had paid their full respects earlier, when the formal meeting had started and the contracts had been signed.

"Ease yourselves," Jabin said, grinning at them. "We are alone, and there is no need for formality now." As both Israelites assumed a normal posture, Jabin's cold smile touched Ard. "You never thought, did you, Ard, that when you fled from me you would someday stand before me like this again?"

"No, my lord king."

The smile lasted on the king's face. "I could have had you killed as a deserter the moment you entered my borders," Jabin said lightly, "but, had I done so, I would have dishonered my own words in the safe-conduct passes and left your fighter without a trainer. It is a good thing"—he scowled suddenly—"that I keep my word."

"Yes, my lord," Ard murmured, wondering why Jabin had summoned them again.

"How soon do you think your fighter will be ready?" Jabin asked of the trainer. "The contracts specified only that the fight would take place and listed the wagers made. Now I will have to know when the combat takes place."

"My fighter needs six or seven weeks to prepare his body for the fight with the Bull, and he——" Ard stopped when he saw Jabin's slow shaking of the bullet-shaped head.

"Three weeks and no more. So shall it be written."

It could have been worse, Ard was thinking. He thanked his caution in having Dael train at the Egyptian gladiator school every day during their stay at Memphis. In three weeks there might be just enough time to——

"You——fighter," Jabin was speaking to Dael. "Have you nothing to say?" With considerable curiosity he looked closer at the Israelite, admiring the physical perfection of the man, his calm demeanor.

"I say only I will do as my lord king commands," Dael answered quietly. "But I do ask one favor. I would like to see the woman Deborah and speak with her."

"No." Jabin pulled his robe closer. "I can understand your desire, fighter, and your concern. To rest your spirit, I tell you that no harm has come to her. She is in comfortable quarters, she has reading material, and she will be delivered safely unto you—if you win the bout with my champion."

"Does she know of my return, my lord?"

"She has so been informed." Jabin nodded. With the robe wrapped tightly against his throat, he leaned forward somewhat, looking intently at Dael. "Some men would consider you a fool of fools," the king remarked without rancor. "To risk all, your fortune, your very life, for a mere woman. Why"—he spread his palms outward—"a man such as you, with your wealth and fame, could have a hundred women from which to choose. Yet you prefer this one." As Dael's dark eyes looked into his unwaveringly, Jabin nodded briefly. "You need not answer. I think I understand. When it comes to women and affairs of heart and love, there is no telling what a man would do. Why, even I once——" he began, breaking off sharply. Once more he regarded Dael steadily.

"And if you lose—you will serve me willingly, so that I need not use force?"

"I have so promised, my lord."

Jabin nodded again, the coldness in his eyes melting for a moment, the blue becoming darker. "And I believe you, Dael ben Abinoam. Perhaps it would be better if you lost. As a soldier and fighter, you can serve Canaan well, perhaps even help bring peace in the land. If your people listen to you, and you hear my words, Israel and Canaan may yet be bound together in common unity against those who threaten from the borders. You could serve on my councils and plan with me against the enemies of Canaan who," he added in a stronger voice, "also are the enemies of Israel. Why does not Israel understand this?" he asked. "Why must Israel and Canaan be at sword's point? Together, Canaan with its armed might, Israel with its books and laws, we could——" Jabin looked down for a moment, rubbed his hands along the robe. When he met Dael's gaze again the king's features had resumed their normal appearance, the eyes cold, the mouth set and determined. "It is not my fashion to discuss politics and religion with fighters," he said shortly. "Go you back now with Ard to the barracks and commence your training. And in three weeks I will behold you again at the arena."

He raised his hands in dismissal as Ard and Dael bowed and began to back away from the throne.

When the news reached Achan of the terms and contents of the signed contracts and wagers made between Dael and Jabin, the shophet's rage knew no bounds.

Jabin must be mad! he stormed to himself when a minor court official had informed him that, if Dael won, both he and Deborah were free to do as they pleased. For a whole night he was unable to sleep, tossing on the pallet, creating schemes and plans in which to thwart Dael, casting them aside as being impractical, then once more searching his mind for other ideas. One thing was certain, he told himself. Dael and Deborah must not be freed. It was quite possible that they already knew of his conspiracy against Israel, his part in Abinoam's death——and thus represented a definite threat to his own life. But with Deborah and Dael defeated, living as prisoners of the king or being executed, Achan's work could go on.

It was at the dawn of another sleepless night that he finally found the scheme he thought best. Early morning saw him at Hazor again—not to visit the king—but to see Kashor, the chief trainer of the Bull of Bashan.

Kashor, a sour-faced man with grizzled white hair cropped close to the skull, gave reluctant time to the excited Achan. The shophet did not waste a moment.

"You want your fighter to win, do you not?" he asked quickly. "And there are many who say he cannot prevail over Dael. Look at the wager-making. It is almost even. The Egyptian officers of the garrison are confident that the Israelite will conquer. And they may be right. For look you, Kashor, this Dael has met the best of the champions in the Grecian islands, has fought many and great fighters. In experience alone he is the better man."

Kashor, who had secretly been worrying about that very factor himself, looked sharply at the shophet. "And just what have you in mind?" he finally asked.

"Certain victory for your fighter," Achan answered smoothly.

"I use no potions nor poisons," Kashor objected mildly. "Others might—but I——"

Achan's smile was broader, more understanding. "Who speaks of poisoning Dael before the fight?" he asked with mild indignation. "There are other ways in which none might suspect."

"And this way is?" Kashor asked carefully, never taking his eyes from the burly Israelite.

"The spiked cuff hidden in the glove," Achan whispered. He

watched Kashor's face for a reaction, was disappointed when the trainer's features remained impassive.

"And why not?" Achan said in a low tone. "The fight has been ordered to be a catch-as-catch-can one. You know what that means. Not only using the fists, but wrestling and kicking and biting and gouging. And during the heat of battle, should Og's hidden cuffs with the iron spikes on them rake Dael's face or crush his skull, who would know? You could remove the illegal cuff immediately after the battle."

Kashor rubbed his cheek thoughtfully. There was something to be said about the plan. In his own heart Kashor had begun to doubt whether Og could win. First of all, his fighter was older—and slower—than Dael. Secondly, Dael had more experience. Thirdly, Og had not been in training for consecutive periods, preferring the wineskins to the long hours of conditioning.

Of course the whole idea was risky. The spiked cuff, outlawed in Canaan, would never be tolerated by Jabin, who wanted a fair fight. If the king ever discovered that a cuff had been used . . . Still—Kashor's hand moved faster over his cheekbones and chin—who was to know? Just before the fight the cuff could be slipped under the thongs which had been wound over Og's palm. And once the combat was over, the cuff could just as swiftly and easily be removed. In view of the odds on the fight, of Og's own condition, Dael's training and experience, it might be worth while to try winning the bout by any means. Kashor thought of the bags of silver and gold rings he had himself wagered on Og and grew a little frightened.

He stopped his stroking hands. "Suppose I agree?" he asked softly. "How much?"

Achan's eyes blazed with anger. "How much?" he demanded hotly. "Do you not want your fighter to win? And yet you demand payment from me for suggesting a way of victory to you?"

"How much?" Kashor insisted quietly. "Remember this, Israelite. I train fighters, not for pleasure, but for gain. I make whatever I can and get what I can from anyone. Remember this, also. Suppose I approached Jabin and told him what you suggested here to me? How would that go with the monarch?"

Unsmilingly Kashor looked at Achan, who finally shrugged, snorted with disgust, and then said: "Four pieces of silver."

"Increase it to five"—Kashor smiled pleasantly now—"and we are partners in this business. After all," he said mockingly, "I have to pay for the illegal spiked cuff."

Dael entered his period of training in the three weeks allotted to him by Jabin with a spirit of grim determination. Luckily, the weather was turning colder, and this kept the fighter working harder to keep from being chilled.

Ard concentrated on running, shadowboxing whenever the sun shone, and footwork at all times. Once or twice a day he had Dael running backward, explaining that it was good to know how to do this, to keep away from a charging Og. Ard also supervised Dael's diet carefully, saw to it that he had enough sleep and rest. And in order to have the fighter worry as little about Deborah as possible, Ard had bribed a guard to bring to them, from time to time, news of her. The reports were good; she was well, the guard told them, and Dael had to be satisfied with that little.

They were lying on their mats one night, close to the end of the training period, when Ard asked idly, "And when you win over Og, Dael—what do you do then?"

"Think not I have not thought often of the future," Dael answered unhappily. "I know what I would like to do. I dream of taking Deborah with me to one of the islands, there to settle, work as a smith and find our happiness. But," he added moodily, "I know she will never consent. Not while the tribes of Israel are without unification and a leader."

Ard absently tugged at a loose reed in the mat. "The leader is no problem," he said without looking at the fighter. "It is no great secret that your name was brought out at the congress at Shiloh. True, you have not been approved, but in emergency leaders are quickly, and without too much questioning, chosen."

Dael, half sitting up, smashed his palm against the sleeping pallet. "Why must it ever be so?" he cried, his face getting stern with anger. "That I must be drawn into conflict, must always be thinking of fighting and be prepared to fight?"

He stared as Ard, whose face had become livid with emotion, arose and with hands on hips looked down upon the fighter. Never before had Dael seen such cold contempt, such bitter scorn, mixed with a headlong fury that raced over the trainer's features now.

"You fool! Fool!" Ard said, trying to control his voice. His fingers trembled as he lifted his hands, ran them over the tufts of hair, and lowered them once more to his hips. "For years I have locked my tongue in silence against your continuous tirades and whining about fighting. But now the bonds have burst. I can keep my speech within me no longer. Hear me, great champion of champions." He bowed mockingly at the surprised Dael. "Hear me and think and remember. Where would you now be were it not for your skill and strength as a fighter?" he demanded hotly. "Back in Kedesh, fearful of Achan, seeking solace in the cave from your books? As a mere scholar and smith, would you have been able to win the applause and favor of Jabin, and thus even be given a *chance* to fight for your woman? Without fighting would you have been able to reach the Nile and secure the money for your wagers? Suppose you had not killed Dargan that night? Or suppose you had gone down in defeat at Gibeah's torch? Think and remember —all you have won, all you are today, and all you hope to gain is only because you have fought. You cry out you want a peaceful land so you can practice your craft without fear or interruption. But I tell you this!" Ard stormed, his hands raised high in the air now, as if to bring them down upon Dael's head. "So long as warfare ravages the land and you must obey the commands of others, you will never labor at your forge without fear or in peace. For first, as it sometimes happens, you must have war before you can have peace. Ask of your father, blessed in name, who gave an eye and his life in his belief that Jehovah would fight until peace was won."

Exhausted, Ard dropped his arms and his head, sinking wearily down upon the pallet once more. "Forgive me," Dael heard him murmur, his voice coming as if from a far distance, "for having spewed out my wrath at you. But I could not prevent it. It was the first time. It was only that——"

Dael's arm slipped around the trainer's shoulders, the fingers digging into the hard flesh. "I have nothing for which to forgive you, old friend," the fighter said softly. "For, contrary to your belief, I am not a fool. Think you that similar thoughts have not plagued my sleep at night, that your words have not echoed and re-echoed a hundred times in my mind?" Dael took his hand away, looking down curiously at it. He bunched the fingers into a hard fist. "That you are right, I now know, perhaps have known for a long time, but was unwilling to accept or even admit to myself. It is good you have talked to me, Ard. Sometimes"—he smiled wistfully—"the words of another sting and drive toward a realization of the truth, more than one's own thoughts."

He took a deep breath and then, almost fiercely, curled the fingers of his left hand, the striking one, so that the knuckles bulged, hard and white, under the pressure. "So be it, then," he said softly, and to Ard it was almost like a vow. "With this hand I have won much, and may it be given me to win more with it."

And then, without further speech, he threw himself full length on the mat, staring silently up at the ceiling until slumber finally weighed his eyelids.

As the first roll of drums sounded outside the stadium of Hazor, the City of Chariots, Ard motioned for Dael to rise and stand for the final inspection in the dressing room, which was located to the rear and under the arches of the arena.

Ard's calculating eyes surveyed the gamor carefully, allowing no emotion of concern or doubt to film them. He had done all he could to prepare Dael for this day of battle, both physically and in spirit, and the rest was up to the fighter and Jehovah. Now the day—yea, the very hour of ordeal—was upon Dael, Ard thought. Twice more would the skin heads of the conical-shaped drums vibrate, and then their thundering summons would bring both fighters parading out into the sanded space before the expectant eyes and screaming throats of the thousands of spectators.

The trainer's gaze went over the body of Dael again, satisfied with the sleek shine the oils and powders gave it, with the closely shaven head and face. He quietly gestured at Dael to tighten the silvered string around his hips. Otherwise, according to the rules, the Lightning from Kedesh was naked. The spiraling strips of leather over knuckles and extending high up to the elbow were his only other covering. Moving closer to him, Ard tightened an end of thong, tugging on it, although he knew it was already well fastened. There was so much he still wanted to tell his fighter, and his mind raced, sorting out what should be revealed and what should not, and he wanted time.

"Remember this," Ard finally said. "The fight today will not be fought under island rules."

Dael nodded. "I have so been informed by many, including your own self."

"You know what that means?" Ard asked. "It will be a catch-as-catch-can battle. A fight not only with fists, but one in which wrestling is allowed, as well as biting and kicking and gouging and pinching. Beware, then, of close combat. Stay away from the Bull as much as you can."

Hopping nervously around on his toes, flexing his fingers, Dael nodded. He ducked, hunched his shoulders, and shot a fist out at an imaginary foe.

"There is little else I can tell you," Ard finished soberly, "save to pray that Jehovah watches over you this day and brings you victory."

Dael suddenly grinned at him. "And if I need Jehovah's help, I will ask for it," he said lightly. But Ard merely frowned as the sharp, rolling thunder of the drums shook the air in the room. Without a further word he picked up Dael's blue-and-gold-embroidered robe of white, throwing it about the fighter's shoulders, fastening the two edges of the collar with a large gold-coated pin. Arranging himself stiffly and carefully at Dael's side, the trainer waited for the third and final signal, a long, sustained series of drumbeats, this time pierced brazenly by trumpets.

"The time has come," Ard said, and, in step with Dael, started to march the few hundred yards to the middle of the arena. At the doorway two of the guards saluted them, their spear tips glittering yellow-red as they dipped into the sands.

Then the two men entered the place of combat.

Dael had long become accustomed to the sounds of crowds at fights before, but not even this experience had prepared him for the roaring, beating welcome that hammered down upon him from every side, that enveloped him and immersed him in an ocean of noise. Wave after wave of stentorian screams, high-pitched yelps, torn from the throats of women, slapped against his eardrums with dizzying force. The drums maintained their reverberating thunder, the trumpets growled in their brassy mouths. As they proceeded to the center of the arena, this clamor became louder, thicker, more insistent.

Only once did Dael look upward and around him to behold the heaving, turbulent mass of crowd. Only patches, squares, circles, and triangles of color met his blurred vision—ovals of pink or red or white faces, glistening flashes of purple, red, gold, or white of gown, blinding ripples of jewels, and at last—almost directly in front of him—the shaded, royal canopy under which sat Jabin and his general, Sisera. The weak breeze, trying to raise itself fitfully, moved in weary little puffs through the limp pennants that, like some multicolored beard, bristled on the lip of the stadium.

Before the canopy Dael and Ard stopped, pivoting sharply to their right, saluting smartly with upraised arms. Sisera and Jabin, also rising, returned the formal salute, remaining standing to await the appearance of Og. And from the suddenly heightened shouts and from Ard's quiet nudge, Dael knew that his famed opponent was approaching, along with his trainer, Kashor.

Red—was Dael's immediate impression of Og; the man is all red—red hair on chest like a brick-colored rug, on thighs and legs, and shining in auburn spots over the shaven skull. Red, too, was the face. Around the mighty arms were bound the strips of horse-hide, which had first been bleached of all color and then dyed a deep crimson. And the robe that lay on the shoulders was shadowed with scarlet.

"Red thongs," Dael heard Ard murmur, "So the blood won't show clearly on them." Inwardly he was thinking that, so far as physical advantages of height and weight were concerned, they were all in the Bull's favor. Og was taller than Dael by at least two inches, and the champion of Og easily outweighed the Naphtalite by twenty pounds. The torso was heavy, the neck small and muscled. And the arms were as large and round as a horse's haunch. Over all this Og's immense shoulders spread like some great blanket.

The Bull of Bashan and his trainer paid their respects to the king and commander of the armies. Then both fighters turned to face each other for the first time.

Dael was aware of a huge, red face, a bulbous nose with widely spread nostrils, and a loose, wet mouth. Then as Ard had done before him, Dael swiftly took inventory of Og's body. Only the legs seemed to be out of proportion, Dael pondered. True, thick and hard-muscled were the thighs, but they tapered down to weak ankles, while the calves of the legs themselves were roped with blue veins that stood out of the red skin. Dael sucked his underlip thoughtfully. In a catch-as-catch-can fight, those veins could be an asset to him.

The referee, bearing his thin wand of ivory topped with a gold head, saluted Jabin and then faced the fighters and their trainers, introducing them to the crowd by their names. Then the fighters made their vows to their gods, Og asking for protection from El and Anath, while Dael again sought the favor of his personal goddess, she of the lamps.

The trainers left the sanded area to the fighters, who again faced each other, with the official's staff laid lightly over their shoulders.

There was a sudden hush in which the referee's bellow: "To begin now!" was heard at the very top rows of the stadium.

As he stood easily in the approved island fighting position, Dael's eyes flickered over Og, who was crouched, his teeth already revealed in a snarl as he lunged forward. The great right arm of Og raised high and came down in a swooping, underhand arc. But Dael skipped aside, brushing past the hammer-like chop—but not swiftly enough. Og's fist grazed his side and a flash of pain came from Dael's ribs. Surprised at the sharpness of what should have been only a glancing blow, he looked down, seeing the four long scratches, one of them already deepening with red.

Og is using a cuff of iron spikes, Dael realized almost at once. Then a fuller meaning swept over him. This was no mere boxing bout. Og was determined to kill.

As he whirled out of the way of a second charge, he calculated his chances. He could of course protest to the referee and demand that Og's hands be examined for the hiden cuff. But by that time the Bull might have a chance to rid himself of the weapon, and Dael would be made to look like fool and coward. As for the scratches, Og could claim they were made by his nails and fingers. There was no other way open to Dael save to continue the fight, now against such desperate odds, he thought. His knees trembled suddenly, but he hardened his face with the iron of resolve, to give Og no inkling of the fear he felt.

One thing was certain. With Og's reach greater than his, with the spiked cuff cleverly palmed in the hand, it would be folly to engage in long-range blows with the Bull of Bashan. The only way, the most certain way, Dael thought savagely, would be to bore in closely to Og, under those powerful, flailing arms, and hammer at heart and belly. Or the muscles of the arms, making them hurt so much that Og would drop his guard. But that, too, was edged with danger. While getting close to and under Og's fists, the Bull could easily slam down one of those great hams he had for hands, with the hidden knuckle bracelet on it, and cut his neck to shreds.

Skipping and dancing out of the way of Og's continued, bull-like charges, Dael reviewed old lessons, sorted out in his memory faded experiences of other fights. He remembered the weak spots of an attacker: the great vein under the left ear and on the throat; the sinew under armpit, which, when tightly pinched, could bring unconsciousness; the quick grind of a foot on the opponent's in-step; the cut, made with the edge of the hand, at the left side of the skull or on the apple of the throat, the thumb and forefingers, which could be used as pincers or wrenchers . . .

Cautiously he backed away from still another lunge of Og, who stopped, sliding his thick neck between the shoulders, and then straightened to his full height. Deliberately and with naked de-rision, he gestured to Dael to fight. Then he turned to the specta-tors, as if to appeal to them to force the combat to go on. Og spread his hands wide in a dramatic gesture.

And Dael took instant advantage of the theatricals of Og.

He struck like an angered serpent, his right arm stabbing at Og's face. As the Bull ducked, bringing both arms around his head, his heaving abdomen was exposed long enough for Dael to whip his left hand twice into the bellow-like ribs. With a howl of pain Og straightened out now, lowering his guard, his hands dropping briefly.

In the silence of the stadium the thudding, slapping sounds of the blows could cleanly and clearly be heard. Three times did the man from Kedesh smash his left hand into the face of the cham-pion of Bashan. Against his exposed thumb and over his fingers, Dael felt the jar of the blows, the sudden, hot spurt of Og's blood. He saw the giant reel back, his throat moving skyward, the mouth lacerated and spouting scarlet. A tooth, hanging by a thread of flesh, wobbled against the lips, broke off, and fell on the sands.

The packed tiers heaved into sudden life and rocked with screams and applause.

Back—back went Og, his heels digging into the sand, breaking the backward impetus of his body. Like the lightning after which he had been named, Dael lashed out unmercifully now, his arms moving in rapid, streaking blurs of brown. The Bull sagged, weaved once, but then recovered his balance, his arms flung wide to aid him. As Dael rushed upon him, one of the great thighs projected sideways, hitting the fighter from Israel, upsetting his balance. Dael felt himself sprawling on all fours. Instantly he sprang up again, prepared to meet any charge from Og, but the latter was using that moment to rest, making no effort to attack.

For a moment both men circled each other warily. Then, breathing heavily, his head lowered once more, Og rushed at Dael. The Bull's arm was raised again for the chopping downward swing. Stepping nimbly to his left, Dael avoided the blow, counterattacking with a smash of his own to the giant's head. Dael's arms went numb to the elbow from the impact with hard bone, and he winced with pain. His right hand momentarily hung useless. And, noticing this, Og screamed once, slid forward, and with all his strength brought his weaponed right fist down upon Dael's head.

He was hardly aware of pain at first. Then a giant circle of flame blazed before his eyes, starting to move, faster and faster, in dizzying, gyrating sparks of fire. He did not feel himself fall, could not hear the horrified and yet delighted roar of the crowd. He was aware only of the taste of sand against his opened mouth and of the blood that dripped into it from his wounded head.

Dael gasped with exploding breath as Og hurled himself upon him, the giant's hands already seeking his eyeballs, his knees thrusting and kicking at Dael's groin. The Israelite, with slowly returning strength, began to twist and squirm, writhing to get away from the cruelly searching fingers, the probing knee. Dael bridged himself into an arc, then lowered his body and flipped it around, hoping in this way to unseat the Bull. But Og held on grimly, one hand now pressing against Dael's throat, the other still jabbing at the eyes.

Muscles swelled and quivered on the bodies of both gladiators In harsh, choking agony, Ard—standing white-faced on the sidelines of the sanded square—saw Og slowly gain supremacy, finally forcing Dael to be spread-eagled on the ground. The Bull's thighs were around Dael's ribs, pressing together in excruciating pain. The jutting fingers, still unable to find the target of the eyes, relaxed.

But the right hand of Og—with the cuff now clearly visible to those who knew of such things—raised itself high to strike down into Dael's face.

The Lightning flicked neck and head back and forth, desperately trying to avoid the coming blow. As Og tried to hold him down and quiet the darting head, his left hand had to ease its pressure. Sensing more than feeling this sudden decrease of weight on his throat, Dael thrashed his body to the left and right more furiously, while his toes and heels dug frenziedly into the sand, puffing up little balls of golden grains which the rising wind scattered in all directions. Finally the Israelite found the foothold he had sought. With every trembling sinew of his tortured body his thighs standing out like great corded sheets of leather, Dael heaved upward, bridging his body in a gigantic thrust.

"May Jehovah help me now!" he moaned between set teeth, the sweat and blood bitter on his lips. He had no time to be surprised at the prayer which had been wrenched from him. He had spoken without thought, without reflection, calling upon aid from the only source he had never before sought.

Slowly, as if drawn up by a sling, Og's body rose with Dael's as the Bull rode him awkwardly and clumsily, frantically trying to cling to the quivering flesh below him. Straining and heaving, his ribs pumping with breath, Dael shivered and then, with a last surge of strength, threw the Bull from him.

Og fell forward, sprawling on his face, and before he could right himself, Dael was upon him. The Israelite seized Og's mouth with his fingers and began to pry the lips open, determined to rip the huge jaws apart. As a fish out of water, Og began to flip and writhe to and fro, his knees doubled under him. Fastened against the Bull's thigh, Dael suddenly saw the throbbing ribbon of blue-edged vein of Og's legs below him, saw the giant's cuffed fist opening and closing helplessly near the limb. Furiously Dael seized the spiked and useless fist, twisted it backward so that the sharp, iron points rested against the fullness of the vein.

Then, with breath that whistled weirdly through his nostrils, Dael began to press the razor-sharp spikes against the vessel of life.

With all the force and strength of his body Dael began to bore the metal into flesh. Through his half-glazed eyes he saw the teeth begin their deadly, sawing bit, saw Og's flesh whiten, stared as the tiny depressions sank deeper and deeper, until they seemed to become part of the vein itself. Lifting Og's hand, Dael savagely raked it again and again over the vein, seeing it burst open, white-edged, quickly becoming streaked with scarlet.

Og quivered but once, his entire body rising in a last and terrible spasm before it sagged back to the saturated sands again, saturated by his own life stream, which flowed out of him from the torn and jagged slash in the vein.

When he no longer felt Og move, Dael, half crawling, half kneeling, began to rise to his feet. Blood curtained his face and chin. Once he weaved, caught himself, and continued to rise. Ard, taut and ready, knew he could not approach Dael until the fighter stood on his own feet and was touched in victory by the staff of the referee.

And it seemed that the very heavens were split apart by the roar from the stadium as the hero from Kedesh remained on his feet and was touched on the shoulder by the referee as the victor. Nor did he stop there. Although Ard was already half supporting him, Dael bent down, removed the bloodied cuff from the corpse of Og, and unsteadily walked to the royal canopy.

Without speaking, he held out the spiked bracelet, his eyes

accusing Jabin. But the monarch's own gaze lay quietly and calmly upon the gladiator.

"I know," Jabin said slowly. "I, too, saw the cuff on Og when he tried to kill you with it. This, however, is not of my doing. I speak to you as a man, Dael ben Abinoam, and not as a king. I have ordered Kashor arrested, and we will learn the truth from him."

Silently Dael faced him. He dropped the bloodied cuff to the ground. Then, after several attempts to speak, his lips finally moved.

"The woman," his voice croaked. "Where is she?"

Jabin nodded, signaled to one of the officers at his back, and before he sank to the ground in dark and blessed senselessness, Dael caught a brief glimpse of the butter-colored hair shining in the sun. . . .

17

WHEN he could open his eyes again, the first thing they beheld were the worried and anxious faces of Deborah and Ard hovering over him. As he recognized them, as his mouth tried to form words, Deborah placed her hand over his lips. "If you are able to hear me, beloved," he heard her say, "nod your head."

Weakly the muscles of his neck obeyed, and he saw the tension in the features lighten somewhat. Deborah, kneeling beside the mat upon which he now lay, moved her hand from his lips, to his cheeks and over his head. He winced with a sudden twinge of pain that resulted from her touch and, with feeble fingers, felt his skull and the tightly wrapped cloths around it.

"I always said you had a hard head"—Ard was trying to smile—"and you have proved it. Fear not. You will recover. The iron spikes caused no really serious damage."

Dael nodded weakly. And this time words made their way to his tongue. "How long have I been thus?" he asked.

"Two days," Ard replied. "And you are back in Golan." As he saw the surprised look flicker in Dael's eyes, Ard went on easily: "It was Deborah's plan. For, although Jabin was a man of honor, kept his word, returned Deborah and the winnings to you, it was still felt you would be safer away from his presence. Sometimes even kings change their minds. So you were taken here, in the ancient old temple of the serpent goddess. Here you will be safe until the strength returns to you."

For a time he looked at each one carefully, his gaze dwelling longest on Deborah, seeing the shadows under her eyes, the drawn lines of her face, symbol of her imprisonment and the mental ordeal she must have gone through. Then his look swept back to Ard.

"And the matter of the cuff?" he asked, his voice stronger now, slowly heated by anger at what had happened.

Ard smiled wryly. "Ah, the cuff!" he remarked. "That bracelet has already caused the death of two men. Og and his trainer, Kashor."

"Kashor too?" Dael asked.

Ard nodded, rubbing his nose. "Kashor was arrested almost as soon as Jabin saw the cuff. Under torture the trainer confessed he had persuaded Og to use it. And just before he died Kashor also confessed that the entire scheme of using the cuff had been born in Achan's mind."

"Achan?"

"The same." Ard nodded. "Thus Jabin immediately ordered the arrest of the shophet as well. He is now a most unwilling house guest of the king. What plans Jabin has for him, none know. But one thing is certain. Actually, Jabin's arrest of Achan is a sort of sanctuary for the judge. For Deborah has released unto all of Israel his name as a traitor and a spy and the instigator of the death of Abinoam. Perhaps that is why Jabin keeps close watch on Achan, knowing that if the judge ever were given his freedom he would be slain by righteous men of Israel."

As Deborah saw Dael try to understand and assimilate all the news and facts, as she realized how confusing and difficult it must be for him now, she rose to her feet. "Leave him to rest, Ard," she said. "Then later we shall talk more of these matters." Tenderly she looked down upon Dael, smiled at him, placed her fingertips over his mouth, and then walked out of the old temple chamber. Ard, lingering behind, winked at Dael. "She is right," the trainer said. "Rest you, eat with appetite and regain your strength. Then we will exchange further words between us."

Aided by rest and sleep and Deborah's care as a nurse, with her herbs and poultices that were placed on his head wounds—and probably most of all by the sheer presence of her around him at all times—Dael began a steady and rapid improvement.

Within two days he was able to forsake the hot lentil soup, in which fat chunks of bread floated, for more solid nourishment of meat and fish. Soon the headaches and nausea left him, and he was able to have breakfasts of fruits and milk and honey-smeared corn cakes. By the end of the week he was clamoring to sit up, and in another day he begged to be allowed to totter along the stone floor.

As his strength returned, as the bandages on his head lightened and the skin formed over the wounds again, he tried—time and time again—to speak to Deborah of her future plans, of the coming struggle with Jabin, of the tribes and the leadership. But each time she would either smile at him and bid him wait and be patient or refuse to discuss the matter entirely. "There will be time later," was all she said.

But on the day when his last bandage was removed and his walk was brisk and steady again, he turned to face her. "But I must know what the future holds for us," he pleaded. "If there is to be battle—it must soon begin. For it is Kislev already, the month of rain, and rain will help us to fight the chariots of Jabin."

Soberly she looked at him. "Then you have had the same thoughts as I? That the rain will bring mud, and the mud will mire the chariots and render them helpless?"

"Yes," he answered quickly. "It is the only way we can overcome the odds against us. As soon as the plains are drenched enough, Israel must strike."

They were seated below the statue of the serpent goddess. It was night, and only a single lamp on the floor flooded its pool of light around them. Deborah reached for his hand, entwining her fingers in it. "It eases my heart," she confided softly, bringing his palm up to her mouth, "to hear your words. I had thought that perhaps you——" She did not finish.

"That I what?" he prompted, moving closer to her now, aware of the scent and warmth of her body, of the nearness of her. A slow excitement began to beat in his blood.

"That you cared not about Israel."

He laughed lightly. His arm slipped around her shoulders, bringing her still closer to him as she yielded to his touch. Her face looked up at him, the eyes half closed. "I tell you this, Deborah. When I thought Og was about to slay me, I called upon Jehovah to help me."

She nodded quickly. "I know. For so Ard, too, informed me. He heard your cry."

"Then why do you doubt?" he asked gently.

Her eyes closed. "Because I still do not know. A man in despair of his life may pray to a god for aid. And then, after it is given, may forget about it."

He made no answer to that, merely holding her tighter, feeling her move still closer against him, snuggling into his arms and sighing softly. "And what of the tribes?" he asked. "Have they chosen a leader?"

He felt her shrug. "It is a mere formality. All they wait for is your word that you will lead them. There is no choice, for there is none other so qualified. That is why I wanted you to wait before you made up your mind, to give you time."

"And you, Deborah, would you want me to lead?" And this time he looked down upon her and saw her nod swiftly.

"Then I so will," he said simply. "For you. Because *you* want me to do it." He smiled. As she looked up at him, startled, not quite sure she had heard correctly, she opened her lips as if to say something, as if to protest. But he was speaking again, one hand reaching into the waistband of his kilt. When he withdrew it, she sat up, staring at what his hand held out to her, her eyes opening wide at the golden bracelet with the tiny lamps on it.

Her hands trembled as she allowed him to encircle her wrist with the metal. She held the bracelet up to the light to inspect it closer, and her breath caught in admiration. The tiny lamps jingled pleasantly.

"Dael . . ." she finally was able to say. "It must have cost a fortune. The workmanship alone is——"

"Of my own." He smiled at her. "I made it for you in Egypt. Have it to wear always and to remember me."

The gray in her eyes darkened as she reached up to him, brought her arms around his neck and forced his face down to meet her lips. When they parted for breath, she whispered, "To remember you? I need no trinkets to remember you, Dael. I need only——"

But then it seemed to both of them that the quiet calm of their being together was suddenly ripped apart by a stroke of lightning that not only flooded them with heat and desire but seemed to weld them together in a single, unlooked-for flash of passion. They had not expected this, had perhaps not even consciously thought of it. But in that single heartbeat of time they were in each other's arms, lying side by side at the feet of the serpent goddess. He felt her arms tighten around his neck, her fingers run softly through the short-cropped hair.

"Dael, Dael . . ." she whispered. "Oh, Dael, I love thee."

He turned and bent over her, his heartbeats loud in his ears now as he let his lips roam over her hair, her forehead, down her cheeks, kissing the corners of her mouth. "Deborah. Deborah . . ." he was saying, his voice thick with the sudden miracle of it. "I have loved thee all this time but never fully knew it, never——"

Her fierce kiss stopped his words, and she withdrew her mouth only to utter, half moaning, "And thee love I. . . . Oh, thee love I, Dael."

And from above, the wise and silent stone eyes of the serpent goddess of Canaan watched them impassively as they repeated the familiar scene she had beheld countless times before, in other years, in other lands, but always with the same beginning and the same, ultimate ending.

And now, too, the only sound in the chamber was the metallic jingling of the tiny lamps of the bracelet.

As Deborah had suggested, the choice of Dael ben Abinoam as the leader of Israel against Canaan was a mere formality. The reason was one of simple necessity. There was no other man better qualified to head the tribes.

Thus, within a week, Nun and Jair of the tribes of Ephraim and Issachar visited Dael at Golan, solemnly conferring the leadership upon him, promising him aid and remaining for two days to discuss the plan of battle with him and Deborah.

"Our only hope, my lords," Dael said gravely to them, "is to wait for the heavy rainfall that the month of Kislev is sure to bring—rainfall which will turn the earth into mud and which will mire the chariots of Jabin. Then will Israel swoop down upon the Canaanites, catch their helpless, immobilized chariots, hamstring their mounts, killing and driving them back to the banks of the River Kishon."

"Why there?" Nun asked with interest, looking up at Dael from the map the latter was drawing on the ground.

"For this reason." Dael's finger tapped the wavy line that indicated the course of the Kishon. "The river is near Harosheth. There Jabin will make his headquarters. From Harosheth he can control the entire Plain of Esdraelon, where he will fight with his chariots. But—when the Canaanites are driven back to Harosheth, they will find the River Kishon to be swollen with the waters of the rain, flood-swollen so that the very Kishon itself will act as a barrier against our fleeing enemy."

"And where will Israel gather?" Jair asked.

Dael indicated two sections of the map. "Israel will strike from two separate places, and at different times," he said crisply. "The northern tribes of the Benzi factions—mainly Naphtali, Issachar, Zebulon, and Western Manasseh—will gather here"—he pointed—"at Mount Tabor. The southern tribes of the coalition, Benjamin and Ephraim, will gather at Taanach, at the south bank of the Kishon. First Benjamin and Ephraim will strike hard at Sisera's and Jabin's chariots, which will be on the Plain of Esdraelon. Then, when the Canaanites least expect it, the northern tribes will storm down from the mountain of Tabor and join in the conflict."

Both Nun and Jair nodded with approval, but Deborah, despite

Dael's calm confidence and scheming, looked worried. True, she thought, the plan was of sound military value, using an attacking force, reserves, surprise, and taking advantage of the weather. But was that enough for victory? she pondered. Could a battle be won on technical and tactical planning alone? Where was the vital spark of idealism, of dedication to a cause, of belief? Dael had, so far, shown none of these. He was planning the battle as he would a combat in the arena. She bit her lip. It was not enough. Not enough at all. A man could lose a battle if the planning went wrong and if he had no spirit, no belief or dedication. To be sure, Dael had said he would undertake the leadership. But she knew why.

Because he was doing it for her.

Not for Israel, not for Jehovah, not for peace—but merely because he wanted to please her and had promised her. It was like giving her a gift, as he had given her the bracelet. But what if the planning bore no fruit? What if the odds against Israel, great as they were, became even more helpless? How would a leader, without dedication or spirit of purpose or ideal react then?

Oh, she thought to herself, if I could only show him, really make him feel that what he is doing is not to please me but to bring peace to the land and to end warfare for all time between Canaan and Israel. If I could only convince him that Jehovah, as a god of peace, has to use war to achieve his end. But how, how, how? her mind, like a clanging bell, kept ringing in her ears.

"Does Israel gather, then, in secrecy?" Nun was asking.

Dael grinned crookedly at him. "No," he said shortly. "No attempt at secrecy will be made. Let the tribes gather openly at their camps on Mount Tabor and at Taanach. In this way Sisera will have to bring his chariots into the open and then wait for *us*. He will have his vehicles come up from the west, from the shadow of Mount Carmel. Then he will have to wait, not knowing whether to attack the Israelites at Taanach, not knowing what the men on Mount Tabor will do. Naturally he cannot send chariots up the mountain of Tabor to fight Israel there."

Again Nun and Jair nodded in agreement. And finally the elder of Ephraim spoke and promised that his warriors would start to gather as soon as he returned. Jair echoed the promise, speaking also for the men of Benjamin and Zebulon and Western Manasseh. As for Naphtali, since Dael was of that tribe, it went without saying that he would lead them.

Thus, before another week went by, the men of Issachar, Zebulon, Naphtali, and Western Manasseh and their families, their wives and children, gathered on the slopes of Mount Tabor and there made their encampment. And with them they also brought up from Shiloh the Ark of the tablets of the Ten Commandments, which always went into battle with Israel.

While the southern tribes of Benjamin and Ephraim—led by the fiery Obed—were slower in their gathering, they, too, kept it no secret, with the result that Jabin's general, Sisera, nervously began to concentrate his chariot forces at Harosheth, determined to meet the Israelites on the Plain of Esdraelon and defeat them and drive them from the land.

Slowly Deborah led Dael down the narrow trail which wound its way to the encampment of Israel on Mount Tabor. The battle, she knew, was but one day—perhaps two at the most—away. The rains had come and the pores of the plain had opened to receive the waters from the sky. Already the normally dry and flat land now was soggy and heavy with the rainfall, mud lay thick over everything, and here and there the earth had sagged under the weight of the fall of rain, creating huge pits and craters. The footing was treacherous, the scouts had reported. Another day of downpour, and Israel would be ready to strike. Deborah took a quick glance at the sky above and breathed a little prayer that all she could see were the low, fat, scudding clouds that hovered ominously over all.

Slowly Dael became aware of the stir of life and the throb and hum of domestic activities around them in the pitched tents or in the natural shelters of caves. As they moved downward, he caught glimpses of family life—here a woman bent over the mortar and pestle of her mill, pounding the corn or barley that would make tomorrow's bread, there a man blowing upon the flames of a small fire, a group seated around an eating mat. Snatches of song, the soft insidious tinkle of the *kinnor* harp and the exotic, lonely wail of wooden flute floated up lazily to them.

At first Dael had debated the virtues of having the warriors accompanied to the mountain by their families. But he had finally decided that to leave them alone in their homes, unprotected, at the mercy of Sisera's raiders, would not only endanger their lives but would fill the spirits of their men with doubt and anxiety. So he had agreed that the wives and children accompany the fighters.

Thicker and more profuse grew the temporary homes and the people who now dwelled in them. Around Dael there swirled the odors of cooking, hot and savory goat's flesh being roasted, the aroma of freshly baked bread, the vinegary pungence of wine. In a small tent a dark-haired mother was nursing her babe, while near her another mother was shoveling food, piled high on a bone spoon, into the smeared and gurgling mouth of an older child.

"The children are everywhere!" Dael mused.

"And why not?" came Deborah's soft answer. "Whom but for the children do we fight? So that their generation may have the peace that ours did not?"

He looked quizzically at her, wondering at a hidden meaning in her answer, whether there was anything personal in it, then decided not to explore further.

When he said he had seen enough of the camp and was satisfied as to its location, she urged him forward. "Only a few paces more," she said, pointing to a wide and unguarded space to their right. There is something I most desire for you to behold." She wet her lips nervously. "The Ark," she added.

He stiffened with surprise, his glance touching hers hotly. "The Ark!" he finally burst out. "What need is there for me to see it?"

"There is need, Dael. You are the chosen leader of Israel," she answered. And in her mind she added: *Chosen but not yet dedicated.* Still, she began to pull him forward, but his feet remained rooted against the stones of the trail. She continued to tug at him and, to gain time, he asked, "Why is not the Ark guarded?"

Deep in her throat the laugh arose, then died as quickly as it had sprung into life. "Because there is no need for man to guard the Ark. For what greater protection than the power of Jehovah Himself can there be?"

Slowly she led him into the open enclosure. There Dael saw a portable tent shrine of the kind he had seen on the walls of certain houses in Memphis that had the picture writing on them. As he neared it, he saw that it was made of ram's skin dyed red, with a domed roof, and large enough to hold two or three persons. As he hesitated, Deborah confidently swung aside the low-hanging canopy and waited for Dael. "Fear not," she encouraged him, "for the Lord is here, and with thee as well."

She pushed him forward gently, and Dael, stopping slightly, entered the interior, surprised to find little more in there than a single lamp, suspended from a pole, blazing heartily against the darkness of the corners of the sanctuary. Directly under the lamp, in the center of the portable shrine, stood a squared box with four rings on each corner.

"For the carrying poles," Deborah explained, pointing to the circlets of metal, "and constructed by some of our finest craftsmen. See for yourself." Her hand indicated the cover of the box, which, Dael noticed at once, gleamed a dull yellow.

"It is made of pure, beaten gold," she went on, "as are these two images."

Dael's interest quickened immediately. As a worker in metals, not as a leader or fighter now, he bent forward, his hands already running with loving and knowing knowledge over the smooth surface which, despite the coolness of the night, still appeared warm to him.

His fingers touched a pair of small statuettes, child-faced and fruited with spread wings, which hovered over the lid. The two little figurines were deftly molded into the gilded cover of the chest of cedarwood by their entwined feet.

"But one is broken!" he exclaimed sharply, pointing to the left wing of one of the cherubim, which had a crack in it and seemed to droop.

Her smile was wan in the pale light. "Remember you how once I spoke of this?" she recalled. "I said then that the Ark needed mending and that no craftsman had been found who could make the repairs."

He nodded, concentrating on the metal figures. It really would not be hard to do, he mused. First to melt the wing off, then shape it carefully to the right size, and then, with infinite care, mold it back onto the body again. Perhaps he would even place the wing a little higher, to make it look more protective, more defiant.

Dael felt Deborah's hand on his. "Now," came her hushed voice, "take your hand and open the lid and gaze within. Come, fear not. With my hand on yours you will open the Ark."

She felt his fingers tremble, then steady themselves as they found the edge of the lid and lifted—slowly, carefully, until the golden cover stood upright on rigid hinges. Together, the close-cropped head close to the butter-haired one, they bent over the box. All Dael could see inside the Ark were two large stone tablets about three feet in length and a foot wide.

"Reach within, take them out and read," she urged. And with a sudden confidence he had not felt before, he obeyed her. He found the tablets stone-cold to his touch. Carefully he brought them out, hugging them to his chest, greatly fearing that he might drop one and shatter it to bits. Deborah, a strange smile on her lips, took one of the flat stones from him. The other he brought closer to the suspended lamp.

"Read, Dael."

He concentrated on the letters which were carved in a beautiful and archaic style. Then, as the phrases combined in familiar groups before his eyes, he began to read in a voice that grew louder and stronger as he mouthed each syllable.

His voice never faltered as he read the Commandments of the covenant made between Jehovah and Moses, how Jehovah was the one and only God and there could be no others but He, how no images of Jehovah should be carved for worship, and His name not to be invoked for evil intent, how to remember the seventh day for Him and keep it holy.

" 'Honor thy father and mother, that you may live long in the land the Lord your God is giving you,' " his voice rang, and then faltered as he remembered Abinoam, his father, and how he had died. *And have I honored him?* he asked himself. He paused. He had come to the bottom of the first tablet. But before he could reach out for the second one in Deborah's arms, her own voice, beautiful in its trained and poetic expression and phrasing, went on for him.

" 'Thou shalt not commit murder.'

" 'Thou shalt not commit adultery.'

" 'Thou must not steal.'

" 'Thou must not bring a false charge against your neighbor.' "

And she finished with the laws that forbade the coveting of a neighbor's wife, his male or female slave, his ox, ass, or anything that was of his possession. And when she had concluded, she gently took the tablet, replaced it within the Ark, while Dael did the same with his. He closed the lid tenderly, his eyes dark with thought.

"Of what you found here, or what you read, does it appear to you that Jehovah is nothing but another blood-smeared war god?" she demanded quietly. "Does a god of war speak thus, and in such terms? Does a war god forbid murder and false witness and theft and adultery and coveting? In what you read was there only blood lust? Do you really believe that Jehovah, who inspires such a philosophy of life as revealed in the commandments, can be nothing but a savage deity of fierce desert tribesmen?"

He made no answer, his head bowed.

"More than that is Jehovah," she insisted. "A whole world will someday live according to the concepts you have seen enscribed here. Jehovah is more than a mere tribal god; He is for *all* to share. And to love. For, yes, Jehovah is a god of love," she continued softly. "You know the phrase. 'In the image of God He created him. Male and female created He them,'" she whispered. "Hear me, Dael. For in those two words 'male and female' speaks the essence of Jehovah. For Jehovah speaks of love now, of love between man and woman and for the children that are born from such unions of love. Therefore, Jehovah is a god of love and so shall forever be for all mankind. Not of war, Dael, but of love. . . ."

He lifted his head and looked at her. For some time now, perhaps since his return from Egypt, he had longed to tell her that he thought she was right. But perhaps pride and stubbornness had tied his tongue with thongs of silence.

His hand caressed the Ark. "Why?" he asked, more of himself than of her, "do the words of the Commandments seem so different now? I knew them, had read them before. But now, at this time . . ." His voice, soft with wonder, faded.

Deborah made no vocal answer at first, her eyes cast downward, with only the insect-shaped eyebrows raised high. A slight smile trembled on her mouth. But when she spoke, she looked at him. "Perhaps," she answered, "you had to live the words before you could understand them."

Slowly he nodded. She was right. Call Him what you might, Jehovah the god of war, or the god of peace, the fact remained that, because of love for this woman, he, Dael, had gone through many ordeals gladly and was prepared to face more. It came upon him again, as it had when Ard's bitter words had lashed at his conscience, that it was necessary to fight first for the love, or peace, a man desired. I know now, he admitted in silent and rueful thought, that I cannot live aloofly in a world, I cannot be an island, not to partake of events and affairs which will lead to a better life for all. No man can so live alone. If I fight for Jehovah, the god of war, so that He may become a god of peace, I will have shared in the struggle of all mankind and shall share in the fruits that later must come.

Deborah was beginning to move out of the sanctuary when he stopped her. "I wait here," he said, his hands running over the broken wing of one of the cherubim. "Have fetched for me a strong hand bellows and a fine chisel. And order a hot fire built for me outside." He grinned at her amazed expression.

"The broken wing," he explained. "I would repair it so it may fly high in victory for Jehovah. . . ."

18

LATER it was told by those who remembered, and mouthed and repeated by countless generations, until it was finally enscribed in the books of the land, that Jehovah had been pleased and gratified that Dael had laid his gifted and gentle craftsman's hands on the Ark of the Lord. For otherwise, asked the chronicles, would Jehovah have opened the heavens that very night and sent forth such a downpour as had never before been beheld by the eyes of man?

For hours the rain never stopped, and with it Jehovah also hurled his lightning bolts, his crashing thunder, the whistling wind, and even great icy stones of hail that shrieked as they rent the sodden clouds and buried themselves in the soggy earth of the plan with great splashes of mud that curtained the scene. And where these hailstones nosed into the soft and yielding ground, other spouts of water streamed upward, so it was as if the rain poured from both above and from within the earth itself. The great plain became riddled with pits, and where there were no depressions on the land, the mud was like a treacherous, clinging sea of brown.

And there were those who huddled in fear that night as the rain and hail drummed against the tent walls or on the stone shelters, and whispered that Jehovah, the God of Israel, and Hadad the weather deity of Canaan, were already locked in a personal, mighty combat of their own.

And when the dawn lanced the eastern horizon, hardly able to pierce the thick, rain-sodden clouds that scudded close to the earth—clouds that were borne on the high wind—Dael ben Abinoam, he who was known as Barak, knew the time for battle was at hand.

He did not need a grim Obed, leader of the Benjamite and Ephraimite forces, already encamped at the south shore of the Kishon, to meet him and tell him the plain was in an almost untenable position and that the river was rising furiously all along its banks.

By the end of the first watch of morning, Obed returned to his men with instructions to select those who were fit for battle and to march openly out on the level ground, where Sisera's scouts would see them, report them, and bring the chariots into the open for the battle.

As Obed returned to the southern camp, Dael ordered his captains and lieutenants gathered unto him to begin the selection of the warriors. In a small valley, part of a cuplike depression grooved against the flank of Mount Tabor, Dael commanded that the northern tribes stand before him for the battle selection. And the men of Naphtali, Issachar, Zebulon, and Western Manasseh heard and obeyed. Under their banners, damp and heavy with water, but still wind-whipped proudly, they stood, the warriors who were this day to meet the might of Jabin and Sisera.

Standing on a low edge of rock, Dael again beheld the banners—the flag of Ephraim, with the single horn on the goat bobbing and darting in the wind; the pennant of Manasseh, the half tribe of the son of Joseph, with its bull's image nodding at the goat; the symbol of Zebulon, its twelve-oared, bird-shaped boat rocking in the gusts; the sign of Issachar, the strong old man, bearded and bent under his pack, but all-eternal, all-wise.

And proudest of all the flags, it seemed to Dael now, was that of Naphtali, of his own tribe and his own people and of his own blood. Great artistry had gone into the creation of that banner, the leaping gazelle who freely and joyously sprang under the protecting rays of a crimson-and-gold sun. The gazelle leaps to freedom, he thought, with proud and quickening heart, a freedom we shall this day wrest from the iron jaws of Canaan.

Yet he knew that under the cold and impersonal scrutiny of any man of war the situation of Israel could be considered hopeless, even with the rain. Nine hundred chariots and twenty thousand of Jabin's best fighters awaited only nine thousand of the warriors of Israel. Canaan was fruitful with horses, vehicles, weapons of bronze and iron, spears, bows, axes, javelins, swords, while Israel had little more than clubs, stones, a few swords, some meager supplies of bows and arrows, flint knives, boomerangs.

And faith . . .

Faith that they would win, that they must win to preserve their integrity, their very way of life, to continue existing, to save the land and keep the peace for their children and their children's children for all time.

But was faith, an ideal enough? Would that be strong enough to hammer down the iron chariots, break through the sturdy shields of Jabin?

Almost unseeingly he stared before him. They *must* believe, his intellect told him, just as he himself now believed. He had come to the road of faith after a long and indifferent detour. But if he did not believe—believe that in Jehovah would be found peace, even if it meant war first—would he be here now? And would the others be with him? They, too, must share the same convictions. There were no mercenaries among the men of Israel. They had come willingly and without coercion. The farmers and the laborers, the artisans and craftsmen and the scribes and poets and musicians had all come when they had been summoned. No officers had, at sword's point, forced them into combat. Even now those who might be faint of heart were free to leave when the selections began. And men who came to fight willingly, he thought, his resolve strengthening, could not easily be defeated.

And there was more, he pondered. For the first time in the history, for the really first, recorded time, the tribes of Israel were uniting against a common foe. True, the great Joshua had invaded the land, but he had come with no great and summoned army; his military achievements had been more in the nature of quick, guerrilla-like raids, infiltrations and the conquest of certain Canaanite settlements. And with him had been no single and unified fighting cohort, merely parts of tribes, of wanderers, of men even foreign to Israel who had attached themselves to the invaders. But now Israel—at least half of it—stood together against the foe, stood as an army, as an individual host. And perhaps, he thought, it was the start, the beginning of many such armies until Israel would be mighty and ready to resist any and all who threatened it. Perhaps in future centuries men would point to this day and say to their children:

"It started then. . . ."

He straightened his shoulders, glanced at his captains. "Let the selections begin," he ordered quietly. He stepped aside as three musicians, lifting the rams' horns to their lips, blew the blasts that rolled and echoed and were hurled against the mountain and then returned to the ears of all. Only dimly he heard the laws of the selection being mouthed by the captains. Those men who had built a new house and had not yet dedicated it, those who had planted a new vineyard or who had a new wife, still virgin, those who were fearful and faint of heart were commanded to step forward and be excused from warfare.

Dael's eyes stung with pride as not a single man stood forth to be counted. He knew, as well as did his officers, that many among the Israelites could have met the requirements but refused. For, he understood now, what good were houses and vineyards and wives and children if there was no peace, if all could be destroyed or taken away?

He stood with the others as the priests and Levites made the dedications to Jehovah and sanctified the fighters for battle. Then, as the sacrifices began, he strode from the ledge, seeking Deborah, finding her huddled against a rock. She was wearing a robe of light wool, and around her shoulder was strapped an inkhorn that swung from her right hip. In the wide belt were stuck several pens, and in her left hand she carried a small untouched and unrolled scroll of horse leather. Her hair was swept back from her forehead by a band of lapis-lazuli-blue, and on her feet she wore long thonged boots.

He frowned as he saw her, his eyes touching her equipment with a severe glance. "You cannot stay here," he finally said. "We sweep down into battle soon after Obed moves out into the plain. Return you with the other women up the mountainside, where it will be safe."

But she smiled at him and shook her head. "I go not with them," she answered quietly, "but venture down with the fighters." She touched the scroll in her fingers. "This day I will write of the great victory I shall see, so that all men may read of it later."

Dael's face was hard. "I so order you to return," he said shortly. "The field of battle is not for women."

She continued to smile at him. "I do not go forth to battle, merely to record," she replied. "I will not be hurt. I will watch and write what I see. And why not?" she mused as if to herself. "Perhaps in other times other women will do as I do today. Write what they see when their men fight." The smile left her lips and she came closer. "Dael, can you not understand? This must be written down as it happens, so that men will remember and have the word before them always. Perhaps there will come times when they will need the spirit of confidence and hope and faith to move them, and they can read what I will this day enscribe, and their hearts will be refreshed."

He looked away from her. "I want you not here," he insisted stubbornly. "It is your life that concerns me. That—and nothing more. I cannot lose you. Not now. Not after——"

Her lips were both cool and clinging against his mouth. When she broke away, her smile was wistful. "Fear not, beloved," she assured him. "For Jehovah is this day with me, as He will be with you. I will be in no danger but watch from a distance. Go now," she added kindly, "for it is time."

He nodded, opened his mouth as if to speak again, then turned sharply on his heel and walked away, hardly hearing her call after him, "I will take care."

And thus the first general of a united Israel and perhaps the first woman ever to witness a battle and enscribe it for the future parted.

And now, having crossed the south bank of the Kishon, the men of Benjamin and Ephraim advanced boldly upon the Plain of Esdraelon.

Watching from their hidden positions near the base of Mount Tabor, Dael and his men saw Obed leading his own fighters as they made their way laboriously through the mud. No mail, no armor weighed them down. They wore loose mantles, kilts, or loincloths as rank by rank they wheeled and faced the high ground to the west where surely the great chariots of Sisera must hurtle upon them. In their hands were clubs, oxgoads, daggers, a few homemade spears. Some of the captains carried awkward and bulky-looking swords. Other men held the wooden boomerangs. A few had their bows slung over their left shoulders.

And some, Dael noticed, had nothing in their hands but stones. . . .

Still onward they went, toward the west, knowing that soon the thunder of the wheels must meet them. Stubbornly, courageously, and yet quietly they moved forward under the murky, wind-swept skies, pierced now by the peaks of Mount Carmel ahead of them and of Mount Tabor to their right.

"Look, my lord." It was Heldai, one of his captains of a hundred, who touched Dael, pointing to his own right. Dael's eyes followed the gesturing finger, and he froze into stiffened attention.

For now the might of Sisera was advancing upon Israel.

From the west they came, from Harosheth, from the place of the setting sun, the picked twenty thousand of Canaan, with their nine hundred terrible war wagons, with their blades already glinting dully in the light as they turned on the hubs, with their trained war horses who knew how to kill, with their drivers and archers and spearmen and cavalry poised for the conflict. Already wheels were churning and working heavily on the drenched upland as they came pouring down toward the soggy plain.

It was an awesome sight to behold, this powerful army of banners and pennants and death. First, approaching slowly, majestically, almost in arrogant defiance, were the great chariots of six spokes, with driver, spearman, and archer on the swaying platforms. In three tightly packed rows of three hundred the massed vehicles neared the host of Israel, each chariot moving panel to panel, each horse's shoulders in line with the others, stepping high, their plumes bobbing, the jingle of the tiny pomegranate bells on their bellybands already reaching the ears of the men at the base of the mountain. Red and gold and blue shone the enameled panels, bronze glinted from spears and swords and mail. As if turned by a single hand, eighteen hundred wheels churned the mud that could not blanket the rising, rolling boom of the oncoming chariots.

Sisera, Dael saw at once, was taking no chances, meeting the nearing Israelites, who were on foot, as if they were a mighty army themselves. For not only was there a solid wall of chariots to the front, but, protecting their rear and front were the checkreined and impatient chargers of the cavalry, the riders sitting stiffly and proudly upon the ornamented saddles, their javelins already naked in their hands.

And behind the chariots and the cavalry trudged the foot soldiers, the spearmen, the archers, the axmen, and the slingers.

Dael's breath caught harshly in his throat and escaped in a trembling sigh. "Sisera is determined to win," he pointed out to Heldai. "The battle formation is perfect. The chariots to break through the front, the cavalry to attack from the flank and to the rear, and the foot soldiers to move in to finish the deadly work." He glanced quickly at the captain beside him and wondered if his own face was as pale as that of Heldai's.

On and on rolled the war wagons, forward trotted the horses of the cavalry, ahead surged the masses of the infantry, some slowly removing their bows and notching the arrows into the strings. And already the sounds of battle were starting, the occasional neigh of a horse, a shrill command, the creak of leather, the sucking sound of hoofs in mud.

But the men of Israel never faltered, also moving forward through the heavy mud into the very jaws of death, heads up, stride confident, shaggy hair flowing in the wind, faces lifted. And leading them was the sturdy figure of Obed, his crude sword already raised.

Watching them, Dael shivered—whether from pride or fear, he was never to know. For a fleeting moment he thought: It is folly, madness, fanatical and fantastic. How can we win against such a war machine? The men of Ephraim and Benjamin will be shattered by the first charge of the chariots, will be crushed in the vise of the cavalry and annihilated by the foot soldiers.

But still the men of Israel marched on, coming ever closer and closer to the chariots, which were picking up speed, the bladed scythes whirling faster now, the figures on the platforms steadying themselves against the lurch and bounce by holding onto the panel straps. And along the flanks, the riders began to spur their horses, lifting their feathered javelins high in the air.

"Soon . . ." Dael heard Heldai breathe beside him.

Shorter grew the distance between Israel and Canaan, closer and closer came the chariots. They had reached the flat plain now and were close enough for Dael to make out clearly the high and protective panels, even the inlaid ornamentation. The tremendous wheels, heavy with steel at the hubs, were churning the heavy mud.

And high rose the hoofs of the charging horses, their flanks already bespattered by mud, their handsome trappings soaked and soggy. The proud crests and haughty plumes still danced on the heads of the beasts, but the constant bouncing and jogging caused these ornaments to act as hindrances now, slipping over the eyes of the horses, blinding some of them until a charioteer had to cut them off with his sword.

The cavalry, too, swung into action, their riders low in the saddles now, the javelins held level as they moved against the advancing Israelites. And from the rear the footmen and archers either stood or knelt as they unstrung their bows. Cloud after cloud of arrows whispered their song of death as they soared skyward and then landed in the midst of the men of Benjamin and Ephraim, no longer walking now, but running into the fray. And the flung spears hissed their own deadly tune as they pierced the air and sought their targets of flesh.

It was becoming a blurred scene now—the rocking chariots, the plunging horses, the running men who closed in against the Canaanites. Almost with bare hands the ragged, lean, gaunt tribesmen leaped upon the war horses, tearing bridles from them, their knives glinting dully as they whipped at tendon and sinew. And the land was covered with sound now, the yelling, the blaspheming, the prayers, the exhortations, the neighing and screaming. With a sickening feeling Dael saw the men of Benjamin and Ephraim fall, like the mown wheat, as the arrows and spears cut them down, as horses' hoofs tramped them into the bloodied mud, as scythed wheels chopped and slashed, as chariot warriors, leaning out of the platform, hacked with sword and ax.

But not a man of Israel turned backward. With bared teeth they leaped upon all who came at them, hanging from bridles, poles, from harness, clambering onto the very chariots themselves, and, while the vehicle was still in motion, engaging the fighters there in hand-to-hand combat. Forward and onward, not to be stopped, sometimes scrambling over their own dead, they flung themselves at the enemy, using oxgoads to pierce eyes and bodies, hammering with the stones in their fists, unmindful of the death around, in front, and above them.

And now the mud began to take its toll. The chariots' wheels were biting helplessly against the soft and yielding ground. Whips flashed over the flanks of the horses, the muscles of their haunches strained as they sought to extricate themselves from the sticky embrace. Here and there a chariot began to founder, then to slip, then overturning entirely, the spokes spinning slowly against the leaden sky. And into these overturned wagons others crashed, borne forward by the momentum of their charge. Loud and terrible were the screams now, the whinnying of horses already entangled in their own harness.

And like lithe cats, the men of Israel leaped upon these stalled vehicles and savagely struck at all before them, at drivers and horses and warriors alike, slashing and cutting. Many were already armed with Canaanite weapons, which they used against their former owners. Others, seizing emptied chariots, were charging frenziedly into the ranks of the Canaanite-manned wagons with smashing impact that crushed and shattered the vehicles. Here and there little piles of chariots, either mired or overturned, began to dot the plain. Furiously—but more helplessly now—the cavalry wheeled, unable to use its lances for fear of killing their own men.

Dael felt Heldai look at him, and the man from Naphtali nodded his head slowly.

"Now," he ordered tersely. As Heldai was about to rise, Dael stopped him with a hand on his elbow. "Before you give the signal, do your chosen ones have the torches hidden in the pitchers?"

Heldai nodded. "And the rams' horns as well, my lord."

Dael also arose, feeling at his waist for the sword. He regarded Heldai soberly. "We will charge down the mountain now," he said quietly. "And may Jehovah be with us." As Heldai nodded, Dael asked, "And the woman, Deborah?"

The tight smile stretched briefly over Heldai's face. "She will be safe. She told me you need have no great fear over her."

Dael nodded again. "So be it," he said. "Now we go into battle. Let the signal be sounded."

And again a ram's horn—five times—called out, and then men of Naphtali, Issachar, Zebulon, and Manasseh, who had been hidden, rose as one and began their wild charge down the mountain side to the plain below.

"*Cherev l'Adonoi!* The word for the Lord!"

By the twenties, then the fifties, then the hundreds and thousands, they stormed down Mount Tabor, screaming their great battle cry—leaping, lean, bearded men, unkempt, with their long hair streaming in back of them, their crude weapons held high before them. In front they were led by Heldai and Dael, closely flanked by those who bore live torches, whose flames were guarded against extinguishing by the pitchers in which the brands had been thrust.

"Cherev l'Adonoi!"

With a roaring fury they sprang and bounded from their ambush upon the field of battle. The Canaanites, already desperately fighting for their lives, heard the new sound with dulled ears and then, with amazed and frightened eyes, beheld the second assault upon them.

In moments, it seemed to Dael, he was closed in battle.

He almost stumbled over the body of a Canaanite officer at his feet. In one smooth and liquid motion he dropped his own sword, retrieved the finer blade of the slain man, waved it high, and urged his men forward. Before him loomed a Canaanite, his teeth bared and grimacing. Dael easily skipped aside, bent his knee slightly, and thrust the sword under and upward. The Canaanite never finished his plunge, whirling once, twisting upon Dael's weapon until the fighter had to force the sword free by jerking at it savagely. As he turned, a spearman charged upon him, the point held low and steady. But Heldai, swinging a battle-ax, let it fly from his hand into the face of the enemy. Grinning at him, Dael plunged ahead, his eyes seeking a free chariot. Already around him the sound of the battle was reaching a maddening pitch, and the torches of the Israelites, which had already made the remaining horses crazed with fear and utterly unmanageable, began to be applied to chariots. Here and there spurting flames raced along panels and pole. Mounds of mired chariots started to burn hotly. Others, set afire and allowed, like mobile torches, to run free on the battlefield, careened into other vehicles, smashing into panting groups of struggling men.

As he ran forward Dael felt a jarring impact on his shoulders, and he crumpled to the ground, trying to roll from under the Canaanite whose hands were reaching for his throat. Over and over both men turned, with Dael's newly found sword knocked from his grasp. With a free hand he tugged at his waist, slipping the bronze dagger out, jabbing fiercely upward again and again. Blood spilled in a sudden tide over him, and the weight was gone from his body. When he rose to his feet he did not even look at the slain warrior below him.

Another figure reared up at him, ax raised high in the air. Bending swiftly, Dael ducked the first blow as the ax thudded into the ground. He whirled, but not in time to prevent his enemy from wrenching the ax from the earth and raising it to strike again. From the corner of his eye Dael beheld part of a broken chariot wheel. Even before the ax could descend, he had lifted the half-moon of jagged spoke and broken scythe blade and hurled it into that screaming mouth.

His eyes smarting from the pall of smoke that was beginning to hover over the field of combat, he still sought for a chariot, finally seeing one, still unbroken and with its two horses under control, managed by a single driver. He ran toward it, waiting as it bore past him, reaching upward with one hand, vaulting onto the platform. Still half crouched, he coiled himself for the spring upon the driver, the blade in his hand ready for the thrust. He was about to leap when the driver turned and stared.

Dael lowered his knife, sagged against the lurching back of the chariot, grinned weakly at Ard—Ard, blood-smeared, soot-streaked, but wearing Canaanite armor, made of leather and circles of iron fastened against it.

"Dael!" Ard began to rein the plunging horses, but Dael merely waved for him to let the beasts continue. He rested for a moment, getting his breath, thankful that Ard, who had gone to fight with his own tribe at the start of the battle, was safe and alive.

"Truly you have the luck of the brave!" Dael shouted. "In one more instant I would have been forced to find a new trainer."

"Or I a fighter!" grinned Ard. He tapped his chest, pointing at the armor. "Behold this. From a Canaanite captain of a hundred. He gave it to me most willingly. This chariot too."

"Gave?" Dael shouted again.

Ard nodded. "In fact, he had no more use of it after my persuasion."

Dael laughed harshly, then looked at the platform of the chariot. There a huge two-bladed sword of iron rattled against the bouncing floor. He picked up the weapon, grunted at its weight, and began to swing it from both hands. "Drive into the footmen!" he ordered.

"What?" Ard screamed with indignation. "Am I your chariot driver then? *I* secured this wagon. Get yourself one of your own!"

But he obeyed Dael, driving into the huddled groups of archers and spearmen who were still valiantly trying to stem the tide of battle. But it was hopeless now. More and more of the Israelites had found chariots and, like Dael and Ard, were thundering into the helpless infantry, hacking at them with sword and ax as they swooped by, returning again and again until they broke whatever ranks they had and began to flee.

To flee westward, toward the city of Harosheth.

To the Kishon, the swollen, flooded Kishon.

And now, as if their very discipline had been shattered by fear, mud, surprise, torch, and blood, the Canaanites began a headlong retreat to their headquarters, hoping to cross the river and thus regroup for another attack. But upon them now from every side, from flank and rear, came the men of Israel, on foot, on horse, in chariots, laden with weapons, carrying torches in pursuit of their foe.

Those Canaanites who still had chariots drove them desperately westward, not stopping to pick up any of their own men who pleaded with them to be spared from the death behind them and at their sides. Although the retreat continued, the battle did not end, with smaller bands of Israelites and Canaanites fighting along the way.

Then, as they neared the Kishon, a new terror unfolded itself before the eyes of the Canaanites. When they had crossed the Kishon four days earlier, it had been a quiet stream, moving slowly, placidly, against its narrow banks. Now, swollen by rain and flood, it was a raging torrent, a turbulent barrier which had spread far beyond its banks and was already pounding against the wheels of the approaching chariots of Jabin.

Dael and Ard, in swift pursuit, knew what faced their enemies. In front of them was this wild and tumultuous stream; to their back came the screaming, battle-maddened, blood-crazed men of Israel.

There was no time for debate or decision now, no moments for planning or deliberation. Without hesitation, the leading chariots plunged into the roaring waters.

For a moment Dael thought they would emerge safely. Horses swam, heads high, and the chariots, although teetering from side to side, still managed to keep afloat. Half carried, half pushed by the angry Kishon, they headed for the middle of the river.

Then it happened.

The weight of the scythed wheels was too much; the burden of the ornaments and tassels and plumes could not combat the snarling, raging waters as they closed over chariot after chariot. One by one they went down, twirling over and over in the water, being tumbled along by the force of the flood before disappearing for all time. But the other chariots still kept coming, rolling or pitching over the banks and into the stream. And behind them raged another storm, that of Israel, who dove into the waters and helped the Canaanites drown, thrusting horses' heads under the surface and keeping them there, clawing at drivers and warriors, wrenching them out of the chariots and then slitting their throats. The banks became heaped with the dead. The Kishon turned ruddy, and its foam was flecked with pink.

Dael and Ard, furiously maneuvering their chariot, were almost charged into by another wagon, whose driver was an Israelite. Splattered with mud, with a sword cut still open on his cheek, this driver made a hasty salute.

"I come from Obed," his voice rasped. "He ordered me to find you and tell you that victory is ours!"

Supporting himself by the strap, Dael leaned out. "In what manner?"

The messenger smiled despite the wound. "In back of us the Canaanites are asking for surrender. And their great general, Sisera, has fled the field."

"Sisera? *Fled?*"

It was inconceivable at first, hard for the mind to grasp or imagine. Sisera, the great general, the genius of the chariots, fleeing?

"This is true?" Dael shouted again.

"Both Obed and Nun confirm it," the messenger screamed back. "The Canaanites want our mercy and plead for surrender."

Dael continued staring at the other for a long time, hardly aware of the diminishing sounds of the battle, not knowing when Ard finally calmed the plunging horses, alighted from his chariot, and stood silently at their heads.

Jabin's lips pursed, his pink jowls shook as he laboriously signed the document, held out his hand silently to the scribe who placed the sand box in his palm. The King of All Canaan dipped stubby fingers into the grained surface, pinched the sand, and scattered it carefully over his signature. He stared at it for a moment, lifted it, and handed it to Dael.

"Here is your peace, Barak," the monarch said.

In back of him, Dael could hear the slight stir made by the Canaanite officials and the elders of Israel who now, four days after the defeat of Canaan on the Plain of Esdraelon, were witnessing the peace pact established between Jabin and the tribes of the children of Abraham.

As Dael started to read, he heard Jabin say: "It is all there. No longer will Canaan raid against Israel. And workers in metal, smiths and craftsmen, can continue their peaceful pursuits."

"And enforcement of the worship of Baal?" Deborah's clear voice rang out.

Jabin glared at her, his pink pate turning a shade darker. Then he shrugged. "Worship of Baal by Israel will not be enforced." He continued to stare at this woman, whom some called sorceress and who, others whispered, could be the first queen of Israel if she so chose. He could not help his resentment. She was a woman, and in his entirely male world there was no position of any authority for a woman at all.

"Peace, at least," Jabin's voice rumbled. And peace, he thought, bought at such a terrible price—nearly his whole army destroyed, his general, Sisera, fleeing from battle, only to be slain by the hand of a Kenite woman in whose tent he had sought sanctuary. And if he were to count the loss of his champion, Og, and his wagers—the price was even greater. Still, he mused, it could have been worse. There would be peace now within the land, and Canaan was still intact. Better yet, perhaps now Israel would unite with Canaan against common foes, since there would no longer be warfare between them.

Dael finished reading the document and folded it carefully before thrusting it into his waistband. Jabin looked at him, a suspicion of a smile on his mouth.

"It is satisfactory, Barak?"

"It is," Dael answered solemnly. "Fair and satisfactory."

"And I will honor it," Jabin said, "and see to it that you do as well, since you are now King of Israel."

Dael, also smiling, shook his head. "I am no king, nor wish I to be one," he said. "But I will honor the peace."

"It is what I desire too," Jabin agreed. "Someday you will see that my words will bear fruits of truth. Canaan and Israel will be as one, with the same cultures and religion merging for the good of all."

Dael regarded him. "And would Canaan have prevailed, would you still have felt this way?"

Jabin shrugged. "Perhaps not. Perhaps, had I been victorious over you, I would have marched forth against Egypt. Although," he continued, shaking his head, "it is no longer Egypt which should be feared, but a new power which is rising in the north."

"The wolf of Assyria?" Dael asked quietly.

Jabin nodded glumly. "A new enemy. Not quite ready, perhaps, but ever growing in strength. And one which we will have to fight one day."

"And perhaps then," Deborah broke in, "it will be *Israel* which will defend Canaan against the invader."

Again Jabin peered at her, his little blue eyes speculative and narrow upon her. Still trying to overcome his suspicion and resentment against her as a woman, he made speech directly with her for the first time.

"I am told you witnessed the battle and recorded it in words," he said. "I would that it were given me to hear this poem. Or at least part of it." His curiosity was natural. He had never before met a woman who could read and write.

Deborah, inclining her head somewhat, murmured that she would be pleased to oblige the king and would recite from memory portions of her descriptions of the combat. Then she lifted her head, her eyes half closed as she began to intone:

"Awake, awake Deborah,
Awake, awake, utter a song
Arise, Barak, and lead thy
captivity captive, thou son of Abinoam. . . .
Then fought the kings of Canaan
In Taanach by the waters of Megiddo
They fought from heaven
The stars in their courses fought
against Sisera.
The brook Kishon swept them away
That ancient brook, the brook Kishon
The earth trembled, the heavens also dropped
Yea, the clouds dropped water

And the mountains quaked at the presence
  of the Lord
Then did the horse hoofs stamp
By reason of the prancings
The prancings of the mighty ones. . . ."

When she had finished, there was only silence in the room. Jabin, his face impassive now, swallowed once, sighed heavily, then looked up at Dael. "Of one more matter I would speak to you," he said, and this time the grin was broad and unashamed on his face, "a matter of law."

Dael looked at him and Jabin seemed to burst with hidden mirth. "I still have an Israelite with me," he revealed, "one for which I know not a manner of disposing. Wait and you will see." He signaled his guards, who bowed, walked to the side door of the throne room. This was quickly opened and, before all, the utterly deflated and dejected figure of Achan was half dragged in.

The former shophet of Kedesh was not only unkempt in appearance, his beard uncombed and snarled, but he was thoroughly frightened, his eyes rolling from Jabin to Dael, back to the king again.

"Behold my guest these many days," Jabin chuckled grimly. "Achan, my former spy." Jabin leaned forward on the throne, enjoying every moment of this. But he was again speaking directly to Deborah. "Tell me, since you, too, are a shophet, is it not the law of Israel to seek a tooth for a tooth and an eye for an eye in revenge?"

"It so is," Deborah answered gravely.

Achan moaned loudly, but Jabin paid him no heed. "Then," the king said almost pleasantly, "here is the betrayer of Abinoam and of all of Israel. Let Abinoam's son now wreak his revenge." And with amused but still cold eyes Jabin unhooked his own long dagger and handed it to Dael. "Go ahead," Jabin said pleasantly, as if he were offering bread and meat. "It is perfectly legal and will be fully witnessed by all," he added, indicating the officials at the rear. He sat back on the throne, hooked his thumbs into his belt, stretched his legs out.

Achan's wild scream sounded in the hall. He fell on his knees, facing both Dael and Jabin. "No, no," he pleaded, his breath heaving, his eyes wild. "I throw myself upon your mercy. Spare my life. I will leave Israel, never to return. I——"

"You will leave Israel—and all the other lands of the earth—so what matters it now?" Jabin asked calmly. He nodded again at Dael. "Go. Strike. Or would you have me think that the great champion and leader is woman-hearted and that all who follow him are so?"

"I think, my lord," Dael began, "that it would be better perhaps to——"

"Strike!" Jabin's voice was hard. "You are still in my throne room. *I* still command here. Strike, and deeply so!"

Dael shrugged, lifted the dagger. He was not quite sure what game this was that Jabin was playing, but he certainly was not going to appear fainthearted before the monarch, not just after a victory. The knife rose higher in his hand.

And it was then that Deborah's voice cut like a sword.

"In whose name kill you now, Dael?" she challenged, her eyes scornful. "Surely not in the name of Jehovah! You have killed enough in His name, and He wants no more deaths now. Nor does He demand Achan's blood from you. It is not yours to take. Let Achan be traitor judged and as traitor executed by the people whom he has betrayed. But not from *your* sword should his death come upon him. Hear me, Dael. For everything there is a time. A time for war, a time for peace, a time for death, a time for life. Now we are through with the war and death, for Jehovah has won the peace for us. Spill no blood here, arouse not the anger of Jehovah."

Dael lowered his hand. Taking the dagger by the blade, he gave it, handle first, to Jabin. The monarch took it back, tapping the metal against his fingertips.

For a long moment the king looked at Dael, then let his glance encompass Deborah as well. He kept staring at her until she had to cover her unease with a little laugh.

"Tell me, what is it you see?" she asked.

"I look for a sorceress," Jabin answered darkly. He turned to look at Dael. "Reveal to me the truth," the king demanded. "Is she sorceress really?"

Deborah laughed again. "You do right, King of Canaan," she said. "Ask of him. He should know."

Gravely Dael turned now to Deborah. He took her hand in his and then, still holding her fingers in his own, made his answer to Jabin:

"I tell you this, King. In so far as matters of the heart and love are concerned, Deborah is, and indeed shall always be for me, the greatest sorceress of them all."